"...AN EVERLASTING RENOWN"

ALEXANDER THE GREAT
July 21st 356 B.C.–June 10th. 323 B.C.

by

Rita Fairchild

Published by

MELROSE BOOKS

An Imprint of Melrose Press Limited
St Thomas Place, Ely
Cambridgeshire
CB7 4GG, UK
www.melrosebooks.com

FIRST EDITION

Cover designed by Jeremy Kay

ISBN 1 905226 68 3

Printed and bound in Great Britain by:
CPI Bath, Lower Bristol Road,
Bath, BA2 3BL, UK

Dedication

Edward A Fairchild, without whose help this book would not have been possible.

My thanks and appreciation for all the hard work by the staff of Melrose Books.

Walter Edwin Bulbeck
Oxford and Bucks Light Infantry
Killed in Action
France and Flanders 23/07/16
Aged 20

Ernest George Bulbeck
The Seaforth Highlanders
Killed in Action
France and Flanders 24/04/17 Aged 19
"At the going down of the sun
And in the morning,
We Will Remember Them"

Dr Frank Marxer
Dr Reuben Sloan
St Joseph's Hospital, Atlanta, Georgia. USA

Dr Scott Pastor
Piedmont Hospital, Atlanta, GA 30309

Dr Winifred Soufi
Northside Hospital, Atlanta, GA 30342

Dr James B Whitesell, D.D.S., P.C.

Maggie Katrek

The Wild Edibles of Georgia USA.
Who Welcomed Strangers
The Georgia Appalachian Trail Club
The Tuesday Hiking Group of Atlanta, GA.

Dr Aytug Tasyurek
Archaeologist

To celebrate the Greeks

PHOTOGRAPHER Edward A Fairchild

Author's Note

The author asks the reader's indulgence for any errors: geographical, historical or factual. My book is a novel, and the characters have been reduced with intent to avoid confusion; others have been created to fit the format. Alexander's story has consumed a great but very enjoyable part of my life as I have been fortunate enough to follow the early parts of his incredible odyssey. His influence stretches down to the present era giving him a unique immortality.

Glossary

Date	Event	Chap.	Country (modern)	Province (ancient)	City mntns.rivers	Modern/ Nearest City
BC						
343		1	Greece	Macedon	Pella	Thessalonika
				Macedon		
359	Philip acceded		Greece	Epiros		
367	Phillip exiled		Albania	Illyria		
364			Greece	Boiotia	Thebes	Thebes
387	King's Peace		Laconia	Attica	Sparta	Sparta
			Greece	Thrace	Athens	Athens
			Greece	Macedon	Amphipolis	ibid
			Greece	Mt. Pangeaus	Pydna	Makrygialos
			Greece	Chalkide	Thrace	
			Greece		Potidea	Kassandra
357	Marriage of Philip		Greece	Aegean Sea	Samothrace	
356	Birth of Alexander		Macedon	Macedon	Pella	Thessalonika
	106th.Olympiad		Greece	Chalkide	Olynthos	ibid
			Greece	Thessaly	Thebes	
			Greece	Thrace		Thrace
			Greece		Phocis	Phocis
			Turkey	Chersonese	Cardia	Gelibolu

Date	Event	No.	Country	Region	Ancient Place	Modern Place
344	Aristotle Alexander's teacher	2	Greece	Macedon	Mieza	Naoussa
		3	Greece	Macedon	Aegae	Edessa
340	110' Olympiad	4	Greece	Peloponnese	Elis	
			Greece	Peloponnese	Mt Olympos	
			Greece	Thessaly	Naupactos	
			Greece	Aetolia	Patras	Patras
			Greece	W. Lokris	Olympia	Elis
			Greece	Archaia	Sardis	Lydia
		5	Greece	Elis	Byzantium	Istanbul
			Turkey	Lydia	Maidis	Alexandro-poulis
			Greece	Euboea	Perinthos	
			Turkey	Thrace	Elatea	Drachmoni
			Greece	Thrace		ibid
			Turkey	Thrace	Amphissa	Thessalonika
			Bulgaria	Hellespontine-Phrygia		
			Greece	Scythia		
			Greece	Phokis		
			Greece	Boietia		
			Greece	W. Lokris		
338	Battle of Chaeronia	6	Greece	Greece	Boitia	Chaeronia
			Greece	Peloponnese	Corinth	Corinth
337	Philip's Marriage to Cleopatra	7	Greece	Macedon	Pella	

Glossary continues overleaf

Glossary continued

Date	Event	Chap.	Country (modern)	Province (ancient)	City mntns.rivers	Modern/ Nearest City
336	Accession of Darius					
336	Murder of Philip	9	Greece	Macedon	Aegai	
336	Accession of Alexander	9	Greece	Macedon	Aegai	
	Lllth	10	Greece	Aetolia		
	Olympiad			Ambracia		
				Aetolia	Argos	
				Epiros		
				Phocis	Mt, Parnassos	ibid
				Phocis	Delphi	ibid
				Thrace	R. Nestos	ibid
				Bulgaria	R.Ister	Danube
335	Thebes destroyed		Greece			
			Turkey	Thrace	Sestos	Abydos
334	Alexander invades Asia	13		Thrace	Hellespont	Dardanelles
			Asia	Troad		Turkey
			Turkey	Troad	Troy	Hisarlik
				R. Granicus		R. Kocabas (Biga)
				Lydia	Sardis	Sardes(Sahlili)
				Ionia	Smyrna	Izmir
				Ionia	Ephesos	Ephesus (Seljuk)
				Ionia	Priene	Turunclar

Map	Country	Region	Ancient name	Modern name
14	Turkey		R. Meander	R. Menderes
		Ionia	Miletos	
		Caria	Halicarnassos	Bodrum
		Ionia	Didyma	Yenihisar
		Lykia	Tehnessos	Fethiye
		Lykia	Patara	Kinik
		Lykia	Myra	Demre
		Lykia	Phaselis	Phaselis
		Pamphyllia	Perge	Aksu
		Pamphyllia	Aspendos	Eelkis
		Pamphyllia	Side	Selimiye
		Pamphyllia	Sillion	Sillion
		Pamphyllia	Termessos	Gullukdagi
		Phrygia	Celaenae	Dinar
		Phrygia	R.Sangarios	R. Sakarya
		Hel-Phrygia	Gordian	Polatii
		Phrygia	Ancyra	Ankara
15		Cappadocia	Cappadocia	Cappadocia
		Cappadocia	Mt. Argaeos	Mt. Ergiyas
		Taurus Mtns	Cilician Gates	Gullekbogazi
		Cilicia	Tarsus	Tarsus
		Cilicia	R. Cydnos	Tarsus Cay
		Cilicia	Soloi	Viransehir
		Cilicia	Olba	Uzuncaburc
		Cilicia	Anchiale	Kazanii (?)
		Cilicia	Margasos	Karatas
		Cilicia	Mallos	Kiziltahta
		Cilicia	Mopsuestia	Misis
		Cilicia	Hieropolis	Hieropolis
		Cilicia	Castabala	
	Turkey	Cilicia	R, Pyramos	R. Ceyhan

Glossary continues overleaf

Glossary continued

Date	Event	Chap.	Country (modern)	Province (ancient)	City mntns.rivers	Modern/Nearest City
333	Battle of Issos	16		Cilicia	Miriandros	Iskinderun
					Plains of Issos	Dortyol
					R. Pinaros	R. Delicay
			Turkey	Daphne	Harbiye (Antakya)	
				Syria	R.Orontes	R.Orontes
			Lebanon	Phoenicia	Ugarit	Ras Shamra
			Syria	Phoenicia	Marathos	Amrit
			Syria	Phoenicia	R. Lycus	Dog River
			Lebanon	Phoenicia	Sidon	Saida
			Lebanon	Phoenicia	Tyre	Tirus
			Lebanon	Phoenicia		
332	Tyre	17				
332	112th. Olympiad		Philistia	Samaria	Rishpon	Apollonia
			Palestine		Aphek	Antipatris
			Palestine	Gaza	Gaza	Gaza
			Israel	Judea	Jerusalem	Jerusalem
			Egypt	Sinai Desert		
			Egypt		Pelusium	Damietta
			Egypt		Memphis	Cairo
			Egypt		Thebes	Luxor
			Egypt		Naucratis	El Niqrash
			Egypt		Alexandria	Alexandria
			Egypt		Siwah	Siwah
			Libya	Cyranaica	Cyrene	Shahats
			Tunisia		Carthage	Tunis
			Libya		Parataetoniun	Mersa Matrub
		18	Sudan	Nubia		Sudan

331	Battle of Gaugemela	Syria		Damascus	Damascus
		Turkey/Iraq		R. Euphrates	R. Firat
		Iraq/Turkey		R. Tigris	R. Dicle
		Iraq	Media	Gaugemela	Irbil
		Iraq	Babylonia	Arbela	Irbil
		Iraq	Mesopotamia	Babylon	Borsippa.
		Iran	Susiana (Elam)	Susa	Susa
331	Burning of Persepolis	Iran	Persis	Persepolis	Persepolis
		Iran	Persis	Darius' Tomb	Naqh i Rustum
		Iran	Persis	Parsagadae	Parsagadae
		Iran	Media	Ecbatana	Hamadan
		Iran	Media.	Rhagae	Tehran
330	Death of Dariusran	Iran	Hyrcania	Zadracarta	Astrahad
		Afghanistan	Areia	Susia	
		Afghanistan	Bactria	Persia	Afghani/Turkestan
		Afghanistan	Areia	Artacoana	Areian Herat
		Afghanistan	Areia	Alexander	
		Afghanistan	Dragiana	Zarangia	Phradra (Nad i Ali)
330	Murder of Parmenion	Afghanistan	Arachosia	Alexander in Arochosia	Ghazni
		Afghanistan	Arachosia	Kophen	Kabul
		Afghanistan	Bactria	Bactra	Wazirabad

19

Glossary continues overleaf

Glossary continued

Date	Event	Chap.	Country (modern)	Province (ancient)	City mntns.rivers	Modern/ Nearest City
328	Black Cleitus Killed Maracanda 113th.		Uzbekistan Tadjikistan	Sogdiana Sogdiana Paratecene	R. Oxus Maracanda R. Jaxartes Alex. Eschate	Amu Darya Samarkand R. Syr Darya Khojend The Pamirs
327	Olympiad marriage to Roxane	21	Uzbekistan Tadjikistan Uzbekistan	Sogdiana Sogdiana Paraetacene (Sogdiana) Rock of Chorienes	Nautaca Sogdian Rock	Karshi Derbent Pamir Mntns.
327	Pages Plot	22	Pakistan Pakistan Pakistan Afghan/Pak Afghan/Pak	Ghandara Ghandara Ghandara Cis-India	Nysa R. Indus Aornos Rock Indian Caucasus Parapamisos(Grk)	R. Indus Pir Sar Hindu Kush Hindu Kush Between Hindu Kush and R. Indus
	Death of	23	Pakistan Pakistan Pakistan	Ghandara Punjab Punjab	Taxila R. Kydaspes Bucephalos	Sirlcap R. Jhelum Jelalpur

Year		Event	Country	Region	Ancient	Modern
326		Bucephalos	Pakistan	Punjab	R. Acesines	R. Qhenab
			Pakistan	Punjab	Sangala	
			Pakistan	Punjab	R. Hydraotes	R. Rav
			Pakistan	Punjab	R. Hyphases	R. Beas
	24	Return	Pakistan	Punjab	Alexandria on the Acesines	Multan
					Multan	Patalla
	25		Pakistan		Alexandria	Bampur
			Pakistan		Patalla	Baluchistan
			Iran	Gedrosia	Pura	Baluchistan (Makran desert)
			Iran	Gedrosia		Baluchistan
	26		Iran	Carmania		Khuzestan
			Iran	Elam	Icaros	Failaka
324		114th Olympiad	Kuwait			Kuwait
			Arabia		Dilmun(Tylos)	Bahrain
			Bahrain		Babylon	Borsippa
323	27	June 13 Death of Alexander	Iraq	Babylonia		

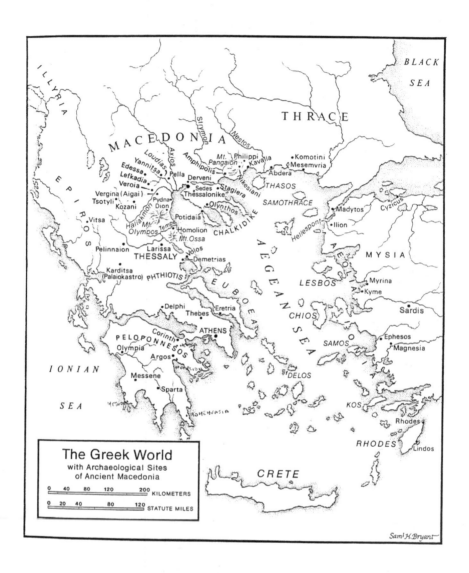

The Greek World
with Archaeological Sites
of Ancient Macedonia

0   40   80   120   200 KILOMETERS

0   20   40   80   120 STATUTE MILES

Sam¹ H. Bryant

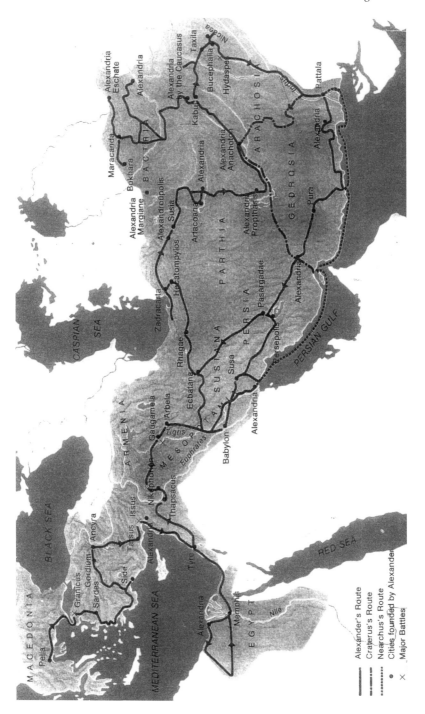

Chapter 1

I, Jason, the son of Nearchos of Macedon, write for my son this epilogue to the years when Alexander was king and ruler of all the earth.

The sun rose today over Babylon, as it did for all Alexander's yesterdays; tonight it will set, never to shine on him again. He was favoured of the gods, the first prince of history, lord of the west and east, soldier and statesman, scholar, philosopher, diplomat and King of the Macedonians.

Alexander died today. He survived marches, battles and grievous wounds only to perish meanly of fever. He carved an empire from Greece to the far ends of the Persian satrapies, into remote tribal lands and beyond to India. To the countries between, Alexander gave a common language, equality before the law, civilisation, science and the arts, the flowers of Greece and wedded them to the barbarians' different ways.

The first rays of the rising sun are slanting across Babylon as I write in desolation of spirit. I am overwhelmed by loss and heavy with fatigue. My mind is plagued with the knowledge of the pestilences which now will fall upon the world.

Alexander was a man above other men. He commanded and was obeyed, he led and was followed, he conquered and plundered and the gods raised him up and confirmed his divine lineage. In triumph, he showed mercy to those who surrendered but annihilated the defiant vanquished. A policy which often gave easy victories, without bloodshed, and secured his rear and supply lines. He paid the price by enduring bitter antagonism from his beloved Macedonians.

I am a soldier, toughened by fifteen seasons of campaigns. I have witnessed treachery, endured the loss of friends in battle and listened to the screams of ravished women and children, victims of wars' insensate horrors. I have sickened at the stench of battlefields and the sight of open, pulsating wounds and felt the merciless sun beating down in the furnace of Asia's summer. I have crossed high mountain passes where the blinding snow concealed the tortuous paths and heard the cries of men and the squeals of horses swept to death in avalanches. In the deserts, I have been cut off in stinging sandstorms with my tongue parched, swollen and blistered. I have gloried in victory and counted my share of plunder. In the taverns of the world I have praised the god Dionysos to excess, not only to shut out what my eye has seen and my mind tried to reject. Had the gods made me a Greek I would have followed the philosophers, but I am a son of a Macedonian general who was high in the late King Philip's favour, and so I bore arms and avoided disgrace to my father's house.

Alexander's generals are now gathered in the quarters of Seleucos, son of Antiochos, dividing between themselves the satrapies of the king's empire. Macedonian resentment has festered against the king for his policies of reconciliation with the Persians and the equality he granted to our former enemies. Professional soldiers are blinded in victory by a lust for power and spoils, and they fail to comprehend the subtleties by which Alexander secured vanquished territories and then advanced to greater conquests. The generals, with their smaller vision, will now squander his achievements and dismember his empire.

My mind will not look to the future. The dream of a world ruled by one prince is over, for it was Alexander's and his alone to achieve.

There is no direct heir. Roxane, the king's first wife, is far gone in pregnancy; both she and the child will be helpless pawns in the hands of ambitious men. The alternative heir to her child is the illegitimate son of King Philip by a Thessalonian woman, Philip Arrhidaeos, known to be half-witted and therefore ineligible by double misfortune. The empire is conquered, but not consolidated, and it must fragment. For ambitious men, power is the stake and they will quarrel in its disposition and by pettiness will destroy the unity created by Alexander.

I look back to the days of my youth in Pella. On my thirteenth birthday, in the seventeenth year of King Philip's reign, I went to court and I enrolled in the Corps of Royal Pages. Our duties were light; we guarded the king at night, collected his horses from the grooms and escorted him on the hunt. We also studied with Greek teachers, exercised at the gymnasia, practised horsemanship and performed our duties to the gods. The days began with sacrifices and, often, a hunt dedicated to Artemis.

I was the same age as Alexander, the king's son, who, at that time, was in the charge of a tutor named Leonidas, a kinsman of his mother, Queen Olympias. I shared some of their lessons with other pages and so became acquainted with the prince at an early age.

Alexander, through Olympias, a daughter of Neoptolemos, late King of Epiros, was descended from Achilles and from the great hero he inherited many princely qualities. He was brave, chivalrous and ruthless. He consciously challenged destiny with a confidence born of self-mastery. Through King Philip, his lineage descended from Herakles, to whom he gave a special devotion and from whom he found his life-long inspiration.

Philip's destiny had changed at the age of twenty-three. He succeeded his brother Perdicass, who was slain in battle against the Illyrians. Philip first acted as regent for Amyntas, the infant son of Perdicass, but ruled so well and successfully quelled the murderous raids of the border tribes, that the army and people proclaimed him king.

Philip was exiled to Thebes during his youth where he stayed in the house of the great Theban leader, Epaminondas. He was taught Greek history and especially studied the wars against Persia. He shared Greek anger at the infamous treaty known as 'The King's Peace', which was signed at Lydian Sardis and imposed by Artaxerxes on all the city states. By its terms, Persians had the right to interfere in Greece at the discretion of their King of Kings.

Philip also studied the causes of Greek weakness, how Persian money bribed and corrupted, leading the cities to internecine war and preventing a coalition against their common enemy. Treacherous Sparta, in 'The King's Peace', was recognised as leader of all the other Greek cities with the right to use force against them, in the name of the Persian king.

Philip also examined the causes of the Peloponnesian War, which ended in the destruction of Athens. He noted how Persia had played off, in turn, one city against the others to foster antagonisms, so that wars and preparation for war consumed

3

their energies and wealth while leaving the Persian Empire strong and unchallenged.

Athens, Sparta and Thebes all tried to gain supremacy and weakened themselves further. Thebes, under Epaminondas and Pelpidas, almost succeeded, but when the former was killed in a victory against Sparta, Thebes collapsed and all Greece was ready to fall to the student of history from outside, Philip of Macedon.

By the time that he became king, Philip observed how the wars against Persia had produced a germ of a common Greek patriotism and he planned to nourish this into a powerful force in his own service.

Nearchos, my father, was a general in King Philip's army and when home from campaigns, he told glorious stories of battles and victories and, less gloriously, of bribery and trickery used as acts of state.

He spoke of the personal bravery of the king when he lost an eye, suffered mutilations of his hand and leg and many other grievous injuries. My father delighted in the king's strategy by which the Greek cities were taken by intrigue, in preference to military conquest.

One of Philip's first acts, as king, was to raise an army and then, to soothe the Athenians, renounce a spurious claim to Amphipolis. He bought off the Paeonians until he was strong enough to defeat them in battle, before he marched to the west, and drove the Illyrians out of Macedon.

With this new-found strength, the king's cunning grew bolder. He sent a secret embassy to Athens, offering to the Athenians Amphipolis in exchange for the free city of Pydna, that was not in his gift. The greedy Athenians accepted, expecting to gain control of the gold and silver mines on Mount Pangaeus owned by Amphipolis.

Before withdrawing from Amphipolis, Philip organised a faction in the city, favourable to Macedon, which later handed it back to him with unopposed ease. He advanced on Pydna and Potidea to secure their ports and returned to Amphipolis to claim the gold and silver with which he bribed his way through other city gates. He also used the timber from the mountain to build a fleet to rival that of Athens.

With cool calculation Philip recruited, victualled and equipped an army. When it was trained, he marched to offer bribes and peace. The cities that accepted his hegemony were shown mercy and those that opposed him were destroyed. Philip turned his attention to the threat from Epiros to the south west of Macedon. Olympias, daughter of the Epirots' dead king, was at that time visiting Samothrace in the Aegean Sea, to take part in the worship of the Kabiroi, in the ancient rites, in the Sanctuary of the Great Gods. Philip, to further his purpose, made the same journey. My father was in the king's party and he told me of the mysteries celebrated there and of the meeting between Philip and Olympias.

He first saw her at the evening celebration of the mysteries. Positioned on the western side of the temple, she stood against the radiance of the setting sun. She was dark of hair and her topaz eyes glittered from an inward fire. Her brow was high and her nose straight, her mouth curved in mockery and her chin was ever tilted in defiance of all men. Her bearing was proud and noble but she was possessed of a temper and jealous rage which made her feared daily by those who served her.

Philip fell wildly in love with the princess, to the chanting of the priests, the erotic dancing of the temple women and the music echoing hauntingly across the mountains. At the age of twenty-six, he made Olympias his fifth wife. The princess was eighteen years of age.

Olympias, and her brother Alexander, had been pushed aside at their father's death by an uncle and, though young, she already burned with ambition for power. She was ripe for opportunity and quickly recognised it in a marriage with the Macedonian king. Olympias was the first of his five wives to become queen and to the marriage she brought her snakes, symbols of regeneration always writhing and coiling within her reach. One year after the marriage, Alexander was born during the one hundred and sixth Olympic Games. It was said that Nectabeno, last of the ancient pharaohs, and an exile in Macedon, held up the birth for the right conjunction of the stars. When the infant was finally born, the Egyptian prophesied to the queen: "Thou hast given birth to a ruler of the world."

Amongst many portents which attended the birth of the prince was the destruction, in a fire, of the great Temple of Artemis at Ephesos, one of the Wonders of the World. People whispered that it had burned because the goddess was absent in attendance at Alexander's birth.

The Fountain of Prophecy at Didyma also gushed again after many dry centuries, and the temple oracle foretold great victories by a flame which would burn Asia. Princess Cleopatra was born the year following the birth of Alexander. The king's ardour had quickly cooled. The queen's snakes in the bedchamber gave the quietus to passion and the marriage had become a battleground for dominance and power between Philip and Olympias. The queen taunted Philip with the claim that she had lain with Zeus, in the form of a snake, and Alexander was the son of this union. She schemed to realise power through the prince and, as he grew older, she constantly influenced him against the king. Alexander was bitterly torn between them and though, in later years, he admired the great deeds of Philip, he never wholly trusted his father. Olympias knew herself to be descended from the gods. She attended the secret rites of Dionysos and she roamed the woods with her maenads, her hair loosed, streaming behind her, naked but for the snakes coiling round her body. The people held her in great awe, and unseasonable storms, bad harvests and many other mysteries were attributed to her powers.

The lady Olympias weaved many tangled webs amongst courtiers and officials. Her bribes corrupted and brought them the slavery of blackmail as she gathered power into her own hands. Philip, with a world to conquer, treated the marriage as a political weapon in her native Epiros and manipulated the queen's influence with the rulers of the Greek states to his own advantage. When love died he found consolation with many other women.

The king was a man of majestic dignity, with a leonine head covered in curls which met his full beard. His strong neck was set on broad shoulders; his face was wide and his jaw firm. His expression was of mocking condescension, except when he dealt with matters of state, and then his good eye reflected an inner concentration and his face grew animated as he gave orders and judgments.

Alexander was the child of these ambitious, ruthless parents. Olympias brooding, mystical and imperious and Philip earthy, brilliant and bold. By his father, Alexander was conditioned for conquest and an imperial destiny and by his mother to be the equal of the Gods.

The king, ignoring the taunts of the queen, always regarded Alexander as his son and heir and watched over his education with devoted pride. Philip gave his son, in his early years, into the care of Lanice, a widow and member of a family devoted to the royal house. She gave the prince warmth and tenderness, otherwise lacking in his life, until she was superseded by Leonidas, who was chosen as his first tutor.

Leonidas was an admirer of Sparta and he and his assistants, in emulation, instituted a rigorous regime for the education of the prince. Olympias and Lanice were obliged to smuggle food to his quarters to make up for his scanty meals. Alexander, due to the physical training imposed on him by Leonidas, ever after disliked exercise for its own sake but he learned well the Spartan virtue of enduring deprivation and hardship.

The king's campaigns, intrigues and conquests ended a Sacred War, which had devastated Greece for ten years and in doing so he gained the balance of power for himself. He demanded the surrender of Olynthos, where two of his brothers lived. When the city refused to submit, he destroyed it and exiled many of the leading citizens.

The remaining Olynthans tried to make common cause with Athens against Philip. Demosthenes, the Athenian orator, thundered approval, but the city vacillated and sent help too late to save the Olynthans. The Olynthans were also betrayed from within, by suborned officials and, when the betrayers later complained to Philip that his Macedonians called them traitors, he answered: "We are a rough people and call a bribe a bribe; how else would you be known?" Confused, they departed in dishonour to take their only consolation from Philip's gold.

With more gold, Philip divided the Thessalonians amongst themselves and then urged them to unite with him against Thebes. Thebes and Thrace were at war with Athens and the opportunist Phocians, plotting to seize an advantage during the confusion, seized Delphi and made an alliance with Athens and Sparta. The Amphityonic Council, composed of the states whose cities had immemorially administered the Oracle and Sanctuary of Delphi, reacted by declaring war on Phocis, Athens and Sparta, which cities had used the temple treasure to recruit a large army and so started another Sacred War.

Philip reacted by marching east and making a new treaty with the Olynthans, the allies of Athens. The Athenians were thoroughly alarmed. Demosthenes, in the public places of the city, denounced Macedon, which he despised, considering us barbarians, descendants of Dorians and little better than slaves. He preached that Athens alone had a sacred mission to protect Greek freedom and scorned the claims of Philip. The king, however, felt a great reverence for Athens and her lawmakers, thinkers, architects and scientists and now courted her with honeyed words, eloquently persuading her citizens of his desire for peace. After years of exhausting wars, many Athenians were enchanted by the prospect that he offered to the city, and her Assembly dispatched ten ambassadors to Pella, including Demosthenes, to draw up a treaty. Philip's terms included a clause requiring Athens to relinquish her claim to Amphipolis and the gold of Mount Pangaeus. He, in turn, agreed not to interfere with the Chersonese, except for Cardia with whom he already had an alliance. The Athenians tried to insert a clause to save the Phocians, their former allies, but they were unsuccessful in their negotiations with the king. The ambassadors returned to Athens to give the city Philip's choice of either accepting his terms or war with Macedon. The Assembly voted for ratification of the treaty and the delegates left again for Pella to obtain Philip's signature. During the journey they learned, in horror, that the Amphityonic Council had invited Philip to come to its members' aid, giving him an excuse to march south as he engaged the Athenians' hopes in diplomacy. The Phocians, in despair, surrendered the pass and Philip arrived at Thermopylae.

The Council destroyed the dependant Phocian cities and awarded her votes to Philip making him guardian of the temple and treasure of Delphi. The members of the Council further confirmed their confidence in his leadership by inviting him to preside over the Pythian Games at Delphi, the most sacred in the calendar. Philip now controlled the major part of Thessaly with the surrounding districts and, allied to Thebes, he was poised to invade Attica.

The Thessalonians appointed Philip their Tagos, or leader, for life. They had the finest cavalry in Greece, after which fell to his command and all Greece took notice of his growing power as he prepared to challenge Persia.

The king had no desire to subject Athens to war, preferring to win her as an ally and thus gain control of her powerful navy. It was essential for his plan to invade Asia and free the Greek cities of Anatolia, ceded to Persia by the terms of 'The King's Peace', and signed with the Persian King at Lydian Sardis.

Isocrates, the great orator and advocate of pan-Hellenic unity, published a work urging peace between the city states and war against Persia, under the leadership of Philip. An advocacy very much to the king's purpose. The rivalries and wars of the contentious Greeks had been the key to Philip's successes and he now prepared to change policy and unite them under his leadership. In all the cities, the parties which he had fostered were ready to seize power and the season was a Macedonian dawn.

Chapter 2

The king brought Athenian scholars, physicians, geographers and scribes to the court at Pella. Many of them despised their Macedonian hosts as barbarians, but not the generous stipends paid for their services. Philip, also, obliged his nobles to speak the Athenian tongue. No hardship for my father who was born of an Athenian mother. He had grown up with its cadences and subtle shades of meaning and married my mother, also a woman of Athens. Philip gave deep consideration to a successor to Leonidas, as Alexander approached his thirteenth birthday. He asked for commendations from many of his nobles, including my father.

As they walked in a palace courtyard, he said: "Nearchos, your son is now at court and sharing some of Alexander's lessons and it is time to find them a new teacher. A score have their protagonists, but I have yet to find one sufficiently accomplished in all the sciences, philosophy and arts to be equal to the prince's education. He must be the right man for the future of Macedon. He should have integrity that he may, by precept, impart the same quality. He must also be able to discard the trivial, live a hard life without luxuries, value loyalty and know how to make decisions for the common good, unswayed by personal inclination. He must inspire both assistants and students and leave such a mark of excellence that it will be a lifetime standard. When I was exiled in Thebes, in the house of Epaminondas, he was just such a man; now where do we find his equal?"

My father knew the king as a man of few words concerning his family, which often provoked the rage and defiance of Olympias. His answer was as considered as the king's question: "Sire, I recommend Aristotle whose father served yours as court physician. He is no stranger to Macedon and is renowned throughout the civilised world; amongst the Greeks he has no equal."

Philip was immediately enthusiastic and arranged for an emissary to leave for the island of Lesbos where Aristotle was planning to open an academy. When he received the king's invitation he recognised a greater destiny in moulding the mind of the king's son and set sail for Pella.

I was present at court for the arrival of Aristotle. He was greeted by the king with great warmth and a feast was held in his honour. Alexander, relieved to be released from the strict and gloomy supervision of Leonidas, expressed his pleasure. The new teacher made an excellent impression on the court. His bearing was full of quiet dignity; he was calm of manner and gently spoken. Aristotle was above average height, with a large head and wide brow above blue eyes. His nose was straight and his jaw firm and he inspired confidence in all who met him. With my father's consent, I had already joined Alexander's classes in Greek and horsemanship. Remote indeed seemed the quiet days of my childhood, now that I was surrounded by the brilliance and intrigue of the court. I had been in the capital for nearly a summer season when Aristotle arrived. My command of the Athenian tongue had brought me notice from the king and I was among those chosen to attend school with Alexander.

A few days after the arrival of Aristotle we left for the nymphaeum of Mieza, where the new school was established, far from Pella and the distractions of the court. Our teachers quickly established a routine. In good weather, our lessons were given out of doors and we strolled in the gardens listening and learning, proposing and disputing in the manner of Plato's Academy. The sessions with Aristotle opened our minds and hearts to the sacredness of truth and to the delights of rhetoric, philosophy and science. We heard of the life and teaching of Socrates, of his noble death and of the torch that he lit, a flame spreading throughout the world, even among the barbarians.

Aristotle was an inspired teacher. Homer and the noble deeds of the heroes lived again for us. He venerated the gods and was full of personal humility. He was a master of many disciplines – zoologist, botanist, astronomer, physician, metaphysician and moralist – and freely did he bestow these gifts upon us. He opened doors to many mysteries and led us on the quest for learning, making my life rich, and giving me a precious antidote for the future against sorrow, hardship and tribulation.

Alexander often walked alone with Aristotle and between them was forged the great spiritual relationship sacred to teacher and student, even above that of father and son. The parent bestows the body and from the teacher proceeds the mind and essence of man. Aristotle taught the prince the precept: 'To rule first be ruled', and into Alexander's hands he placed the future of the world. During the time at Mieza, we visited the Grotto of the Nymphs and took part in the Orphic rites. Aristotle encouraged our devotion to religion and now I wonder if he interpreted the king's wishes rather than his own convictions.

Periodically, we visited Pella. We joined in army manoeuvres and such was the quality of our training, we were easily assimilated into the cavalry. The king had reorganised the army. The infantry, as well as the cavalry, were now professional soldiers, instead of being raised from the districts only in time of war. The methods of training introduced by Philip were mainly developed from the teaching of Epaminondas, learned during the king's exile in Thebes. He introduced the oblique order of the phalanx as a further advance, dividing the front line into a strong offensive weapon which advanced to the attack as the second defensive line moved slowly forward. When battle was joined, the phalanx moved into the oblique position. The king armed the men with spears twice as long as those carried by the Persian infantry. They carried round shields by a ring on the arm and wore helmets and greaves and jerkins protected with metal. At either end of the phalanx (known as the pezhetairoi) the hypaspists took up their positions. They were lightly armed infantry who marched into battle between the cavalry and the phalanxes.

The cavalry was the main offensive wing and the infantry was the line of defence. Their positions were altered in battle, to confuse the enemy. The mounted squadrons of hetairoi were increased from the original King's Companions to several regiments and they were armed with helmets, corslets, swords and thrusting spears. Our visits to court were exciting interludes from the quiet routine of Mieza. The news from the front was always good and there was a confident air at the palace. Sometimes I was fortunate, and I saw my father when he was not away at war. Queen Olympias was hysterically happy whenever she greeted Alexander. The prince bore her attentions with kindness and listened to her constant complaints against Philip in silence. He was much less affected by her attempts to alienate him from his father as he grew older and he gave the king ungrudging admiration for his military and diplomatic successes.

In conversation, Alexander spoke of his ambition to unite Greece and avenge her ancient wrongs on Persia. He studied geography with concentrated attention and applied himself to the sciences of tactics and strategy so that he mastered them in theory and practice.

Aristotle had also introduced study of the arts, thus opening the door to out an appreciation of sculpture and painting. Alexander became a patron and counted many artists among his friends. The prince was sometimes remote and the mysticism, which he inherited from his mother, was never far below the surface. In appearance, Alexander was of medium height and powerful build. His features were delicately moulded over a clear bone structure. His hair was corn-coloured, perhaps a Dorian legacy, and when he raced his horse Bucephalos, it streamed out behind him in harmony with the horse's long mane and tail, a picture to excite the skill of artists in paint, mosaic and stone.

The palace was full of works of art and we were free to roam, except in the royal quarters. Amongst the treasures were intricate mosaic floors, some depicting the hunt with lively realism and one of Dionysos riding a leopard which I particularly liked. Aristotle aroused our interest in the craft and we visited the workshops where new mosaics were designed. I recall, most vividly, from this time the day when Bucephalos was brought to Pella and offered to the king for the huge sum of fifteen talents. The great, black horse was marked with a white blaze on his forehead, from which came his name the Bull-headed. Philip was so intrigued by his outrageous price that he cried: "I must see this horse, worth a king's ransom."

And he strode from the palace with his courtiers, Alexander and me, with other pages streaming behind us.

A crowd gathered, and watched as first officers and then grooms from the stables, tried unsuccessfully to mount the wild and rearing beast. Groans went up when the king turned him down as too unmanageable. Alexander approached his father and asked his permission to mount. At first the king hesitated and then, with a slight smile, he inclined his head and Alexander stepped forward to soothe the beast. He took the bridle as the horse reared, calmed him and gently led him away from the crowd. The groans ceased and all stood statue still. Alexander turned Bucephalos into the sun. His purpose was obvious as the horse, no longer disturbed by its own shadow, grew calm.

Alexander gently mounted, and then gave free rein to the end of the field. As he returned, congratulatory cheers broke out and I heard the king remark: "Macedon is too small a kingdom for such a prince."

I felt that he spoke in jest, but when his words were repeated to Alexander later that day, he seriously replied: "Kingdoms are parts of empires and my concern is with empires."

I often remembered his words and they made me think of home. The mountains, valleys and plains of Macedon are ever in my heart. I often dream of my father's country estate where life was pleasant and tranquil. I recall the song of the birds at sunset. I can see, in my mind's eye, the poppies and the yellow mustard glowing under the hot sun, the wheat, golden at harvest time, and the white cotton crop ready to be delivered into the hands of skilled craftsmen for weaving into cloth.

Macedon is a fair land, the sheep and goats are fat, the olives plump and crops heavy. The people are well fed, and live pleasant lives. I weep afresh that Alexander will not return to receive the honours due to him. The gods first raised him up and showed favour to all his undertakings and then, growing jealous of his power and prestige, took away his life and will now destroy his work.

Chapter 3

Court life was exciting after the tranquility of Mieza, especially when the king came home. There was feasting, music and laughter, lasting far into the night. Philip gave much of his time to Alexander and encouraged his questions. He brought the prince into discussions with foreign ambassadors and to meetings with his generals. In a lesser way, the pages were included. It was always the policy of the king to trust his advisors and men, in return, gave him unquestioning devotion.

During the absence of the king from Pella, Alexander received the foreign embassies. Completely in Philip's confidence, he dealt with them with subtle authority. Gymnasiums had been built at both the palace and at the school in Mieza and we had daily training sessions. We also used the public gymnasium in Pella, where there were a great many more men available to test our skills.

Closest amongst us to Alexander in affection and shared confidences was Hephaestion. There was a warmth and trust between them, which neither ever betrayed. Hephaestion was a natural leader, excelling in games, philosophy and the arts. He was older and taller than the prince, more obviously handsome, but without the gentle spirituality of Alexander. The prince first admired Hephaestion because he often surpassed him where others held back in competitions. Alexander would take no part in public games after he was humiliated by a spurious victory.

Alexander treated us all with gracious courtesy, but he was always conscious of his kingly destiny and it was only with Hephaestion that he was completely at ease. Craterus, a noble's son, was the second in Alexander's affections. He excelled at hunting and often he and the prince, with a small party, would go into the mountains for days to follow their sport. He was a brilliant student of politics and the arts of war and many were the hours he spent with Alexander and Aristotle discussing the world's mysteries. Alexander valued Craterus for his astute mind and ability to make swift decisions for he was swayed by neither personal feeling nor personal ambition, good qualities in a king's advisor. Craterus and Hephaestion were rivals for the prince's favour.

The latter often displayed jealous spite, to which Craterus showed good-humoured indifference. He was the friend of many men while Hephaestion had no companion other than the prince. Others amongst us were Ptolemy, the son of Lagos, Seleucos, the son of Antiochos, and Antigonos and Coenos, all sons of nobles or generals and personally selected by the king. Aristotle and his assistants taught that we were 'the chosen companions and darlings of the gods'.

In Greece, the cities were fragmented, weakened by war and bankrupt. Macedon grew stronger every day. Greek problems were constantly discussed; we thought in military terms of alliances, war and victories and dreamed that our future empire would extend into Asia and far beyond.

At Pella I met old Parmenion, the king's Chief of Staff. He was a close friend of my father and I was privileged to know the famous warrior personally. His three sons were also in the army but apart from Philotas, the oldest, they were absent on campaigns. Parmenion was a soldier and man of honour. He conducted expeditions with efficiency and discipline and was totally loyal to the house of Philip.

Apart from the king, the strongest person at court was Olympias. She was beautiful, still young with an aura of mystery which I found oddly fascinating. She made a very bad enemy and banished from court a page whom she discovered in a lie. At the feast of Dionysos, she disappeared from the palace and was seen roaming naked in the woods with her snakes and the maenads. It was whispered that she took part in all their most secret rites.

The queen claimed her house to be the superior of Philip's family, because it was founded by Achilles and she constantly told Alexander that he was sired by Zeus and not by the king. Alexander was influenced by, and shared in his mother's religious mysticism, but he realised that Zeus as a father questioned his own legitimacy and inheritance and he forbade his mother to make her claim public.

To the Macedonians, especially those most under Greek influence, Olympias was a savage barbarian. To me she was a goddess, though I detested her snakes and lived in fear of her sharp tongue.

The queen's relations with Philip were tempestuous. His women were legion, to which she seemed indifferent as long as neither her position nor that of Alexander were threatened. Philip had a son, Philip Arrhidaeus, by a Thessalonian woman. He was feeble-minded, as well as illegitimate, and ignored by Olympias. On great ceremonial occasions the court moved to Aegai, our ancient Macedonian capital. The city is perched in the crystal air of the northern foothills of Mount Olympos, above the fertile plain which sweeps down to the sea. From the time before the Greeks razed Troy, it was the burial place of Macedonian kings and the royal tombs give great dignity and serenity to the lovely place. We swam in the small river at Aegai, just before it plunges into a sparkling waterfall. It was a paradise to remember when the sun scorches above shimmering deserts and my throat is parched beyond endurance in Asia's burning furnace. And now, when I look back to the idyll of our lives at that time, I feel that the favour of the gods has left Macedon and that my son must grow accustomed to a very different world as the civilisation, power and wealth won by Philip and Alexander are dissipated by men with very different ambitions from those which spurred them both.

Chapter 4

The heralds came to Pella, to announce the Sacred Truce before the 110th Olympic Games. Alexander was asked to compete for Macedon, but he refused, with the comment: "Only if all the other competitors are princes."

He well remembered the deep humiliation of a spurious victory in the past; he also despised professional athletes and he refused to compete against them. Alexander never sought praise or flattery but he did like to be compared with the best. Hephaestion was a competitor, and he practised long hours for his events. Competitors were required to train in Elis for the last month before the games and he left Pella to fulfill this obligation. Amongst my most vivid memories are the days when we travelled to the Peloponnese, under the command of Cleitus, known as the Black. Cleitus was the commander of the Royal Squadron and the brother of Lanice, the prince's old nurse, and he was a close companion of the king. Philip was always careful to surround Alexander with old and trusted friends who gave him, not only protection, but were also examples of the best soldierly qualities.

We were a carefree band when we left Pella on the way to the festival. Olympias watched our departure, the only woman in the crowd of well-wishers. The queen revelled in the challenging world of men and, although but a woman, compelled the admiration of many by her imperious arrogance. Alexander's deference to her in particular was remarkable. Mounted on Bucephalos, he now tenderly looked down upon her and it was obvious that the bonds of his childhood were not yet broken nor her influence at an end.

We set out from Pella for high adventure on our first

Expedition into the world of men. Leaving the city behind, we galloped across the plain racing each other and shouting in joyous freedom. We also left, far behind, the tranquil calm of Mieza and the protocol and intrigues of the court in the capital. Cleitus and the men under his command were indulgent, but watchful. I think that they too shared our festive mood for they were on holiday from the battlefield.

From the time of the arrival at Pella of the heralds and ambassadors announcing the Sacred Truce, the ancient peace before the games was honoured and it was safe to travel all over Greece. Alexander might otherwise have been seized and used as a hostage since it was obvious that there was no ransom that the king would not meet for his safe return.

Camp at night was relaxed and informal. We sat around the fires and talked of war with Persia, of the stars in the night sky, of philosophy, of the nature of the gods and of happiness and destiny. Alexander loved conversation and listened to the men on the arts of war, but he led the discussions on the arts of peace. He closely questioned the stratagems of the newly-organised army, the purpose of the enlarged cavalry squadrons and the oblique phalanx formations. He constantly referred Craterus to the details of engineering, the construction of siege machines, transportation by land and sea and the other sundry logistic problems discussed by the king's men.

On the borders of Thessaly the ground began to rise, and soon we saw Mount Olympos, Home of the Gods, ascending to massive, craggy heights. That night we camped on the plain below the towering pinnacles and the local people brought us their sweet honey and rough wine to supplement our evening meal. We broke camp as dawn was rising over the mountains. I remember feeling some surprise, for the terrain was stony and dry, very different from Macedon with its orchards and farms and this was my first journey into a foreign world.

We continued on through the mountain passes of Thessaly into Aetolia, to the port of Naupactos, where we embarked to cross the Corinthian Gulf. Philip's naval commander, Nicanor, was waiting for us with a small fleet to make the crossing. Sotelis, son of a ship's captain, replaced Craterus at the side of Alexander and Nicanor instructed us all on the principles of naval warfare, its strategies and limitations. He explained that the main functions of the fleet were to blockade ports and destroy enemy fleets, to protect shipyards which already clanged with the sounds of the construction of our future navy, and to carry supplies to the army.

When we arrived at Patrai, in Achaia, we had reached hostile country. King Philip had subdued Greece only as far as Thessaly. The farther south that we rode, the more sullen the people appeared when they discovered that we were from Macedon. Without the immunity from attack bestowed by the Sacred Truce, it would have been impossible for us to make that journey. Cleitus kept us close together and he and the other men were never far from the side of Alexander.

Our arrival at Olympia was greeted with polite cheers but little enthusiasm from most of the other delegations. The Spartans, of course, remained aloof. Since signing 'The King's Peace' with the Persians at Sardis of Lydia, Sparta's status was compromised and the other Peloponnesian states were careful not to offend Alexander too deeply; Macedonian conquests haunted them all.

We found Hephaestion and went with him to the Temple of Zeus where, at the altar, he took the oath to compete fairly and affirmed that he had been training for the required ten months. He was competing in the pentathlon for boys and we all hoped for a wild, olive crown to escort home to Macedon in triumph.

We came to honour Zeus and Hera, but we desired honour for Macedon. We keenly felt the slighting tolerance of the Greeks and knew that they considered us barbarians, hardly qualified to compete in their sacred games. The temples of Olympia are magnificent and the statue to Zeus of unsurpassed splendour. Made from gold and ivory, it awed and humbled in its majesty. I now understood why contentious states made peace for the games. In honouring the gods, all things are made possible, even an end to war.

The stadium was near to the temple and very uncomfortable under the hot sun. Once the games began however, excitement possessed the crowds and they shouted for their favourites. The tumult echoed across the plain to the sparkling waters of the River Alpheos. The pines grew everywhere and the air was heavily scented with their aromatic perfume. When the competitors came from the altis, through the sacred arch, bets were laid on the favourites and the atmosphere was charged with a throbbing tension, as of a vast crowd celebrating a religious sacrifice in satisfaction of a barbaric god's threatening power.

The Priestess of Demeter, in her official capacity, was the only woman present in the stands, except for a few unmarried girls. The judges, and other officials, sat on marble benches at the south side of the stadium. They were lavishly attired in robes of eastern extravagance. Every event was accompanied by religious rites and ceremonies, some originating in the past before the first Olympic Games. The road leading into the stadium was lined with a row of statues of past competitors who had cheated in the races, conspicuously placed there as a warning against a repetition of the crime. Some were of such elegant workmanship that the effect of the warning was diminished by their beauty.

The pan-Hellenic Oration was of special interest to we Macedonians. Alexander listened with great attention and many in the crowd stared insolently at our section. I heard a few dissident mutterings but it must have been obvious to all that only King Philip could impose peace between the city-states and unite Greece against the Persian threat, even if this was not to the liking of all Greeks.

I enjoyed the music and poetry contests but the odes written in praise of the victors commanded better prices than they were worth. We were disappointed that Hephaestion did not win a first place, but watching the fine competitors, the best in Greece, was exciting and we cheered enthusiastically.

Cleitus ordered us to be ready for an immediate departure at the conclusion of the Olympics. He had left the king during a campaign and he was anxious to return to his military duties. Professional soldiers are reluctant to take time off from war and we made good speed back to Macedon.

Chapter 5

We returned to the routine of the school at Mieza for a short period of time. Aristotle gave a warm welcome to Alexander and greeted us all with affection. We found that army officers had arrived from Pella to join the staff, and amongst them was Philotas, the oldest son of Parmenion, who added lessons in diplomacy to the curriculum.

Philip's prestige was rising in Greece. Some of the cities were beginning to feel the benefits of the peace which he had imposed upon them. In Athens, however, there was intense disagreement between many of the leading citizens. Speudippus, Plato's nephew, advocated unity amongst the Greek states and a national war against Persia, even under the leadership of Philip. Demosthenes, the famous Athenian statesman and orator, on the other hand, worked hard to gain allies in Euboea and he tried to persuade the Peloponnesian states to go to the aid of Byzantium, in a move to protect the Attic corn route from the Euxine Sea. At the same time, he plotted war against Macedon, but Athens was not strong enough to resist the rising tide of King Philip's conquests.

The king returned to Pella and sent for Alexander to join him in the capital, and the school was disbanded. With Aristotle, and the other teachers, we all returned to the city. With scant ceremony, Alexander was made regent of Macedon and the king left the city to conclude the pacification of the Greeks. News reached Pella of a tribal revolt in Thrace. Alexander, immediately, organised an expeditionary force under his own leadership. He quickly subdued the tribesmen on what seemed little more than a hunting trip, for they were a hopeless match against well-disciplined Macedonian troops.

Philip meanwhile had called on Perinthos, in eastern Thrace, and Byzantium, at the entrance to the Euxine Sea, to come to his aid and, when they both refused, he laid siege to Perinthos. He was now campaigning dangerously close to the Persian Empire and Artaxerxes, King of Kings, responded by ordering his satrap of Hellespontine-Phrygia, across the narrow water-way, to support the Perinthians. Athens, also, reacted to the king's move against Perinthos, as the city was a port on the Athenian grain-route from the Euxine Sea. She had moved a large naval force to protect this vital interest. Philip, therefore, risked a possible alliance between Persia and Athens and he made a strategic withdrawal from Perinthos to march east to seize Byzantium.

The Athenian naval squadrons immediately sailed to protect this even more indispensable port. The Macedonian fleet was still under construction and unable to meet any challenge from the sea, and Philip prudently abandoned his position and struck instead against Scythian tribes who were harassing our northern border. He thus ensured that his soldiers were rewarded with some spoils of victory before they returned home to Pella.

The Amphityonic Council sent an embassy to Philip, inviting him to come south and, although winter gripped the land, he rode out from Pella, at the head of the army, to the ruined fortress of Platea, which commanded the main road into Boeotia and Attica. From there, he sent a proposal to Thebes and suggested a joint campaign against Athens. At the same time, he dispatched orders to Pella for Alexander to join him. We had two days in which to prepare. Alexander, no longer in the position of a subordinate, had become a cool and organised leader. He took over from the senior officer and drew a little apart from his former companions.

Our last duty was our farewells to Aristotle. Alexander approached him first and received the present of our teacher's own copy of *The Iliad*, annotated by Aristotle himself. It was the supreme gift and the one prized above all others by Alexander for the rest of his life.

When my turn came, I approached Aristotle. He took my hands and said: "Jason, son of Nearchos, use your courage, keep a silent tongue, listen and watch and, above all, always be constant when Alexander needs a friend."

Our teacher had a private word for each of us and then, raising his hands in farewell, he walked slowly away. Aristotle prepared us for the world and in that debt which binds a student to his teacher, he forged links as strong as those in a chain of iron, tempered in the fires of Damascus.

At this departure, Alexander did not allow Olympias a public farewell. When we rode away he was at the head of the column and there was no racing, or high-spirited shouts, or laughter within the group of pages, as on the journey to Olympia. The officers were familiar with the road south and we made good progress. They knew where the streams and rivers offered the best camping places and, as we approached Elatea, excitement rippled through our small party. We had been trained and had waited many years for just this day, and Alexander had become a man. I felt less difference in myself, perhaps because soldiering was not my choice, and I had left my soul with Aristotle and the other teachers.

However, I was happy to be joining my father and we all felt a sense of history and the favour of the gods in our destiny. I did not then know that war destroys people, cities, and the land and brings famine and pestilence and spoils the earth for unborn generations. With eighteen summers behind me, and a life spent happily in pleasant places with gifted companions, I knew nothing of that different world where people live in want and die in misery.

Alexander's arrival at the king's camp was greeted with respect. He was untried on the battlefield, but all the men knew of his bravery and prowess in the hunt, of the rigorous training he had undertaken, and none ever forgot the taming of Bucephalos.

Escorted by four pages, Alexander walked straight to the king's quarters. The pages withdrew to leave king and prince alone together.

My father heard of our arrival and came to see me. I was saddened to see how he had aged and after greeting me he said: "Jason, my son, I am glad that you are here. You will take my place in service to the king and I can retire to my home. All my life, I have been a soldier and for the last few years granted to me by the gods, I hope to enjoy peace raising crops and living by the seasons."

His words affected me for I had always thought that we should serve together. My father was a good man, with qualities of compassion and gentleness unusual in a soldier. I honoured him, not only as his due from me, but because he gave to others far more than he received, and he asked favours of no man.

The day after our arrival Philip held a council. Alexander sat at his right and Parmenion on his left. The king began by announcing the ceremonies which would end our term as royal pages and begin our enlistment in the King's Companions. He then turned to the war and outlined his successes. He spoke of a secret treaty that he had made with Hermios of Atarneus, across the Hellespont, his first contact in Anatolia and the farthest east that his influence reached. All the cities and tribes in north and central Greece were now in the king's alliance and he was ready to treat with, or subdue the south and the Peloponnese. After a pause he continued: "Macedon alone will never be strong enough to attack Persia so, for the common good in forever ending the Persian threat, we shall make common cause with all willing Greeks, and treat them as allies rather than as subject people. We shall thereby gain military support and security at home as we campaign in Asia. Generosity in victory is our policy, and victory always our final goal!"

Philip now defined a new role for a conqueror. He forbade us to loot a conquered city and he demanded that his army treat a defeated enemy with respect. I heard some mutterings of opposition, but none who disagreed with the king's policies dared make his voice too loud and the king ignored them. He continued when all was quiet again: "I have allowed a signed dispatch to fall into the hands of the Athenians. It falsely states that I intend to withdraw the army to deal with an uprising in Thrace and that if we continue south, we can expect to face an army of Athenian mercenaries between here and Amphissa. I expect the Athenians to be duped and I intend to march against them.

"This campaign is now on the road which, eventually, will lead to the Hellespont and once across the straits, we shall take rich spoils from the Persians, and every soldier will have a share of the wealth."

The king turned to Parmenion and continued: "We shall treat the Athenians with respect. They are a wonderfully clever people and I prefer them as allies rather than as an enemy. Every year they produce ten generals whereas, in my lifetime, I have found only one, my friend, Parmenion."

The old soldier's expression scarcely changed as he bowed acknowledgement of the king's words, to the murmur of approval from around the tent. Loyal, fair, incorruptible as well as being a brilliant general, his were qualities to rouse the admiration of everyone present. Parmenion was an honest man.

The conference ended and we swiftly returned to our quarters to prepare for the battle. There was a great deal of noise and shouting from the courtyard as the slaves brought the horses to us. This was our first major battle and I felt a chill of apprehension. Alexander had prepared, all his life, to fulfill his destiny. The prince showed no emotion but his eyes glittered with excitement as he mounted Bucephalos. Man and horse were disciplined to a pitch of military splendour.

The king faced the column. Alexander, with the pages, was in a group on his right. Philip nodded to Parmenion, who ordered us to advance before the king, and we were invested with the helmet, corslet, sword and thrusting spear of the King's Companions. Alexander took his place at the king's side and the rest of us were scattered throughout the Companions to benefit from the guidance of experienced officers.

First in the column rode the cavalry, known by the ancient Greek name as the hetairoi. Behind the cavalry were the hoplites of the heavy infantry, with their long spears and round shields. Then came the lightly armed infantry, the peltasts, and finally the pezhetairoi of the phalanx formations.

The army was a balance between the aristocratic cavalry and household footguards, and the peasantry of the infantry and phalanx. Philip always planned that no faction grew strong enough to independently challenge his authority. I had often watched the army leave Pella, and now I was part of it and about to be tried in battle. I hoped, for my father's sake, that I would acquit myself, but I had small stomach for war and my imagination vividly anticipated bloody scenes of brutal violence.

The Athenians with their Theban, Corinthian and other allies were camped on the western border of Boeotia. They had deployed ten thousand mercenaries at the pass leading into Amphissa. We bypassed their main army and surprised the mercenaries. The false dispatch, previously sent by the king, had left them unprepared for our arrival. It was all over before they could make battle formation and they surrendered a shattered mob. Amphissa and Naupactos on the Gulf of Corinth were left undefended and Philip received envoys bringing their surrender from both cities. For me, this was an easy introduction to war and an example of the king's skill as strategist, general and diplomat.

From his strong position, Philip offered Athens peace. The city refused his terms and we moved east again towards the south of the fortress at Elatea, on the Plain of Kephessos, where the main Athenian army was encamped.

We camped overnight in a narrow defile leading to the plain. Double guards were posted and spies were sent out amongst the Athenians.

The king held a council of field commanders to give his battle orders. Craterus, Hephaestion and I waited in Alexander's tent for his return. We stood as he approached and he came with news of his promotion to the command of the offensive left wing; the king had taken the defensive right side. He looked supremely confident and his eyes, one black and the other grey, sparkled in suppressed excitement. He held his head to one side, due to an old injury, as he received our congratulations. The prince was groomed with great care, and with his impressively powerful build he was a leader confident and calm, a man born to command all other men.

He gestured for us to be seated and paused a moment before saying: "Friends, tomorrow we shall fight and win and afterwards, if we cannot have the hearts of the Athenians, we must win their minds for the great enterprise in Asia. We do not want their casualties, for we need soldiers. We do not plan the destruction of Athens but rather wish that she should carry the civilisation of the Greeks to the far corners of the world, even to Ocean. We want the goodwill of the Athenian teachers; we need her geographers and engineers, scientists and philosophers. Our friendship has been refused. We must fight only to increase our strength, not to destroy what is noblest in the world."

Alexander spoke of a new concept. War had always been a bloody and ruinous game played for glory and greed. Now it must be fought to achieve Greek unity and an end to the external Persian threat forever. Hephaestion and Craterus were silent. Hephaestion was especially deep in thought, but Craterus looked puzzled. I think for him, at that time, war was the great adventure with all spoils to the victor, no matter that with each victory the spoils grow smaller and both victor and vanquished are so weakened that they are unable to resist outside aggression.

27

I answered Alexander: "Prince, in war, you offer lasting peace, an opportunity for children to grow up knowing their fathers, educated in the arts of peace with a proper inheritance for the strength of the family. Here is a chance for the people to cultivate the land knowing that they will benefit from the crops and not have them destroyed or seized by an invading army. Perhaps you bring us to the threshold of another Golden Age. Our strength can bring protection to the weak, a respect for the law and the rights and duties of all men. May our victory be swift, our casualties light and our compassion great."

Hephaestion then spoke: "If Jason is making the ends of war an ideal rather than plunder, what reward will you promise to the soldiers to make them fight to win if, in victory, they are to be denied spoils?"

Alexander answered him: "There will always be spoils, but they will be provided by the rulers of the vanquished. The common people will only pay an assessment which will leave them enough to survive and rebuild. The crops will be unharmed and business encouraged so that we can collect taxes for government administration. By this policy, we shall gain the loyalty of subject people, rid them of despots, establish just and equitable laws and in the general prosperity the entire country will benefit."

Hephaestion seemed impressed, but Craterus, the born soldier, noble in descent and disposition, found the exchanges irritating rather than practical politics. Both he and Hephaestion were Alexander's men and both were necessary to him. Hephaestion spoke to the prince with gentle reason, and they were the closest companions; Craterus shared with the prince the dangers of the hunt and soldiering in which Alexander exulted. Together they gloried in pushing physical endurance to its limit; Craterus scorned the weak and inefficient until he was mellowed in the pains of experience.

He remained unconvinced by the new philosophy; for him, a soldier's business was to win wars, subdue the vanquished, reward the army and enjoy the spoils and glory of victory. A simple ethos which made him a happy man and good companion. He was admired by all other men for his honesty and single-minded purpose.

It was early morning before we parted. Alexander's tent was pitched near the king's pavilion and we left him to walk the short distance to the cavalry encampment. There was a full moon and the stars glittered in the dark bowl of the night. It was a setting for poets and dreamers rather than soldiers and I went reluctantly to bed, to find rest before the next day's battle. The entire camp stirred before dawn, making as little noise as possible to avoid alerting enemy spies. The horses were fed and bridled and the men put on their armour and tested their weapons. Food was distributed to them and they washed it down with barley beer or rough wine. When the army moved out, a detachment remained behind to restore order in the camp after our hurried departure.

The army was marshalled into columns under the command of King Philip, who was flanked by generals and members of the King's Companions; Alexander rode at the head of the cavalry. We moved out of the narrow defile on to the Plain of Kephessos, in an eerie silence, to avoid giving the alarm to the Athenians and their allies; but news of our approach must have reached the enemy for, as we crossed the plain, we could see them drawn up and waiting for us along the banks of the Haimon Brook. In the distance, we could make out the silhouette of the acropolis of Khaironeia on the twin peaks of Mount Petrachos, over in the west.

When all the Macedonian army was in battle order on the plain, the king gave the order to advance. He led the phalanxes of some 30,000 men with Alexander in command of 2,000 cavalry. We approached the Athenians and Thebans at a steady pace. Alexander proceeded slightly ahead, to attack from the left and as we grew close, he shouted the order and we charged towards the famed Theban cavalry. We held our thrusting spears in the ready position and increased our speed, until the air was full of pounding hoof-beats, and joined battle. It was a confused hell. Soon the groans of injured men, the clash of weapons and the horrifying screams of wounded horses reached to the heavens, which were filled with the smell of blood and other wrenching odours.

Philip halted the hoplites on the right and then retreated slightly, as though in flight. It was a successful feint, the Athenians advanced, shouting: "Drive them back to Macedon."

Alexander wheeled round and attacked as Philip went over to the offensive. It was the end of the battle. Philip allowed the enemy to retreat and he did not pursue them, expecting to gain the enemy's submission and then their co-operation, rather than following the ancient rules of war and annihilating vanquished armies and their cities. Demosthenes, the orator and Philip's bitter adversary, was with the Athenian army. He had spent the latter part of his life warning Athens of the city's total destruction if Philip prevailed in battle, and he was now proved a false prophet and he fled the battlefield.

Philip's victory at the Battle of Khaironeia made southern Greece open to his advance. Neither Philip nor Alexander stooped to personal revenge. They both admired a brave foe and used their military successes to gain political victories over conquered lands and cities. It was too new a strategy for most of the army to accept for soldiers lust for the spoils of war. Later, Alexander paid dearly for continuing this policy with bitter opposition from the Macedonian army. We counted our dead and our losses were light. We buried them in a mass grave on the battlefield, with full military honours, and covered their remains with a mound of protecting earth. We helped the wounded back to our base camp and Alexander went amongst them; he thanked them and assured them that they would receive land in Macedon and stipends for their support. In the king's name, he also promised that the families of the dead would receive a similar bounty.

Philip sent emissaries to the defeated Athenians and Thebans and their allies. From the Athenians, he demanded the Thracian Chersonese, the abandonment of her naval league with other cities, and an adjustment of her borders with Thebes. This last condition was very much to the Thebans' disadvantage. The Athenian prisoners were sent home and the Athenian dead were cremated according to all the proper rites and their ashes reserved for burial in their own city.

The Thebans, as renegade allies of Macedon, suffered a much harsher fate. Philip ordered the execution of the Theban leaders. He sold her citizens into slavery and cancelled the city's votes in the Boeotian League. He sent a Macedonian detachment to occupy the Kadmeia, their central fortress, named for Kadmos, founder of the city. The king's strategies in his dealings with Athens and Thebes were very different. Athens was a great naval power and he planned to use her fleet, in an alliance, under his own command. He also recognised that Athens had sufficient strength to offer further resistance and to rally support amongst the other cities, which would prolong his campaign in Greece and give the Persians time to build up their army and defences, and he planned instead to make the Athenians his allies.

Thebes was a very different case as they had been Macedonian allies and his harsh treatment of the city was a warning against treachery to other states already allied to Macedon. No Macedonian voice was raised to challenge the king. He now ruled the army and dispensed justice with absolute power and senior promotions came only on his orders. If he had been a different man, the people would have felt the yoke of the despot but Philip, the king, was dedicated to his kingly office and duty always overrode privilege. By his achievements, Macedonians were now leaders of Greece, a heady position for 'barbarians' and one that we found very much to our liking.

Chapter 6

As a sign of his desire for reconciliation with the Athenians, the king gave Alexander command of the escort taking the Athenian ashes home. Because of my fluency in Athenian Greek, to my delight I was chosen to be in the prince's party for I longed to see my mother's native city. As we made ready to leave, the king instructed his ambassadors to visit the Greek states and summon them to a congress at Corinth. It was high summer and to give all the delegates time to assemble, he convened the conference for the beginning of winter.

Alexander rode at the head of the escort, as we left for Athens, with Parmenion at his side. When he wished to discuss our reception in Athens and the reactions of the Athenians, he invited me to join them. I was once again privileged to listen to Parmenion and I learned much wisdom from the old soldier.

The prince showed traces of irritation when he spoke to the general. I concluded that Alexander was impatient with old ideas, which contrasted seriously with the king's new policies. It was harvest time in Attica. The countryside was ablaze with gold, green and red. The grapes hung rich and full on the vines, ready to be picked and dried for storage or trampled underfoot to make wine. The olives were ripe and the peasants were gathering crops in all the fields. Above the earth, there was a light of dazzling clarity. It reached to the heavens in crystalline brightness, illuminating the land in glowing radiance. I marvelled in light-headed ecstasy, intoxicated by the elemental power of the divine Apollo. When we arrived at the gates of Athens, a great crowd had gathered to give us a tumultuous welcome in gratitude for the city's escape from destruction. We were royally housed and cheers followed Alexander wherever he passed. The Athenians gave splendid feasts in our honour and we made a ceremonial visit to the Acropolis in a procession of priests. The feeling of relief, amongst the citizens that their city was spared was so great that both Alexander and Philip were made citizens. Through it all Alexander maintained his princely dignity. He had qualities very different from the republicans who ruled Athens. His power to command and inspire seemed to come from when the gods first shaped the earth. Daily he grew in stature and his dignity converted the Athenians to his leadership.

One night I slipped away to climb a solitary path to the Acropolis. The moon was riding full across the sky and, in that place of unearthly magnificence, I stood alone and breathed into my soul the transcendent spirit, which is the essence of divinity held captive on this sacred site. The marble of the Parthenon gleamed in pale gold reflecting the radiance of the moon, in contrast to the dark shadows, and it was as if the temple floated in air above the earth. I would most happily have remained in Athens dedicated to the service of the gods, but I had laid aside my personal inclinations in service to Alexander when I was charged by Aristotle.

When we returned to Philip's headquarters, we found that embassies from the Greek states had arrived to make arrangements for the Congress at Corinth. Part of the Macedonian army was now garrisoning Thebes and, in sad exchange for the city, there were many Thebans detained in the camp as slaves and Theban women were the solace of Macedonians serving far from home. Some of our men had been sent on leave to Macedon by the king, with orders to return before the opening of the Conference in distant Corinth. Philip intended to have a strong army on display in that city and to use the opportunity to integrate the armies of the conquered cities with that of Macedon.

The king had summoned delegates from all the islands, the former members of the Hellenic League and all the states up to the Macedonian border. Alexander was constantly at his father's side and, at every opportunity, the king continued to advise the prince in the arts of diplomacy and leadership.

Sparta alone refused the king's invitation to attend the Congress. Philip responded to this insolence by sending troops to destroy her crops and he adjusted her borders. She was isolated from the rest of Greece, not only by the harsh idealism which had always set her apart, but in trade and the confinement of her citizens within her walls.

We moved to Corinth and the Congress opened with the pomp of great military displays and ceremonies. At their conclusion, Philip presided at a meeting of all the delegates. He invited them to form an alliance to attack Persia, recover the Greek cities of Anatolia and to avenge the burning of Athens and her temples by the Persians when they invaded Greece, some one hundred and fifty full seasons earlier.

The king announced to the delegates that Macedon would not join the Congress but that he, as his country's King Commander, would personally conduct negotiations with the League. The delegates properly elected Philip their Hegemon and they gave him command, in war, of the ships and men, which they would contribute to the common cause. They established a federal council with plans to meet at all the great pan-Hellenic festivals, with a provision, if circumstances demanded, to allow an additional extraordinary meeting to be convened in Corinth. Philip granted all members of the League exemption from payment of tribute and, in the event of an attack against any one of them, he guaranteed the support of Macedonian troops. He forbade all acts of piracy at sea, and he ruled that all naval actions should come under the command of the League. In return for these generous terms, the League members swore to give money and soldiers to the common cause. They took an oath never to attempt to overthrow Philip, or his descendants, and to keep the peace amongst themselves.

Philip had treated his defeated enemies so well that their delegates voted to approve his proposals and, with this achieved, he re-convened the Congress for the early summer following the coming winter after their cities had ratified the treaty. The king had brilliantly legalised his position, and he had made his cause the common cause of all Greece, except Sparta, and he now controlled armies strong enough to challenge Persia. Philip's last act at Corinth was to send stonemasons to prepare marble for sculptors to carve a colossal lion at Khaironeia to commemorate the fallen and his own victory in the battle against Athens and her allies.

Chapter 7

At the conclusion of the first Congress of Corinth, the king left Parmenion in command of the army in that city as a show of strength to all the allied states. The king returned to Macedon, accompanied by Alexander, and escorted by a detachment of the cavalry and a few pages. As we travelled north, General Attalos rode at the king's side, in Parmenion's customary place, with Alexander and Hephaestion immediately behind them. The prince was silent and deep in thought. I had heard rumours of a breach in the royal family but the king had given Alexander full recognition for his successful leadership in battle, command of the mission to Athens and the position at his right hand during the conference in Corinth, honour enough for so young a prince.

I knew, too well, the folly of conjecture in the affairs of the royal household for they were wild and unpredictable in their private lives. The king, faithless to Olympia, was a drunk and violent man although a great leader and an incomparable strategist with a mind so cunning that often his victories were as much by outwitting his enemies as defeating them on the battlefield.

Olympias was a goddess and no less ruthless. She was tempestuous, proud and much less concerned with men than with gods and she made herself their willing instrument. She was as beautiful as the wild creatures of the mountains and forests and almost a part of the divine order. She could enslave or destroy any man and her titanic rages doomed everyone who opposed her. Her snakes, always coiling within her reach, were a terrifying manifestation of her close communion with the gods and the vital role that she played in the mysteries was a measure of the way in which they possessed her. She was most feared when she danced naked in the woods and there were rumours, fed by Olympias herself, that Zeus had fathered Alexander in the manifestation of a snake. Such stories provoked the king's rage but he never allowed them to alienate himself from his son.

Alexander loved to gather with friends for food, wine and conversation and we often sat together far into the night. Occasionally, the prince seemed absent in spirit and lost in his own thoughts and, rarely, he fell into rages which were usually provoked by his capricious family. He possessed unique qualities of leadership, courage and endurance leavened with mystical beliefs which found expression in faith in his own destiny. From his father, he learned statecraft, and Aristotle had schooled him in logic and taught him science, recreated the heroic deeds of history and opened his eyes to the mysteries of life and all these disciplines were the foundation of Alexander's intellect and character. The king had also shown, by his example, the secrets of the command of men and the arts of military strategy and the importance of winning men's minds, if not their hearts, as vital to a lasting victory in war and peace.

Cleopatra, the king's daughter, played little part in the life of the court. She was terrified of her mother and hardly noticed by her father. She worshipped Alexander from a distance and was rarely seen. She attended a school with a group of girls who lived in the palace and amongst them were the daughters of Theocritos and Cleitus and the niece of General Attalos, who was also named Cleopatra. My mother's niece and the sister of Ptolemy also attended the school. I supposed that they were all waiting for marriage and an opportunity to manage their own estates and families. Many years later, a second illegitimate daughter had been born to the king and she was named Thessalonike in celebration of his victory over the Thessalonians.

This was the family to whom we owed our loyalty. Personal defects in princes are often not of great consequence to a kingdom, if they exercise their royal office with justice and honour so that they may command our allegiance. That is the divine order of life and a bad king may well succeed a good king as the ancients recognised. Many of the internecine wars of the Greeks can be traced to republican forms of government. Politicians are usually blinded by their own self-importance and they are in pursuit of fame and fortune, whereas a king inherits these trappings of office and even if his dedication is to his own welfare this is bound in the welfare of his kingdom, or so I reflected. Long before we reached the gates of Pella, excited crowds met us on the road leading to the city. They tore down pine branches and picked flowers to strew in our path and Alexander rode beside the king. The people were wild with delight when they saw him and the sun, on his hair, made a halo of light round his head and he looked like a hero from an ancient odyssey. He made no acknowledgement to the crowd, which only increased the excitement. He was already a hero, receiving a hero's welcome but he was also an isolated figure as he proudly rode on the high-striding Bucephalos.

When we reached the palace, the queen, her daughter, Cleopatra, and their women waited in a group outside the entrance. They were gorgeously dressed and their jewels glittered in the brilliant sunlight. It was heady wine for victorious soldiers and probably the greatest welcome ever given to the army in Pella.

The king had sent swift messengers, with lists of the dead, after the Battle of Khaeronia, and their families were in places of honour at the foot of the palace steps. Some of the bereaved women were wailing and the king let them know that he intended to give them an equal share of the spoils to compensate them for their fallen men. We were drawn up in battle order and dismissed; the pages and companions formed a group to escort the king and Alexander into the palace. Philip barely paused to acknowledge Olympias and marched straight on; we were bound to follow him, but I felt my anger rise against him for such a slight against the queen.

That night, Philip gave a splendid feast in the palace at Pella. Alexander sat at the king's right hand and the oily Attalos was on his left and Cleopatra, his niece, sat on the general's right side. The queen was to Alexander's right and she held her head high and her lips formed a tight, straight line; she neither ate nor drank during the celebration. Philip, on the other hand, drank an enormous quantity of wine and rose unsteadily to his feet at the end of the banquet. As he began to speak, a hush settled over the crowd and his words were slightly slurred as he said: "This night, we all have cause to praise the gods and to rejoice in our great victories which have resulted in peace, at last amongst the Greeks, and prosperity for Macedon as we take the leadership of the great enterprises of the future. I also give you another good reason for happiness for tomorrow I shall wed the beautiful lady Cleopatra, who is the niece of Attalos."

He sat down amid a tense silence. I looked towards Olympias and saw her rise to her feet and Alexander supported her and together, with every eye upon them, they walked from the banqueting hall. The king's liaisons were prodigious but this was a different story. Philip was attempting a semblance of legality in an affair which threatened the position of Olympias, as queen, and Alexander as heir to the throne. The assembly remained seated in an awful silence until the last sounds of the queen's departure faded. The hall was then filled with the buzzing sound as of angry bees as everyone fell to discussing the implications of the king's words. Some people rose to offer their congratulations to Philip and even to the malicious uncle, smiling in undisguised triumph. They were indeed hasty to show the king approval and, in my youth, I marvelled as I watched the sycophants and noted their easy duplicity and disloyalty towards both Olympias and Alexander. My father was one of the first, amongst others of his generation, to leave the banquet and I hastened to follow and caught up with him just outside the palace. He looked tired and frail and he turned to me, saying: "My son, I intend to leave Pella at once and retire from the king's service. I have seen enough this night to want no part of it. You, however, are now a man and you must make up your own mind about your personal opinions and loyalties. Whichever way you decide can mean trouble, even danger, for the king has already shown you many preferences and in return he might reasonably expect your fidelity, but Alexander is your friend and he is naturally with the queen. You cannot at this time be loyal to both of them and a choice is forced upon you."

I tried to think carefully as I answered him: "I am grateful, father, that you do not try to influence me for I must support Alexander and the Lady Olympias but I pray to the gods that there will be a peaceful end to this quarrel."

My father replied, his voice strained with emotion: "You have chosen well for Alexander is the future of Macedon and Greece."

We quickly embraced and I left him standing alone to hasten to the queen's quarters in the palace. The guard at the entrance allowed me to pass when I answered his challenge and once inside I ordered the page on duty to announce my arrival.

Hephaestion received me and beyond him I could see gathered in the room Craterus, Coenos, Amyntas, Ptolemy, Philotas, the son of Carsis, Nicanor, the grandson of Parmenion, Antigonus, Pausanius and Perdicass and we were all from the school at Mieza. Alexander stood alone beside a statue of Achilles intently watching the queen as she paced up and down the room. Her eyes glittered in fury and her hands, clenched in rage, were held before her. She stood still as I approached her and I said: "Madam, my life belongs to you and to the prince. I ask for no greater honour than to serve you both and may the gods be witness to my oath."

As she replied her eyes flashed with fire and she said: "Jason, son of my old friend Nearchos, I ask you to be a true Companion to Alexander, to guard him, to support him against all enemies, until death relieves you of this responsibility."

I was overcome with emotion in that moment and I took her hand in mine before making room for others to follow me and I turned to the side of Alexander. He placed his hands in mine and said with undisguised feeling: "Jason, this day will ever remain in our memories, but it shall not alter my father's plans for Macedon and the unity of the Greeks as we prepare to cross the Hellespont, to defeat the Persians and destroy the Persian King of Kings on his own ground. I am convinced that the follies of my father will long be forgotten even as Alexander's name will be famous throughout the world even to distant Ocean."

Turning to the queen, he spoke decisively as he said to her: "Mother, I shall attend the king at this famous marriage that we shall know his intentions and be in a better position to make our own plans."

Olympias was still for a moment and then she answered him in anger: "Alexander, by your father, Zeus, set Philip's cunning to naught. Let your wits be far sharper than his that you may destroy him before he destroys you. We shall then reign together more successfully than any others in our long history for we are descended from the gods."

Alexander seemed about to answer the queen and then changed his mind and left the room. I followed him and walked on my solitary way beyond the palace courtyard. Olympias had once again claimed the paternity of Zeus for Alexander. I tried to think that the god was the common father of us all and of all the other gods, but the queen went far beyond this simple religious belief. She created, by risking his legitimacy as Philip's son and heir, a ready excuse for the king to disinherit him. Olympias had also spoken of a joint rule with Alexander. A queen she was, as a king's wife, but a ruler in her own right she could never be, especially as joint ruler with Alexander for they were both incapable of sharing power.

I thought of the prince's hesitation as she spoke for the significance of her words had not escaped him. He must have considered it better to humour her strange fancies rather than argue when greater issues must be resolved. I walked in the peace of the garden and the fragrance of roses was all about me as the full moon shone down from heaven. The sounds of frogs and cicadas kept my thoughts company, for when princes quarrel a great deal of hardship may come to the land and lives and property are often lost in their differences and many families are torn apart in factional loyalty.

Ptolemy, son of Lagos, was also in the garden and, as we met, I saw that his craggy features, beneath his curly hair, were drawn into an expression of distaste. He was a quiet man, scholarly and totally indifferent to palace gossip or intrigue. We walked together and talked, but not of the royal family, but rather of Nectanebo, the Egyptian seer, who had told us many stories of his native land. Ptolemy had promised himself to visit the Nile and personally see if the Egyptian had spoken truly of strange gods and their vast temples and pyramids, and of the unimaginable beauty of the palaces of the pharaohs and especially of the annual inundation of the Nile.

Chapter 8

Very early the next morning, a messenger brought me word to join Alexander. By the time that I reached his quarters, all the Companions who had gathered there the previous evening had already arrived. The prince dismissed the pages and asked Craterus to guard the door before he spoke to us, saying: "My friends, between us there are few secrets, no grudges of which I am aware and we have pledged our mutual loyalty to each other. I now count on you, not only through the events of to-day but wherever we find ourselves in the immediate future. We will all go to my father's nuptials, although I intend to spare the queen from so insulting a farce. I ask you to be especially alert to danger and to carry concealed weapons throughout this day and lastly to have your horses bridled for a swift departure from the city. Pausanios now wishes to speak to you."

Pausanios was a quiet, dull man and not given to pushing himself forward or promoting his own interests. Silence fell as he told us in bitter words: "Alexander, the lady whom the king intends to marry is my longstanding betrothed. Since our return from Corinth, I have had no opportunity to hear her wishes concerning this marriage to the king and I learned of it only when he gave his speech last night.

"The lady's uncle, Attalos, as you will recall, rode with the king throughout the march north from Corinth and they left Alexander as much in the dark about their plans as myself. I therefore pledge myself to the service of the prince and I intend to avenge my honour. If the parents of Cleopatra were still alive, I am confident that they would have refused the king's suit. Attalos, on the other hand, is an ambitious man and he would use any method to gain favour with the king. This, I warn, is but a beginning of his schemes."

Pausanios stepped back against the wall as he ended his speech and his face was angry with humiliation and lost pride.

We were all bewildered by his words, which joined us in a dangerous, personal quarrel with the king. We had answered Alexander's call for our loyalty only in support of his legitimacy and right to succeed to Macedon's throne. For Pausanios I felt no call to sacrifice or service. His words made me uneasy and I doubted that any good could come to Alexander with this man in our party, nursing so great but private a grievance. Alexander broke into the tense silence and said: "Now, my friends, you see more clearly how the king's affairs stand. He has a passion for the lady, Cleopatra. In exchange for her favours, Attalos has held out for a marriage between them and a throne for his niece that his may be the voice whispering to the king and controlling the succession. I invite you all to the wedding so that together we can witness a king's folly."

I hurried to my father's house and found his servants packing for his move to the country. He had already sent his resignation to the king and his retirement caused no comment amongst other members of Philip's court who were consumed by gossip at the word of the king's new marriage. My father was in his library and he was supervising the packing of his statues, precious books and other treasures. He had already received Philip's message accepting his resignation and he told me that he planned to leave that day to avoid attendance at the king's marriage. I wondered if Philip could understand his old friend's disapproval and if he was making it easy for him to leave Pella in quiet dignity?

I told my father of the words of Pausanios. He surprised me and revealed that the parents of Cleopatra and Pausanios had signed a marriage contract during the infancy of their children. They were elderly, and intended to unite their two estates. He also told me that Attalos, through his mother's family, could make a claim to the patrimony of Pausanios so that he was also in danger of losing his wealth and lands to the ambitious general. My father then advised me, saying: "Try not to become involved in this separate business with Pausanios. It is enough for you to be loyal to Alexander's interests. The king can hardly fault you there, as it is by his command that you ride at the side of the prince. The favour of kings is often fickle and its recipients more likely to feel the chill of disfavour than the citizens of a republic.

Who indeed may question a king? They are often self-serving and ambitious and they can easily remove all who stand in their way."

My father was wise with years and service in the army and I most carefully heeded his advice as I said goodbye to him. I walked into Pella and paid my bills with money given to me by my father. The vintner was especially happy to see me as I had owed him money from before the Battle of Khaeronia. A few of my creditors were willing to wait for settlement as they added a rate of interest to the outstanding bill and so, by immoral custom, they increased my debt by an escalating amount, but I needed to hold some money in reserve to cover the expenses of the next few days.

I returned to the palace and ordered my groom to bridle and saddle my horse to be ready from sunset onwards. I packed money, with other necessities, in my saddlebag and I told my slave to wait for my return with my outer garments for the nights were raw and cold.

I next walked to the house of Theocritos, an old friend of my father, to let him know my father's plans. An attraction for me was to try and see his daughter, Penelope. She was much favoured by the Muses and by me and I thought that she might be in her father's house. She lived at the palace and attended school with the princess but, with the return of the army and Philip's marriage, there seemed a chance that she would be with her parents.

Tyche favoured me and I found Penelope, with her father, sitting in their courtyard. Theocritos greeted me affectionately and I inquired for his health and that of Penelope, which was truly radiant. I took the opportunity to study her face as she made her reply to me. Her eyes were unusually blue and deeply expressive and they slanted upward a little towards the outer point. Her hair was fair and dressed back from her high forehead and her skin was the palest olive and her mouth was full and smiling. She was dressed in a long white chiton and she wore no jewels, for her beauty needed none. Theocritos beckoned to a slave and ordered him to bring out refreshments and, when the man returned, we drank a cup of wine together from his own vineyards. He was proud of the quality and I gave it appropriate praise for it was very good and carried the taste of the earth of Macedon.

I looked at the gentle Penelope, and she seemed so pale and fragile until unbidden, thoughts of the dark, imperious queen came surging into my mind and it was difficult to dismiss the corrupting image of Olympias.

Penelope spoke of the king's marriage. She had grown up with the niece of Attalos and knew of her betrothal to Pausanios. She chattered on, as girls do, and seemed not to notice my lack of comment. Her father, cautiously, was against the king's marriage for he disliked Attalos and distrusted his new position near to the throne. He asked me how Alexander had taken the news, but I was excused replying to him by the arrival of his wife. I took my leave of this good family and made my way back to the palace. It was noon before I arrived and food was laid out for us in the dining-hall. Alexander, Craterus, Hephaestion and several other Companions were gathered there and we had a simple meal of fish, olives, cheese and fruits and we washed them down with barley beer. We were unusually quiet, even Alexander spoke little and Hephaestion, as was his custom, took his direction from the prince. Craterus and I talked together but of the king's marriage we said nothing for it is prudent not to be overheard, when servants may spy, especially during a time of bitter controversies in the royal family. We did not doubt that the king had us watched in an attempt to discover Alexander's plans. We talked of Mieza and Aristotle and our service in the army until Craterus asked me: "Will you join the hunt when we leave shortly?"

I knew nothing of this plan and so replied in the same spirit: "My father is retiring today and is leaving Pella for the country. As soon as Alexander can spare me, I intend to join him and all the Companions are welcome at my father's house."

I hoped to let him know that there was a safe haven for all of Alexander's Companions but, at the same time, I was concerned to protect my father from accusations of plotting with us and against the king.

Craterus thought and then nodded in understanding and said: "Speaking only for myself, I hope to accept your invitation and I shall let the others know of your father's kindness."

After the hurried meal, we separated. I went to my quarters in the palace to rest. I slept well and when I woke up I saw that my slave was preparing a finely woven chiton suitable for me to wear for the king's wedding. Wine stood on a side table but

I drank none in order to keep a clear head during the marriage feast and for whatever might follow it.

I dressed with care in the gold-embroidered chiton and underneath it I carried a dagger and I wore another small weapon concealed in the thongs of my sandal.

My slave had been born on my family's estates and I felt confident that he was trustworthy, but this was the first time that I had been dependant on the goodwill of another person for my safety, apart from on the battlefield. I was only too well aware that the king could reward him handsomely for betraying any part of what he knew to be Alexander's plans. I was therefore silent as he combed my hair and carefully arranged it. As he did so he quietly said: "Master, now that my lord, your father, has left Pella, I ask your permission to follow him. I should like to see my own family and live in the peace of the country and once again serve your father."

The man had been given to me when Aristotle had opened the school in Mieza and he had been with me throughout the recent campaigns. He could not leave the city without my written authority and this I gladly gave to him. If I stayed in Pella, I could easily go to my father's house and take one of the other servants or, alternatively, if I left the city with Alexander, it was better that he was not available for questioning by the king. I felt a twinge of regret that I had not thought of his welfare for I had known him all my life and he was a good servant and faithful to my family. We had an unspoken understanding and with the pass he could leave Pella without any danger of being picked up as a runaway slave.

I went to Alexander's quarters and found that I was one of the first to arrive. Several of the prince's Companions were orphans and absent making arrangements for the care of their houses and estates. Alexander greeted me briefly. His smile was tense and his eyes smouldered in anger, his golden hair was arranged with care and the intensity of his gaze was accented by the disparity in the colour of his eyes. He was dressed in a white silk chiton, a gift of rare and fragile beauty from his mother. The mysterious material came from the very ends of the earth, far beyond the limits of the Persian Empire, and it must have cost a king's ransom. The prince also wore a costly dagger, with a magnificent gold handle encrusted with jewels, in his sandal thong. On his shoulder there was a clasp with an

45

image of Achilles, his ancestor, carved in a great cameo relief and Alexander, in that moment, radiated such princely qualities that we were all willing to follow his lead to the ends of the earth. As the other Companions gathered, I felt the general strain amongst us. It was one thing to attack an enemy on the battlefield and quite a different matter to act against the king. We spoke in hushed voices, or were silent, knowing that we were watched and, possibly, risking our lives.

When all were present, Alexander began to speak: "My friends, I greet you. If any of you have pressing affairs, the care of which must take priority over tonight's business and its consequences, you must go and see to them. It is not my wish either to bind myself to anyone of you who has a different opinion about the king's marriage, or about anything that I may do as a consequence of his folly, nor should I want such a companion and neither can I predict how this night will end ..."

He paused and as none of us moved or spoke he continued: "Should we be separated during my father's marriage feast, you will proceed along the south-western road for 80 stades and there you will wait for me. If I should die, or I do not join you by dawn, return to your homes immediately so that the king's attention will not be directed towards you and he will not hold you accountable for your loyalty to Alexander."

He smiled as he spoke and relieved some of the tension. I am sure that he had no serious thought of his own death and that he was considering only our safety. He ended by saying ironically: "If none of you wish to leave, or if you have no questions, let us join my father and his bride, the niece of the crafty Attalos."

Alexander led us to the great banqueting hall. The noise died down as we approached his father who was seated between Attalos and Cleopatra. The prince bore Philip's drunken scrutiny with great dignity and saluting the king, Alexander addressed him with irony: "I am here father and as you see without my mother."

Philip's one good eye rested on him uneasily and he replied: "Take your seat Alexander and join me in the festivities for my marriage. Tonight I overlook your discourtesies toward the new queen. From tomorrow, see to it that I have no further cause for complaint."

Before Alexander could move, Attalos rose to his feet and looking straight at Alexander said that Macedonians ought to pray to the gods for a legitimate heir from the king's new marriage. In great fury, Alexander hurled his wine-cup at the head of Attalos and Attalos threw his goblet at the prince. The king drew his sword and threatened Alexander but he stumbled and fell from the effects of too much wine. Alexander stood over him and shouted that Macedonians should look carefully upon the man who would cross into Asia and defeat the Persians and yet fall crossing from one couch to another.

The prince then strode from the hall leaving an appalled silence. All his Companions followed him and we could hear a great din from the banquet as people rushed to help the king or shouted comments with their neighbours about the scandalous scene before them. I walked to my own quarters and I gathered up my cloak and money and hurried to the stables.

Craterus was already there and he told me that Alexander, with Hephaestion, intended to take Olympias away from Macedon. We were assisted by the grooms to mount as we waited for them. When they joined us, we left Pella by the western gate. Once beyond the city, we made great speed before the king might discover our flight. He would surely pursue Olympias and Alexander and probably kill them, to prevent them becoming a rallying point for revolt. After riding hard for many stades, we caught up with the other Companions. Alexander and Hephaestion now rode on either side of the queen, Craterus and I followed them and the rest covered our rear, at some little distance, to shout a warning if we were overtaken by the king's men. By the next evening, without any sound of pursuit, we were approaching the passes over the Pindos Mountains and travelling towards the Epirot border.

Olympias was magnificent. She rode as hard as Alexander and uttered no complaints. She ate dried fruit, goat's cheese and unleavened bread twice daily, washed down with rough barley beer or water from the streams, vulgar food for a queen to endure. In three days we reached the Epirot border. The horses were desperately tired, except for the great Bucephalos. We also were weary as we turned from the road, on a track to an estate owned by one of the queen's kinsmen; where we rested for two days. Word of our arrival in the country was sent to her brother, also named Alexander, and now the King of Epiros.

By the standards of the court at Pella, amenities in this prince's palace were rough and the food was coarse and ill-prepared, but after the hard journey it served as a flea-ridden haven for us all. The dialect of the people was uncivilised and crude and they kept conversation to a minimum, except for Olympias. She was so much at home and showed great enjoyment amongst these barbarian people; Epiros was all that she knew before her marriage to King Philip. It occurred to me that she had done well to exchange such rough living for the comforts of Pella and the jewels, clothes, food, gold, silver, fine sculptures and beautiful cities, to say nothing of the Macedons, their conversation and courtesy to each other.

Epirot mountains are lofty, wild and desolate and made more so by the constant bad weather. We experienced driving sleet in winds that cut like a dagger. We were trained soldiers and hardened to rigorous conditions and Olympias always kept up with our pace. I assumed that the desolation was partly to blame for her wild character, having been born in such a remote and untamed place.

We left our hideout at daybreak and continued the ride over the bleak mountains until we descended into the western foothills and the king's palace in a small, unkempt town. I was told that we were not far north of Dodona, the most ancient sanctuary in Greece and beyond this was the Ionian Sea. The king's welcome to us lacked warmth. He was probably reluctant to attract Philip's fury or even risk an attack from so powerful a quarter. He could, however, hardly do less than show hospitality to his sister and his nephew and express outrage for the insults which they had endured.

We bathed, and were supplied with fresh clothes and escorted to the banqueting hall to a meal of skewered goat, unleavened bread and grapes and wine, in the presence of the king and his court. Conversation was at a minimum until, at the conclusion of the meal, Alexander spoke to his uncle, but he looked at his mother: "My friends and I are grateful for your hospitality and I feel confident that my mother will have a safe refuge here in Epiros for tomorrow I must leave for Illyria."

His words shocked us all and Olympias angrily asked: How long shall you be gone and how long shall I remain here? What other plans have you made without consulting me?"

Alexander answered her: "Mother, your honour and your safety are my first concern and this is your home. I must leave as it is to our advantage to be separated for the king, my father, to take one of us only would give him small satisfaction. I shall send word to you as often as my circumstances allow. I am going to seek the loyalty of the northern tribes and to make preparations to recruit an army, if my father forces me to fight against him."

There was a tense hush over the assembly at Alexander's words. I do not think that any of the Macedonians had thought of civil war and we all must have wondered if we had chosen the losing side. The prince then parted from his mother and uncle and, with the Companions trailing behind, he made for his quarters. Once there, he invited us to join him and he asked for a volunteer to return to Pella and to keep him informed of King Philip's plans.

After a little thought, I offered to return to Macedon. To campaign in war is one thing but to exile oneself from home and engage in civil war against the king, and such a king as Philip, risked not only my life but that of my father and of his close friends.

As no-one else spoke, Alexander accepted my offer. I parted from the other Macedonians with very sad feelings. They were going on to other distant lands to find adventure in Alexander's cause. They had been my constant companions for six years; now I might be facing great personal danger and I well knew that Philip would not hesitate to use torture to extract information from me.

I decided first to go to see my father. Perhaps the king would then assume that I had left Pella with him, rather than with Alexander. I rose the next day before daybreak. I found a guide willing to take me through the mountains of Epiros and a spare horse to carry supplies and so that I could rest my own mount when he tired of the pace. I did not intend to stop, except for very short periods to sleep, until I reached my father's house.

It was a dreadful journey. The sleet changed to snow, making it difficult for even the guide to find the way. The falls were light or I think it very unlikely that I should ever have returned to Macedon alive. Winters at home can be bitterly cold but in the loneliness of those mountains, it was far worse than anything that I had previously experienced.

Chapter 9

My father was delighted to see me. My slave had arrived from Pella and I was soon made comfortable and enjoying a meal of fish, olives, stuffed chicken, lamb, pork, salads, fruits, bread and wine. I was very hungry after my journey and my father smiled as he watched the quantities of food, which I consumed. When the servants withdrew, I gave him an account of all that had happened in the short time since our parting in Pella. He listened with care, and he told me the little news which had reached him from the palace.

The king did not discover the flight of Alexander and Olympias until the morning after his wedding feast. It was then too late for pursuit as there was no indication of the route by which they had left the capital.

He sent emissaries in all directions and was in a monumental rage over their flight. Attalos was out of favour for causing a public breach in the family, but otherwise, the king was delighted with his bride and ready to indulge her whims, provided that they did not interfere with his plans for Macedon, Greece and Asia. Philip had convened a second congress in Corinth and a messenger arrived inviting my father to join the king on the journey south.

My father suggested that the invitation was an easy opportunity for me to appear at court and offer myself in his place and so present myself to King Philip. I agreed, and I prepared for another journey but this time with servants, baggage and food. I arrived at the palace in Pella and I asked to see the king. One of the slaves escorted me into the council chamber and as I approached him, silence fell over the crowd gathered there. He stared at me with his one good eye, until I felt very uncomfortable and he finally said: "Well, well Jason, the son of Nearchos, it is a great surprise to see you here; what news do you have of Alexander?"

I answered as my father had advised: "Your Majesty, I have just come from my father's house in the country and I am ignorant of all that has happened since my departure from Pella. My father is ailing in health and asks that I may serve you in his place."

Philip did not immediately reply but the colour in his face turned red and everyone was very quiet as they listened when he spoke: "I shall allow you to come to Corinth for I wish that Alexander will have accurate reports of all that occurs at the Congress and I am confident that you will undertake that duty. He is still my son and heir and his childish action in leaving Pella must not be allowed to interfere with his right to know state affairs. From now on, the succession is more important than this prince, whose position may alter in the future."

We seemed to understand each other, although the king's words held a threat against Alexander, but I was relieved, as I had feared close questioning or even imprisonment. The king had now turned the situation to his own advantage and he intended to use me to communicate with the prince. This could only mean that I would be given a report of all the facts that Philip meant to be passed on to Alexander.

My situation was much better than I had dared to anticipate. Preparations were under way for the departure of the court for Corinth. I missed Alexander and the Companions but I used the time to organise a trustworthy source in Pella, through whom I could send secret messages to the prince.

Philip played down his family's quarrel in the cause of Macedonian unity. Out of public view, Demaratos of Corinth was in his confidence and preparing to act as mediator between the king and Alexander. During this time, I also called at the house of Theocritos several times and I was fortunate to find Penelope at home on two occasions. Now that Olympias was away from Pella, I was more aware of Penelope's charms. She seemed pleased to see me and we strolled in the garden of her father's house and I was delighted by her knowledge of flowers, herbs and shrubs and their uses in food and medicine. I had no sisters and knew few other girls and her company was a new and gentle experience.

The king, court and army travelled south and arrived in

Corinth after all the other delegates had assembled. The court and a contingent of the army accompanied Philip into the great council chamber and he opened the proceedings with a tremendous speech in which he condemned the infamous 'King's Peace' dictated by the Persian King of Kings at Sardis of Lydia. He once more pledged to the Congress that he would lead the Greek states to conquer Persia and forever end Persian interference in Greek affairs, free the Greek cities of Anatolia and guarantee peace throughout Greece. He roused the delegates to great emotional heights by promising vengeance for Persia's destruction of Greek shrines and temples and all their insults to the gods of Greece.

The king ended his speech with a proposal to ratify the treaty, creating the League of Corinth, to tumultuous applause. Venerable Isocrates of Athens had already prepared the delegates by previously writing an open letter to Philip proposing war against the Persians under the king's leadership. The delegates unanimously voted for an alliance with Macedon under the hegemony of Philip and even to give the money, arms and men necessary for the campaign. Sparta alone was absent from Corinth, as an otherwise united Greece declared war on Persia. By the terms of 'The King's Peace' signed at Sardis, such a union was expressly forbidden and Sparta was a Persian ally.

I wrote a letter to Alexander detailing the momentous events at Corinth, which I sent by messenger to Epiros that same day. I was confident that it would be intercepted by the king's men, and I wrote a second, secret account, which I dispatched through a friend in Pella. I reported to the prince that the king was eager for reconciliation and that his own status remained unchanged. I added that Philip had easily discovered his refuge and that he was sending Demaratos as a mediator between them. I also advised the prince that the king would delay the invasion of Asia until Alexander returned to Pella. Philip well knew that Alexander was high in the public affection and could pose a great threat to himself if the prince remained in Macedon, should the expedition march from Greece with their differences unresolved. In the great events now unfolding, with all Greek eyes, save Sparta's, turned towards the Hellespont, I thought that it was a moment in history which might easily rival that of any tales from the ancient epics.

Immediately after the vote in Corinth, Philip prepared to

return to Macedon. He left a small group of civilians, backed by part of the army, to run the day to day business of the Congress. In great heart, we marched north for our king was lord of all Greece with the title of Hegemon of the League. We enjoyed our new status and power and we spoke, carelessly, of new battles and gloated over the riches that we might gain in the future. The men sang and everywhere along our route people came out of their houses to hang garlands round our necks and welcome us with food and wine. Political victories seemed sweeter than those of war with its cruel waste of life and resources and devastation of the cities and land. Parmenion rode north beside King Philip and thus the king began to remove the cause of his quarrel with Alexander and he eased the way for a reconciliation with the prince. When we reached Pella, the king ordered Parmenion to recruit and train a mighty army for the crossing of the Hellespont.

Demaratos returned from meeting Alexander and Olympias to continue negotiations, which were progressing towards a resolution. One firm condition proposed by the queen was to marry off her only daughter, Cleopatra, to her brother Alexander, King of Epiros. A suggestion very acceptable to the king. It would bind the Epirots closer to Macedon and they would more likely help to defend us from diversionary attacks by border tribes in the north. The king concealed his enthusiasm for the absent queen's stipulation, using it instead as a concession by him as the bargaining continued.

I wrote a secret letter to Alexander, which I dispatched before Demaratos left Pella once more. I thought that the prince would welcome time to plan his next move and to prepare a reply before the return of Philip's mediator. I then felt free to visit my father and I asked him to negotiate with Theocritos for the hand of his daughter. Pella was a lonely place without my friends and I knew that my father desired me to marry before I left with the army for Asia. So warmly had I been received by Penelope's family that I hoped that my proposal would be accepted. It was most agreeable to be pleasing so many people, including myself, that I made sacrifices to the gods for the pleasantness of my life in this interlude.

My father was delighted with my plan and he returned with me to Pella. Theocritos gave his consent and my father and I walked to the palace to observe the courtesy of telling the king of my intended marriage. He received us cordially and he offered me his congratulations and wished me many children.

Shortly after, Olympias, Alexander and the Companions returned to Pella. Philip gave the prince a military parade and a banquet at which he spoke of his son and heir with deliberate emphasis as his successor. He also announced the forthcoming marriage of his daughter to the King of Epiros, planned to take place before we marched for the campaign in Asia.

Olympias was restored to her position as queen and the now pregnant Cleopatra, niece of Attalos, was rarely seen in the palace. Preparations were made for an extravagant wedding ceremony and feast at the nuptials of the king's daughter. Philip never missed an opportunity to display pomp as a facet of power. Reports of an army of trained and armed soldiers were calculated to make a potential enemy hesitate before planning a revolt against Macedon. It was at this time that word reached the king of the murder of the Persian King of Kings by his wazir, a eunuch named Bogaos, and the accession of his cousin Darius, which had resulted in disorders in the Persian satrapies, welcome news indeed! The court was a happy place with the celebrations of the wedding of Philip's daughter and the news from Asia, especially so for me, with my own marriage to Penelope already arranged. Olympias, as if to show her own importance to Philip and Macedon, received the King of Epiros with an excessive show of welcome, although I think that her poor daughter was only thankful to marry and escape the mediocrity of her life in Pella to her new position as Queen of the Epirots and of the ruling Mossolian House.

Seven days before the wedding, the court moved to Aegae, our ancient capital, where the royal family always returned for ceremonial occasions and family funerals. It lies below the mountains which shelter it from incursions from the sea and commands the roads to Pella and south west across the Pindos Mountains. There is about the city a mystery, and communion with the gods, which is lacking in modern Pella. A long columned avenue leads to the palace and official buildings, which stretch extensively over a high plateau, and below, on the plain, are the tombs of Macedon's kings. The city is a short distance from the Grotto of Mieza, where I had spent happy years at school with Aristotle. Olympias was feline in her satisfaction at the wedding between her daughter and brother; her influence was now extended into Epiros and in the absence of Philip, Alexander and the army in Asia, her power would be the first in Macedon. I saw her walking in the garden with Pausanios on the morning of the wedding. They had their heads together and I imagined Philip's new wife was the subject of their conversation. The queen wanted her out of her way, but a common cause between Olympias and Pausanios seemed an unlikely alliance. He had been morose and angry since Philip's marriage to Cleopatra even though his friends in the Companions urged him to seek another bride, for nurturing a grudge against a king must surely bring a miserable end?

I bathed and dressed and walked to the house of Theocritos to escort Penelope, her parents and my father to the royal wedding. We arrived at the palace in time to join the vast throng of guests as they waited for the ceremonial procession to arrive. It was a clear, moonlit night and the clothes and jewels of the women dazzled the eye. This was the most brilliant occasion ever staged in Macedon and the new wealth, gained through war, was on display to honour the bridal pair. Penelope was exquisite with gold in her hair and jewels on her fingers, and her skin was white alabaster clear in the pale radiance of the moon. We heard the sound of trumpets from the king's private quarters and there was a great flurry of excitement amongst us all. The townspeople and peasants were also crowded into the courtyard to catch a glimpse of the wedding and share in the happy occasion.

As the kings approached, walking side by side, great cheers of acclamation broke from the people. Everything was going well for Macedon and this was an occasion on which to express joy. Then came a great roar: "Alexander! Alexander!" It was constantly repeated and as he exited the palace, everyone went wild with excitement for his homecoming. Now that their quarrel was over who, indeed, could halt Philip and Alexander from the conquest of the world? We followed the procession into the audience hall for the ceremony. I pitied the princess. She seemed carved from marble and showed no sign of happiness, in contrast to her mother who wore a smile of triumph, covering a thousand hidden thoughts. I always came under her spell. My feelings were unrelated to goodness; perhaps that was the fascination. Evil allied to power attracts, where virtue passes unnoticed.

I wondered if Princess Cleopatra had heard the story brought back from Epiros which alleged that, in the absence of Alexander,

Olympias had passed the long nights of exile warming her brother's bed and between them they had schemed up this marriage to open their way to each other. They claimed descent from the gods; explanation enough to set them apart in unnatural behavior. After the wedding ceremony there was a great feast, with food enough for all Greece. None was wasted, for what remained was given to the crowds outside the palace. None of the wine or beer was sent out to them. A populace can become drunken enough, without royal encouragement, and speedily change into an ugly mob.

Philip made a speech at the end of the banquet. At the conclusion, images of the twelve Olympic gods were brought in and he took his place beside them. This caused muttering in the crowd. It appeared as though he intended to take divine status and Macedonians did not care to be ruled by a god on earth. It is easier for a god than for man to abuse power and the gods are ever jealous and could visit terrible punishments on mortals who assume divinity, as I had heard was the case in Egypt. The pages and Companions formed up behind the king and other members of his family were taking their positions as Penelope and I slipped out to the courtyard to watch the procession. We took our places as the trumpets sounded. The king walked, with immense dignity, from the palace, followed by the images of the gods raised on high. As Philip came fully into my sight, a man dashed forward, raised his right hand and stabbed the king. He fell dead. The man dashed towards the gate and I saw, in horror, that it was Pausanios. Companions rushed after him and he stumbled and they were on him. In a few seconds, it was all over. He also lay dead, mutilated beyond questioning and beyond the truth. I saw Theocritos and I left Penelope in his care. My duty was now with Alexander. As the news spread the confusion was horrible. I heard the cry: "Alexander is king". And I thought that I heard the voice of Craterus.

Alexander assumed command and gave immediate orders to the army to patrol the city and control the people. He called for a bier and a door was brought in makeshift haste. He asked four of the Companions to place the king's body upon it and take his father to his own chamber and he ordered servants to bring a table into the courtyard. When it was in position, he leapt upon it and called for silence amongst the people gathered there. He announced the death of the king and he was answered by a roar from the army present: "Alexander is king!"

He was twenty years old. His father was murdered in his forty-seventh year. It was a terrible night. Riots and looting in the city were savagely put down by soldiers. The army won the day and Alexander was indeed King of the Macedonians. Olympias stayed up all night. I thought of the walk which she and Pausanios had taken that same morning but I hastily banished such thoughts. They had the germ of another Atrean tragedy, with Macedon finished as Mycenae died when the House of Agamemnon destroyed itself.

By morning, Alexander exercised sole command, not even Parmenion could be at his side. He ordered an inquiry into Philip's murder and sent dispatches to Parmenion, Pella and the Congress at Corinth with the awful news. The king requested Alexander of Epiros to return home, with his bride, to maintain order there, and he dispatched detachments of the army to Thrace and Illyria to quell any further uprisings. He ordered the army to stand on alert and cancelled all leave. Alexander then sent Nearchos of Crete, Admiral of the Navy, back to the fleet with orders to patrol the coast and he sent word to Isocrates, Philip's advocate in Athens, affirming his own dedication to his father's policies.

When all these things were done, Alexander spoke to his mother and in a firm tone invited her to his quarters. Whether they discussed funeral arrangements, or whether he questioned her or connived with her at this terrible act of violence, is a secret of history. No explanation or motive, or proof of conspiracy has ever been discovered. Pausanios alone is convicted of personal, petty revenge in the murder of King Philip of Macedon.

We cremated Philip's body, according to the ancient rites, and interred the bones in a box of gold and buried him in a tomb at Aegae, with golden diadems, his greaves of uneven length to fit his leg shortened by a battle injury, and many family treasures. It was quickly done and there were now mutterings against Alexander and Olympias with most suspicion falling on the queen. Some spoke in favour of Alexander but against Olympias. I thanked the gods that I alone had witnessed the early morning walk that she had taken with Pausanios. For the unity of Macedon, and all Greece, it was necessary that Pausanios should take the truth to his grave.

Any other explanation would neither restore the king's life

nor produce a prince capable of commanding universal loyalty. Alexander was potentially a greater leader than his father, if he came to the throne untarnished by accusations of patricide. The army put down all rumours against Alexander. In a monarchy the succession rests with very few contenders; in a republic, with politician against politician, soldier against soldier and the people against everyone with a vestige of power, a murdered leader is often followed by a despot. Alexander vigorously inquired into the death of Philip. He suspected the princes of Lyncestis of being implicated and signed a warrant for their execution, excepting the son-in-law of Antipater. He was given proof that Attalos had conspired with Demosthenes, when his niece was replaced once more by Olympia, after her return from Epiros, and he sent orders for his death. Parmenion was the father-in-law of Attalos, but he helped carry out the order when shown proof of his treachery. Alexander also suspected Darius, the new Persian king who owed his crown to the Persian wazir, Bogaos. He had murdered the previous Great King, and bargained his throne to Darius, but no truth was found in the death of Philip of Macedon.

Chapter 10

Alexander, at the age of twenty, became King of Macedon. He was committed, by his inheritance and his personal dedication, to a war of conquest against the great power of Persia's King of Kings. Since the time of Cyrus the Great, the Persians had held most of the known world within their empire. Daily the king's confidence increased. He had inherited the invincible Macedonian army, which was disciplined to hard standards and included the superbly trained, oblique phalanxes. The army was backed by a civilian service unsurpassed in history in organisation and efficiency, to maintain the supplies of food and weapons essential for every military campaign. Alexander held three interlocking positions as King of Macedon. He was Hegemon of the Greek states, through the Corinthian League, and military commander of both, which gave him absolute power over all Greece, except for Sparta. His father had raised armies from all the subject city-states and his combined command was large enough to challenge Persia. In our tradition, the king was the chief judge and chief priest in Macedon. Alexander was also a subtle diplomat with an inborn sense of his own royalty. His vision was much larger than King Philip's for we knew that he secretly planned to unite the world in peace and spread the civilisation of the Greeks into the furthest places in the unknown world.

The envoys from the Greek states, attending the wedding at Aegae, had brought messages of loyalty which they now transferred from Philip to Alexander, in the inviolable terms of the treaty signed at Corinth. For a short time, the king's position seemed assured but then voices were raised against his youth and, more secretly, suspicions of his possible involvement in King Philip's murder were whispered amongst the people of

Macedon. Some now favoured the accession of Amyntas who, during his infancy, was replaced by his uncle, Philip. Various other names were proposed but none gained sufficient support to challenge Alexander.

News reached us, which was much more ominous, of rejoicing in Athens when the people heard of the death of Philip. The citizens danced in the streets and feasted all night and they flocked to their agora and passed a vote of thanks to Philip's assassin. Demosthenes, once again, surfaced in public and he called Alexander a braggart and proposed to the Athenians that they should withdraw from the League of Corinth and seek a separate peace with Persia. Reports came in of unrest in Aetolia and Ambracia. Thebes and Argos, with some of the smaller states, were plotting to withdraw from the League and, in Thessaly, the Macedonian party was defeated in a referendum. Advisors now appeared at court on every side. Many of them urged Alexander to abandon Greece on the grounds of threats of attack on the Macedonian border from Thrace in the east, from Paeonia to the north and from Illyria in the west. Alexander listened to all of them and then he struck. Many men were put to death for their lack of confidence and loyalty and the voices of unrest and opposition grew very faint. The king replaced the dead with men who had proved their loyalty and he gave them positions of importance in Macedon and when he was ready, he ordered the army to march south into Thessaly.

We were halted by the Thessalonians, who held the northern entrance to the Vale of Tempi, which led through the mountains, near the coast under Mount Olympos. Alexander, immediately, ordered the engineers to cut steps over the mountain and leaving a strong force in our rear, the rest of the army climbed the heights and trapped the Thessalonians in the pass. They surrendered without a fight and rushed to elect Alexander to all the positions previously held by Philip, including the command of their famous cavalry. The king swept into Thessaly, where the Amphityonic Council was in session. Thoroughly frightened, the Council elected Alexander as their new Hegemon, and they summoned all the members of the League to a meeting in Corinth. The Athenian delegation left Thessaly to return to their city, with a copy of this new treaty, to seek ratification of its terms. They found that Athens, under the powerful influence of Demosthenes, who had returned from exile after Philip's death, was preparing to go to war with Alexander rather than fulfill the city's treaty obligations, entered into at Corinth. News of this new Athenian treachery soon reached us and Alexander marched the army into Boeotia and halted only when he was a short distance from Thebes. The Athenians were thoroughly frightened when they discovered that Alexander was now so close to their city and they sent a new delegation to the king, which included the treacherous Demosthenes, to beg for mercy.

An alliance with Athens was vital, first to Philip and now to Alexander and, making a virtue of necessity, he pardoned the city, which in return, confirmed him as Hegemon for life and commander of all the Greek forces. Demosthenes was exiled again with his chief supporters, a mild punishment for a lifetime spent denouncing Macedon's kings. As soon as he had dealt with the Athenians, the king invited those of his father's generals who were present in the camp – Hephaestion, Craterus, Nearchos and other Companions, including myself – to his tent. For the first time, his own generation was given equal recognition with the older men and for the first time, also, Alexander spoke of a permanent empire in Asia. It was a stunning new development. Philip's policies had been limited to revenge for the black deeds of Xerxes and to gain security from any future Persian attacks on Greece.

Alexander spoke with the assurance of a god-hero. He had proved his courage and he was bold, ingenious and usually slow to anger, although from his mother he inherited a passionate and occasionally violent nature. He endured privation without complaint or loss of spirit, and he used it as a challenge to his own mortality. It was, always, by the exercise of tremendous self-control that he achieved great ends. At the end of the evening, Alexander invited Hephaestion, Craterus and me to go with him to consult the Delphic Oracle while the army was ordered back to Macedon.

Escorted by a small bodyguard, we rode for Delphi the following day. As we approached the mighty Mount Parnassos, a mood of reverence and awe descended on us. The climb to the great temple-sanctuary took us through wild and rugged passes into landscapes of infinite magnitude, I felt myself dwarfed into insignificance. The others, except Alexander, seemed similarly affected and he commented: "I am come to Delphi to the centre of the world and shall myself be Apollo's light on earth."

His words were blasphemous and the gods are ever jealous of mortal power and they can mock mortal ambition with terrible retribution, when men claim even a small part of their divinity.

We ascended the Parnassos, ever higher, until it seemed that we must reach the very heavens. We rested for one night in a village dizzily perched on a ledge of rock, and drank of the local wine. It was dark red and flavoured as if by the gods for themselves. It brought a little madness to our senses but Alexander drew apart from us as if to weigh, in solitude, the scene before us of towering peaks, deep, mysterious chasms and forests of olive trees, which stretched down in a dense, silvery carpet to the sea far below. It seemed that he must subdue the very elements and make them all subject to his will. We mounted the horses early the next morning and continued the ascent until suddenly looming up, as I had heard, were the Phaedriades, the two sheer rocks which guard Apollo's sanctuary. We paused and washed in the Sacred Kastilian Spring, which flows between the cliffs, and purified ourselves. We continued up the rough pathway of the Sacred Way and passed the treasuries of the cities which supported the sanctuary. They had all been plundered by the Phocians in their war against the Amphytionic Council and they now stood bare and empty. We saw the other magnificent monuments and statues which decorated the road and we paused at the Sibylline Rocks and read the Delphic Inscription: 'Know Thyself and Nothing to Excess'. And then I saw, high over the mountains, the most brilliant light of the sun, a radiance of fire, the very essence of the god Apollo manifesting himself here on earth above us, and in this fire attendants came to greet us and Alexander stepped forward and said: "I am Alexander and I have come to consult the Oracle."

They shook their heads and the chief amongst them replied to him: "It is not a lawful day for a consultation and the Oracle will refuse to see even Alexander of Macedon."

At his words, the king dashed past the priests into the temple and reached the Oracle whom he dragged to the sacred Tripod where he made her sit upon the stool beside the mystical, carved stone, which is the 'Navel of the Earth'. To our amazement, she did not resist the king's unprecedented attack, but she inhaled the rising vapours as they ascended from the hole and, after a pause, she spoke directly to the king: "Alexander of Macedon, thou art invincible."

Hephaestion, Craterus and I were witnesses and her words spread quickly to Macedon, to all Greece, the islands and to the Greek cities beyond the seas. We walked away in awe and wonder from the great temple and an eagle soared above our heads to confirm Alexander, son of Philip of Macedon, the future ruler of the world, even to most distant Ocean.

We visited the gymnasium, the theatre and the lofty stadium where King Philip had presided at the Pythian Games and finally we walked to Athena's own sanctuary far below. Philip had built his tholos, or round temple, amongst the olive groves in an enchanting setting, which is full of the spirit of the goddess and we rode away from Delphi. Alexander had heard the Oracle and he was ready to return to the army and prepare for the campaign across the Hellespont. Sparta, alone, remained outside the League of Cities in his alliance. Philip had already reduced her boundaries and destroyed her power but Alexander was always aware that, as an ally of Persia, she was a threat to his rear.

We swiftly returned to the army still camped in Boeotia and we marched for Macedon where we heard of revolts amongst some of the northern tribes. Alexander sent orders to Nearchos with the the fleet, which was anchored in Byzantium, to sail through the Bosphorus to the Euxine Sea, as far north as the Ister and then along the river to a position north of the Nestos. Swift detachments of the army also prepared to march to the Ister and within fourteen days, we left Macedon. Alexander rode on great Bucephalos at the head of the expedition, and after his recent successes, there was a new and greater pride in his bearing and we all shared his confidence and some of his glory was also ours.

We reached the Nestos and followed its course north and rode across the plains where we fought a few skirmishes against local tribes, until we found the fleet tied up on the steep, south bank of the Ister. Nearchos reported that his ships had made a great show of strength in all the cities along his route, and that he had been welcomed and given food and water by the citizens.

The bank of the river was so steep that we were unable to board the ships. Alexander dispatched the sailors to collect the boats owned by the local fishermen. The soldiers filled tents with hay to make them buoyant for use as rafts and engineers cut steps into the river bank. Alexander gave orders to work in silence and by dawn a detachment was across the river, with their reluctant horses swimming against the current. We reached an island where the king of the Triballians had found refuge. As soon as a sufficiently large detachment was across the river, we quietly marched to the Getae camp pitched outside their small town. The element of surprise gave us an easy victory. Alexander destroyed the town before we returned to the river where he made sacrifices to the gods, for our victory, before we crossed again to the south bank, and all was accomplished without the loss of a single Macedonian life. The Triballians now surrendered, without a fight, and the rest of the tribes along the river sent ambassadors, with their submissions, to the king. Even the fearsome Celts asked for Alexander's friendship and our northern borders were secured. That night we celebrated round the campfires, until a messenger rode into our camp with the news that Cleitus, the king of Illyria, had rebelled against the king. Soon after dawn, we were on the road until we reached his fortress at Pellion. Cleitus was well-prepared behind his stone-built walls and the Illyrians showered us with arrows and came out from different gates to fight separate battles and then retreat behind the walls. We won the day, but Alexander was injured and, while his wound was being dressed, news reached us that Darius, the new Persian king, in true Archaemenid tradition, was offering gold to the Greeks to destroy the Macedonian alliance.

Sparta, alone of the cities, accepted the Persian gold and Demosthenes accepted his share for using his influence against Alexander. The messenger also reported that wild rumours had reached the Greek cities telling of the death of Alexander in battle. Demosthenes was swift to use them in the Persian cause. He thundered that Macedon had no heir and therefore the Treaty of Corinth was dead and that Athens and all the Greek cities could go back to their wars. The Thebans believed the rumours. They recalled their exiles from Athens and attacked the Macedonian garrison stationed in the Kadmeia. Athens sent them arms and other cities joined in their rebellion. A furious Alexander dismissed his doctors, dressed with help and strode out from his tent to speak to the army drawn up in parade order before him. In a strong voice he said: "I would like to acknowledge the hard campaign which you have just fought and won and I must tell you that when the Greeks received news of my death ..."

He was interrupted by a great roar of laughter and the men

cheered as they broke ranks and crowded round the injured king and their devotion showed in their rough voices as they spoke to him. When order was restored, Alexander continued his speech: "With the news of my 'death', the Greeks are already breaking their oaths sworn to my father and they plan to destroy the alliance, which we made with them, and all Greece will once again be open to attack by the Persians. Shall we therefore delay our return?"

The men roared in answer: "March for Greece! March for Greece!"

We immediately made preparations to leave Illyria, and the Illyrians, after they had formally submitted to Alexander of Macedon. We reached the Boeotian border on the thirteenth day and, by the next sunset, we were before the walls of Thebes to the citizens' great alarm, surprise and confusion. They first speculated that another, unknown Alexander had usurped the Macedonian throne and he was now before their gates or that this was an army commanded by Antipater. Once convinced of the king's survival, they allowed his envoys into their city. They offered the Thebans peace in exchange for their surrender to Alexander as Hegemon of the League of Corinth. The envoys also informed the Thebans that many delegations from other Greek cities had arrived in Alexander's camp with promises of men and arms to support the League of Corinth. The brave but foolish Thebans decided on war not peace and they attacked the Macedonian garrison occupying their fortress, known as the Kadmeia. The following day Alexander moved his best troops to the high point nearest to the fortress, hoping by a show of strength to change their minds. He sent a further offer of peace but this time in exchange for the leaders of Thebes. Their insolent reply demanded the surrender of the Macedonian garrison and they called upon all the other Greek cities to join their revolt. Alexander immediately ordered the attack upon Thebes. Perdicass led the first assault but he and his men were driven back by the Theban defenders. The king ordered all units into an attack on the city. The Thebans bravely defended their position and we fought hard to break through their defences and, gradually, we forced our way in and by night Thebes was taken.

Alexander called a meeting of the members of the Corinthian League and gave the city's fate into their hands. The Phocians were ferocious in their hatred of Thebes. They clamoured for the destruction of the city and proposed selling the women and children into slavery and sending the men into exile from all of Greece. No other voices were raised and Alexander confirmed the sentence, saving only the house of the great poet Pindar. He made a terrible example of the Theban revolt, and the city's end haunted him for the rest of his life, and ever after he showed kindness to Thebans whenever he chanced upon them.

The Athenians had promised an army of support to Thebes, which failed to arrive, and now that city dispatched an ambassador to congratulate the king, a contemptible move as Athens was the instigator of the Theban revolt.

Alexander needed the Athenians' naval power and he forgave their crimes. He could not risk their ships falling into the hands of the Persians but many Athenians deserted their city and left for Persia and some became Persian mercenaries, advisors and administrators and the worthless were lured by Persian gold.

Chapter 11

With peace and unity, at least temporarily, restored in Greece, the Macedonian army marched north to Pella. It was autumn and the time of softening light after the glare of summer. Golden days turned our journey home into an idyll, for the harvest was almost gathered and many of the villagers were making wine and the air was heavy with the perfume of grapes. The peasants were also working hard, pressing oil from their olives. There was a languorous ease in the air with time for us to enjoy the sun before sharp winter cut across our land.

We were welcomed by the people at their wine-making festivals for, unlike most armies in the histories, our men were disciplined and theft or vandalism was severely punished. Villages had no need to fear our passing. The king gave payment for all requisitioned stores and fodder, and compensation for lodgings or accidental damage to land and buildings. We reached Pella, to a great welcome from the people who cheered Alexander's entry into the city. As soon as we were released by the army, I went to my father's house to bathe and for a meal of meats and fruit, and I then walked to the house of Theocritos where I was greeted by him and the lady Penelope. We spoke of our marriage plans and other private matters and at the end of the evening I left the gentle family, a very happy man.

I walked to the palace where I discovered, from my servant, that Alexander required my presence. I hastened to the royal apartment to find that Antipater, Hephaestion, Craterus, Coenos and Ptolemy were already there and that Alexander was in a great rage. He had returned to Pella only to be told that Olympias had ordered the murder of the infant born to Cleopatra, the niece of Attalos and sometime queen, and she had forced her rival to kill herself. There was no room for personal and private vengeance in the king's great plans, for it churns up bitter enemies who evermore threaten treachery. Olympias had also tried to rule during his absence and he was determined to force her to acknowledge that he alone was king in Macedon and that he would tolerate no rival authority. He recognised that a strong hand was needed to curb the queen, especially in his absence. We also discussed and argued for and against candidates to leave in charge in Pella when we marched for Asia. Alexander spoke in an even harder voice: "It appears that we are threatened, not only by the Greek cities, but from within my own house. I must therefore act in Macedon with the severity that I showed against Thebes. Craterus, arrange for the removal of my father's nephew, Amyntas, my father's bastard sons and all of the male members of the family of Attalos. I ask you to do it for the safety of our great enterprise and the victories still to be won."

We were all very still and silent at the conclusion of his words. I must have refused such a duty and I silently wondered if conscience alone could refuse such a command, or if expediency creates a bitter weal when men are driven into shameful deeds, which must poison their souls in the decay of corruption?

Antipater, one of Philip's generals and the most trusted of his friends, rose to his feet. He was a good soldier, competent in all that he did, plain-spoken and without personal ambition and he usually asked few questions but he now addressed Alexander: "O! King, for the good of Macedon, you might consider your decision most carefully. If you die without an heir, the state will fall in confusion and rivals from within will dismember your empire. Amyntas would now be king, if his father had survived his infancy but he was replaced by King Philip. Despite this, he has been loyal to your father and, since his death, to you. His claim to the throne is far above those of your father's other sons. At least wait to act in the matter of his life; should he change in the future, it may then be forfeit. Men will judge you harshly if you order his death and even the innocent will fear for their lives and may plot against you. As for the others whom you plan to kill, you may well be rid of them and the nuisance of their conspiracies ..."

Antipater paused in an uncomfortable silence, and Alexander thought for a moment before he replied: "My father's friend and respected general, I have given a great deal of thought to the security of Macedon, and all of Greece, when I leave for Asia, I anticipate that factions will arise and they will plot to replace me here at home and, while Amyntas lives, they may declare him 'King of the Macedons'. He is not in the army and I cannot force him to join the campaign; therefore, he must die with my father's bastards and the family of the treacherous Attalos. After this evening's discussions, I intend that you shall stay behind and rule in Pella and in Corinth, in my absence. I plan to leave you without any declared enemies, although some may well emerge from their secret places when the Hellespont divides me from Greece."

Antipater replied to Alexander: "So be it! I served Perdicass, the father of Amyntas and, after his death, Philip, his brother, and now you, Alexander. My loyalty is to your house as Kings of Macedon and I regret that you have decided for the death of Amyntas. I, personally, do not believe that he would seek your throne or give comfort to those others who might be tempted to seize it. For himself, he would accept it reluctantly, at your natural death should you leave no heir. He is a gentle man, with a liking for books, architecture and all the other arts and he would refuse to lend his name to any act of treason. You may therefore have more to fear by his death than if he lives."

He stopped speaking and Alexander growing impatient with argument turned to Craterus and said: "You all have my orders. Hire people to help you who are unconnected to the palace and now I give you all goodnight."

We left the royal apartment and I returned to my father's house to a very restless night. Amyntas was only my senior by a few years and I liked him well enough. His close friends were Cassander, the son of Antipater, Callisthenes, the nephew of Aristotle, and the three sons of Parmenion who were all in the army. They were professionals in the service of the king and they would deeply resent the murder of Amyntas. I tended to agree with Antipater that kings have enough enemies without inciting even greater numbers to rebellion. I thought that King Philip might still be alive but for his marriage to Cleopatra for whoever had used Pausanius had found a very willing tool. He burned with vengeance against the king. I was, also, personally grieved that Alexander had ordered the death of his dead uncle's son only for political convenience. He was too young to make such hard decisions and, if he found them easy, I reflected, then maybe so much the worse for the future of us all.

Alexander had given orders that we were to be available for immediate consultations with him. I rose early the following day and I decided to move back to the palace for my greater convenience. I first wrote to my father, prudently omitting any reference to Alexander's latest orders. Letters have a way of falling into the wrong hands, and now that he was retired, I thought to protect him from too much unpleasant knowledge of events in Pella. He had been one of the prime movers in the election of Philip to the crown, when Amyntas was still an infant. He would probably intervene on that prince's behalf if the king's orders reached him in time for him to act against them at his own great peril. I next told my slave to bring my clothes and equipment to the palace. When I arrived, I walked straight to the king's council hall. Antipater, Hephaestion, Craterus, Ptolemy, Philotas and Nicanor, two of the sons of Parmenion, Cleitus the Black, the brother of Lanice and his nephews, and Antigonus and Ptolemy, with Coenos, Nearchos and Callisthenes, the nephew of Aristotle, were amongst those gathered in the chamber. Perdicass followed me and finally Alexander entered the hall. Immediately, silence fell and the king dismissed the slaves and servants and ordered the doors closed before he spoke to us in a calm and even voice: "My friends, the time has come when I must brief you all for our campaign in Asia. First, put your own affairs in order by appointing administrators for your estates. If you are married, arrange for the education of your children, for who amongst us knows how long our great enterprise may last?" Then, with a slight inclination of his head towards me, he continued: "Those of you who are not married, marry and leave sons that the empire that we shall win will be secure in our future generations.

"As to our strategy, the Persian fleets control the seas. We do have an efficient navy, under the command of Nearchos, to support the army in our own coastal waters but we do not have enough ships to defeat those of the Persians. The sea is our weakness. The Athenian navy is ours by right of conquest and the terms of the treaty, signed in Corinth but we have no guarantee that it will be loyal to us, and I shall therefore make use of it only when I have no alternative.

"I have sent orders to Parmenion to return here leaving a large enough garrison to defend his present position across the

Hellespont. From him, we shall learn of the loyalties of the Greek cities in Asia, and if we can count on them as allies. We shall easily gain the coast and advance until we control the ports of Phoenicia and Canaan. The Persian navy will be unable to halt us and it will be as driftwood against our progress as far as Egypt. If the cities on our route are hostile, we shall take them by force against our best hopes for peace with them. I plan to avoid battles and avoid shedding blood, especially Macedonian and Greek blood, and the fewer enemies that we leave in our rear, the more secure will be our supply lines.

"My father, King Philip, trained an invincible army and to it we can now add mercenaries from the border tribes as well as those from each of the cities of the Corinthian League. At first, they will be small detachments; so that they can be smoothly assimilated into units of the Macedonian army, they will also serve as hostages against rebellion in their native cities.

"The success of our war against the Persians truly depends upon my Macedonians. The Gods are with us, as I heard from the Oracle at Delphi, and victory will be ours to the ends of the earth, until we reach Ocean. I have given each of you a special task. Antipater will remain in Pella, with half the Macedonian army, to maintain peace here at home and throughout Greece. Parmenion will be my Chief-of-Staff of the army in Asia; Craterus and Hephaestion will each command half of the army under Parmenion. Nicanor will serve under Nearchos who will command the navy. They will recruit geographers to make charts of the seas, and commission swift ships, to carry dispatches between Macedon and the expedition. Harpalos, who is not in the army, will serve as the chief financial advisor to the expedition, and always raise enough funds to finance our advance. Philotas will command the cavalry and Cleitus the Black will continue in command of the Royal Squadron of cavalry. Perdicass will be in charge of supplies, Callisthenes will write the history of the expedition and he will arrange the relay posts for dispatches between army units. He will also be in charge of the surveyors who will measure and record the distances that we cover each day. Eumenes will keep a daily journal and Jason, the son of Nearchos, Ptolemy, the son of Lagos, Antigonus and the nephews of Cleitus, will serve on the general staff and they will be given appointments as vacancies occur.

"We shall recruit geographers, botanists, engineers, steppers to measure distances, and every other kind of expert in the arts and sciences in the civilian train and enough men to find water and food supplies, horses and all our other necessities. And now go and recruit the staffs that you need, and let us begin the final training of our integrated army, taking advantage of the winter to accustom the men to arduous conditions.

"You must anticipate bitter cold and snow, mountainous terrain and low-lying swamps, disease, heat and pestilential insects and a shortage of food, although we must always find fodder for the horses. We are dependant upon them for our survival. The engineers will manufacture easily assembled siege machines to break down the walls of fortified cities, and you must discipline the men that they will neither loot nor plunder, unless the order is given, after we take a rebellious city. The Persian Empire is weak; I have reports of revolts against Darius, the King of Kings, in Egypt and other distant Persian provinces. Darius received his throne after a treacherous eunuch, named Bogaos, murdered Artaxerxes Ochus, the rightful heir, and Arses, his youngest son, whom Bogaos poisoned. Darius was not a direct heir when he seized the throne, and many factions have risen against him. We shall make allies as we advance, and enemies only of those who refuse our friendship and their freedom from our hands. Now, in the name of the gods, go and prepare reports for me of every contingency in our preparations that our strengths may be balanced and our weaknesses remedied."

Alexander strode from the council hall and we all followed him. King Philip would have consulted his council and invited suggestions. Now, it seemed that Alexander was absolute, the second Achilles, and he used divine authority as his personal command. Craterus was at my side and quietly told me that Alexander had cancelled the order to kill Amyntas and his relief, shared by myself, was evident on his face. Within a short time, Parmenion returned to Pella. He urged the king to marry and to leave a Macedonian heir. Alexander had advised on us the same course but he was angered by the suggestion applied to himself. I thought that he felt himself invincible and above the earthly need of family for his mistress was the beautiful Pancaste, whose wit and charm were legendary.

Parmenion reported that before he left his camp on the Hellespont, he had won the Asian coast as far south as Ephesos and Magnesia, before he was driven back by the Persians.

Alexander was undisturbed by this news for now his would be the glory of permanently liberating the Greek cities of Anatolia.

My father returned to Pella for my marriage to Penelope. I was happy until I left in Alexander's army in the spring of the following year. Penelope was pregnant when I rode from Pella and I was reluctant to leave her and, not for the first time, I regretted that I could not live peacefully in Macedon for the rest of my life. I arranged to leave Penelope in my father's care. I had purchased several slaves to attend to her every need. Now she is dead and I have only faint, perfumed memories, except for her son who is more real, though unknown to me, than all the realities in my life, since Alexander led his army away from Macedon.

My father, disturbed by rumours of the murder of Amyntas, told me of his plans to return to his country house after the birth of my child. He wanted no part of public life, which condoned political murder, and he was not reassured when he learned that Antipater and Craterus had persuaded the king to spare the life of Amyntas who had sadly learned of Alexander's plan to assassinate him and was evermore embittered against the king for doubting his loyalty. Two nights before we marched from Pella, the king gave a feast for all his generals and the leading citizens of the city. When I arrived at the banqueting hall I took my place on a low couch as Alexander was speaking and he asked everyone present to discuss the most difficult problems which faced us and to offer our solutions to them. Parmenion was the first to speak and with great deliberation he once more asked Alexander to marry and leave an heir for, in the event of the king's death, factions would immediately begin a civil war, he reasoned. Antipater, and several of the older men, thrust back their heads in agreement but in the quiet that followed no-one else spoke. Alexander paused before directly addressing the two senior generals and he ignored the suggestion of Parmenion: "You, indeed, as becomes soldiers and statesmen, are anxious for the future and not without reason, for it is a very difficult task that we undertake. If we should advance with the purpose of conquering the Persian Empire without adequate preparation and training then we must surely fail and we shall see our whole enterprise ground into the yielding dust of Asia. Our regrets would be too late for all Greece must then fall to Darius, the King of Kings. We must take council together and plan to the last detail for men, horses, ships, weapons and supplies."

A sigh of relief went up from everyone present as we all realised that Alexander intended to take us into his confidence. He continued after a slight pause: "It is essential that before we set sail across the Hellespont, we must finally decide if we are ready for so great an adventure or if, indeed, we should undertake so large an enterprise at any time. Once we are exposed to the winds and the waves of the sea we are at the mercy of Poseidon and once again on land, the challenges that we must face may temporarily overcome us; therefore, I ask for your frankest opinions and advice. Friends of kings, to be worthy of that name, must advise without regard to possible favours from their king, but must rather speak with all conviction and honesty. A man who recommends any course of action different from that which he would personally pursue is no friend but a servile flatterer.

"I am sure that nothing is less favourable to my plans than unnecessary delays, for in addition to the uprisings in the Persian Empire, all the barbarian tribes on our borders are conquered. The Greeks are united and we should seize this opportunity and not allow our victorious army to waste away in inaction; rather we must lead it to the riches of Asia, possession of which we have all enjoyed in our hearts. We shall take from the spoils of Persia the rewards for our labours for the long years the men served under my father and now under the second year of my rule. The reign of Darius is still young and, because he made the eunuch Bogaos drink his own poison, after he discovered that the slave was plotting his murder, he has incurred, amongst his own subjects in Persia, suspicions of cruelty and ingratitude which can fill the most loyal of subjects with hatred for their rulers and make them slow to obey their orders. My friends, shall we sit idly until Darius regains his authority at home, for then I am convinced that he will bring war into Macedon and Greece? There are many rewards for the victor which, if we delay, will belong to the enemy.

"Again, with how great a danger to my own reputation shall I disappoint the hopes of the Greeks? They gave me the honour of command in my youth, when my father, a great commander, after many proofs of valour, only received it a little before his death. Certainly, the assembly of the Greeks did not elect me to their command in order that a slothful Macedon, devoted to pleasure and the base acquisition of wealth, would neglect the wrongs formerly inflicted on us all, but rather that I should make the Persians pay the penalty for those crimes, which they committed against us. In addition, what must I say to those Greek cities of Asia who endure the intolerable slavery of barbarian oppressors? You all remember the prayers and arguments with which Delius of Ephesos pleaded their cause. I believe that it is a sure outcome that all those cities, as soon as they see our standards, will immediately open their gates to us, and they will vigorously support their liberators against their present severe and unjust masters.

"We, who subdued all Greece, except Sparta, in so many hard campaigns and with our small numbers inflicted great losses on our enemies and who have either slain the Greeks' bravest men or now have them in our own army, shall we fear Asia?"

Alexander paused and then he continued with evermore eloquent words and he so moved everyone present, even Parmenion who had advised that the war should be postponed until we were better prepared, that we agreed to use all possible speed to cross the Hellespont. The king, showing great satisfaction, gave orders for the army to leave Pella in nine days' time. Alexander, during this time, made many sacrifices to the gods in which he used vast quantities of costly incense. Before our departure he gave a banquet, in a magnificently decorated tent, and there was enough food remaining to distribute throughout the army.

Chapter 12

It was a proud day when the army assembled at Pella to march away from the city for the conquest of Asia and Darius, the King of Kings, in the second year of Alexander's reign. The people gathered in great multitudes to cheer our departure and many were the tears of parting and the last whispered words to us from our families and friends.

The king had one final duty to undertake in Macedon and that was to pray and offer sacrifices to the Gods at Dion, the most sacred of all Macedonian cities, where we especially honour Zeus and his daughters, the Muses. We have no priests to conduct relations with the Gods and this is the King of Macedon's first duty. King Philip had made a similar journey to give thanks and celebrate the destruction of Olynthos.

We travelled south until we reached the city, which is sheltered under the massive, protecting heights of Mount Olympos where the land is flat and marshy as it stretches towards the Thermaic Gulf. We rested the first night and, at dawn the next day, Alexander performed ritual purifications and sacrifices in the Temple of Zeus.

During the next nine days he visited the Asklepeion, the Sanctuary of Demeter, and the Nympheon on the banks of the Baphyra. He distributed the sacrificial animals to the army and held feasts for his friends and senior officers in his tent as night fell in Dion. We stayed about fifteen days in the Holy City before we marched for Amphipolis to find army contingents, from many of the Greek cities, already assembled there. The town had grown into a considerable city since it was first seized by King Philip and the gold mines on Mount Pangaeus were worked continuously throughout the day and night. The king was heavily in debt and his first priority was to establish a mint to process the gold into coins, to finance the expedition. The goldsmiths worked long hours to fill bags and boxes with the gleaming metal.

Amphipolis was a noisy place; the air echoed with the clatter of the smiths as they laboured to change base metal into swords and armour, and the engineers feverishly constructed and dismantled siege machines in an effort to simplify their designs, and to reduce parts into a size more easily transported by an army on the march. Recruits from all over Greece arrived daily and men and horses were drilled on every spare piece of ground. Alexander set agents to find Persian spies in the camp, in an effort to keep his preparations secret from the enemy. He planned to finance the liberation of the cities of Asia with money stored in their treasuries before any could be moved east into Persia's homeland.

The king invited many famous artists to Amphipolis and he commissioned several portraits of himself from Arpelles which were sent to Pella and other cities. Lysippus sculptured elegant bronze heads and Pyrgoteles engraved miniatures on precious jewels of many of the officers, which were given to their wives. Finally all Alexander's preparations were complete and he convened a council of Macedonians to speak to us for the last time before we marched to the Hellespont. He entered the hall with Parmenion, as Commander in Chief, on his right side and Eumenes at his left, as if to emphasise that conquered cities would be governed by civilians as well as soldiers. Silence fell as the king began to speak: "My friends! Winter is over and we march to fulfill our destiny in twenty days. Nearchos will command the fleet and meet us at the Hellespont. He will promote Macedonians to command his ships and make sure that the Athenians neither rebel against us nor sail for home.

"Our cavalry numbers 1,000 Macedonians and 1,800 Thessalonians and it will be under the command of Calas. My Macedonian infantry has 24,000 men, supplemented by about 7,000 more supplied by members of the League of Corinth. We are strong enough to subdue all the satraps of the Persian Empire, especially if we take them one by one. We march as an avenging army, but we shall take peace to all the cities that open their gates to us and destroy only those that oppose our advance. The army, under Parmenion, will begin to leave Amphipolis at first light after twenty days. We shall triumph over every obstacle as we advance to conquer the King of Kings and the navy will command the seas and be our lifeline to Macedon.

"We must also consider the civilian train and the poets and writers who will record our deeds, the geographers who make maps to guide our advance and chart our progress, the scientists who will study the trees, plants and animals, and the geologists who will examine the earth and hunt for metals for our weapons. Our philosophers will dispute with Chaldeans, the wise men of the Persian Empire, and learn their secrets, artists will paint their pictures and interpret in marble and stone the wonders that we shall discover in Asia. They will create memorials to celebrate the noble deeds of my army. The politicians and orators will make laws and govern according to our customs and tax collectors will find the wealth by which our conquests and government will be financed.

"Whomsoever is with the army of Alexander walks with destiny, and great histories will be written of our deeds. We shall create a new world of peace, united by the language and ideals of the Greeks. Cities and states will no longer destroy each other in war, and their wealth will be used for trade and the prosperity of all, and none shall go hungry or uneducated. The gods march with us, and the light of Apollo will shine over the whole world. Whomsever is against us is against the gods and will perish. We shall be across the Hellespont in twenty-one days."

A noble speech. I had also heard of the thousands in the service of Darius who would defend their king to the death. At the outset, in Hellespontine-Phrygia, we risked losing the whole campaign against forces twice our size. We were a small army, conquerors of Greece, but now we challenged the might of the King of Kings in his own empire. We would indeed need the favour of the gods for so brave an enterprise. I returned to Pella during this time to say goodbye to Penelope and my father. I left them both in sorrow against a final parting for death has seared me twice in its scorching flame and taken them both from me. Alexander also returned to the city to see Antipater and his mother, the queen. Hephaestion and Craterus were with him and on the sixth morning after my arrival I walked to the palace, waited on Olympias, and then joined the king's party. We left Pella to the cheers of the assembled people as word had quickly spread that, at last, we marched for Asia.

On the ride back to Amphipolis, the king was withdrawn and silent, possessed by an inner fire until the first night round the campfire, when he spoke of his mother's last words to him before we rode from Pella. She had repeated her old story that he was the son of Zeus when the god had appeared to her in the guise of a snake. I, personally, hoped that she spoke in revenge to alienate Alexander from his father's memory; a son of a capricious god might have very different qualities from those we needed from our king. I suspected that her wild claims were the reason why Philip had rejected the queen so early in their marriage; repelled by her storied fantasies and coiling snakes. The earthy king must have preferred more human company in his bed. Philip had never denied Alexander as his son and heir, even during his disastrous marriage to Cleopatra; rather he showed great pride in the prince's achievements and always ignored the queen's wild claims. Hephaestion readily accepted them, however, but Craterus commented: "I think that the lady Olympias mistakes fantasy for reality for she is a very devout lady and sometimes, in religious ecstasy, dreams are born, which seem more real than proven fact. Alexander, you have a destiny to fulfill far greater than the most powerful dream, and you should be content with that. Let women have their dreams, and do not allow your resolve to be obscured or your plans destroyed by this fable, for men such as you must rule without the luxury of visions."

The good sense of Craterus shone on his rugged face and I hoped that Alexander would forget the queen's whispered words. Many lives depended on his cool judgement and the success of our whole adventure was placed in jeopardy by too many signs from the gods. We needed cool leadership, untainted by fantasy.

When we rode into Amphipolis, we found that the army was ready for the march towards the Hellespont. The men had trained hard and their excitement ran high as the hour for the fulfilment of our plans was now and their enthusiasm spilled over as they crowded round the king shouting his name: "Alexander! Alexander!" as he walked amongst them.

He laughed, swept up in the glory of the hour, and his excitement reflected on all of us as his clear eyes swept across his army in confidence and pride. The king had matured in the last two years from boyishness to the beauty of a marble Apollo, carved by an inspired hand. He was clean-shaven and so denied a beard as a handle to the enemy in battle. All his con- temporaries followed his lead, but Philip's men, such as Cleitus the Black, refused to shave to honour the memory of the murdered King Philip. Cleitus was so named for his dark, shining hair and great beard, and his black, glittering eyes which were as chips of obsidian. He was the brother of Lanice, Alexander's nurse, and the beloved companion of our late King Philip and he held a special status amongst us all.

Alexander called a conference on the day following our arrival, to which he also invited all the leaders of the allied armies. He questioned us closely about the preparations for our departure and he took a special interest in our weapons, equipment and stores. He gave to the unit commanders their positions in the column and he ordered Parmenion, and the leading units, to march towards the Hellespont in three days, leaving at dawn. Alexander separated the allied units amongst the Macedonians. He never wholly trusted them and they were taken along, almost as hostages, for the co-operation of their native cities in the king's absence.

There were people of many professional skills in the civilian train as well as sutlers to supply wine in drinkable condition, merchants to buy supplies, men who claimed skills in the healing arts, together with their hospitals; musicians and tumblers to entertain in camp, builders and craftsmen to settle in conquered cities and personal attendants to supply some of the comforts familiar to us in Macedon. The army was far outnumbered by the civilian train, with its thousands of pack animals, which carried the vast stores, and they stretched out into a noisy, polyglot, sprawling column.

Alexander rode Bucephalos at the head of his army and marched from Amphipolis confident of winning the world. The training and discipline of the men was very apparent, in their tightly drilled columns; it was an inspiring moment leading us to a noble enterprise. We moved into the rising sun as the early dawn spread an incandescent glow, which lighted our road from the heavens, and pressed the darkness of night behind us into the western horizon. I reflected that in the great moments in Alexander's life, Apollo sent his approval in glorious light; if Alexander was not a god, he enjoyed their blessings in all his undertakings, especially now that he rode to defeat the might of Persia. We marched along the coast road towards the east and reached Sestos on the Hellespont in eleven days; excellent time for an army hampered by a vast supply column and the multitude of civilians unskilled in campaign conditions.

Nearchos and the fleet were waiting for us in the harbour of Sestos. He had already requisitioned merchant ships to ferry the campaign across the strait to Asia. He reported to Alexander that he had sighted Persians on land but that he had seen no sign of their ships at sea, a good omen for a smooth crossing for the expedition. We camped overnight, and the king gave orders for the crossing of the Hellespont to begin at dawn the following day. The excitement was intense amongst the men; they showed no signs of fatigue although the civilians groaned their complaints far into the night. We met, that evening, in Alexander's tent. As I walked through the olive groves, my thoughts were of Macedon and all that we were leaving behind us. It was a night of soft warmth; the stars glittered in the bowl of the heavens and the moon shaded a golden, topaz path across the phosphorescent sea. I listened to the sounds of the night creatures mingling with the sibilance of the gentle movement of the water. I was part of Alexander's mighty enterprise, eager for conquests, for travel to see the mysteries and wonders of the Persian Empire and to test myself in the challenges of battle. I missed my wife and all that made life dear to me and I knew the paradox in my nature – when I had home and family, I longed for high adventure and to share in the world of Alexander's vision. Yet my placid life in Macedon lured me back with siren sweetness. This night I would gladly have had the Hellespont as the furthest limit of my personal enterprise.

The next day, Alexander had no such wayward thoughts. He was vitally alive, strong in purpose and I felt his personal power engulf me as he sat before a table covered with reports and charts. Nearchos was at his side, and they discussed the invasion of Asia with intense concentration. When all the commanders were present, Alexander laid aside his charts and spoke to us: "And now, my friends and commanders, we stand at the bridge to Asia, at last. I shall command the first ship to sail across the Hellespont. With me will come Hephaestion, Craterus, Eumenes, Jason and my bodyguard.

"The army will be under the orders of Parmenion and the

navy, with the Athenian fleet and the requisitioned merchant ships, will be under the command of Nearchos. When the landing is complete, Nearchos will disband the merchant fleet. I regret that there is no money to keep his ships in commission. However, we shall not need them, for I shall take the coast all the way to Egypt and, from the land, deny the Great King's ships the use of all his harbours. I expect an attack from the sea when we reach the Hellespont but, either because the Persians are asleep, or they underestimate their danger, we shall all land without incident. The small army left in Asia by Parmenion, before my father's death, will guard our landing on the Asian side. The gods favour the bold and have given our enterprise divine authority. Lead your men to victory and let us right all the ancient wrongs visited on us by Persia. From our victories will stand a united and independent Greece, from now on the mentor of the world."

The embarkation began at first light. Alexander took the helm of the leading ship until we reached mid-channel and there he sacrificed to Poseidon, Amphitrite and the Nereids. Behind us sailed the rest of the fleet. It was a brave and lovely sight. The sun dazzled on the glittering sea and, as the oars dipped and rose in rhythm, drops of water cascaded from their surfaces with the fluid brightness of mercury.

Alexander was the first to leap ashore. He thrust his sword into the ground and paused, momentarily, as the waves curled round his feet and then he bounded forward with his arms outstretched, as if to embrace the whole world, crying: "Asia is taken by the sword."

The sun shone upon him and anointed him with light and his ashy hair haloed his head. Myself I do not know the part which the gods play in human affairs, but in that moment, I thought that I beheld a god.

Chapter 13

In order to complete the ferry of the entire expedition, we found that it was necessary for each ship to make several trips across the Hellespont and, as there were no Persian ships or men to threaten the crossing, Alexander invited Hephaestion, Craterus and several members of the Companions, including myself, to visit Troy. I noticed that as we rode off, the king carried Aristotle's gift of *The Iliad*. He spoke to us of Hermias, our teacher's friend, who rather than betray King Philip's plans for the invasion of Asia was, by the orders of the Persian king, vilely tortured and then crucified. He also spoke reverently of Achilles, his own ancestor and the great hero of the Trojan War, and of Herakles, that other ancestor, whose labours for mankind fired his thoughts and whose noble example inspired his own life.

And so we rode, preparing ourselves for our pilgrimage and amongst the ancient stones of Troy Alexander of Macedon dedicated his armour to Athene and ceremoniously exchanged his shield for that which had belonged to Achilles and now rested in the temple on this ancient site. The beautiful, finely-crafted shield was inlaid with representations of the sun, moon and stars and of marriage feasts and dancing peasants and it was hallowed by time and the noble deeds of all the men who had died upon this famous battlefield. They lived again for us as Alexander read from Homer's mighty epic, as we sat in the fading light, dreaming of our own great enterprise in Asia's vast lands.

The next day we visited the tombs of Patroclus and Achilles in the plains, which stretched out below the city of Troy. Alexander laid a wreath on each grave and cried: "O! fortunate Achilles to have found such a friend as Patroclus and Homer as the herald of your glories." We danced naked round the tombs in traditional, holy dedication. When the dance was over we sat near the sacred place and we quietly spoke of Aristotle and of his teachings, especially those from *The Iliad*, until it was time to ride back and join the expedition on the southern shores of the Hellespont. When we reached the sea, we found that the ferrying of the expedition was almost completed; even the civilians and pack animals were spread over the Asian shore. Parmenion was interviewing our spies to discover the strength and positions of units of the Persian army in the province of Hellespontine-Phrygia. Alexander, unsatisfied with their contradictory reports, joined him, and closely questioned them. He ordered them to leave again and return with more accurate accounts of enemy movements, especially sightings of the Persian fleet.

The grooms collected our horses and we separated to the tents which had been erected during our visit to Troy. I put on clean clothes and my groom brought a fresh horse for me to ride to the makeshift parade ground. When the army was assembled Alexander, riding Bucephalos, rode out to address us, saying: "I have learned that the local satraps are massing their men on the River Granicus, two days' march to our east. The traitor, Memnon of Rhodes, has advised Darius to withdraw his armies far into Asia, destroying the crops as they retreat, and at the same time to send orders to his fleet to invade Greece and Macedon. Were I Darius of Persia, this would be my strategy for then the expedition of Alexander must fail, when we turn back to protect Macedon. However, we have Persian pride on our side, for the Great King plans to defeat us in a single pitched encounter on the River Granicus.

"We march for the river and my invincible army will take the field to win our first battle, for I set no limits of labour or worth to a man of spirit, save only that the labours lead on to noble enterprises. It is a lovely thing to live with courage and to die leaving 'AN EVERLASTING RENOWN'."

The men shouted and cheered their pride in Alexander and the land rang with the great voices of Macedon as we left the parade ground.

The camp echoed with the sounds of preparation until after the moon had risen and then a quiet settled over the fields as men and horses rested before the next day's march to Abydos. The following morning, Alexander ordered the army into battle formation and we marched at first light. We, of the King's Companions, surrounded Alexander as we grew closer to the enemy.

The Persians were drawn up on the high east bank of the Granicus and we looked up to their army of some 12,000 cavalry and 8,000 of their infantry. Our cavalry was far outnumbered but, with the detachments from the League of Corinth, the numbers in our infantry must have been nearly three times greater than those of our Persian enemy. Darius, the King of Kings, was absent. The Royal Guard of Medes and Persians, drawn from their nobility, was a force constituted of 2,000 cavalry and the same number of infantry. They were armed with lances, ornamented with golden apples, pikes and bows and arrows, and the 10,000 famed Immortals carried lances in their hands.

Parmenion advised the king to wait overnight before crossing the river which flowed between us. He anticipated that the Persians would withdraw during the hours of darkness, and so lose the advantage of their position high above us when we attacked. He argued that we would be very vulnerable if we lost formation fording the river. Alexander answered him: "We crossed the Hellespont. Should this little ditch detain us, we would stand shamed."

He raised his spear and ordered the cavalry to charge and he galloped forward followed by the Companions. The Persians, waiting for this moment, rushed down to attack us in the river and from behind their first wave of men came a separate charge, led by Mithridates, the son-in-law of Darius. It was directed against the person of the king who, in his white-plumed helmet, riding on the magnificent Bucephalos, was an unmistakable target. Alexander met Mithridates head-on with his spear raised and he ran the enemy through the head. As Mithridates fell, other members of the Persian nobility charged towards Alexander. The king's spear broke against the armour of the leading man and his page, at his side, handed him a replacement. Then the king's helmet was sheared by a Persian lance and his neck exposed and I saw a Persian arm raised to decapitate Alexander with his sword. I looked in horror, but at that moment Cleitus the Black rushed forward and severed the Persian's arm.

Alexander downed another Persian and shouted the order to charge up the river bank. Suddenly, the Persian line broke and we attacked with victory in our hearts. The battle was swiftly over and the Persians fled. Our casualties were great, especially amongst the cavalry, which had taken the brunt of the fighting. However, the Persian losses were much greater; many of their generals were dead, though Memnon, the Greek traitor, escaped. The Greek mercenaries in the Persian service were largely slaughtered; only about 2,000 were sent back in traitors' chains to Macedon.

Alexander walked amongst the wounded and asked them how their injuries were inflicted. He allowed them to exaggerate and treated each one with gentle courtesy, personally bathing many of their wounds. That night we dined on the swans which proliferated in the country. We ate beside the Granicus turned red with Greek and Persian blood. The stench of mud, sweat, blood and smoke was a thick blanket round us and the air was filled with the moans of wounded men and horses and the whine of clouds of insects. Victory, fatigue and wine dulled our senses.

We slept where we ate and the following day the king ordered three hundred suits of armour to be stripped from dead Persians; these he sent to Athens with the message: 'From Alexander and the Greeks, except the Spartans, in tribute to Athena, and taken from the Persians who dwell in Asia'.

His gesture was one of recompense for the destruction by Persians of the Athenian temples and it was not lost on all the troops from the Corinthian League. The king had given them an honourable role in the battle and recognition for their part in our victory. Alexander grieved for his friends, the twenty-five Companions of the cavalry, slain in the battle, and he ordered the famed sculptor, Lysippos, to cast their images in bronze for a permanent memorial to be installed in the Holy City of Dion.

The king, after this battle, followed the Persian system for the administration of conquered provinces and thereby effected the smoothest transfer of power to Macedonian rule. A civilian satrap administered the provincial capital – a secretary, who reported directly to the king – and a military governor commanded the army detachments, left behind to guarantee the peace. Alexander also created a corps of inspectors, known as the 'Eyes and Ears of the King'. Persian laws and standards of justice remained in place until these slowly evolved into our Greek customs. The tribute assessed on all the people of each region was now remitted to Alexander's treasury to pay for the campaign. Eumenes advised the king that greater tribute should be extracted from so wealthy an empire but in reply Alexander observed: "I hate the gardener who cuts to the root the vegetables of which he ought to cull only the leaves."

Calas, the commander of the Thessalonian cavalry, was appointed governor of Hellespontine-Phrygia and remained in the province when we marched south to Sardis, the opulent Lydian capital and terminal of the Royal Road from Susa; where once was signed the infamous 'King's Peace'. As we approached the city, the military commander came out to surrender Sardis and to give the keys of the treasury to the king. Alexander rode to the centre of Sardis and, after a brief ceremony, he ruled to the enormous joy of the mostly Greek inhabitants and, because of the 'King's Peace', our occupation was a potent, symbolic moment in history to nullify the hated document for Macedon and all the city-states of Greece.

We found, in the citadel, to the great anger of Alexander, records of the large amounts of gold sent by the Persians as payment to Demosthenes in Athens, to foster war against Macedon in the reign of King Philip, his honoured, but murdered father. Sardis was the home of many poets and philosophers and an important market for trade between east and west. The city is on the banks of the gold-bearing River Pactolus and, in its waters, the ass-eared King Midas bathed and successfully cured himself of the Golden Touch.

Croesos, of fabled wealth, was the last native king of Lydia. He had once shown off his vast treasure to Solon visiting him from Athens and he inquired of the famous philosopher, if he did not think that he, Croesos, was the happiest man in the world?

"No man can be called happy before his death," the Athenian replied.

Croesos found this to be true when he later consulted the Delphic Oracle, who cautioned him that an empire would fall if he crossed the River Halys. Confident that the Oracle prophesied the end of the Persian Empire and its expansion, Croesos crossed the river and he was defeated by Cyrus, founder of the Persian Empire, who condemned him to death. Cyrus heard Croesos lament, as he was led off to his execution: "O! Solon, Solon!" in melancholy memory. The Great King asked his meaning and when Croesos told his story, Cyrus pondered life's uncertainties, even those of kings, and he spared the life of Croesos and retained the Lydian as his advisor.

The Persians had fortified Sardis with a triple row of walls which Alexander inspected and greatly admired as a superb defensive system. He then climbed the high peak of the acropolis where he planned to build a temple to Zeus. As he reached the summit, a powerful thunderstorm rocked the earth. It was centred on the site of the ancient palace of the Lydian kings on the plain below. Alexander took this as a sign from the god to build his temple on that historic site and not on the high place.

The king initiated his policy of reconciliation with the people of Asia, in Sardis of Lydia. He gave them the right to keep their own ancient form of government and freedom to practise their religion, which was devoted to Kybele, the Great Earth Mother of Asia, whom we identify with Artemis. He appointed a Macedonian satrap to govern in Sardis and the province of Lydia; a Macedonian to command the garrison, which he planned to leave in the city, and a Greek civilian to collect tribute, a wise move for the Greeks are crafty with money and find many ways to collect taxes. Sardis, surrounded by a fertile plain, was a rich city, with plentiful gold from the River Pactolos. The king ordered the people to mint money from their gold, with which he paid a bounty to the army and the Greek civilians, but for himself, he kept nothing.

Calas, the governor of Hellespontine Phrygia, arrived in Sardis, to report to the king that he had restored order in the province, after the Battle of Granicus. Alexander now sent him, together with Alexander of Lyncestis, on a hazardous expedition into the mountains south of Sardis. He was in command of troops from cities which were least loyal to the League of Corinth and, therefore, least likely to be missed if they were killed in battle, except for the Argives who remained to garrison Sardis. Calas was ordered to advance into territory controlled by Memnon, whom we expected to defend it to his last man.

The king made a ceremonial visit to the ruins of the Temple of Kybele. It had been the gift of King Midas and was destroyed by the Persians when they conquered and occupied the city. Alexander promised the ecstatic people enough money to rebuild their temple in the original rose-red granite. The citizens fervently acclaimed the king, overlooking the fact that the money would come from tribute collected by a foreign Greek and paid by themselves.

We left the people of Sardis at peace and dedicated to the rebuilding of the temple to their beloved goddess. We marched the road west to the site of the ancient city of Smyrna on the Aegean coast. Since it was destroyed by the Persians, the people had lived in scattered communities in the surrounding district. They gave Alexander a joyful welcome anticipating a far better future, free of Persian domination. The city was especially dear to Alexander as the birthplace of Homer. Alexander hunted on the mountain, which towered above the ruined city. He sat on the summit, beneath a plane tree, to rest during the midday heat and to celebrate the great poet, he read from his copy of *The Iliad*, until he fell asleep. He dreamed that the goddess, Nemesis, appeared to him and she asked him to build a new city on the top of the mountain. He returned to ancient Smyrna and sent messengers to all the citizens to return home and he gave them enough money to build a new city. He found a site much easier to defend than the old city round the harbour, but beneath the mountain, with the added advantage that it was in a cool, shady wood.

When all this was accomplished, we marched south to the exquisite, marble city of Ephesos, site of the great temple of Artemis and ruined and looted by Persian invaders. Alexander received another tumultuous welcome. The people had already massacred some of their Persian masters, especially those whom they suspected of looting their temple. The king stopped the killing, and executed only those of the enemy whom he found guilty of destroying a statue of his father, King Philip of Macedon. Alexander restored all the civil liberties of the people of Ephesos. He cancelled their tribute to the Persian King of Kings, and ordered that the money should be paid instead to the priests of Artemis and his popularity was assured in Ephesos and all Greek Ionia.

We heard, from the people in the city, of the stories told on the night of Alexander's birth when the temple of Artemis, or Kybele of more ancient worship, had burned to the ground. The priests claimed that the fire occurred during the absence of the Goddess at the royal birth in Macedon. There were also rumours that a madman, named Herostratos, had sought eternal fame for himself or, some said, that he was jealous for his Goddess, Kybele, to whom he gave his devotion in the venerable worship before the Greeks came to Ionia, and for her, he had lighted his arsonist's torch. Many other gods and goddesses are still worshipped in these lands of Asia and, whichever story held the truth, Herostratos found his fame when his name became synonymous with destruction. Alexander attended many religious ceremonies in the ruins of the temple and he offered to pay for the restoration of the building. Unlike the people of Sardis, the proud Ephesians declined with smooth cunning, telling the king in honeyed words that: "It is not fitting for a god to build a temple to another god."

Alexander praised them and thanked them for their loyalty and further added that he shared their joy in the new shrine to their goddess and he ended his speech to them saying: "God is the common father of all mankind, but more particularly of the good and virtuous." A strange comment to people who worshipped Artemis and all the other gods of Greece.

After the conclusion of the ceremonies, the Ephesians celebrated for four days and there was a huge market for small statues of their many-breasted goddess, which more closely resembled Phrygian Kybele than Greek Artemis. I bought and dispatched to my father in Macedon an exquisite silver copy.

Parmenion left the expedition to ride in the king's name on a visit to all the cities in the north of Anatolia, and Alexander sent runners carrying orders to Nearchos to bring the fleet to the Persian port of Miletos to our south.

The famous painter, Apelles, lived in Ephesos and the king gave him commissions, amongst them was a representation of Aphrodite. The artist used Pancaste, the king's mistress, as a model for the goddess and while the work was in progress they fell deeply in love. When Alexander was informed, he gave Pancaste to Apelles and, as she was beautiful and intelligent, it was a most generous gift. Alexander always surrendered pleasures with detachment and an easy grace, regardless of the pain that he suffered and Pancaste, of course, was delighted to exchange the rigours of the campaign for the comforts and elegance of Apelles' beautiful house in the lovely city of Ephesos.

Alexander restored democratic government to the people of Ephesos and retrained the army for the hard battle to take Miletos, a city heavily fortified by the Persians and their most important naval base in the west. He also equipped the baggage train from the resources of the district of Ephesos, scrupulously paying the fair market price for all the supplies and, when all was ready, we moved south to Priene to rest and train during the winter months.

Priene was a new city, built by the architect Hippodamus, with money donated by the people of Athens. It sat high on a mountain ledge above the valley of the wandering River Meander, and looked south across the plain to Miletos. The people of the city were in the process of building their new temple, which they dedicated to Athene in Ionia. Alexander gave them funds to complete the construction and in gratitude after our departure they made the house, where he had lodged, into a temple dedicated to the king.

We marched across the plain to reach the walls of Miletos and found that Nearchos, with the fleet, was already anchored in the mouth of the Meander effectively protecting the approach to the city from the Persian navy riding the waves, out to sea, beyond his position. Nicanor had effectively taken over the command of the fleet from Nearchos. Parmenion, during an inspection of the sea defences of Miletos, observed an eagle sitting on the shore and taking this as an infallible sign, he advised Alexander to immediately attack the Persian fleet. The king, however, reasoned that if the allied fleet, which was mostly manned by Athenians suffered a defeat, the men serving in the ships might easily defect to the Persians and thus endanger the whole campaign. We Macedonians are not natural sailors and Alexander depended on naval forces only as a last resort as he never fully trusted the Greeks, especially the Athenians. He therefore declared that the eagle was clearly a sign that our victory would be on land.

We camped outside Miletos, and engineers, under the Thessalonian Diades, worked for many days and nights to build siege machines. We had brought from Greece only parts already fabricated, which were too difficult to manufacture in the field. When this work was completed, Alexander ordered them to be brought up against the walls of the city.

The king stationed an infantry detachment on the beach to attack Persian sailors landing for essential water and supplies. A lesson learned by Memnon of Rhodes, as he sailed away, one night, under cover of darkness. Spies soon brought in reports that he was taking the Aegean islands one by one, planning to cut Alexander off from Macedon and all Greece.

The large colony of Persians living in Miletos found themselves trapped between our army and navy and many panicked in the face of danger. Some fled or committed suicide and others of them were killed by Greeks living in the city and some surrendered and swore allegiance to Alexander. He offered them a truce on condition that Persians joined his expedition as hostages for the rest of their people in the city. He held a council to explain this strategy to his commanders saying: "The importance of Miletos, as a port, and possible base for Memnon, makes it imperative for us to leave the city pacified and allied. I shall therefore appoint some of the leading Persians to positions of authority in the army and government. Their experience will be of great value to us, in administering the city and surrounding district ..."

His speech was interrupted by angry murmurings. Macedonians had reluctantly accepted a similar policy for fellow Greeks but neither they, nor many of the Greeks with us, viewed Persians as anything but enemies and they certainly did not welcome them in positions of power; plunder of Persian wealth was more to their expectations. Alexander ignored the interruptions and continued, "...The fleet has now fulfilled its mission. I shall leave about twenty ships only, in commission, to transport siege equipment and supplies along the coast; all the rest will be decommissioned and the men will be enlisted in the army."

Nearchos was present and led the noisy protests. I sympathised with him; after many years of preparation and training, his command was to dissolve as flotsam in the sea.

Alexander answered him personally: "Nearchos, you have magnificently finished your task but I have no money to pay for a navy. You will remain with the twenty ships, however, and be ready to expand your fleet whenever I send you the order. To take the south from here, and the rest of Anatolia, and secure our rear with garrisons, we need every available man. And I say that none may question the orders of Alexander for I alone must lead the entire campaign, avert disaster and prepare for our final victory. Every one of you must make his full contribution for this end, regardless of any personal sacrifice of power and prestige."

Nearchos had to be content with this and he returned to his ship to give orders for paying off the fleet with the exception of the twenty ships spared by the king. We then heard that Memnon was also deprived of his effective strength, as Darius had reassigned the Greek mercenaries serving with the enemy fleet and in the Persian army. He probably blamed them for the loss of Miletos, which was a severe defeat for the famed invincibility of Persian might. It was also a great strategic defeat; Darius lived far from the sea and probably failed to understand the importance of sea power to guard his distant coast and provinces.

Prior to the arrival of the expedition, the Greeks of Miletos had lived well under Persian rule, even enjoying a measure of independence. The city was prosperous with its own mint and many of the Greeks were employed in the service of the Persian fleet as technicians, artificers, geographers and chart makers. They were therefore reluctant to exchange their easy Persian servitude for unknown Macedonian rule. When the Greeks first settled in Anatolia, they carried with them their traditional prejudice against Macedonians and called us barbarians. Their descendants judged the Corinthian League merely a device to give legitimacy to the ambitions, first of Philip, and now of Alexander. The king, in response, set faction against faction to prevent them forming a coalition strong enough to challenge his government in the city, when he marched away. Skilful politics learned from his father and now applied by his own authority. We were in daily contact with Persians and I found it curious that they could not pronounce the name of Alexander and they spoke of him as 'Iskander'.

They paid him homage in a prostration which they called 'proskynesis', detestable to both Macedonians and Greeks. From us, Alexander received the honour due to the first amongst equals; the Persian obeisance lifted him up to the gods. Ominously, he did not forbid the enemy from grovelling to him, as he planned to adopt local customs to win allies amongst the defeated enemy. Many Macedonians were angered by the king's acceptance of such homage and they secretly speculated how long it would be before he demanded our obeisance as his due as he claimed to be descended from the gods. I hoped that that bad day would never come for men are men and the jealousy of the gods can swiftly destroy those amongst us whom they raise most high.

Alexander appointed Eumenes to bring Persians into the secretariat of Miletos. Hephaestion and Eumenes were old rivals and as his influence with the king increased, Hephaestion's hostility towards him increased. He was not alone in this amongst the Macedonian and Greek generals. Eumenes foolishly affected the supercilious superiority of many civilians in government service, which is ever an irritant to military men. He was short and oily and his complexion was unburned by the sun as he spent his days writing his diaries, sheltered in his tent.

Soldiers are ever contemptuous of civilians who follow the army, organise their supplies, record their actions and then share in the booty, without ever exposing themselves to danger. Civilians, in their turn, regard fighting men as half savage, bloodthirsty and ignorant, and war a ridiculous waste of resources. I found myself uncomfortably positioned between these two extremes.

Philip was the first general in history to conduct winter campaigns and Alexander intended to follow his successful lead and to gain advantage from a swift advance, which this would give to him. His spies now reported that the main Persian army was far to our east and that their navy was sailing off the Phoenician coast. He reasoned that to continue the march would gain us southern Anatolia, free of the threat of any major battles.

Chapter 14

It was late summer before we left Miletos to move south towards Halicarnassos in Caria; the native city of the great storyteller, Herodotus, from whom Aristotle had taught us so much of the history and geography of these lands of Anatolia. At the end of the first day's march we reached the desolate ruins of the great Temple of Apollo at Didyma. It was burned, by the Persians, long years before. They carried off the cult figure of Kanochos, deported the Branchidian priests, and sent their plunder from the temple to enrich their treasury at Persepolis. Alexander visited the vast remains and he sat in contemplation by the Sacred Spring, known since ancient times as the Fountain of Prophecy. The story was well-known to us that on the night of Alexander's birth, the spring had gushed again after many dry centuries and the Oracle knew this as a sign from the gods and he prophesied for the infant: "A victory over all the world".

An ancient crone, muttering spells and curses, still wandered round the temple ruins on moonlit nights.

Alexander, in gratitude for the famous prophecy, ordered Eumenes to donate the necessary money for the restoration of the great temple and to include funds for the support of the Oracle and attendant priests. We arrived before the mighty walls of Halicarnassos to find that Memnon of Rhodes commanded the city's defences. He had brought the Persian fleet into the harbour and reinforced the large garrison with sailors from his ships. Alexander prepared for a long siege of the city. To provide us with food, our men gathered the ripe harvest from the rich, fertile fields surrounding Halicarnassos. We built a great camp, complete with granaries and cooking facilities, but our most important work was to build forges so that the smiths could make us new weapons and repair damaged swords, shields and armour. As soon as the soldiers had finished building the camp, the king ordered the army to resume normal training in preparation for an attack on Halicarnassos.

The mornings were cool, after the heat of summer, and the longer nights gave us many opportunities to discuss strategy for storming the defences of the city as we gathered in Alexander's tent. During the days, I used every opportunity to explore the shore and countryside, now barren after we had gathered the harvest. The engineers spent many days assembling the siege machines and as soon as these were ready, they were brought up against the city's walls in the east. A small force of Persians came through the gate to attack us, but we quickly drove them back behind their own defences with few losses on either side. The king detailed a small force to guard the eastern gate and he led the rest of the army to the Myndos Gate, on the western side of the city. We filled in the moat, with the help of local peasants, and brought up our battering rams and siege machines against the walls of the city. We continuously attacked the heavily defended fortifications and, during our assault, the Persians opened the gates and galloped out to attack us. Each time we drove them back until, one night, they closed the gate before all their men had retreated inside and they were left to die miserably, if swiftly, at our hands.

Memnon's last and most horrible deed in Halicarnassos was to set the city on fire. When Alexander saw the flames, he ordered us into an immediate attack. It was a black night but the fires soon lit the darkness as the screams of men, women and children tore through the air and rivers of blood flowed from both sides of the battle. The city was razed to the ground in the flames, but Memnon and his sailors escaped by ship to a fortified island just beyond the harbour as the city fell to Alexander.

Pixadarus, the satrap of Caria, had survived the battle. He had recently succeeded his brother, Idrieus, and married his wife, Ada, who was sister to both men. They both appeared before Alexander when Ada exiled Pixadarus from Caria for failing to protect the city. There was an immediate bond between the queen and Alexander and she found in him a substitute for a son whom she had recently lost in death, and they spent many long days in each other's company.

Escorted by the Companions, Alexander made a ceremonial

visit to the enormous tomb of Mausolus, the uncle of Ada. This was one of the Wonders of the World. The queen told us the story of his wife, who in an excess of mourning after his cremation, had taken his ashes and drunk them in a sweet-tasting nectar. The tomb dominated the land of Caria and the money to raise such a monument must have impoverished all the people of the province.

Alexander, impatient to continue the campaign, quickly established a democratic government in Halicarnassos, and he appointed Eumenes the chief administrator of the city. Parmenion and some of the older generals spoke out bitterly against a civilian usurping the fruits of a military victory, as they plotted the downfall of the diarist until their complaints reached the king and he quickly advised them that: "Victory belongs to Alexander and responsibility for securing the peace is mine also. The methods that I choose are for the success of the expedition and any one of you who cannot serve me should declare himself and return to Macedon without honours or spoils. The army is not a democratic institution and therefore there is no other authority but mine and if you are not with me you are against me and my cause would be better served by your departure."

Parmenion stiffened in anger at the king's words. He had enjoyed the confidence and close friendship of King Philip and now Philip's son clearly told him that he was no longer necessary to the campaign. He, who had been the architect of so many Macedonian victories on our borders, in the cities of Greece and here in the east. In a tense atmosphere, he drew himself up and left the king's tent. We shared his humiliation for our loyalty to Parmenion was second only to our loyalty to Alexander.

After Parmenion's departure, the king continued to speak: "We now hold the cities of most of the west coast of Anatolia and we must advance into the interior. Parmenion will take the army and the civilian train to Gordion in the north. I shall take a small force into Lykia, to our south, and then into Pamphyllia and Pisidia to our east. I am informed that the local tribespeople spend the winter in the mountain valleys or on the coast and, due to deep snow, they have no escape from either. We shall make peace with them so that they will not attack our rear and we shall join Parmenion in Gordion in the spring.

"I have decided that all the young men who married before we left Pella may return on leave to Macedon and they will rejoin the expedition in Gordion. I tell them to give their wives sons to keep Macedon strong. To take to the Macedonians greetings from Alexander and report to them that the Persian yoke is lifted from Hellespontine-Phrygia, south as far as Caria."

All the young men, including myself, were delighted by the king's command. I instructed my slave, who was enraptured by the good news, to prepare for the journey. He was a narrow-minded man and he refused to enjoy any travel away from Macedon. He had been born and raised on my father's land and he had women, children and other family. He went off in great haste, promising to be ready by dawn the next day. I had purchased Persian trinkets for my father and Penelope. I knew that he would enjoy the statues of Artemis from Ephesos, the small bronze figurines, coins, the gold pieces and the strange seals which I had been able to purchase. I had bought exquisite jewellery for Penelope It was barbaric in design and I thought how well it would suit her delicate beauty.

I was happy beyond words to be going home and I rushed to arrange a relief for my command. I walked to the secretariat for my men's pay and fat bounty before clasping friends' hands in farewell. My mind calculated the shortest time until we rode into Pella. Alexander had sent runners to announce our arrival, and I was confident that my father and Penelope would be in Pella to greet me. I had felt deep concern during my wife's pregnancy, and I hoped to be present for the birth of our child.

That night I retired early. We were quartered in the shattered public buildings of the town, but I found that city noises were much more disturbing than the country sounds familiar in camp and sleep eluded me. My thoughts were very happy and I was delighted when my slave entered my room before dawn, carrying a letter from my father. I broke the seal and now I quote from his letter for I have kept it these many years and his words are forever etched on my soul: "Greetings to Jason from Nearchos. I write in sorrow and mourning. Yesterday Penelope gave birth to a son but gave up her own life. Would that I could bear this for you. Would that my hand be severed before I must write of this tragedy and would that the gods had taken me in her stead.

"My son, she was the light which brought gladness to my old age. Tomorrow, when I have made all arrangements for the care of the child, I shall leave for Pella to comfort her parents. I shall write again from there, but for now my heart is heavy and words will give you no comfort."

I felt a shock go through my body as lightning from heaven and then a cold numbness which prevented my tears from flowing. I know not what I did thereafter. I was lost in the black darkness engulfing me. Death had come to destroy my wife and with her had gone my happiness and very heart. A finality in my life without compromise in hope, a consuming sorrow which destroyed my reason.

Thoughts of my journey to Pella had gone and when my slave came to call me, I was sitting as he had left me. He took the letter and read the contents and squatted at my feet to take my hands and, by his touch, convey compassion. My soldier's training helped me through those first hours.

I presented myself before the king and I gave him the letter and reported that I wanted to stay with the army. There was something within me which stopped me going home to share my father's grief. I was too small for that or to see my son, the stranger who had taken the life of my wife. I felt nothing for his orphan plight. I needed to be alone, to take my misery and let it engulf me. To cry for Penelope in sad privacy and shut the world out from any part of me. Alexander was all kindness. My slave had followed me and the king gave him orders to cancel my journey. He then sent for Craterus and he asked him to relieve me of all my responsibilities. A special messenger left Halicarnassos, with letters from Alexander, for my father, Olympias and to my wife's parents I still thought of them in that relationship for I could not accept her death and my thoughts were clouded in wild fantasies.

I returned to my quarters and told my slave to refuse everyone admittance. He brought me a draught of a strange, Persian remedy made from the poppy seed heads which grow on the high Anatolian Plateau. It gave me a wanton stupor adding to my fantasies, blunting my senses and mocking my tragedy. Many of our men became addicted to the potion and the king severely punished those who were found using it. Soldiers could not fight under its influence nor could we maintain discipline in the army; only physicians were allowed to prescribe the poppy for the wounded to deaden their pain.

The day after I received my father's letter, Parmenion came to see me and he urged me to leave Halicarnassos for Macedon. His thoughts were with his old friend, my father, and he advised me to go and comfort him. The old general would not see that I had enough to bear and that I could not open my wound even for my father. Soon afterwards, he marched out, with the army, for Sardis and Gordion in Phrygia. Alexander and Craterus, with the swiftest troops, and a small cavalry detachment, left for Lykia.

Ptolemy was appointed Satrap of Caria and he remained in Halicarnassos, with a garrison, to defend the city, where I also, with Alexander's permission, chose to stay.

The weeks dragged by without any decrease in my grief. I wrote to my father, but I could not mention the child. I wrote to Theocritos and to Aristotle. I refused all invitations, and I spent the days roaming the country, trying to reconcile myself to my loss; as a wounded animal will seek solitude, so also did I. I was afraid of other men's problems. I had nothing left to give them; for all her fragile beauty, Penelope had been my strength and without her I was lost. I blamed myself for her death and I walked in the mawkishness of self-pity. And now the years have passed and I look back to regret the awful selfishness of my youth. To my father, I abandoned the responsibility of my son, his care and education and I sent no word to lessen the load, much less return to Macedon to do my part. I was fortunate that winter had halted the campaign against the Persians for my uselessness was obvious but, with the help of Ptolemy, in this respite at Halicarnassos, I was able to regain some measure of peace.

And then, one day before the chill of winter had turned to the balmy days of spring, Craterus rode into the city to recall me. He brought a bottle of clear liquid, which with the addition of water turned cloudy and tasted of anise. Together we drank and I was able to speak of my loss. We had been friends since our youth in Pella and few words were, usually, necessary between us, but now I talked until I felt relief from my grief. Craterus, the hunter, athlete and soldier, reached out a healing hand to my sick soul and dragged me back into the campaign of Alexander where I must do my part or part from it. We talked until the sun was setting across the sea. I thought that Apollo and Dionysos were competing to light the world. The reds, golds and orange of the Sun God were turned into the purples and reds of wine as they struck the water. Homer, himself, wrote of 'the wine-dark sea'; it was so magnificent that it dwarfed the affairs of finite men and turned each one of us into no more than a drop of rain in the storms of history.

We watched in silence the ever-changing majesty of the spectacle until the light faded beyond the western horizon and the stars stealthily brightened in the darkening sky. Craterus spoke: "Jason, it is time for you to join Alexander. He sent me to offer you the choice of returning to Macedon on the staff of Antipater or riding on with me. We have had a hard campaign in Lykia. To cross the mountains we followed rivers and streams many miles inland before we could find a passage over the rocky peaks. We were often deprived of food and water. We met people who inhabit this lonely land who make their livelihood by piracy, they speak strange languages and are as rough as their country.

"We saw great tombs, built with facades like temples, carved into the rock and others roofed, massive and free-standing, all tributes to death, for there is nothing in life the Lykians fear. When the Persians invaded the country, the men of Lykian Xanthos killed their women and children and fought the Persians until the last man fell, rather than submit to the invader.

"Alexander has received a letter from Parmenion, which was captured from a Persian courier. It reveals a plot between the Persians and Alexander of Lyncestis against the life of Alexander. If successful, the Macedonian throne would be given to Amyntas. Darius offers 1,000 talents for the murder of the king. Alexander of Lyncestis has been seized. The king now regrets that his earlier plan to kill Amyntas was not carried through, and that he gave the command of the Thessalonians into his hands during the absence of Calas.

"Where we have campaigned, the countryside is beautiful and there is a great deal of history to interest us. I have even heard of a peasant man named Gordios who claimed to have received a sign from Zeus, as he drove his ox cart along a road in central Anatolia. He swore that an eagle had alighted on the shaft of his cart and Gordios interpreted this as an omen that he would succeed a king who had recently died without leaving an heir. When he reached the River Sangarios he learned of the death of the King of Phrygia and beyond that place, he founded the city of Gordion and received the acclamation of the people of that country. Gordios built a temple to his ox cart and, at the dedication ceremonies, he tied the yoke to its shaft with a concealed knot. The Lykian Oracle at his court predicted that the man who could untie the knot would become 'the Master of all Asia'."

Craterus told me of many other Anatolian legends until I finally felt compelled to say: "My period of mourning must end. I have already been away from the army far too long, let us ride to join Alexander, after we have seen Ptolemy and collected his report to the king on conditions here in Halicarnassos and all Caria."

He clasped my hand and we filled our cups again, we saluted each other and then we parted for the night. At last I wrote to my father and told him of my plans.

The first town that we reached in Lykia was Telmessos, the city of seers. Craterus told me that at the approach of Alexander, Telmessos had surrendered to the king and that night we rested in civilised surroundings which were undamaged by war. The city was the birthplace of Aristander, Alexander's famous seer, and of snake men, and many other wise men practised their rituals in secret places, even in caves and grottoes outside the walls, for the town was full of strange religions.

The people of Lykia claimed that they came from Crete and had been allies of Troy during the Trojan War. We found many graves cut into the rock faces just as Craterus had described them to me. They were carved with temple facades and there were also more massive free-standing stone tombs which were finished with high-pointed roofs. We left Telmessos and stopped the following night at Patara, a busy port in a small valley between hills above the sea. The next day we climbed the mountain, which soared above the city, to the ruined city of Xanthos from where the view sweeps gloriously down to the sea. There are more wonderful tombs in Xanthos, which are decorated with strange myths and they speak of ancient gods in an unknown language, and the sun shines on the desolation of deserted temples, a theatre and tombs, one of which is said to belong to the Harpies. When Alexander had visited Xanthos, he left a small garrison to attract people to return to the city and bring it back to life. Greek soldiers were at work restoring the buildings and they brought new hope to the few people who lived amongst the ruins. We watched the work until the setting of the sun, for the place was haunted and full of death and I was thankful to leave; it was night before we reached the road to take us east along the Lykian coast.

We reached Myra in three days, to find more tombs carved into the high cliffs above the city. They were decorated with columns, entablatures and ornamented architraves and they spoke eloquently of the Lykian obsession with death, and we rode on speedily to escape their sad message and to find life with Alexander.

We reached the king's camp above the cliffs of Lykia's eastern shore and I heard of the dangers, which the men had faced from many hostile tribes throughout this wild and beautiful land. Now the land and tribes were pacified and in a few days we continued the march north following a track along the coast. We were soon met by a group of citizens from Phaselis and they brought Alexander a golden crown, and they offered him their city. We arrived outside Phaselis to the cheers of the excited people, who escorted us inside their walls for two days and two nights of noisy revelry. With calm restored, Alexander appointed Nearchos as the satrap of Lykia, a difficult task but one worthy of his integrity and talents, as a commander on land and at sea.

Phaselis is built from white marble and nestles in a pine forest, which reaches down to the sea. The mountains soar into the sky above. It is a beautiful place, made prosperous with two excellent harbours and the people are far less barbarous than those of Lykian towns. They prized their Greek heritage and spoke in a dialect that we could all understand. The citizens soon complained to the king that their neighbours of Pisidia had built a fortress high above their town and constantly raided their ports and stole their merchandise. The king sent an expedition to destroy the stronghold, and so bound Phaselis to his cause.

Craterus and I climbed their Mount Olympos, to the place where Bellerophon slew the dragon. The creature's flame still burns on the mountainside and it was visible from Phaselis during the hours of darkness. Alexander was impatient to continue the campaign to Perge and the other cities of the Pamphyllian coast before the heat of summer exacted its cost on the men. After a short rest, he sent most of the army north, through the mountains, and the king led only a small unit to explore the difficult coastal path. At one point, we found our way completely cut off by the sea as it crashed against the rocky cliffs. Fortuitously, the wind veered to the north and separated the water from the cliffs and gave us a passage around them. As soon as the last man had passed this place, the wind changed again and the sea once more thundered against the rocky shore. Many people say that this was another miracle in the life of Alexander and the cliffs are named Chelidonia.

We found that Perge was a fully independent Greek city protected by a wall and imposing gates. We camped outside the wall and the people welcomed us and held many feasts to honour Alexander. The columned agora, with the market section, was filled with throngs of people from dawn until after dark each evening. We enjoyed the theatre, stadium, baths, taverns and many other civilised pleasures in Perge, but this interlude soon ended, and we took the short road to Aspendos on the banks of the River Eurymedon.

The great Taurus Mountains loom up in the north filling distant horizons, paralleling the coastal road and between the mountains and the coast is the lush Pamphyllian plain on which the sun, it seemed, shone every day. The Taurus Mountains stretch across Anatolia as far as Syria and I heard that there are only four passes through the towering heights and all of them impassable during the snow of winter.

Aspendos is well inland but, as the Eurymedon is navigable, ships brought supplies up to the city and carried away, to many distant markets, the bountiful, surplus harvest gathered by the citizens in their surrounding countryside. We camped on the banks of the river. Aspendos is famous for its stables and the hundreds of horses the citizens bred by a mutually advantageous, special arrangement, for the King of Kings. The animals were stabled and exercised in the large area between the outer and inner walls of the city. We urgently needed to replace many of our animals, which we had lost in battle, or to the hardships of the campaign. Alexander intended to appropriate them from the stables of Darius. The citizens of Aspendos sent a delegation to the king and they asked him not to leave a garrison in their city. He agreed to this request on condition that Aspendos gave him the Persian horses and that the city paid fifty talents as tribute. The delegation argued for some time amongst themselves and finally accepted the king's terms. It seemed an excellent bargain for us and we marched away from Aspendos, leaving only a few Macedonians in the city to collect the horses and the fifty talents.

With business concluded in Aspendos, we returned to the coast road and continued east for the short distance to Side. The city fathers prudently welcomed Alexander and we enjoyed a short respite in their city. The people believed that it had been founded by Aeolians; it must have been in the far distant past for they speak a language quite unknown to Greeks or even other Pamphyllians, which has isolated them from all the surrounding people in that part of Asia. Side is a large coastal city with a very prosperous port and it is surrounded by a fertile plain, which stretches north to the Taurus Mountains. The city has many magnificent buildings, including baths made from marble, and a large theatre, all near to the agora. Alexander left only a small garrison in Side, for the people were far more interested in peaceful commerce than waging war against Macedon.

We marched inland to Sillion. It is built on a flat-topped hill rising straight up out of the plain. We heard that the Persians had a strong garrison in the town and I did learn that the Laws of Pamphyllia are inscribed on a wall in the city.

We camped on the plain below Sillion and Alexander sent scouts to climb up to the wide ramparts leading to the city's gate. They returned to report that high, massive walls rise straight from its hill top and give strong protection to the city, and that it would be impossible to breach them without siege machines, which were all with Parmenion on the way to Gordion. As the king listened to the report, a messenger arrived from the Macedonians, left in Aspendos, with the news that Aspendos was in revolt against the king and had refused to hand over either horses or tribute. At this news, Alexander quickly concluded that not even the isolated Persian garrison in Sillion was strong enough to threaten our small expedition and that the city could be safely bypassed and we hastened back to rebellious Aspendos. We warily moved inside the outer walls and occupied the abandoned houses and Alexander waited. He was soon rewarded by a delegation from the citizens begging him to allow them to honour their original treaty with him. The king had to consider that we were only a small contingent of the army, we had no siege machines or heavily armoured troops and the people of Aspendos were safe behind their wall until their food supplies were exhausted.

However, he scornfully rejected their petition and demanded that as the price of a new treaty, they must turn over their leading citizens as hostages to their good faith. He doubled the sum for tribute and added a stiff annual amount and he appointed a

Macedonian governor to rule the city. To our surprise, Aspendos accepted all Alexander's new terms and, after many formal ceremonies, designed to impress the chastened people with the king's power, we left the city and returned to the coastal road, marching this time into the setting sun.

We came to the crossroads where the road turned south to follow the coast but we continued west along a difficult track, through craggy mountains until, coming through a gorge and only with the help of a local spy, we found the city of Termessos perched on the highest peak, which only an eagle should occupy. The city was so high that we could only make out the faint outline of walls after climbing the steep lower slopes. Alexander decided that we were too small a force to undertake the siege of such a site and that the city was so isolated that it could never threaten the security of the campaign. We therefore returned along the road to the east until we reached the pass through the Taurus Mountains. We made good progress, despite the cold, snow and miserable condition of the track through the mountains. We left Pamphyllia and passed through Pisidia until we reached the city of Celenae where we stopped to rest and Alexander appointed administrators for all the newly conquered territories. Antigonus the One-Eyed, a general from the days of King Philip, was appointed satrap of Pisidia, and he stayed in Celenae when the expedition left the city. We continued endlessly on across the wastelands of the central Anatolian plateau. We saw few settlements or even living creatures and we had to exist on our own meagre supplies; it was a time of hunger and hardship but we always found fodder for the horses.

The ordeal ended when we reached the River Sangarios where we learned from a Greek-speaking peasant that we were only a day's march from Gordion. We rejoiced as we made camp and prepared horses, equipment, men and our clothes for a triumphal entry into the city and our reunion with Parmenion and the army. We rode into Gordion and our comrades greeted us with wild shouts and joyful laughter and they surrounded Alexander and cheered him to the skies in joyous relief for his safety. We feasted together for many days, exchanging news of our conquests and of Macedon and of Greeks and Persians, but we only privately remembered the men who had died in battle. Scribes, under Callisthenes, diligently wrote down all that we told them of the campaign in the south, but they lacked the genius of Homer and I silently wondered if by their works alone the deeds of Alexander would live on to unborn generations?

The botanists and geologists had collected many samples from the earth of Anatolia, and these were now sent to Aristotle, even the poppies which gave relief from pain or turned men into haunted spirits. I felt that we had been absent for too many seasons from Macedon as I tried to absorb all that I now heard from old friends, not only of the progress of the army, but also the news from home. Once we had settled into a routine in Gordion Alexander, riding Bucephalos, in full armour and escorted by the Companions, visited the temple of the Ox Cart and before the excited crowd he unsheathed his sword, held it on high and, with a clean sweep, cut the Knot of Gordios, shouting, "I have done it!" as he pulled the pin, which had secured the yoke, and he gave notice to Darius, King of Kings, and to all his subjects that a new Great King claimed Asia. The people of Gordion were wild with excitement, and shouted again and again: "Alexander! Alexander! Liberator! Lord of the East and Fulfiller of the Prophecy!"

Many libations were poured that day and the celebrations continued far into the night in the city.

The young men returned from leave in Macedon and they brought supplies, trained horses and new recruits who were immediately incorporated into the army and we resumed daily training to bring the army back to full efficiency. I felt in full health and vigour and I could even remember Penelope with less sickening sorrow. Eumenes also arrived in Gordion. We spent the late spring and early summer in the city, long enough for old rivalries to flare again. Hephaestion and Eumenes quarrelled, even openly before the king. Hephaestion despised the administrator and his scribely function and he refused to give him an account of the Lykian campaign for his journal. Callisthenes fared better for his publications and he sent back copies of the details of every part of the expedition to Antipater and the Corinthian Council.

Craterus and I spent time together. We visited the taverns, wine shops and pleasure houses; I often nursed a head wracked by a night of excess. Alexander waited in Gordion to test the strength of the governments which he had established in the conquered territories but no reports of any uprisings reached the king. He also expected Darius to march north to attack us but the

Great King missed his opportunity, either from an overwhelming confidence or because he feared his doom and knew that every decision which he made hastened his end.

Alexander had a deep faith in Persian astrologers and their predictions and he praised their excellent physicians. He learnt of all the plants, which they used for curing the sick, and he often prescribed their concoctions for the wounded military. The king employed more and more Persians throughout the expedition in permanent positions. Macedonian anger grew throughout the army, for all the Persians who voluntarily surrendered to us were given their equivalent status amongst the Macedonians and Greeks.

Persian women also arrived in great numbers in Gordion. They were welcomed by many of our men, but scorned by Macedonian women in the expedition and, as opposition to Persians grew louder, it seemed that Alexander was indifferent to our fears. He even planned to use them in the great battle which we must fight against Darius, their Persian king.

One of the branches of the Persian Royal Road from Susa, the capital of their empire, terminated at Gordion; the southern branch extended to Sardis of Lydia. Gordion is on the high plateau near the banks of the River Sangarios. During the spring, the air of the plateau is fragrant with the scent of flowers, including the poppy whose opion juice had soothed my sorrow in Halicarnassos. Poppies grow in great carpets in Asian lands and they are cultivated by the people for their medicinal qualities and their profit.

Huge earthen mounds dominate Gordion. They had been built by the people of the city to cover the tombs of their Phrygian kings, with access to the burial chambers through open passages from the outside world. Alexander made a ceremonial visit to the tomb of King Midas of the Golden Touch. He was the son of Gordios who had tied the prophetic knot. We heard that Midas had travelled to Sardis to bathe in the River Pactolus and successfully cured himself of his terrible affliction by which everything that he touched, even his food, had turned to gold. Alexander went to the temple of Gordion and offered sacrifices and libations in honour of both kings and especially that of Gordios and of his Knot and the prophecy which, by acclamation, the king now fulfilled.

Alexander and Craterus, as a relief from the cares of the

campaign, several times went off to hunt lions and boar in the country surrounding Gordion. The king's headquarters were always filled with embassies and petitioners arriving in the city to plead their masters' causes and pledge their loyalty. It was arduous work, but Alexander always received them with dignity and courtesy and thanked them for their many gifts. He kept none of these for himself and most were given into the custody of the treasury.

One day Arbas, a Syrian, came to offer his camel trains for hire. Alexander tried out these strange beasts to carry some of our baggage, but Greeks found them difficult to control as we could not imitate the guttural commands used by the camel drivers, which were about all the creatures seemed to understand. Jews also arrived from that part of Syria called Judea or Canaan or Philistia and they came to trade with the expedition. They were able to supply us with every necessity and many luxuries. We were an army rich with spoils. There was a large community of their kinsmen in Sardis and a few of these had left their home to follow Alexander. He spoke to them quite often and he listened to their religious theories of a single deity. They also told him stories from their long history, which had been written during an exile in Babylon, before their Persian liberation.

The king held many conferences in Gordion and we frequently stayed with him until the dawn broke over the steppes in the east. We all found a great deal to fascinate us, even to admire, in the Empire of the Persians. I especially liked the Persian gift for compassion and I saw its mellowing effect on Alexander. The Persians, as well as the Jews, also worshipped only one god, but in several manifestations; he was dedicated to man's spiritual advancement, quite unlike our capricious Olympians. Alexander deeply revered Achilles, but he took for his personal model Herakles, the Doer of Good Works, his own paternal ancestor and from whom he found an echo in the ethics of the Persians.

Nearly all the members of the school at Mieza were united at Gordion. Ptolemy was missing, for he governed in Halicarnassos of Caria and Seleucos was with the navy. We reminisced together about our teacher Aristotle and the gentle life that we had known under his care and we listened as Alexander unfolded his dreams as they turned to grand ambition. He knew himself in many roles as King of the Macedonians, Hegemon of the League of Corinth and so overlord of all Greece, except for Sparta, also as the liberator of the Ionians, Carians, Lykians, Pamphyllians and Phrygians, and he saw himself in the future, emperor of all the Persian satrapies with these separate components, in a grand alliance united by a common allegiance to himself. His vision was titanic; in any other man dangerous in its concentration of power. He was, however, a very different prince and he now worked to end destructive wars and to bring, to all men, a common civilisation and the religion of one god. Some amongst us reflected that should Alexander die, he left no heir and the disintegration of all his dreams must surely follow, but we were young and death seemed a very distant threat, and we were part of Alexander's great enterprise with a life of very heady promise.

The king ordered the artists with the expedition to make sketches and paintings from our daily life. Some of the sketches were sent to Pella and we heard that they were used by artisans for copies in mosaics. Other artists designed new coins using the king's head, which were minted in great quantities from our stores of silver and gold and they were used to pay the army and for all the supplies and services which the expedition purchased from local people. Gordion rang with the sounds of shouted commands and the incessant clang of forges making armour and weapons all mingled with the cries of the marketplace, where business never ceased night or day. Wagonloads of money and treasure left Gordion for Macedon for the families and friends of members of the expedition, some of it to be stored against the owners' return home.

I bought trinkets and manuscripts for my father. He could not, of course, read Persian, Phoenician or any of the other hieroglyphics in which they were written; but I planned to send keys to their mysteries as soon as I could find translators. There were many Greeks in the camp whom we had captured, or who had deserted from the Persians, and a few had learned the local languages and I intended to find some of these to do this work for me.

And then one day, as balmy spring changed and the land was seared with the heat of high summer, Alexander called a Council of War. We assembled in the ruins of an ancient temple and we heard the king speak: "I have waited this long in Gordion to be sure that the pacification is completed of all the territories which we have taken. Now that these reports have arrived, I do not think that any city is strong enough to attack our rear, except for Halicarnassos where Ptolemy reports incipient revolution and which he has taken all necessary action to control.

"Gordion will be the first permanent staging post on the road from Macedon, for the expedition, as we continue to advance. We shall leave strong detachments of the army in the city, from where they can swiftly move as necessary to maintain peace in the captured cities or reinforce the army on the march. I have news that the traitor Memnon has been killed and with him his plan for the conquest of the Aegean islands, Euboea and Macedon, in the name of Darius, has been abandoned. Thus do the gods favour Alexander and send many auguries for our expedition and as the gods have favoured me this far, so shall we pay them great honours and give sacrifices before we leave Gordion for without them my work is nothing and I am as a bridle without a horse.

"I have also heard that Darius has commanded Pharnazabus, whom he has appointed to succeed Memnon of Rhodes, to sail for Syria with his Greek mercenaries, where he now awaits us, to personally command the Persian army and halt our advance. In three days we shall march east to Ancyra and from there we go south to Syria, not only to defeat Pharnazarbus but Darius himself who styles himself King of Kings."

As Alexander finished speaking to us, a buzz of excitement filled the air. So far, we had fought and won battles but this was war and the professional soldiers amongst us were anxious to prove their men, their arms and strategy and we all looked forward to the spoils of battle. The years of training, first under King Philip and since under Alexander, found every unit of the army functioning cohesively and as the word of our departure quickly spread throughout the camp, the atmosphere was charged with enthusiasm and we felt that we were an army at the greatest moment in history; dull indeed would be the man who did not respond to such a destiny.

Immediately before we marched from Gordion an Athenian embassy arrived in the city with a request for the release of all the Greek prisoners taken by Alexander. The king sent the delegation back to Athens to report that our prisoners would be returned to their cities immediately after he defeated Darius, when they would no longer be tempted to rejoin the Persian army and so fight against us for pay in Persian gold.

Chapter 15

Ambassadors from Pamphlagonia, on the Euxine Sea, were waiting for Alexander when we arrived in Ancyra. They brought the submission of their government to the king and the king responded by assuring them that he would not invade their country. Alexander had no intention of wasting time, men and resources on remote provinces of the Persian Empire. The control of south and central Anatolia (Land of the Rising Sun) was sufficient to ensure our supply lines and establish peace across the land between the army and Macedon; diplomacy once more brought us a bloodless victory with the return of the embassy to their homeland.

From Ancyra we marched south for Cappadocia, the Cilician Gates in the northern heights of the Taurus, and the passes leading to Tarsus and the Cilician Plain and to Darius, the King of Kings, and his army waiting for us somewhere in the mountains beyond. Cappadocia is a hostile, burning land of dust storms and foetid winds. I rode, in Alexander's name, with a small detachment of cavalry, to receive the homage of the people who live in the shadow of the snow-capped peaks of Mount Argaeos. The winds have carved strange forms out of the soft, tufa rock of the area into which the people have dug caves for their use as homes. They provide a cool refuge in the fires of summer, and protection in the bitter cold of winter.

With this accomplished, we rejoined the expedition and, anticipating relief from the heat, we were happy when we saw the great heights of the Taurus Mountains looming out of the dusty haze and stretching to either horizon. The earth on which we marched was criss-crossed with tracks and the guides had done well to bring us straight to the pass known as the Cilician Gates.

When we first entered the mountains, we were in a pleasant valley, which ran south between high and sharply pointed pinnacles of rock. The lower slopes were verdant and animals grazed on the grass, but it was a hostile place and at night we listened to the howl of wolves and the roar of bears as they approached our camp. The trees provided wood for our fires and local people brought goats, sheep, vegetables and fruit for us to purchase. The air was clean and cool and some of the men, who had been ill with high fevers, began to recover.

As we marched deeper into the mountains, the path narrowed and the sun failed to reach down to us. We followed a river, which we had to ford as we were forced to cross from bank to bank. Alexander took advantage of a grassy meadow as it opened out before us to rest the army for a few days. Our scouts rode back to report that the Persians occupied a position on high rocks above the narrow summit of the pass known as the Cilician Gates. The king immediately picked the swiftest, mounted units to ride ahead with him and surprise the enemy.

We left the camp under a full moon. The residual path led between towering cliffs and through deep ravines and finally we came to a tortuous trail, through a narrow gorge, where we crossed a wooden bridge over the fast-flowing river. By this point, the moon had set and we paused to drink from the river, cloaking our movements in silence to avoid an ambush, until dawn's light broke the thick dark of night and crept between high cliffs and showed us the path. We rode on, and we were about to leave the defile, when we surprised the sentries left by Arsames, the Satrap of Cilicia, to guard the pass. The cowards fled at our approach, although we were trapped between the sheer cliffs where only two horsemen or four foot soldiers could proceed in rank and we could easily have been killed by the enemy.

The Persians always failed to take advantage of their natural, defensive positions and, in their haste to retreat, they often failed, also, to destroy the crops and stores in our advancing path or to turn to their own advantage, their victories at sea.

We waited for the main column to reach our position and we then began the tortuous descent down the mountains. After ten days, we were thankful to reach the Taurus foothills where we were met by an embassy of frightened citizens from Tarsus. They begged Alexander to make great speed to save their city from destruction by Arsames, the Satrap. The king ordered Parmenion to ride at full gallop, with a picked force from the cavalry, to protect the city. Arsames fled at our approach and we marched into Tarsus the following night. The citizens expressed their gratitude with tears and acclamations and when the king arrived, they gave him the keys of their mint and they ordered their sculptors to make heads of Alexander in marble, to celebrate his arrival in their city. We were glad to rest, bathe, change our clothes and explore the city. It is the principal port of Cilicia and it is situated amongst lush orchards; altogether a busy and prosperous place where diverse cultures mingle. The colourful inhabitants were from many distant countries. There were Persians, Greeks, Arabians, Armenians, Jews, Philistines, Phoenicians, Canaanites and Assyrians and they all mingled in the market place with people from the mountains, whom I understood were Hatti or Hittites, and their dress was as varied as their speech.

Alexander, burning from the forced march, plunged into the River Cydnos to cool off. It was fed by icy water from the mountains, and by the next day he lay racked with a high fever. When I heard the news, I hastened to the king's tent and I was deeply shocked by his condition for he looked close to death. Philip of Arcania, a physician and friend of King Philip, was at his side and he personally prepared many potions and liniments for his patient. He remained constantly by Alexander's couch, even sleeping within the royal tent.

Two days later, I was again at the king's bedside. Philip approached with yet another draught, as a messenger came in from Parmenion. Alexander roused himself and opened a letter and I saw his white face turn to wax; without a word he handed it to Philip. He watched the physician as he read the letter and he whispered: "Better to die from another's crime than from fear." as he swallowed the potion. Philip passed the letter to Hephaestion and said to the king: "Alexander, son of Philip, as you have taken my medicine follow my advice and you will soon be restored to health."

Hephaestion gave the letter to me and I read in horror of Parmenion's warning that Darius had bribed Philip to poison the king, offering as a reward one of his daughters in marriage and a considerable fortune in gold.

Alexander's faith in the physician was the turning point in his sickness and his slow recovery began. It was Parmenion's misfortune to have intercepted false information, inevitably increasing the distance between himself and the king. Parmenion had no personal enmity towards Philip; they had often campaigned together. I could only regret yet another cause for the old general's fall from the king's grace, especially as it followed his successful ride to save Tarsus, which had been commended by Alexander as an example of courage and military discipline. As his strength gradually returned, the king planned his next moves in the campaign. He sent Parmenion, in command of a strong force from the cavalry, to the east, to occupy the Syrian Gates, the pass leading from the Mediterranean over the Amanus Mountains into the valley of the River Orontes and greater Syria. The main army, under Philotas, marched to make camp at Mopsuestia on the River Pyramos, not far to our east. Alexander, with a small expedition, left Tarsus west for the coast road towards the mountains in the north, to subdue that part of the country known as Cilicia the Rough for it was entirely made from rocks and rugged hills where nothing grows.

Before we reached this harsh land, we rested at the lovely, marble port city of Soloi where we found a few Greeks settled amongst the mixed population. A hostile crowd greeted our arrival and enduring their sullen murmurs, Alexander stiffly rode Bucephalos along the columned Sacred Way to offer sacrifices at the city's shrine. He imposed a heavy fine on the wealthy citizens for their token resistance and ordered them to build a mole in the sea, out from the port, for the use of Nearchos and the fleet. He also established a small garrison in the city, not only to maintain order in Soloi, but also to prevent the Persian navy from using the facilities of the port.

We were ready to ride from the city, when unfortunately, in defiance of Alexander's orders, a few soldiers lit a fire under some olive trees in the surrounding orchards and started a blaze in the grove. The outraged citizens whispered amongst themselves, accusing the king of arson until they discovered that he had severely punished the culprits who had disobeyed his orders.

We left Soloi and took Olba and other mountain villages without too much loss of life and then returned to Soloi.

115

Alexander received a message from Ptolemy, in Halicarnassos of Caria, reporting that the Persians had organised a revolt in Halicarnassos, which he had completely vanquished. Alexander was delighted with the good news and held games and a musical competition in celebration. Those were pleasant days in Soloi. As well as the shady orchards, the mountains towered distantly across the northern horizon, above the Cilician Plain, and the sea sparkled in the warm sunshine. Ports are always rich in taverns and amusements and the people of the city were much given to pleasure and idleness.

With so few Greeks in Soloi, their language was impure and their manners rough. We later asked people of similar hostile disposition if by chance they were natives of that city and henceforth jokingly referred to corruption of language as a solecism. We left Soloi and returned to Tarsus, stopping overnight on the way at Anchiale. In that city we saw the famous tomb of the Assyrian king Ashurbanipul (whom we call Sardanapalos). The tomb supported a statue of the king in the attitude of a man striking his hands together in mocking tolerance and underneath his figure was an inscription which read: 'I, Ashurbanipal, son of Anakynarxes, built, in one day, Tarsus and Anchiale. O Stranger! Eat, drink and play for everything else in the life of man is not worth this'.

We made sacrifices of thanks for the recovery of Alexander in Tarsus and prepared to catch up with the army. Alexander, as at Gordion, established a permanent secretariat and depot in the city to serve our extended supply routes. Runners left with reports of the expedition's progress for Antipater and he always responded to Alexander's orders, for men and supplies, in a minimum period of time.

The mint at Tarsus had produced coinage for both trade in Cilicia and to pay the city's Persian tribute. The old dies were destroyed and were replaced with new ones, manufactured in Gordion. The coins which were minted depicted the head of Alexander wearing, in emulation, the skin of the fierce Nemean lion slain by Herakles when performing the first of his twelve labours. The king now had a simple means of paying the army and members of the expedition and, when the coins were distributed, of receiving the tribute of the conquered cities. It was a great simplification of the system of barter in goods and services which we had used before the new coins were minted and the mint in Tarsus also produced Alexander's coins in profile.

When Alexander was satisfied that the military and civil governments which he had previously established in Tarsus were functioning well enough to control all western Cilicia, we marched on the road going east, across the lush plain below the Taurus Mountains, which was known by the name of Cilicia the Smooth. Many of the towns of the plain were quite large, especially those built on river crossings where communities had built temples to their many different gods. The king paused long enough at these towns to meet the leading citizens, to offer sacrifices in their temples and to receive their tribute in the newly minted coins. We came across a few villages in which people whom we had met before in Gordion and Ancyra had settled. I heard from Greeks living in the area that these people, also, had towns and fortresses high in the mountain passes. Many thought them remnants of the Assyrians but they looked more like Dorians or other northern tribesmen and they spoke their own distinctive language. Indeed, many people had swept across the Cilician Plain since Homer wrote of Troy, amongst them Aryans, Celts, Medes, Assyrians, Babylonians, Persians and Greeks. They had all conquered, plundered and then settled and left their marks in language, art, architecture and religion. The people seemed resigned to invaders but they quickly submitted to each new conqueror to avoid the destruction of their cities and land.

I studied the works of art in Asia and I began to learn the Persian text but I could not find a teacher for the local hieroglyphs. I did discover a man fluent in Phoenician words but he knew no Persian or Greek and we could not easily communicate with one another.

We once more reached the coast, at the town of Margasos, where the king was well received. We stayed in the city only long enough for Alexander to make sacrifices to Athena and Kybele and then we followed the Pyramos north along the bank of the river. Spines of rocky hills jutted out of the plain in this fertile and beautiful land and we passed through villages along the river until we reached the town of Mallos on the west side of the Pyramos.

That night, we sat round the campfire with Alexander and discussed all that we knew of the history of this ancient land.

The farther that we marched from Greece, the stranger to us were the customs of the local people. Their rulers had far greater powers than any held by king or archon in Greece and they could condemn people to prison, or even death, after only a cursory trial. Greek laws are superior for the ordinary people, so we decided, and our system of taxation rests upon them more easily.

The rich, amongst the conquered, were made to pay taxes to finance their liberation and Alexander's expedition. This method diminished their power, allied the people with the king, and so reduced the danger of rebellion in our rear.

We were all reclining one night in the tent of the king discussing the philosophy of the Assyrians, which made no mention of the gods, when a messenger rode into our small camp to report that Darius and his army were on this side of the Euphrates River and only two days' march from the Syrian Gates. With this news, we immediately dispersed to sleep before an early morning departure. We arrived at Mopsuestia, a city founded by Mopsus, a hero of the Trojan War, where we joined Philotas and the main army already in camp and waiting for our arrival. Near to Mopsuestia, above the east bank of the River Pyramos, we saw a strange rock relief of a king. Local Greeks told me that he was Muwattali, of the ancient Hittites or Hatti, a mountain people, remnants of whom lived far up the river valley. Many reports were sent from Cilicia to Pella and regular dispatches were sent of our progress and all that we saw on the expedition to Aristotle, who was now living in Athens. Alexander collected animals, rocks and especially plants, for our teacher's research into the ingredients of eastern remedies for sickness and injuries. We knew that we were close to Darius but we saw no sign of the Persians on our next march to Hieropolis, where we rested for two days on the banks of the Pyramos. Parmenion and his small force had returned and were camped at Hieropolis and the united army moved south to Issos where we left our sick and wounded in the care of physicians.

We continued south, across the Plain of Issos. At several points the Amanus Mountains reach down to the sea and the road was only wide enough for the passage of four horsemen in file and our progress was much slower than across the Cilician Plain.

We camped at Miriandros, below the pass called the Syrian Gates, where we left the civilians and most of the supply train.

Nearchos had brought the ships round the coast to the port and Alexander sent him back to keep watch for any sign of the Persian navy or army. We were up long before the end of night and we began the ascent above Miriandros at dawn. Looking back over Amanus our view was filled with mountainous peaks reaching to the sky in grim and lonely solitude and many were already snow-capped. At last we reached the Syrian Gates where at the top of the pass we met our spies who reported that they had seen no sign of the Persians on the southern side of the mountains. We started the descent and we soon looked far down the slopes to the River Orontes curving across the Syrian plain. It was a limitless view and so green and fertile in great contrast to the barren, snow-crested heights which towered above us. Both men and horses were tired as we followed the turns and twists on the mountain's flank. We were suddenly halted by a storm of wild ferocity. Lightning streaked from horizon to horizon, thunder roared in a continuous fury, and the rain, mixed with snow, lashed down as though the heavens had opened up to submerge the world in its violent fury.

When the storm was over, we lit fires under a sky just as suddenly blue again. The sun drew the moisture from the earth and turned the whole world into a steaming mirage. From men and horses rose strong, bitter odours. We put the equipment out to dry and erected tents and not even the discomforts upset morale or the methodical routine, which we adopted to restore a half-drowned rabble into an army once more.

We were thankful that, except for a few scribes needed to keep the Journal for Eumenes and write dispatches to Antipater, the civilians were at Miriandros and not with the expedition. It was early winter and one and a half seasons since we had crossed the Hellespont to fulfill the dreams of Alexander and Philip.

My slave attended to my horse and raised my tent and he found some clothes stored in a copper-lined box that had escaped the deluge. I gratefully changed into clean linen and walked to Alexander's quarters. Approaching his tents, I saw horses drawn up and tethered at the entrance and I quickened my pace, anticipating new developments. The animals were normally kept away from our living areas, both to save the ground from being churned up and fouled, and to reduce the misery of mud or dust and insects. I walked inside the king's reception tent and I was immediately admitted to the audience section. The place was a beehive of activity, despite the recent storm. Alexander, with Parmenion, Hephaestion, Craterus, Cleitus the Black, and several other people I cannot now remember, were interviewing strangely dressed Greeks; they looked more like Persians.

Craterus came to my side to say: "These Greeks are deserters from Darius and come to join us. They bring us news that he is camped in our rear. He came from the east, through the Amanus Mountains and is now at Issos, where he found our wounded and many of them he tortured and killed. These men also report that most of the Greeks serving with the Persians are ready to desert to our army and, of great interest, several of the Greek leaders, led by Amyntas, the son of Antiochus, a deserter from our army, advised Darius to stay on the wide plain east of the mountains where his huge army might easily overwhelm our much smaller force. Advice which he foolishly ignored. They also report that many of the Persian courtiers had persuaded Darius, King of Kings, that Alexander faked his illness in Tarsus, that he had taken Soloi and attacked the mountain tribes, and that he held games at Soloi. He also spent days offering elaborate sacrifices along his route, all to gain time from cowardice and fear at the prospect of meeting the might of the Persian army.

I felt sorry for Darius for he readily believed his Persians. I joined the group near Alexander and we heard that the enemy had further flattered their king by maintaining that his cavalry alone could ride over the puny Macedonians and totally annihilate Alexander and his army. Amyntas opposed them, courageously asserting that Alexander was loved by all his men, especially for his courage and daring, and that they would follow him unquestioningly in seeking out their enemy. He again advised Darius, at great risk to himself, that in the wide plain his huge army could advance from both sides to encircle the Macedonians, whereas in the narrow plains of Issos only a small part of his forces might engage the enemy at any one point. The Persians privately accused Amyntas to Darius of being Alexander's spy and suggested that his advice was tainted to gain favour with the Macedonian king. Darius, after much thought, decided not to expose his men to the possibility of a Greek trap. He ignored a reminder by his magi that when he changed the Persian scimitar to the Grecian sword that they had prophesied that Persia would fall to the enemy whom he had imitated. Darius was much influenced, also, by a dream, in which he saw Alexander brought to him in chains and he foolishly listened when his advisors interpreted this omen as favouring an advance for a decisive battle against the king.

And so, as was the Persian custom, when the sun was risen in the sky, we heard that Darius ordered the ceremonial horn blown from by his tent and it sounded for the advance of his Persian army. The image of the sun shone in a crystal carried on high in front, as the Persians formed into their marching columns, east of the Amanus Gates. Then first, aloft, went the sacred fire attended by the chanting magi. This was followed by 365 young men robed in purple, one for each day of the Persian year. They were followed by the chariot dedicated to their god, Ahuru-Mazda, a great horse was next, known as the 'Steed of the Sun'. Ten chariots burnished in gold were followed by twelve horsemen who represented the twelve nations of the Persian Empire. After the chariots came the famous Immortals in all their barbaric splendour, and behind them, the unit known as the King's Kindred, followed by the Minders of the Royal Robes, and all preceded the majesty of the King of Kings in a chariot of gold, his person arrayed in jewelled robes of such purple magnificence that every eye was dazzled.

The royal chariot was followed by 30,000 soldiers of the infantry, the cavalry and chariots bearing the king's mother, wife, children, attendants, eunuchs, slaves and concubines. The whole procession of such royal splendour as was never before assembled. More convincing as a spectacle of royal extravagance rather than an army dedicated to the destruction of great Alexander.

Many of the Greeks, with the Persians, always realists, had scorned the spectacle and fled to report to us and for a more certain victory with the Macedonian army. We listened to their talk, giving careful attention to military details, as they described the Persians with jeering laughter, until Alexander turned from them in disgust for they were traitors twice over and he spoke to us: "I am calling a council of war, but first the men must have a period of rest in which they are to be served a meal. Tonight we march north again and down to Issos to surprise Darius."

As he spoke, the king's face was set in firm lines, his eyes shone in anticipation of the challenge he faced and his bearing was full of brave courage. He was a leader born to inspire, especially our little army. We left Alexander's tent to pass on his orders and the stories told by the Greek mercenaries in Alexander's tent. I ate a meal, but refused wine to keep a clear head. My slave had foraged fresh fruits and their sweet juice eased my thirst. I returned to Alexander's headquarters. All the commanders were assembling and the noise of many voices could be heard from some distance as I approached. The king had already ordered detachments of cavalry and archery to leave immediately, some to remain at the top of the pass and the rest to go as far as Miriandros to protect the civilian train encamped there. When we were all present the king addressed us in calm and assured words: "I have now received confirmation that Darius has reached the River Pinaros. The messenger came from Nearchos. He reports that as he sailed up the coast, he saw in the distance the Persian fires, and he heard a great noise of the Persian camp. We march tonight and I plan to give Darius a decisive battle. When we reach the summit of the pass, now held by our advance troops, we shall remain there until the sun gives us our first light.

"You have stared many dangers in the face and triumphed, and we shall win again, for God, himself, favours us by bringing the Persians to a narrow battlefield, which better suits our small army. This time we are a victorious army facing a defeated enemy. We fight the Persians and Medes, who for generations have lived soft lives on the bounty of their empire. We Macedonians are hardened by danger and war. We are also free men and they are slaves and we fight for Greece.

"Our foreign troops, from the borders of Macedon, are the finest in the world. The soldiers of the enemy fight for pay and are soft from easy living. And what, finally, of the two men in command? You have Alexander, they Darius!"

After a pause, Alexander continued to speak of our advantages and he recounted our past successes, speaking directly to those of us who had given distinguished service and thanking each of us for our loyalty and courage. When he finished speaking, we left to parade the men under the command of Parmenion. His tall frame slumped slightly over his horse. His beard was grown grey, his eyes were reddened and tiny veins showed in his face. His hands now were gnarled and he looked tired from hard service for Macedon's kings.

Alexander, on Bucephalos, rode before the army. Turning to face it, he raised his voice: "Macedonians and Greeks of my beloved army, you have all heard the news, that as we marched south through the Syrian Gates, Darius and his Persians, with his Greek mercenaries, were behind us on a plain east of the Amanus Mountains. This was incorrect. They are camped on the River Pinaros. I have to report to you that Darius found our wounded at Issos and he has mutilated and murdered them. This foul deed shall be avenged in the coming battle.

"Darius planned to chase us into Syria, where the vast valley of the Orontes would favour his great numbers, giving him an opportunity to surround us. However, we shall turn to meet him where he is bounded by the mountains to his east and north and the sea to his west. Here our superior quality in men and training and our invincible phalanx will win the day against barbarians.

"As at Granicus the Persians are on a river, but not the Hellespont or the Granicus, or the Pinaros, or any other ditch will halt Alexander.

"Our spies report that the Persian treasure has gone to Damascus and there it waits for your coming."

As he finished speaking, the army let out a mighty cheer. Before it died down, Alexander had wheeled Bucephalos to lead his army north. We reached the summit of the pass and rested until the guards called the first streak of dawn. The army rose without noise. No fires were lit to avoid giving the alarm to Darius if he had advanced nearer our position or sent spies to watch our movements.

Scouts went ahead as we began the descent until we looked across the plain, bordered by the sea and, in the fading night, from the great distance, we saw the Persian fires. They lit the narrow plain in hundreds of separate flames and their smoke rose straight up into the sky. A mighty army awaited Alexander to turn his boast of victory into proud fulfilment or to finish the king by nightfall. Winter was fast approaching and we were stung by the early winds which curse the mountains. We marched as swiftly as men and horses might travel over the narrow, rocky path. Precipices gaped below our way and with every turn we saw the terrible Persian fires lighting up the distant sky. By mid-morning, we were well along the plain. At times the army had to thin ranks in the narrow passage between the sea and mountains. Scouts, sent ahead, brought back reports of the Persian army battle positions. And then they brought us a straggle of our men seized by Darius at Issos. They were brutally mutilated. Their hands had been cut off and the stumps dipped in boiling oil. We stopped to hear, in horror, how vilely men had died from hideous tortures. We swore a terrible revenge and Alexander went amongst them and put lotions on their wounds and gave them opion to dull their pain. We left volunteers to nurse them and to give the small comfort the healthy are allowed to bestow on the permanently deformed.

Before we rounded the last cliffs between us and the Persians, Alexander halted the army and addressed us: "You have seen the barbarous deeds of Darius. Now it is your turn to deal with him in similar coinage.

"There has been no rain below the mountain, but the gods sent a storm to halt us, so that we could turn and choose the battlefield and now we go in the name of the gods to defeat not Persian satraps but the King of Kings himself.

"From today the 'King's Peace', signed at Sardis of Lydia, is dead and all of Greece will be avenged for every past insult received by us from the Persians.

"Once before, led by Xenephon, Greeks defeated vast Persian forces on Persian soil, for the gods also favoured his enterprise."

The king continued to relate the story of the Ten Thousand. It inspired the men, quieted their fears, and set the mood for victory. He ended by telling them that their fame would be the greatest in the long history of Greek heroes and predicted that men would remember their deeds at Issos round campfires to be lit in all the generations to come.

We marched until the sun was well past the zenith. The great mountains had squeezed us into a narrow passage between them and the sea. They towered above us, snow-capped, craggy and mournful and across the sea, we saw more peaks on the western horizon.

I am oppressed by the forbidding majesty of mountains and made lonely by their inaccessible heights, territory of predators and of birds of prey. In this land, before we fought at Issos, I already had had my fill of high places. The sight of rocky outcroppings and sparse vegetation made me uneasy and I felt pity for the people who lived in their hidden valleys in such barren and hostile surroundings.

The infantry led our column as we drew near to Persian might. The enemy was drawn up on the north bank of the River

Pinaros. Our Thessalonian and Peloponnesian cavalry moved to our left wing, under Parmenion. The Royal Squadron was on the right wing as we faced the Persians on the opposite river bank. Darius himself, the King of Kings, was before us, gorgeously dressed in robes edged with purple. He rode in a gold chariot, with a great, golden eagle perched on the front, it was drawn by four white horses, which he held statue still before his army. We moved into battle position. Parmenion led the cavalry into the sea, to prevent the Persians outflanking our western position. The phalanx moved at an angle to protect our eastern front. In vain, Alexander hoped to lure the Persians across the river. They stayed in position and he gave the order to advance.

The Persian cavalry, under Narbazanes, satrap of an eastern province, was drawn up opposite Parmenion. In the centre was the Persian infantry with the Greek mercenaries behind Darius, watched by his bodyguard. Then came the archers and more infantry, positioned in the mountains, ready to bring an encircling movement on our right flank. Their army stretched far into the distance but, as Alexander had pointed out, they were limited by the confines of the plain between the mountains and the sea. They could only engage to the limits of the battlefield.

We moved slowly forward to meet a glittering forest of spears. The dazzle of the Persians' brilliant clothing, the gleam of Darius' golden chariot, and his army filled the space between the mountains and the sea and covered the land as far as the eye could see.

Alexander halted us every few yards, to allow straight lines to reform as we passed natural obstacles. We drew closer, and I saw Asiatic soldiers in the Persian rear. I had seen their rock reliefs and steles and decorated pottery in Anatolia and I recognised them by their clothes. I remembered their reputation for cruelty and I held them responsible for the torture of our men.

Perdicass, Craterus, Nicanor, son of Seleucos, Amyntas, and myself were among the phalanx commanders. The king directly commanded the Companions, so that he could move them swiftly to support any part of the army in difficult combat with the enemy. We finally halted so near to the Persians' Greek mercenaries, across the river, that a discus thrower could easily have spanned the distance. Alexander rode along the entire length of the army, calling affectionately by name the commanders (even of the Greeks) and mentioning the various units. The intense heat of summer had passed, yet the air was suspended round us in shimmering prisms which bent our vision. Alexander, himself, was surrounded by light. It touched his golden hair, glinted on his armour and on Bucephalos, and it seemed that he rode the sky, rather than a Persian plain. The men were hypnotised and would have followed him to the infernal regions over the Styx, in far distant Epiros. The Persians, too, seemed mesmerized. Had they charged, their superior numbers might have won the day. Instead, in that hour, they were the audience to the prologue of their own tragedy.

Alexander returned to the front of the Companions and his order to charge rang out over the still armies. The phalanx moved as a single man, but became ragged as we broke through the river and up the steep bank opposite. We were quickly engaged in violent hand to hand fighting with the Persians' hired Greeks. They were men who bitterly resented the surrender of Greece to Alexander and showed it in the fury of their fighting.

On our left, the Persian cavalry crossed the river to attack our cavalry as Alexander urged Bucephalos forward to strike at Darius. Then the incredible happened. Darius turned and fled the field, his golden chariot lit by the rays of the declining sun.

In the noise and confusion, my impressions were like pieces of mosaic, in a jumbled pile, before assembly into a complete picture. The clamour was deafening, the cries of men and the screams of horses, the clash of weapon against weapon and mixed with it all, the sickening stench of blood and sweat and fear. Alexander was bleeding from a leg wound, of which he seemed unaware, as he struck amongst the enemy.

Then many Persians discovered Darius had fled. They panicked and wheeled as a flock of carrion birds after prey and sped away breaking through their own rear ranks. Alexander dashed into the breach, which they had left, and attacked the Persian centre. The fighting was hard and violent, but inch by inch we overcame Persian resistance.

With victory assured, Alexander turned Bucephalos in pursuit of Darius. Hephaestion, Amyntas, Philotas and myself, with other Companions, raced after the king to protect him from an enemy attack. We galloped through a pass where the mountains almost reached the sea to find the ravine filled with Persian dead. Wounded horses whinnied and neighed at our approach, and we came upon the abandoned chariot of Darius, with the splendid cloak, the symbol of his royalty, trailing to the dusty ground in the declining light.

Alexander left the search as the day grew dark. He assumed that Darius had taken the horses and that he would be many miles from Issos. He knew that it was more important to return to the scene of victory and share the moment with the army and leave Darius to the future. Not to pursue the enemy was a break with long tradition, but Alexander's purpose of seizing the coast and neutralizing the Persian navy had been achieved. Darius could wait.

Ordering grooms to bring the chariot back to Issos, we returned to the pavilion of the King of Kings, on the banks of the River Pinaros. His treasure had already been assembled and the sight caused Alexander to exclaim: "So this is what it means to be a king!"

He ordered that the treasure be shared between the men, setting aside the portion belonging to the dead for dispatch to their families, and another portion for the cities of Plataea and Phayllos in memory of their part at Marathon and Salamis. Alexander kept for himself only a jewelled box of exquisite beauty and, with reverent care, laid his *Iliad* (the gift of Aristotle) within its aromatic lining.

The heavens crowned Alexander's majesty the night of his victory at Issos. The setting sun blazed across the sky, triumphantly charging the heavens with green, gold, orange and red. The sea turned incarnadine, deep as the red of blood. In the distance to the south, the heights of the Syrian Gates were misted in purple. The mountains to the east of Issos towered above, their snowy summits, in the sunset's glow, made pink. The gathering dark changed to blackened green the forested lower slopes. To the north and west across the sea more mountains, darkly shadowed, slumbered but the brilliant light shone on the battlefield, cruelly exposing the starkly postured dead. The gaudy Persian tents and discarded clothing were tawdry amongst the carnage. Weapons, strewn across the ground, gleamed dully and the river ran red between banks made sodden with blood.

The king arranged a banquet in celebration. In preparation, I walked upstream and bathed in the river. My slave had erected my tent and found me clean clothes. Before joining Alexander, I wrote to my father. I knew runners would leave that night and I wished him to have news of my safety with that of our victory.

I listed the friends who had survived and mentioned the newly dead, including Nicanor, the son of Seleucos, so that word could reach their families by the compassionate hand of my father.

I mourned our dead and could not exult in the Persian losses, but I was thankful that the victory was ours for, had the battle gone the other way, our fate must have been a tortured death.

Chapter 16

A banquet was laid out in the King of Kings' royal tent. Entering, I saw exquisitely wrought gold and silver vessels arranged for our use. They caught and reflected the light from a thousand flickering lamps. The low divans were covered in sumptuous silks and the stony earth of Issos was hidden under jewel-bright carpets of sensuous comfort, which had been woven in the villages of every distant part of the Persian Empire. Their colours ravished our senses in the chill night after the horrors of the battle.

Resplendent as peacocks, the Persian royal servants brought us exotic foods as we lounged in such comfort. Frightened girls, huddling together, were brought in for our choosing but these Alexander dismissed, telling us that we could take our pick at a later time. They had no appeal for the king who, in revulsion from the excesses of his father, lived in almost celibate abstention, especially since Pancaste was left behind in Ephesos.

Suddenly, great wailing and lamentations disturbed our feasting. Alexander sent to know the cause and dramatically we heard that the mother, wife, daughters and small son of Darius were in their tent close by in the camp. They had just been informed that Darius was dead and they were mourning him in the Persian fashion. The king ordered a steward to inform them that, although he now possessed his cloak and chariot, Darius lived and that they might retire for the night quite undisturbed by grief. There were, however, many less fortunate women in the Persian camp, who suffered vilely at the hands of our soldiers. Alexander, when made aware of this outrage, ordered his guards to restore order immediately, using every means necessary to free the women. Sickened by all the excesses of the day, at the end of the banquet I returned alone to my tent.

As soon as daylight made the grim work possible, we first counted our Macedonian dead and then the Persian fallen. Their losses were extremely high, made wanton by the flight of Darius. To die in battle is a sacrifice but, in a coward's name, a senseless sacrifice. We also estimated that about 8,000 Greek mercenaries in the enemy army had escaped south through our ranks in the confusion, after Darius had fled. Later, we heard that some had made their way back to Greece where they had joined the Spartans in an unsuccessful battle against Antipater. Others amongst them fled to rejoin the Persian army but many more were left wounded or dead on the battlefield.

After the dead were taken from the battlefield for the funeral rites, Alexander ordered a steward, and the Greek interpreter, to announce his arrival to the Persian Royal Family. Splendidly dressed in his white, silk chiton and surrounded by his closest friends, he made his way towards the pavilion where they waited. His wounded leg was bound, but he walked unaided and there was a new dignity about the king after this victory on the battlefield of Issos. He walked into the presence of Queen Statira, her daughters, Statira and Drypetis, her small son, Ochus, and Sisigambis, the mother of both Darius and the queen. The Queen Mother, in mistake, made a deep obeisance to Hephaestion. He was taller, more handsome, and a little older than Alexander but with a less open face. In that awkward moment, he quickly stepped towards the noble lady and turned to indicate the king. As soon as she realised her error, Sisigambis was overcome with shame but Alexander immediately stepped towards her, raised her up, and gently said: "Mother, do not be disturbed, you were indeed correct for Alexander is Hephaestion and Hephaestion is Alexander."

I saw Craterus stiffen at the king's words and Eumenes took them down with a barely disguised sniff of disdain. Alexander, however, had shown such graciousness to the Queen Mother that he was evermore to find a champion in the Lady Sisigambis and she showed preference to him even over her own son, Darius. The king then took the small boy, Ochus, into his arms and as the child clung to him round his neck, he gently stroked his head.

We left the royal pavilion to attend to the funeral rites of our dead. They were first cremated and then buried on the battlefield with full military honours. At the end of this sombre duty, Alexander visited the wounded and dressed their injuries with his own salves and ointments. He listened, indulgently, to their claims of heroism and spoke words of comfort and praise to each; his own leg injury he ignored. The Persian dead were buried in deference to the wishes of Queen Statira according to the Persian rites.

We rested for a few days on the plains of Issos and Alexander appointed Balacross, son of Nicanor, as the governor of the rich province of Cilicia. The army then returned south to Miriandros, where the civilian train waited for us below the Syrian Gates. We shared our victory in noisy celebration and the women were quickly decked out in Persian jewellery and the fine clothes looted by our men from the battlefield. Two days later, we ascended the heights of the Syrian Gates once more. We knew that the Persian cavalry, which had escaped from Issos, was in our rear and across our supply lines. The Persian fleet was at sea and fomenting trouble in Greece with bribes of gold and promises of freedom to our fickle allies, and some Greek mercenaries had fled south to find sanctuary in the coastal cities of Phoenicia.

Alexander sent spies to report on their movements and to establish a watch on the coast for any movements of the Persian navy to our south. Several spies returned to Anatolia to check on Darius and all the activities of the enemy armies. We marched in high spirits. There were many Persian women with us, in addition to the family of Darius. We had been gone from Macedon for more than a campaign season and we had won two important victories. It was a long season without private comforts for our men but victory and its spoils are sweet recompense to those who have endured the danger of war, and a campaign of hardship and privation.

We rested on the Syrian plain in the cool shade of the groves and the waterfalls of the Sanctuary of Aphrodite, not far from the River Orontes. It was here that the nymph, Daphne, was turned into a laurel tree as she ran to escape from the pursuit of Apollo. The bush, re-named in her honour, covers the hillsides and its leaves are dried and used for a bittersweet flavour in the food of the people. Alexander left money in this sanctuary for the priests to build a temple to Zeus in gratitude for our victory on the Plains of Issos.

We left Daphne to march west on the road leading into

Phoenicia. We camped in ancient ruins on the coast and the people told us that they were the remains of Ugarit, a city founded by the people of Canaan. They also claimed that the Canaanites had invented the alphabet, which was hard to believe as our rounded Greek characters scarcely resemble the chicken scratches the Phoenicians manage to decipher. Phoenicia is a land of artists, scholars and traders who live in fabled cities. Its famed seamen chart unknown seas by reading the stars and bring back fabulous treasures from lands, even beyond Ocean, or so we were told.

We saw many camel trains on the road. They were led by Arab men with brown, hawk-like and bearded faces. They speak a fierce and guttural language and they wear a cloth upon their heads, secured with a circlet of cords as a protection against sun and sand. They are nomads and for shelter they pitch black goat-hair tents, designed to close from either side against the prevailing wind, and they line them with brightly coloured rugs and hangings of wool woven from their flocks of sheep.

The Arab men were immensely dignified and looked down on us from their swaying camels and, although they acknowledged that we came as conquerors, they allowed no man's law to rule their caravans. We heard that they lived in the empty deserts which stretched to the east and far to the south. They travelled to trade their camels, sheep and goats and they brought incense, myrrh and spices to the markets of the Persian world and they named their home 'Jazirah al Arabiyah' or 'Island of the Arabs'.

Their horses were small and wiry; they were bred for stamina. We tried to buy them, but Arabs will sell only the stallions; the mares have multiple owners and they are valued above the price of gold. The men were armed with knives and daggers, which were strong and sharp and forged in the fires of Damascus and they were not for sale at any price. Their women they kept apart, and they were usually veiled in black; many had tattoo marks on their faces which, I later learned, were distinctive to each tribe. For the rest, Phoenicia was mountainous, but the fertile valleys grew rich crops of fruits and grains and the people were well-fed and housed in comfort.

When the wind blew from the south it brought great sandstorms, more trying than snow, heat or rain. The grains found their way into our food, our clothes and our mouths and caused sores in the creases of our skin. Fortunately, as the year came to a close, this evil season passed. We were camped at the city of Marathus, when Alexander received a letter from Darius expressed in the most arrogant terms and certainly not those of a defeated enemy. Alexander called us to his tent and read it to us in disdainful anger. Darius wrote as 'King of Kings'. He gave no title to Alexander and he complained that his country had been invaded and that he was forced to take up arms in its defence. He suggested that if Alexander either would fight him or would bring himself to listen to good advice then he would be satisfied with his own realm and leave what did not belong to him and that he would enter into an alliance with Darius. He also demanded the return of his family and he offered a vast sum of money, enough to enrich all Macedon, in exchange for them. He concluded that his letter showed that he was prepared to sign guarantees on every concession that he offered. Alexander had already drafted his reply, which he now read in a voice filled with contempt and anger: "His Majesty, King Alexander, to Darius: Greetings! I am here to exact revenge for the evil deeds of Xerxes and that Darius, whose name you have taken, of the same house. They both brought terrible destruction on the Greeks of Ionia and on our homeland and I am here especially to avenge the terrible tortures that you inflicted on my soldiers at Issos. You gained your throne illegally by hiring Bogaos to kill the son and heir of Artaxerxes, King of Persia. I come as King of Macedon to avenge the deeds of you and your forefathers against my country and against my father, King Philip, whom you boast was murdered by your hired assassins. You aided and paid his enemies and plotted against our country and spread falsehoods about me to alienate the Greeks and offered money for my death. I am the elected Hegemon of the Greek League and I am now in possession of your land. I shall henceforth be addressed as 'King of Asia' by you and all your people.

"You may, personally, collect your family and anything else that you request, in perfect safety, but not for money, for I am not a merchant and I have nothing to sell. You may try, alternatively, to win your family back in battle but I, Alexander, will defeat you wherever we meet."

We dispersed, without comment, to our own tents and Alexander, we knew, was lord of three separate estates and the people of each had no influence in either of the others without the sanction of the king and he grew apart in the loneliness of his power. Spies brought Alexander reports that Persians were stealing from the great treasure sent, for safety, by Darius to Damascus. The king immediately dispatched Parmenion to seize the fabled riches and recover all the missing items and with orders to send a small part of the minted coins to finance his own campaign. This would relieve him of the severe financial strains which had plagued him since the death of his father.

Parmenion remained at Damascus. He sent, under close escort, the envoys to the Persian court from treacherous Thebes, Athens and, of course, Sparta, whom he found cowering in that city. They were all extremely frightened now that the duplicity of their cities was uncovered but Alexander always held, in honour, the traditions of diplomacy, even in the face of his allies' treachery. He treated the Athenians as allies and he sent them home, as though they were of no consequence to him, and greatly humiliated them. The king always remembered and regretted the destruction of Thebes and he released the Thebans to freedom. The Spartans were held captive, but allowed the freedom of the camp and their chief envoy developed friendships with such men as Callisthenes and Eumenes.

A runner arrived in the camp from Macedon bringing news of fervent rejoicing when Macedonians had received word of our victory on the River Pinaros. There was, however, also a report from Antipater of some of the Greeks' disappointment with our success. A few of them, led by Demosthenes, had taken Persian money and plotted revolution against Macedon and the overthrow of Alexander. The king listened to the scribe, and then he praised all the brave Greek forces with our army and once more recommended their gallantry and loyalty. He did not stoop to blaming the hapless Greeks in the camp. They were not responsible for their cities' treason in breaking their oaths of allegiance. The Greek soldiers, impressed by this generosity, now reasoned that if the Greek states were not independent it was far better to be under the light hand of Macedon than the heavy fist of Persia. They also enjoyed their share of the spoils of victory, for money is ever a great argument with Greeks; they love to possess it, especially do they enjoy the gleam of newly minted coins.

I received a letter from my father who wrote of the son whom I could not realise was mine. He told me of the details and disposition of our family estates in the event that I failed to return from Asia and he named the lawyer who would take care of the inheritance for my son. He included my share of the spoils, which I had dispatched to him after our victorious battles. I was pleased that he thanked me and valued my gifts and he said that it was now the fashion in Macedon to employ Persian scribes, who had deserted Darius and fled to Macedon. They were making translations of the manuscripts and inscriptions that many of us had sent home.

Alexander, also, received letters from Olympias, who raged against Antipater, complaining that he restrained her efforts to govern Macedon.

The king was very satisfied with this news but I did not altogether understand how even Alexander, so far away, could successfully prevent the queen's determination to rule, in his name, in Pella. Antipater sent a report of more troubles in Greece. He said that the Spartans were in a new alliance with the Persian admirals, and that the dispossessed were travelling all over the country, spreading resentment against Alexander. He wrote, also, advising the king that our victories had persuaded most of the Greeks not to make alliances with the Persians. They recognised Macedon's strength from the battles on the Granicus and the plains of Issos and our rapid advance into enemy territory, especially the Athenians who had been roused to revolt by the silvery tongue of Demosthenes, their eloquent if false prophet.

News, also, was brought into the camp of the movements of the Persian fleet, which still controlled the seas and threatened our rear. Until every port from the Hellespont to Egypt was in our hands, the Persians were free to sail and foment trouble amongst the Greeks, to interfere with our supply lines and to force us inland to meet a challenge from Darius on a battlefield not of our choosing.

Alexander called a Council of War to give his new orders, saying: "The Phoenicians are of many diverse people with many different languages and customs and it is my wish that we shall respect their gods, their women and their property, unless they resist our advance and then their punishment will be severe.

"I have received information that the cities of Aradus, Byblos and Sidon will submit to us peacefully but Tyre, which has ambitions to rule all Phoenicia, may prove more stubborn. Anticipating their resistance, we shall advance as far as Sidon.

When we reach that city, we shall check our weapons and siege machines and manufacture any missing parts, and all our arms will be repaired in readiness for a fight to take Tyre. The Persian fleet is largely manned by Phoenicians. Each city has its petty king, whom we must either bribe or vanquish. At our approach, the men will desert their ships or risk our vengeance on their homes and families. We march to take the Phoenician ports in three days."

The season was fast ending and the nights were cold although, by day, the sun shone on us bright and warm. To our right, as we marched, the sea glittered in a sparkling iridescence and on our left the towering, snow-capped mountains of Lebanon rose in splendour. From their great heights comes the wood of the mighty cedars prized by Solomon, the kings of Persia and Egypt's pharaohs.

The envoys from Aradus, Byblos and Sidon came to meet us as we moved south, and they offered their cities to Alexander of Macedon; representatives from Tyre failed to arrive in our camp. The king greeted them all as valued allies and when we entered their gates, he sacrificed to their gods in the temples. He easily identified them with the Greek Olympians and he feasted with their kings. Alexander left a small Macedonian force in each of the Phoenician cities to ensure their loyalty and to deny their ports to Persian ships.

As we marched the road between the sea and the mountains, I remembered Adonis; he was reborn each year in a high grove where the River Lycos gushes out of the land to descend to the sea. When we reached the river, the mountains came down to the shore leaving only a narrow path and we climbed up in single file and saw inscriptions carved on the rocky gorge recording the passage of other armies that had marched this way during the long courses of history. We camped at Sidon, as the king had planned, and we prepared for war against rebellious Tyre. Sidon's population was very mixed; there were even a few Greeks, mostly sailors who had come to trade and then settled in the city. There were also dark men from the southern deserts, Egyptians, and Jews who worshipped one god and lived apart in their own quarter, except to conduct business, which was mostly in their families' hands. There were many Babylonians, dressed in vivid clothes, and they were great artists and craftsmen. There were also Hittites, known as the Hatti people in Cilicia, where remnants of them dwelt in the high, mountain passes of the Taurus. Every satrapy and city of the Persian Empire seemed represented in Sidon and the babble of tongues gave employment to many interpreters.

Alexander, before we left Sidon, deposed Straton, the unctuous and subservient king, and he ordered Hephaestion to appoint his successor and to establish a new government in the city. Hephaestion first offered the throne successively to two young men who enjoyed great public esteem but they both refused the honour and they explained that their king must be of royal blood. Hephaestion commended them for declining what so many other men fought and murdered to obtain. They led him to a member of the royal house, a man named Abdalonymus, reduced by his own honesty to work as a gardener. They dressed him in robes of purple, edged in gold, and Hephaestion installed him as King of Sidon. There were many dissident voices raised in the city against Abdalonymus, which caused Alexander to give him an audience. The king gazed at him for a long time before he said: "Your bearing suggests your royal origins and I am glad to hear of the patience with which you endured your years of privation."

Abdalonymus replied: "I only hope that I may be able to endure sovereignty with the same resignation with which my hands have satisfied my previous desires, for having nothing, I lacked for nothing."

Alexander was much pleased by the words and the bearing of the new king, and to his sceptre and crown he added wealth and adjacent territory to Sidon and in return he gained a devoted friend. The lower slopes of the mountains of the Lebanon range are covered in junipers, figs, carobs, pines, olives and maples and cereals grow in the valleys and plains of this beautiful land. Fuel and food were in plenteous supply and the gold we gave in payment for their goods and harvests satisfied our peasant suppliers.

When we reached the city of Tyre, we found that the people had retreated to an offshore island, which they had fortified, and they had built harbours to its north and south. The city was a great naval port and, since the ruin of Sidon by the Persians, it was again the premier trading centre of Phoenicia. We easily occupied the old town on the mainland, with its few inhabitants, and Alexander sent a local embassy to Azemilkos, King of

Tyre, on his island, stating that he wished to offer a sacrifice in the island temple to his god, Melkarth. Alexander identified Melkarth with his own ancestor, Herakles. The ambassadors returned, after two days, and they were accompanied by envoys from Azelmilkos bringing his reply to the king.

Alexander broke the seal on the document and he then read aloud to his council the words of the Tyrian king: "To Alexander greetings from Azelmilkos and the citizens of Tyre. We offer you our friendship and we invite you to make sacrifice to your god in the temple of the city on the mainland. We cannot admit either Greek or Persian within our citadel for in the dispute between you we are neutral. We have known many wars between Egypt and Persia and we have suffered in each one of them. Therefore we say, go in peace and we will place no obstacle in your way".

Alexander feigned great surprise and hurt to the Tyrian ambassadors as he closely questioned them. He asked them especially why he was refused the privilege of making a sacrifice to Melkarth when he himself was a descendant of their god. The envoys in great agitation replied that in the east only a king may offer the sacrifice to a god and by this duty, he is acknowledged to be the ruler of the city. They also told Alexander that Tyre had been besieged many times, not least by Ashurbanipal, King of Assyria, who had remained before their walls for thirteen unsuccessful seasons before he retreated back to his city on the River Tigris.

They spoke with great delicacy, although they obviously wished to point out the failure of Ashurbanipal, known to us as Sardanapalos, and their words were translated by a Greek of Tyre. Alexander accused Azelmilkos of resisting his request and he angrily dismissed the embassy. He allowed the members to embark for their island, to honour diplomatic custom by their safe return.

High walls encircled the island fortress of Tyre and it was completely surrounded by the sea. It appeared impregnable from the shore. The Egyptian harbour in the south and the Sidonian harbour in the north sheltered the city's fleet which, even now, could escape and sail the seas to trade for supplies. A siege seemed unlikely to succeed. After the departure of the embassy, Alexander called a full council and said: "I am denied the courtesy by these barbarians of sacrificing to Herakles. I am denied the use of their ports and most important to the expedition, I cannot secure these against Persian occupation nor can I leave a garrison to defend the island against an attack by Darius … all this by Azelmilkos across his strip of sea.

"It is clear that without Tyre we cannot continue our march to Egypt. The people of Tyre may well change their neutral minds, if we depart without taking their island, and then give shelter to the Persians or, if Egypt revolts against us, they may ally themselves with the Egyptians.

"We must consider, also, the situation in Greece where we are at war with Sparta, and Athens has proved a false ally by sending an embassy to Darius in Damascus. Darius already occupies Cyprus and commands the Cypriot navy and still holds many of the other Greek islands. We must take Tyre; it is vital for our campaign that Darius is denied the two harbours on the island to use against us.

"When we conquer Tyre, we shall have the harbours and the Tyrian fleets and the navies of all the other Phoenician cities and we shall be ready to liberate Egypt. From there we shall march to the Euphrates River and take Babylon. This strip of sea between us and the island of Tyre is the only real obstacle in our path and the engineers must immediately begin the repair of an existing causeway to join the city to the mainland."

Alexander had considered his strategy and he rejected Parmenion's advice to return north from where we received news that the Persian cavalry was reforming and threatening our communication lines to Macedon. The king received a report from Egypt that the Greek mercenaries, who had fled the Persian army at Issos, had now arrived in that country and that they planned to sail to Sparta to enlist in their war against Antipater. We also heard that Darius was in Babylon and he was busy recruiting and training a new army to launch an attack against us. None of it welcome news, but Alexander was indifferent, as always, to adverse reports. The following day, the engineers started to demolish the old city of Tyre on the mainland. I was sad to see the women and children weep as their rock homes were demolished and carried away to the shore, to construct the mole to the island city.

Men exposed to the sun in the height of summer may fall suddenly sick with a high fever, and even die that same day. We were fortunate that it was mid-winter or our casualties would have been much greater, especially when the work reached deeper water. The men continued their work in the high winds, which blew up abruptly and lashed the sea into huge waves that knocked them over onto the hidden danger of rocks and debris that were washed into the surging water from the mole.

Alexander was confident of victory against Tyre. It was forecast to him in a dream one night, in which Herakles led him into the island citadel. This, he related to the men during their hard labours and so encouraged them to even greater endeavours. As the causeway relentlessly reached towards their island, the Tyrians built floating towers, which they launched to attack our men. They jeered at our soldiers as they worked and they seemed as equally confident of their own victory as we were of ours in the coming battle between us.

Alexander was unable to endure the long months of inactivity during the building of the mole. He left Craterus in charge, and took a small force over the mountains into the lush valleys beyond where Arab tribesmen ruled the Canaanites from their goat-hair tents. I rode along with them, to keep a record for Eumenes and I had the advantage of being a soldier and able to fight if we experienced hostile action.

As we sat round their campfires, Alexander negotiated treaties with the tribal chiefs. A politic course for, unless breached by Alexander, they would be honoured, in perpetuity, by the Arabs according to their own codes. They were hostile to the Persians and they usually made very willing alliances with the king. Strangely, Arabs could not pronounce his name, and they called him 'Iskander'. They will surely remember him in generations yet unborn, when they gather round their campfires to tell each other stories of mighty deeds of great men. I noticed that there was a natural sympathy between the tribesmen and Alexander; they felt a mutual respect and the equality of men born in freedom. It was in great contrast to his usual function as conqueror of subject cities when the conquered often grovelled before him.

As winter turned to spring, we returned to Tyre. The causeway had progressed far into the sea. Alexander immediately walked out to one of our towers and observed the Tyrians as they built a large raft. Day by day, we watched them work and as it was completed we saw them load the raft with timber and erect beams, which extended over the sides from which they suspended leather buckets. They towed the raft towards the causeway. In haste, we returned to the shore to collect our weapons, leaving only the guards in the watchtowers and on the mole. We were not quick enough; we were still on the shore as we saw the Tyrians ignite fuel in the buckets. They untied the raft, which the wind carried against the mole and ignited our towers. They disappeared in flames, in an instant, burning our men in the conflagration. The bold Tyrians sailed their ships to the causeway and seized our men who were watching in horror and, as we rushed back to try and defend them, the prisoners were taken up to the walls, murdered before our eyes and their bodies were thrown into the sea.

From this gruesome spectacle, the king returned to his quarters. He was so fiercely angry that he shook and he was unable to speak. By the next morning, his rage had calmed but it was a calm in which vengeance on Tyre was bred.

When Parmenion had secured the country surrounding Damascus, he came to Tyre. He described the city as a priceless pearl in a desert oasis and he reported that the influence of the Greeks inland was much weaker than on the coast. He spoke of huge carpet and silk bazaars, of the market in gold and spices and of the furnaces in which the famed smiths temper iron and their skill is unequalled anywhere in the world. He told us of schools in all the sciences and he reported that the astronomers of Damascus were far more advanced than the Greeks in their knowledge of the sun, stars and moon, which they used to navigate the seas and I wrote to Aristotle all Parmenion's words.

One day, we were surprised by the arrival of an embassy from Darius. The members were gorgeously attired and lavishly attended by a small army of slaves, as if to demonstrate the full glory and power of the Persian Empire. Dressed in a simple linen chiton, Alexander received the embassy. He accepted a letter from Darius and, after breaking the seal, he read aloud the contents: "To Alexander from Darius,

"I offer you 10,000 talents, as ransom, for the queen, her children and the lady Sisigambis. I offer my daughter, Drypetis, in marriage to you, Alexander, as a hostage for my good faith in any agreement that we may reach and, finally, for her dowry, I will give to Alexander all the land west of the River Euphrates together with my bond from attack by land or sea from any of my forces."

141

Alexander paused and addressed the embassy: "Since the Battle of Issos, I claim the whole Persian Empire. My father planned only to free Greece from all danger of Persian interference in our affairs and to liberate the Greeks of Anatolia from Persian domination. He created the Corinthian League for this purpose and he would have been content with a border secured by the Euphrates. Had Darius met our most reasonable demand, we, also, would have been satisfied with this goal. He has, however, forced us to campaign and fight him and, now that we are the victors, we shall make our own terms. For members of the Corinthian League, we have achieved their objective but Alexander reaches out to the end of the world and the encircling Ocean to bring peace and unity throughout all the lands of the earth. Our empire will be unlimited and in it all men will be free." And the embassy was escorted away from Alexander's presence.

When he paused, Parmenion spoke: "The men have been away from home for two full seasons. Now that we have taken the treasure hoarded by Darius at Damascus we have enough wealth to maintain our present frontier. It will be easy to hold, as most of the people are somewhat Hellenised and our supply lines will be secure. Any further territory that we take will be full of hostile people who will always plot to revolt against us. Darius now offers us vastly more treasure and a political alliance, secured through your marriage with his daughter, as a guarantee of peace. Were I Alexander, I would accept."

The king answered him scornfully as he had on other occasions: "And were I Parmenion, I too would accept."

The old general was crushed by Alexander's words. The dreams and plans that he had shared with Philip were largely fulfilled. He had no ambition beyond their limits and now Alexander declared for a new empire. The king risked the loss of all that had been gained and the great perils of unknown lands. Parmenion, I felt silently, suspected that the campaign was redirected for the personal glory of Alexander and that every further sacrifice and effort would be made for that purpose. Many of King Philip's friends agreed with Parmenion, but the younger men were with the king and the arguments grew fierce until Alexander intervened and he ordered a page to escort the Persian Ambassadors back before him in the council chamber. When they were standing stiffly in front of him he spoke: "The ambassadors shall return to Darius and tell him that I refuse his money for I have enough and I am a king not a trader. I challenge him to meet the Macedonian army once more in battle, without running away from us, to finally decide matters between us. I already hold most of the territory, which he offers to me and the princess is in my hands so that I may marry her, or dispose of her as I wish. Darius may claim his family and anything else he desires by greeting me as 'King of Kings' in person and then making his requests. He may no longer address me as an equal, for what he formerly possessed is now mine. Should he fear for his safety, he may send ambassadors for proper guarantees from me but, if he rejects my terms, he can stand and fight and if he refuses then, wherever he may hide, I shall seek him out.

"I am here to avenge the aid that he gave King Philip's enemies and the part that he played in hiring an assassin to murder my father. I think also of all our Macedonian and Greek dead and of the men sent home injured beyond further service in my army. Many of Darius' people have already voluntarily taken service with me and I expect many more to join them. I am now also responsible for their safety. Therefore let Darius accept my terms or be hunted as a criminal."

We all separated; the Persian Ambassadors were free to remain in the camp or find their own accommodation; they chose to stay with us. The night was loud with the heated debates amongst the Macedonians as they argued for and against Alexander's declared ambitions. I had no personal desire to return to Macedon, but there were many men who wanted to return home and enjoy the fruits of their victories. Criticism was strong against the king at Tyre and it was never again entirely stilled.

When Alexander's reply to Darius was written and signed by the king, the ambassadors returned to Darius. The king now turned to all the final preparations necessary to defeat Tyre. The navies of the cities of Phoenicia were already anchored in Sidon to offer their submission to Alexander and, when this news reached us, the king, with a small escort, rode north to receive their formal surrender and oaths of loyalty. They were joined, surprisingly, by the navy of Cyprus, which also brought many men from the islands to enlist in Alexander's army and all of them had lost faith in a final Persian victory. The Cypriot ships had slipped away at night, as the Persians on the island slept, to join the other navies anchored in Sidon. Alexander ordered the combined navies to sail and blockade the harbours of Tyre, bringing with them all the new recruits to work and speed up construction of the mole to the island. The king himself, very confident of victory, returned to Tyre to direct the final assault on the island city.

Night was turned to day by the flares burning to illuminate the endless work and preparations when we reached the city. The clamour from the forges rang out in an endless racket and men toiled, preparing all the materials necessary to widen, strengthen and finish the mole. Small children watched in wide-eyed wonder, hardly aware of the titanic struggle about to begin between Macedon and Tyre.

Alexander was impatient for the mole to be finished. We all felt the mounting tension and we worked hard, until we dropped in exhaustion. And then one day, as night was turning to morning, we were amazed to see that a great curtain had been placed across the Sidonian harbour obstructing our view of the entrance. Two days later we understood its meaning as the curtain parted and out sailed a fleet of Tyrian ships. The enemy made a brave and gallant attempt to defeat us. The Cypriots' were the closest to the harbour and they were taken completely by surprise and several of their ships were sunk when attacked by the Tyrians and many more broke up under the enemy's assault. A report was taken to Alexander who was with the Phoenician navies at the entrance to the southern, Egyptian, harbour. He ordered the Phoenicians into action against the Tyrians. I watched from the shore and felt a surge of pity for Tyre's inevitable defeat. Many of their sailors, when their ships sank, managed to swim to temporary safety behind the island walls but the majority were captured and Alexander sold them into slavery.

A few days later, our battering rams were in position on the mole, ready to pound the walls of Tyre. They were supported by ships armed with catapults. More ships stood by, with troops on board, and they were poised to land on the island at the first breach in the walls, which finally came in the south. The combined navies sailed into the harbour and the army, led by Alexander, swarmed into the opening to a bitter and costly battle. The sea turned dark red with the blood of the slain. Hundreds of men, on both sides, were injured and dropped into the depths of the sea, where they drowned pitifully for none of us could rescue them in the heat of battle.

We had been at Tyre for more than 200 days. When the city finally fell to us, those of the enemy, who had died were given the better fate, for thousands were sold into slavery and, for free people, that is life devoid of hope or meaning.

King Azemilkos, with some of the leading citizens of Tyre, together with the ambassadors from foreign rulers, had taken refuge in the temple and their lives were spared. Alexander had an innate sense of royalty and he treated defeated kings, and accredited ambassadors, as equal to himself in rank. This policy maintained the people's respect for the kingly office and they more readily accepted his own royal status. Aristotle had taught us that authority will ever support authority and combine against the common people; by such understandings do kings, tyrants and archons hope to maintain their ruling positions, no matter how diverse their individual interests.

Alexander paraded his fully armed soldiers before the temple and he advanced into the building with a full guard and he, finally, fulfilled his desire to offer sacrifice to Herakles in the Temple of Melkarth of Tyre. Games followed this symbolic act and in the presence of Azemilkos, Alexander received the submission of all the people of the city. The city of Carthage, near the Pillars of Herakles in distant Africa, had been founded by Tyre and we flushed from hiding an ambassador from that city who had been sent to support Azemilkos. When he appeared before the king, Alexander treated him as a rebellious Tyrian and he dispatched him home with a declaration of war against his city.

It was again reported to the king that the men were very much against his decision to continue the war and especially against his assumption of the titles of the Persian Empire. He called a council to discuss their discontent, on the eve of our departure from Tyre, and he raised many other subjects. He reviewed his achievements until he reached our present position. Everyone present closely attended his next words: "... and so you see that our policy to take the Phoenician ports has been successful. However, I am convinced, from studying the histories of all these countries of the east, that Egypt is essential for the security of our campaign. Without it, we have an Achilles' heel in their ports, which Darius will surely exploit in attacks against us. We therefore first march south, rather than to the east, and I have many reasons to believe that Egypt is an overripe fruit ready to fall to us. All her vast treasure, accumulated through aeons of time when the pharaohs ruled Egypt, will pass to us. It will be used to finance the liberation of the country and the campaign and to divide amongst the army. Surely there will be enough to compensate every man for any hardship or absence from home, which he has endured? Darius can wait, for daily we grow stronger as he grows weaker, and when the final reckoning comes, we shall be the rulers of the world."

The king, remembering his wanton destruction of Thebes, spared Tyre the same fate. He encouraged settlers into the depopulated city and organised a government to administer civil rule in his name. Alexander celebrated his twenty-fourth birthday when Tyre fell. It was four harvests since the death of King Philip and the season of the 112th Olympic Games.

Ptolemy, the son of Lagos, came from Lykia to Tyre to rejoin the king and we all rejoiced to see him and as we sat round the campfire we exchanged stories of our high adventures since we had parted. And, when the men heard that Alexander had promised to distribute Egypt's fabled wealth, their mutterings were temporarily quieted; to complain and grumble is every soldier's prerogative since the history of warfare was first recorded by Homer and the scribes.

Chapter 17

My days, since the fall of Tyre, were haunted by memories of blood running in sticky excess along the streets of the city and I saw again in my sleep the stark misery of the citizens, slain or dragged into bitter slavery. Many of them were emaciated from the long siege and miserable were the children, now parted from their mothers, and the wives who were left to starving widowhood. I had no liking for the unrestrained cruelty of war on hapless civilian populations; however, in the long history of Greece, it was Greek cities which had fallen to Persian oppressors and if Alexander imposed his will to create peace, that would be some recompense for man's accumulated miseries in the name of war. Alexander, riding Bucephalos, and leading detachments of the army, marched from Tyre; this was a victory parade, accompanied by drums and trumpets. It was notice to the rest of Phoenicia, Egypt and the Persian king that Alexander came either as liberator or conqueror, with Byblos and Tyre to point the difference between capitulation or resistance. The expedition next came to the land of the Philistines which was known in ancient times as Canaan. A land invaded and partly conquered by the Jews before they in turn were taken into captivity by Babylon. Nebuchadnezar, one Babylonian king, destroyed the great temple in Jerusalem but it was rebuilt a few seasons later on a much smaller scale.

The Jews were freed by Cyrus, son of Cambyses, when Persia defeated Babylon. Many chose to remain in Babylon and those who returned to Jerusalem continued to build the new temple in honour of their god. They placed no image within its walls of their single deity who had no representation amongst his people and he exercised a morbid and gloomy hold on them all for they rarely laughed. They were preoccupied with religious observances and they lived apart in houses near their temples, scattered throughout the Persian Empire. They also lived in the past, bewailing the captivities of their people in Egypt and Babylon.

The coastal plain grew wider and our progress swifter as we moved south. Alexander sent an embassy in advance to the Persian general in command at Gaza. He was an Arab eunuch named Batis, and he commanded an army of mercenary troops who were mainly from southern Arabia. When the envoys arrived before the walls of the city, Batis promptly closed the gates and prepared for a siege. The Macedonians returned to report the insolence of Batis and the strength of the city's defenders to Alexander. The allied navies and the siege machines, with large units of the army, had been left at Tyre. The king ordered them south to our position at Rishpon, renamed Apollonia by the Greeks. The city was built on a low cliff above the sea and we passed the time waiting for them by bathing in the cooling water at every opportunity.

I rode with Alexander to explore the countryside and we visited ancient Aphek, a city a short distance from the coast. The elders there told us many stories of their tragic history of invasions by Assyrians, Babylonians and Persians and they expressed their gratitude to Alexander for the promise of peace, which he brought to them.

By coincidence, the chief priest from Jerusalem was present in Aphek. He attended a banquet given by the king and he told Alexander that none but a Jew is permitted to enter or worship in their temple. His statement was received by the king in silence and I thought again of the fate of Tyre when that city defied Alexander.

It was late summer when we marched from Apollonia and we all suffered great misery from the intense heat and sandstorms. We were relieved to end the march before the walls of Gaza which was but a short distance inland from the sea.

The army prepared a camp and scouts were sent along the coast to look for harbours. They returned and reported that the sea was shallow and silted up with the eternal sand brought on the south wind that plagued this region. It affected us daily; our food spoiled and our bodies were constantly irritated by the tons of grit. Once more, sand penetrated into our clothes, scratched our eyes and cloaked us in a coating of dust which settled in the creases of our skin, causing sores to open and fester. They only healed when we reached Egypt and cooler weather.

The people of Gaza, and those who inhabit the deserts, wear loose-flowing garments and they use their headcloths to cover their faces against the sand. We had no such protection and flies, scorpions and mosquitoes added to our accumulating woes. Alexander alone made no complaint. As usual, he mastered every hardship and welcomed every threat as a challenge to his leadership and courage.

The navy sailed into port and anchored in the shallow sea and the captains had to wade ashore, with much difficulty, over the sandy shoals. The people of Gaza climbed their walls and mocked the impotence of the ships and seeing this, the king ordered them to sail for Egypt, and wait there for his arrival after the fall of Gaza. A few of the captains he sent to Macedon to transport home the portions of the bounty of our dead from Tyre, and to carry the official reports of the campaign to Antipater and personal letters to our families.

Before the ships sailed, many of the men were brought ashore to strengthen the army. They audaciously claimed our victory at Tyre as theirs, and they adopted a superior attitude towards the soldiers, which caused many fights and led to hard disciplinary actions, to maintain military cohesion in the coming battle against Batis. During the siege of Gaza, an embassy arrived in the camp, from the Corinthian League, with surprising messages of loyalty from the members. They carried a wreath of honour for Alexander, which was voted for him at the Isthmian Games. The king duly held a ceremonial parade to receive this new and welcome symbol of Greek solidarity.

In addition to the dispatches from the members of the League, Olympias, Antipater and the people of Thrace also sent congratulatory messages to the king for the victory at Tyre. Sparta alone was silent and from Antipater we learned that the Lacedaemonians were once more preparing for war against Macedon. Their threat was no more than the buzzing of mosquitoes in the desert twilight to Alexander, but a letter from Olympias affected him far more. She bitterly complained that Antipater interfered with her regency and exercise of power and she asked the king to remove him from his command of the army in Macedon. Alexander ignored her request, once more, and sent an order to Antipater to deal with both the queen and the Spartans.

Gaza was built on a tel, or hill, and the defences rose high above its peak. The engineers constructed a ramp up to the walls of the city, as we waited for the siege machines, battering rams and men to arrive from Apollonia. The ramp was completed in four days, before all the reinforcements arrived and we then had to wait again until the soldiers assembled their machines, and repaired the parts which had broken on the march. Cereal crops grew in the surrounding country to the edge of the desert, which we harvested to victual the army, as the work progressed.

During this time, the king invited the Companions to join him in offering a sacrifice to the gods for a victory in the assault on Gaza. We assembled before the city for the ceremonies and, as they were about to begin, a great hawk wheeled overhead and suddenly swooped, dropping a small stone on Alexander's head. Aristander, the Seer of Telmessos, was standing at his side and he interpreted the powerful sign as a proof that Gaza would fall. After a pause, he continued to explain that the omen also warned the king to avoid being wounded in the battle. Alexander was elated by the first part of Aristander's prophecy and, characteristically, he ignored the latter, more ominous revelation.

Finally, the engineers were ready. The king ordered the siege machines into position on the ramp against the walls. The defenders, within the city, poured down blazing oil from above and succeeded in burning a few of our machines and in pushing a small number of men down the tel. The enemy fought bravely as we breached the walls, but our superior strength overcame their resistance. Alexander led the attack into the city. As we moved forward, I saw a missile strike the king with such force that it penetrated his armour and inflicted a deep wound in his shoulder. I, and many others, rushed to his side but, with the blood pouring from his wound, he waved us on. I was one of the first Macedonians to enter the city of Gaza.

The Arabs surrendered Batis, who was executed, and the population either was slaughtered or enslaved. Alexander, sickened by our own losses throughout the campaign, was blind to mercy. The people of Gaza had already endured great hardships. Their water and food had been exhausted during our sixty-day siege and disease had taken a large toll. Their treasury, however, yielded enough booty to install a government of Macedonians and the king sent messengers to all the Phoenician cities offering a bounty to people willing to settle in Gaza and repopulate the city.

Alexander rested the army after the battle and the civilian train arrived outside the walls of the city. Our casualties were heavy and the men with severe injuries were given the option of either settling in Gaza or returning to their homes in Greece and Macedon. We cremated our dead. We buried them with full military honours and we carefully set aside their share of the plunder, to carry with us on the march to Egypt, from where the navy would sail, and transport part of this newly acquired wealth to the bereaved families in Macedon and Greece. Alexander left Gaza during the preparations by the army and civilian train for the journey to Egypt. He was accompanied by Parmenion, a small group of Companions and a detachment of the cavalry, under the command of Cleitus the Black. He planned to punish the Jews of Jerusalem for their stiff-necked refusal of his invitation to send a delegation to meet him in Tyre, with their mocking excuse, we believed, that they had already signed a treaty with Darius and that they understood that the Persian king would protect them.

The people must have had a change of heart, for as we approached within sight of the walls of Jerusalem they poured out from the gate to greet the king. The huge procession was led by Jaddus, the High Priest, and he and they were all dressed in white. Alexander, sickened by killing and destruction, was deeply moved by the people of Jerusalem. He leapt from Bucephalos and walked towards them. He spoke to Jaddus and venerated the name of God, inscribed on the mitre worn by the High Priest and, with great reverence, he saluted him and clasped his hands. We were all mystified when Alexander greeted Jaddus with such gentle courtesy. Parmenion led us towards the king and he asked Alexander why he paid homage to such a recalcitrant people. The king spoke, in quiet tones, of a dream which he had had before we left Macedon, in which a priest, of high and venerable appearance, had advised him to march into Asia and overthrow the Persian Empire and that he recognised Jaddus as that priest. The king walked up the hill, at the side of the High Priest, and entered the temple of Jerusalem. It was a small building and had been constructed partly by the people after they had returned from captivity in Babylon. Alexander, despite the protests of the priest, marched inside and into the Holy of Holies and stared round the sanctum before demanding to know: "Where is the god?"

Jaddus explained that his people used no images to represent their deity and Alexander was allowed to offer a sacrifice of a live sheep, according to the custom of the Jews, and he spared the building and the city from any harm.

Jaddus told us of an earlier, great temple, built by their King Solomon on the same site. It was destroyed by King Nebuchadnezar of Babylon, who then exiled the people of Jerusalem to that city. He showed us the scrolls of his people's laws and histories which had been written down by their priests, during their captivity. They were freed by Cyrus of Persia when he conquered Babylon, after they had signed a peace treaty and submitted to the new King of Kings.

Later that day, Alexander again saw Jaddus and other priests, and learned more of the exclusive, monotheistic religion of the Jews and the God who gave his laws to them on a mountain top in the Sinai desert. The king was deeply interested by all that he heard of this strange religion and he paid especial attention to the law which rested the land after every seventh harvest and thereby increased future crops. He absolved the Jews from paying tribute or taxes during this fallow season and he gave them his permission to practise all their rites and laws in freedom from interference. He also told Jaddus that he now understood his people's reluctance to send a delegation to meet him in Tyre and so betray their treaty with the Persians, to whom they owed a debt of gratitude from the time when they were released from the Babylonian bondage.

We departed from Jerusalem and returned to Gaza of Philistia and the army was ready to march for Egypt. We crossed the rocky, barren Sinai desert, where nothing grew and nothing lived, save only birds of prey, foxes and tiny creatures, which survive on insects, snakes and poisonous scorpions. The white heat of that inferno cooled at night, but it was still hard to sleep and we marched for many days before we sighted the city of Pelusium, the gateway to Egypt, which was already occupied by our navy.

Alexander held a Council of War, before we advanced into the city, when he summed up our position, saying: "Commanders and Companions of the King, behind us Greece is secured, except for Sparta, as are all the countries and provinces of Anatolia, Phoenicia and Philistia. The Persian fleet is at sea without access to any port save those before us in Egypt. The Persian king is our virtual prisoner in the hinterlands of his empire. I have received reports that some of the Greek mercenaries who fled before us at Issos, led by Amyntas, son of Antiochus, have tried to take Egypt. We certainly cannot allow so great a prize to be a refuge for traitors, either Greek or Persian, nor can we allow the Persian fleet shelter in Egypt's ports. Therefore, to all our other titles, I intend to add that of Pharaoh of both Upper and Lower Egypt. We come as liberators to a people hungry for their freedom from the Persian tyrant. We are prepared to fight but I am assured that we shall find a great welcome here. In addition to such a welcome, there are enough Persian spoils in Egypt to satisfy an army far greater than Alexander's, which will be used to finance the campaign and to distribute amongst all the members of the expedition, as was done after the Battle of Issos."

The king continued speaking, giving us all appointments and instructions for the march on Pelusium. He was confident and feared no man, for before conquering others, he had conquered himself, which gave him power to bend all men to his will.

At the end of the Council meeting, the king invited several of his friends to remain with him. The conversation flowed between us and the wine cups passed as we remembered all our great moments since we had crossed the Hellespont. Aeons of time seemed to have gone by and many of our men had perished and we remembered them but we were also proud of our victories on that day, in the tent of Alexander of Macedon, the new ruler of the world.

Alexander forecast a great welcome for us in the city of Pelusium, which we entered on the following day. The citizens flocked out to greet us for they hated the Persians and had been victims of war since before history had been written down, and they treated Alexander as their friend and liberator.

Once the welcoming ceremonies were concluded, Alexander ordered the sailors to return to their ships, now anchored in the harbour of Pelusium. He intended to prevent the fights which always broke out between the navy's men and the soldiers in defiance of their commanders, and the apprehension of local civilian populations. Some of the ships were ordered to sail for Macedon carrying dispatches from Alexander to Antipater and specimens of plants, animals, sand, rocks and insects for Aristotle in Athens, and personal letters to our families. They also carried melancholy lists of our casualties and the part of the campaign treasury given to their families. It was a small and sad compensation for their losses but no doubt welcome relief from problems of survival. The king appointed an administrator for the port and city of Pelusium and, under his command, a few units of the army followed the road to the delta of the Nile where we enjoyed the luxury of fresh water with more than enough to bathe and clean our clothes and we finally rid ourselves and our possessions of desert sand. The rest of the expedition remained at Pelusium under the command of Parmenion. The king, with a lightly armed detachment of the army, sailed up the Nile to Memphis, the capital city of Egypt and ancient from long before the time from when our Grecian history began. I looked forward to all its treasures, for who amongst men has not heard of the wonders of the Pharaoh's city?

When we reached the city's limits, Mazaces, the acting Satrap of Egypt, since the death of Sabaces, who had fallen in the Battle of Issos, was waiting to surrender the country to Alexander. At the conclusion of the formal ceremonies, Mazaces reported to the king that he had fought against the rebel Amyntas, the son of Antiochus, when he arrived in Egypt, leading his 4,000 Greek mercenaries who had deserted from the Persian army. He had defeated this army of traitors and Amyntas, with most of his men, was slain in the battle. The news pleased Alexander as we were not a strong enough force in Memphis to have fought a battle against Amyntas, and thus the transfer of power to the king was entirely peaceful.

Once inside the city, we found it partly ruined by the Persians but, despite the destruction, this was a city of such luxury as we had never dreamed existed. There were wonderful temples, public buildings, schools where craftsmen were trained in the arts of Egypt, statues, wall carvings and ravishing paintings in the temples and tombs of the pharaohs, which told the story of the land of Egypt. The pharaohs were buried with everything necessary from this world for their comfort in the next.

The king visited the great temple of the Egyptian god, Ptah, whom we identified with our Greek, Hephaistos, where he offered prayers and sacrifices at the god's altar and when he emerged from the temple, a great crowd had gathered and Alexander was acclaimed by the excited multitude. I even heard cries of "Pharaoh! Pharaoh!" under the hard light of the winter sunshine and in that applause the king was accepted as ruler of a vast new land. From the temple we walked to the treasury and found it bulging with Persian and Egyptian treasures. Our eyes could hardly take in the wealth of gold, lapis lazuli, jewels of glittering worth and minted coins beyond counting.

Alexander held a sumptuous banquet in Memphis for the leaders of the Greek community, Mazaces, now confirmed as Satrap, and the great Egyptian lords that first exciting night in the city. We feasted on the foods of Egypt, the ducks of the marshes, unleavened bread, rice, camel, gazelle, lamb, beans ground into a paste with sesame, dried wheat crushed and flavoured with mint and parsley, persimmons, dates, pomegranates, melons and sweet pastries. The king ate sparingly and diluted his wine until it was mostly water. He rose to speak, at the end of the feast, and over the great assembly silence fell over the noise, as if an enormous flock of chattering birds had roosted for the night when the sun is vanished below the rim of the world, and all the earth is quiet, in that pause before the night noises begin. Alexander looked over his assembled guests and he spoke these words to us all: "I, Alexander, speak to give my gratitude to the gods, for it is they who have led us to Egypt, to liberate you from the Persian yoke and for us to see the beauty of your land and to marvel at the great buildings and monuments, evidence of your long history and learning. Your doctors and seers are famous throughout the world. Indeed! your last pharaoh, Nectabeno, came as a seer to my father and guided him through many years of his turbulent reign; he even attended my birth, when he prophesied this day to my mother. Now we shall join the worship of your gods to those of Greece, for they are the same and to them we owe every good in our lives.

"We have taken an empire from the Persians and destroyed a despot. We shall establish our administration and teach the Greek Koine as a common language to unite the world under one government and one god. Under this god, I bring you peace and restore to you your ancient independence, free from the Persian yoke. I bring you freedom and prosperity, for you shall trade wherever ships sail the seas. The Persians plundered treasure from your temples and, when we march against Darius again, Egyptians will march with us to identify and restore what rightfully belongs to your nation."

Alexander was forced to be silent until the tumult died down as the people of Egypt heard his words and he continued: "You will now only pay taxes, which are fair and just and you may restore the treasuries of your temples, that you may hold, in the secure knowledge that Alexander offers to the gods all that is rightfully theirs and, separately, taxes only what is necessary for your good government."

These words brought the banquet to a close and I left the great hall to walk with Ptolemy, the son of Lagos, along the banks of the Nile. The river was lit by thousands of torches, and lined by ships, and all the hurried activity of men loading and unloading the commerce of the world. The waterside taverns were noisy with the rejoicing of the people as Alexander's words spread amongst them. The indigo sky was hung with the shimmering light of a million stars and the pale radiance of the moon turned the world to silver and slanted across the Nile in a path resembling molten glass. The air was sweet and mildly disturbed by breezes, coming gently from the distant sea. As we walked, we talked of many things for we had been companions for the greater part of our lives, first in Aristotle's school and later in our common service to Philip and Alexander and there was an easy understanding between us.

Ptolemy was captivated by this land and he was already familiar with details of its history; he even spoke of a mighty pharaoh, Ramses the Second, who had ruled before the Trojan War and built a great empire, much like Alexander of Macedon. He also said that from the day when Alexander first ruled, Egypt was vital to our enterprise. He told me that he had studied the writing, language and religion of the country and said that he had found the Egyptians worshipped many gods who were readily identified with those of Greece, as Alexander believed.

Ptolemy was a keen observer, and he confided that he was writing a journal of Alexander's expedition. I felt that it would make good reading when we were safely home in Macedon and our memories were weakened by time.

We had seen many beautiful cities on our way from the Hellespont, but the marvels of Egypt surpass them all. The vast pyramids and temples are magnificent and all the public buildings of such size and architectural merit that even Athens is dwarfed by their splendour. Within a few days of Alexander's acceptance in Memphis, he sailed to Thebes, accompanied by Ptolemy and a group of Companions. In that city, we visited the vast temples which are supported by a forest of soaring pillars. We saw glorious sculptures of gods and pharaohs subduing their prisoners and we marvelled at the inscriptions, which represent the laws and wars of the pharaohs' reigns.

We crossed the river to the rugged, barren valley where Egypt's kings were buried in secret tombs, although robbers had already plundered many of them, in defiance of the anger of the gods, and we spoke of those other tombs, the great pyramids, which were famed throughout the world. We had seen them as we first neared Memphis for they soared into the hard, blue sky on the west bank of the Nile now far to our north. Their origins are shrouded in myth and wonder and we thought that they were probably built by the Titans to honour dead pharaohs. Ptolemy spent his days visiting the schools of Thebes and he learned some of the secrets of Egyptian seers and took lessons from temple priests in their hieroglyphic writings.

Part of the civilian train joined us in the city, and an army of scribes and officials were set to work. The king commissioned many artists in paint and stone and all of them used their skills to celebrate Alexander in Egypt.

The king received a letter from Aristotle, in which the great teacher suggested sending an expedition to explore further up the Nile to determine the cause of the annual inundation of the valley. It was of vital importance to the agriculture of that otherwise overheated, dry and barren land. Alexander enthusiastically commissioned a large river boat for the purpose. Once provisioned, he held ceremonies and sacrifices to solicit the gods' protection for the expedition and crew, and they sailed off to bring back the answer to the mysteries of the great floods of Egypt.

And Alexander announced that he would hold celebratory games to mark the liberation of Egypt. He sent to the cities of the Greeks requesting that their best athletes take part in the sacred contests.

The king then held a council and he spoke to us these words: "Some of the army and civilians will remain here in Thebes to administer Upper Egypt. The rest will return to Memphis with me. From there, with a few companions, a company of hypaspists and a company of archers, we shall follow the Nile north to the river's delta. I shall also take a group of architects who will work under Deinocrates and Callisthenes. Scribes will come with me to record all that we shall see and do, and we shall also have with us geographers, surveyors and scientists and we march at first light in three days."

The king planned to leave Ptolemy in charge of Memphis and he and I left the conference together and we once more walked along the bank of the Nile.

"Jason," he said, "I could happily remain in Egypt for the rest of life. I have heard that Darius built a canal between the Nile and the Red Sea, which I should like to see and to restore shipping to that waterway. I plan, during the absence of Alexander, to penetrate to the limits of the desert in the west. This is truly a fabulous and mythical land, made especially so because I found a girl in Memphis who is already close to my soul and from whom I shall find it very hard to part."

Ptolemy was a quiet man, at peace with himself. He had a scholar's mind combined with soldierly qualities and his speech was always sober and restrained. Now his rugged face was full of pleasure as he anticipated great new opportunities to explore this legendary land of Egypt.

When I returned to my tent, I found a letter from my father in which he spoke of my son, whose existence was still unreal to me. Bitterness, however, was beginning to leave my soul, for if time cannot erase memory, it softens grief and makes hard sorrows easier to bear.

We returned to Memphis and from there, the king and his chosen men continued along the western bank of the Nile. We camped in the shadow of the mighty pyramids and we quietly spoke of Egypt's religion, which dedicates the lives of the living to the service of the dead. The pyramids rise out of the desert. Their size dwarfs every living creature into a speck of sand, and they are watched over by a giant sphinx and it looked as though they were all created by the hand of a god. We reached Naucratis, a Greek city, in the delta of the Nile; it seemed like home in this alien land, and then we marched to Canapos where we turned west to follow the coast towards Libya. We came to Rhacotis, a native city built on a strip of land lying between an inland salt lake in the south, and an island in the sea to the north. We made camp outside this city and that night Alexander studied his charts and marked a site on them, as we assembled in his tent, when dusk was creeping over the earth, and the king said in explanation: "I have marked the position where I intend to found a new city, which shall be named Alexandria. To secure Egypt, we must rule in Memphis, but to expand trade, attract Greek settlers and introduce Hellenism to the people of this land, we must build a great city on the coast with many temples, schools and libraries, marketplaces and a port to serve all Egypt for the import and export of the world's commerce. Deinocrates of Rhodes will be the architect of the new Greek city. He will also develop Rhacotis as a city where Egyptians may proudly live and feel at home, with temples for their gods, and the two cities will together thrive and attract merchants and trade even from distant Ocean."

We talked until dawn of the new cities and the prosperity that they would bring to Greece, together with the spread of civilisation. When the sun came up, I walked with Callisthenes beyond our camp to a haunted place of reed-filled marshes. It was alive with the cries of wild birds as they circled in the misty light and shadows of the early day. The earth, upon which we walked between the lake and the sea, was constantly renewed by the waters of the annual flood of the Nile and it made the soil sufficiently fertile to grow crops and feed any new settlers to the site, as the city rose from its foundations.

When the air cleared of the cloying mist, we returned to the camp with our minds full of the new city, which would rise in Egypt as the most permanent memorial to the arrival of Alexander, son of Philip of Macedon. The king had planned for his city before we left Memphis for Thebes. His architect, Deinocrates, surveyed the land and he made all the necessary adjustments to his plans so that they agreed with the actual site. Alexander ordered him to use grain from our military stores to mark out all the streets with the two principal roads crossing each other at right angles and the rest paralleling them to form geometric squares. Next, public buildings were laid out in the same manner. The king decided which gods to honour and he personally supervised the siting of their temples, and all of them were close to the agora. Alexander was completely absorbed by the work and he only left the side of Deinocrates, his charts and the building sites, to receive the most important emissaries. One of these was Hegelochus, the admiral in command of operations in the Aegean Islands. He arrived with the good news that he had recaptured all of them and that Alexander finally controlled the seas between Greece and Egypt. The admiral brought, as captives, many of the leading citizens of the islands who had treasonously surrendered to the Persians. They were sent to Memphis to await trial for their crimes. We next learned, from runners, that Darius had succeeded in recruiting a huge new army which was already training in Babylon. The king, pre-occupied with Egypt, was in no hurry to meet the Persians, although it might have been to our advantage to fight them before they reached their peak of military efficiency.

The day after the runners arrived in camp, Alexander held a conference during which he ignored the Persian threat. Deinocrates was present and Craterus, Coenus, Hephaestion, Callisthenes and myself were in attendance. The king opened the discussion with a report on the building of the new city and, after a long pause, he said: "Last night, I had a dream of Perseus and Herakles. I must follow where they led, to honour Zeus at the temple of Ammon, in the oasis of Siwah. I understand that Siwah is far out in the Libyan desert but, despite all the difficulties that we may experience travelling there, I shall not only honour Zeus, but consult the temple oracle, for I must know from the gods how fortune favours me. My dream means that at the Egyptian shrine, also sacred to all the Greeks, secret knowledge will be revealed to me.

"I shall now entrust the building of this great city, which will be called Alexandria, to Deinocrates and tomorrow, taking a small force, I ride for Siwah. I shall return to Memphis by the direct route, east across the desert. Therefore, the rest of the army here, which is not working on the construction of the city, will return to Memphis."

We left the king and hurried to give his orders and to make our own preparations for the journey. We needed guides, and the Arabs were the best available, for their lives are spent travelling on desert journeys. I had a little knowledge of their language, and it fell to me to employ them and supervise their purchases of supplies for the road to Siwah. I have heard that long ago Cambyses, a Persian King of Kings, had sent a force to Siwah to destroy the temple of Ammon. The vengeance of the god, for his insolence, was indeed terrible for every Persian in the expedition was lost in the desert wilderness in a ferocious sandstorm sent by the gods to destroy them. Throughout their history, the Persians had descended on Egypt and destroyed temples and banned the religion of the people, by whom they were truly hated. Alexander, the new pharaoh, before he left, gave the people religious freedom, new laws and a just government, for which he received their grateful acclamation.

Before we rode from Alexandria, the king sent orders to Memphis to prepare for the games, which he planned to celebrate on his return to the city. He sent emissaries to Greece and those parts of Asia under his control, to announce his holy pilgrimage to Siwah and to proclaim the games in Memphis; the leaders were instructed to invite the best athletes to compete and the finest artists to paint all the wonders of this incredible land. They must also report to the governments in each city his new conquests and describe their significance for the final defeat of the Persians. Also, with the newly captured wealth, of Alexander's increased power and, most importantly, to describe how Hellenism and civilisation were reaching into all the cities which were previously in the Persian Empire. By these proclamations Alexander gave the Persians and the world notice of his growing authority and a warning to conquered cities to keep the peace. He also conveyed to Darius that the next battle between them would bring Macedon a decisive victory. As the king grew in royal stature in the world, he became more remote from his friends. He was completely absorbed in consolidating his gains and creating a permanent government and, especially, in building the city of Alexandria. Even Hephaestion, closest to the king's heart, did not share in every part of Alexander's plans.

The king reached ever towards the spiritual and the gods and away from the affairs of men. He was still a sympathetic friend, sensitive and compassionate and he expected nothing from us in exchange, except our loyalty. Alexander's gift of self-sufficiency made him independent of the chains which shackle most men in a quest for acceptance. We prepared, carefully, for the expedition to Siwah. The journey across the hazardous desert would be a new experience and we were mindful of other expeditions lost in the shifting sands, especially of that of the Persians under Cambyses. There was one great consolation as most of the men with whom I had shared my life since childhood were again united after separations due to our differing duties to the king. I missed Ptolemy, son of Lagos, left behind in Memphis.

It was now winter. By day, the sun was warm but the nights chilled us to aching cold and we were glad of our woollen cloaks and blankets. We doubled the number of horses and paid good money for the use of camels to carry food, water and fodder. Our guides lived on a handful of dried dates and they cooked unleavened bread over campfires. I wished that my needs were so simple, and I grew to like and esteem the men of the desert and I respected their knowledge of desert ways, born in the hardships of their lives. We rode west along the coast road towards Libya. Alexander was on Bucephalos and he was happy to be surrounded by his close friends and behind us rode the Arabs on camels or on their small, sturdy horses. Round the warm fires of our camps at night, we remembered the battles of the past, our time with Aristotle, the journey to the Olympic Games, and our families and homes. For the last time we felt special comfort in our comrades as we knew that the fates would soon change us forever. The nomads sat with us, although they did not understand our speech. They are proud men, and do not know the relationship of master and servant; in desert law they were our teachers and without them we were lost forever.

One day we came to the tribal camp of our guides and, at our approach, the men slaughtered many of their animals and prepared a great feast for our benefit. In those aching, lonely wastes to them hospitality was a sacred duty and we were welcomed with a warmth and dignity which conferred great honour on their people and on us; it was unequalled in all my experience.

After we had travelled some way from the site of Alexandria, we were met by an embassy from Cyrene, a Greek colony, established for trade westwards along the African coast. They brought costly gifts to Alexander, an invitation to visit their city and inspect their state, and the alluring prospect of an alliance to mount an expedition to the Pillars of Herakles. The king thanked them, but he refused their invitation, remembering only that the campaign had been planned with Antipater, Parmenion and other generals, with the objective of destroying the Persian tyrant and not even Alexander of Macedon might change this plan. We reached the city of Paraetonium and there, we turned to the south west. Our passage across the desert was extremely difficult, especially for the horses in the shifting sands and suddenly the sky and earth were blocked out in the ochre gloom and filth of a sandstorm. It separated us from each other, covered the track before us and we were helpless in the stinging, blinding fury of the earth blackened out by clouds of choking particles of dust. We lost direction and we were as doomed as a sailor when he hears the siren's song.

The hell lasted three days, in which we neither ate nor drank and then, once more, the gods favoured Alexander. The wind veered round to the north and the dust returned to the earth. Our guides searched and found us all, but several of the pack animals were missing and we were now without water and threatened by death. We watched, in awe, the miracle of a small cloud grow in this awful, arid region, until it filled the skies and the heavens opened up and blessed rain poured down upon us. Soon rivulets turned into tiny lakes and we filled our goatskin bags and we gave heartfelt thanks to Zeus and all the gods for our salvation. The rain stopped as suddenly as it had begun, but our road was lost in the sand of that god-forsaken wilderness. Two ravens now appeared in the sky and the king, taking them as a sign of welcome from Zeus-Ammon, ordered us to follow them until, in that desolation, we found the road clear before us.

We travelled on until, at last, like a mirage, stood the citadel of Ammon, gaunt in its surrounding desert. An emissary from the High Priest of the temple came out to greet us. He addressed Alexander as 'Son of Ammon' and said that only the king, as Pharaoh of Egypt, might enter the inner sanctuary of the temple and he must wear the same clothes in which he had made the journey to Siwah. As for the rest of us, he told us that we must stay in the outer courtyard of the shrine and before entering even this enclosure, that we must change only certain of our garments.

We arrived at the great sanctuary as dedicated pilgrims. Priests came out from the Holy of Holies to escort Alexander into the presence of the god. He was lost from our view until much later in the day and when he emerged again, his countenance shone and his hair was lighted by the sun and became a halo of radiance round his head. We were awestruck, until Hephaestion advanced towards Alexander and spoke for all of us when he asked: "Lord, how does the god answer you?"

The king replied: "I have heard that which I most desired."

163

The priests carried their god out from the temple. He was mounted on a boat, made from purest gold, which they held on high for all of us to see and the deity was a hemisphere of stone set in glittering gemstones. The procession of priests was followed by girls and matrons and they all chanted a melancholy hymn in very low tones. The High Priest halted before the king and addressed Alexander once again as "Son of Ammon" and he told the king that the god, his father, bestowed this name upon him.

Alexander of Macedon accepted the title and every other Macedonian present that day in the temple at Siwah was uneasy with his claim to divinity. We felt, at that time, it was a challenge to our own Greek gods.

At the conclusion of this ceremony, the rest of us were given the opportunity to ask questions of the god and the priests interpreted the movements of the swaying image, and gave each of us answers and from that day we knew our destinies given to us by Ammon of Siwah. We were assigned quarters in the town. Alexander wrote, immediately, a letter to his mother and he told her that the god had revealed a prophecy, which he would keep secret until their next meeting, but Death has cruelly taken the king and with him, the prophecy revealed by Zeus-Ammon at Siwah. Alexander truly believed that he was the son of Zeus and he confided in me that he wished to be buried in Siwah to be near his father. His destiny has been played out before all men and bold indeed, in the face of the gods, would be he who questions the divinity of Alexander, son of Philip of Macedon, revealed at Siwah. I wrote to my father a full account of our pilgrimage to Zeus-Ammon and to Ptolemy in Memphis. Callisthenes wrote his official diary, but none knew, nor will ever know, the prophecy revealed to Alexander at Siwah.

We explored the oasis of the god; it was planted with olive trees and date palms and many springs and lakes made the desert fertile. The place was a miracle of nature, rising in the sandy wasteland but a lonely place set aside in service to Zeus-Ammon.

We departed from Siwah, and turned to face the rising sun on the return journey to Memphis. We travelled for twenty days and they were full of the light of Apollo. At night, the moon shadowed the sands into haunted shapes and in the deep dark, the bellowing of camels and the whinnying of horses mingled with the soft cadences of Greek and the guttural sounds of the Aramaic spoken by our guides. I often remember the peace of those nights in which I accepted the sorrows that are man's destiny, as I followed in the path of Alexander of Macedon. Memphis throbbed with the life of a great metropolis. Many embassies, from distant lands, were waiting to be received by the king. News had also arrived from Miletos that when word reached the city that Alexander had been proclaimed 'Son of Ammon' at Siwah the Sacred Spring of the Temple of Didyma had flowed again. The Spring had dried up during the reign of the Persian Xerxes and gushed, for a brief period, when Alexander was born in Pella twenty-four seasons ago. Surely confirmation of his divine status?

Many new recruits had arrived for the army from Macedon and Greece. They were already training in Memphis, with their units, when we returned to the city. There were also several hundred Thracian mounted men and they were a welcome replacement for our dead cavalry and the horses which we had lost in battle and from the hardships of the expedition. Alexander wished to offer sacrifices to Egypt's gods. In the east, the sole prerogative of a king, as we had discovered was the custom at Tyre. Mazaces, the Persian satrap, consulted his local advisors. He announced, in order to observe this sacred custom, that he proposed to offer the king, on behalf of all the Egyptian people, the title of the Pharaoh, together with all the privileges of that high office, including offering sacrifices to the gods. The Egyptian priests arranged the ceremonies and they crowned Alexander of Macedon with the double crown of Upper and Lower Egypt and he wore the royal robes decorated with all the royal insignia as he sat on the throne in the great Temple of Ptah at Memphis. His deification and new styles and titles were called in sonorous tones by the High Priest of Ptah in ceremonies of great pageantry and splendour and in Egypt, Alexander was now a god. Recognition by the Egyptians of Alexander as their pharaoh and that god gave him powers, in this land, far beyond any of those rooted in Greece or in Asia, as the victorious King of the Macedons or Hegemon of the League of Corinth. Macedonians bitterly opposed the deification of their King and they accused him, in muttered and sullen tones, of blasphemy. Our kings are not gods, they are men, merely the first amongst equals and accountable for their exercise of authority. The Greeks were doubly resentful.

Macedonian authority extended over all their states, except for
Sparta, and they were surrounded from the north, through the
east, to the south by hostile seas and now ruled by a god into
the very heavens. For three days Egyptians celebrated their new
pharaoh until the joyous crowd became a drunken mob. Robbers
roamed the streets, forcing the women to stay in their houses;
men were murdered for a handful of copper coins and many old
scores were settled in the general disorder. The king announced
that, with the assumption of his new titles of Horus and Son
of Ra, he would sacrifice, in the temple, to the Egyptian gods.
Order was restored in the streets for the ceremonial procession
but with uneasy hearts we Macedonians watched Alexander
sacrifice to Ra/Ammon and Apis the Bull, sacred to the cult of
Ptah. The Egyptians reverenced the mystical nature of animals,
for us a most barbaric concept, and their unrestrained emotion,
after the ceremonies, increased our anger and opposition to the
king's assumption of the pharaohs' powers. It did not escape us
that he was the first to assume those powers since Nectanebo
had fled Egypt and arrived in Pella, to prophesy great marvels
at Alexander's birth.

The king's authority was now assured and the people of
Memphis were delirious with delight in their new pharaoh, from
whom they expected enlightened government, after the harsh
rule of the Persian satraps. They would not be disappointed;
Alexander planned to reform their government and the onerous
system of taxation in both Upper and Lower Egypt. The Egyptian
priests arranged for the king to offer additional ritual sacrifices
in the temple and, after these, Alexander held the celebratory
games. They were made glorious by the competition between
the best Greek athletes, who had all arrived in Memphis, with
fourteen days to spare for their additional training. It was a
magnificent spectacle and the festivities continued for many days
and nights on the banks of the Nile.

The expedition which Alexander had sent up the Nile
returned to Memphis with the news that the annual inundation
of the river across the land was caused by rains falling in the
southern mountains of Nubia. They prepared a report of their
journey, in which they included maps, and they made a copy
to send to Antipater in Pella. A second copy was also prepared
and dispatched to Aristotle with local specimens of plants, for
his research into their properties and their potential medicinal

purposes. About this time Hector, the youngest son of Parmenion, and a companion from the school in Mieza, drowned in the Nile. He was very close to the king and Alexander was stricken with grief at the loss of his friend. Parmenion, always a professional soldier, aged again overnight but he spoke no words of so private a sorrow. The king's grief was doubled when runners arrived in Memphis to report that the Samaritans had burned Andromachos alive – another close friend, whom he had left as governor of Syria. Alexander immediately ended the festivities and we prepared to leave for that country to avenge the murder of Andromachos. Before we left Egypt, the king announced his arrangements for the government of the new provinces. Ptolemy had hoped to be chosen as satrap on the Nile, but Alexander needed his great qualities close to him, and he appointed Egyptians to head the civil governments, in both Upper and Lower Egypt. Greek military commanders were appointed over the garrisons, and they were ordered to send their reports directly to the king on the campaign route.

The Delta of the Nile was also divided into two satrapies and governed by Apollonius and Cleomenese, both of whom were Greeks, and once again Alexander divided authority as a guarantee against revolt and any opposition to his rule, as he left Egypt to hunt for Darius, the Persian King of Kings.

Chapter 18

We marched from Egypt as winter turned to spring and we left a people rejoicing to have changed Persian rule for that of Alexander's less brutal hegemony. They had made the king their pharaoh and a god and they venerated him with all the honours due to a deity. They wished him a great victory over Darius, by which they anticipated peace and prosperity for themselves, free from the threat of a new Persian invasion. Alexander's relationship with the people of Egypt was personal and, as their king, very different from his authority rooted in Macedon and Corinth, by which he had, so far, ruled all his conquests.

Many Egyptians had protested against the foundation of the city of Alexandria. They are a xenophobic people and they resented a foreign city in their midst. The king reasoned with them that there were many other Greek enclaves in Egyptian cities, which had secured special rights and privileges, but the people were unconvinced and complained that the new city, with its own satrap, was not under Egyptian control, as his official reported directly to the king and bypassed their own governors. Alexander was indifferent to these complaints. Ptolemy was the most reluctant Macedonian to leave Egypt. We rode out from Memphis together, and he spoke to me of his deep interest in the country and her people. He had most unwillingly left his Egyptian mistress in the city. She continued to live in a house, which he had purchased on the Nile, where she waited for his return. She was as beautiful as a gazelle and very different from our strong-minded Macedonian women.

We returned to Gaza and requisitioned what public buildings were habitable in the razed city. The nights were chill and often damp and we welcomed any shelter from the elements. A few people wandered amongst the ruins and they were thin and gaunt from lack of food. Messengers arrived from Antipater to announce a victory over the Spartans. We all cheered and embraced each other in celebration. The Spartan, King Agis, had fallen in the battle, but Alexander was silent until he commented that it was a battle of mice. I think that he had wanted that particular victory for himself and not delegated to even Antipater.

A delegation also arrived from the Greek mercenaries who had fled the battlefield of Issos and returned to Greece. They now begged forgiveness and gave their unconditional surrender to the king. They had also fomented and supported unrest in the Greek cities and many of them had joined the Spartans but he forgave them because their surrender was unconditional. The League of Corinth praised Alexander for this act of clemency and he invited the mercenaries to rejoin the army. Now, at last, the king was free to continue the campaign in Asia without the constant threat of a revolt in Greece.

Alexander sent a detachment of troops to reinforce the unit left on the mole at Tyre with orders to prevent Tyrians from returning to their city and fomenting unrest in that part of Canaan. Macedonians, also, led detachments to strengthen the king's government in Phoenicia, Cilicia and the lands beyond the Taurus, as far as the Hellespont. He intended to deal with Syria in person to punish the Syrians for the murder of his friend and their appointed governor.

One unit of the army, operating near Jericho, found a great store of Tyrian gold and precious purple dye, hidden in a cave on the shores of the Dead Sea. This was a welcome addition to the treasury and it was used to help finance the soldiers' pay and purchase necessary stores, fodder and food. Spies arrived in Gaza bringing news that Darius was recruiting and training a mighty army in distant Babylon. Truly, we wondered if the resources of the Great King were limitless? We heard that Bessus, the Prince of Bactria, and a member of the Archaemenid dynasty, commanded a huge army and there were other armies led by Satropates, the famed Persian cavalry commander, Orsines, the son-in-law of the slain Mithradates, and Mazaeus, the very efficient former satrap of Syria and Mesopotamia, and many other Persian nobles. We also heard that there were with Darius as well the Persians, Medes, Hyrcanians, Areians, Indian volunteers and contingents from every other part of the Persian

Empire and all were training in his army in camps, night and day, in Babylon.

The Medes used scythed chariots bristling with blades from every surface in all directions and the Indians had their elephants, and these were weapons of which we had no experience. The army of the Persians was also much larger than when we fought them on the River Granicus and on the Plains of Issos. The Macedonian and Greek recruits, on the other hand, who joined the Macedonian army, only replaced our battle losses. The king's confidence never wavered whatever the news, which poured into Gaza until the expedition was ready to continue the march, when he held a Council of War and addressed us, saying: "My commanders and friends, I am pleased to report to you that Darius lies in wait for us on the banks of the River Tigris. He has burned the land called Mesopotamia between the Tigris and Euphrates Rivers. We shall therefore take stores to supply our needs as if we planned to cross a desert. Darius has also destroyed the bridges across the Euphrates, but our engineers are already in position on the river constructing replacements. We are experienced in the ways of the Persian and we have already taken from him many lands and cities. He has been defeated in small battles and two major engagements and we shall now be swept along on a great tide of victory, and by the favour of the gods, the excellence of our men, their superior training and weapons. Let no man doubt that we march to scatter the Persian hordes and Greece shall be forever free of the Persian yoke, when Darius is our captive or dies in battle at our hands.

"We are a smaller army and therefore more mobile than his. Our phalanx is invincible and the courage of our men already legendary. We fight for our freedom against the Persian army, which is a rabble of mercenaries and impressed men, with little stomach for their Persian king. We, on the other hand, march with the Sword of Ares and it shall be sheathed only when we have brought certain peace to the world."

From ruined Gaza we marched to Samaria, where the men guilty of the murder of Andromachos were brought to justice and executed. A delegation from the Athenians arrived in the Macedonian camp in Samaria. They brought with them the congratulations of their city for Alexander's victories and they begged the king to return all our Greek prisoners, a request that the king now granted. Greece, even Sparta, was pacified, and by clemency, he reduced the number of mouths that he must feed and guard.

Before we left Samaria, Alexander sent generous gifts to the people of Mitylene for their fierce loyalty to him and as recompense for all the money which the city had spent in his cause. The king also sent generous gifts and honours to the Cypriots as payment for deserting the Persians and for dispatching their fleet during the siege of Tyre. He received many other delegations from different rulers and messengers from the Macedonian military commanders across his conquered lands before we marched to Damascus. When we arrived, we camped on the outskirts of that ancient city and, I regret, with not enough time to enjoy the delights available in this most fabled of cities.

The expedition marched north and we followed the valley of the River Orontes until we arrived at the road which turned east towards Thapsacus on the River Euphrates. Our spies were already in the ruined city and they reported to the king that Mazaeus was camped on the east bank of the river. Half his satrapy in Syria was in Alexander's hands and we now threatened the other half in Mesopotamia. We heard that Darius burned for vengeance against the Macedonian army and Macedon's king. Alexander, after listening to the spies' reports, walked to survey the ruined bridge across the river, destroyed by the retreating Persians. As he stood on the bank one of our scouts swam across the river from the east, and reported that the Persian satrap and his army had vanished in the night. Alexander immediately ordered the engineers to mend the bridge with all speed, and due to their efforts, in a few days we were in Mesopotamia (or the Land Between Two Rivers) and on the ancient Persian road leading to a crossing over the River Tigris, which name I understood was a Persian word meaning 'as swift and straight as an arrow'. Many more spies rode in as we marched; they brought news that Darius himself was on the west bank of the Tigris. Alexander force marched the expedition until we learned that this information was false. The king put the spies in chains for the trouble and haste which their untrue reports had caused him.

Queen Statira, the wife and sister of Darius, died as we crossed Mesopotamia. She was the most beautiful and gentle woman in all Asia, and deeply mourned by Alexander, although he had not seen her since the battlefield of Issos. He expressed sorrow for holding so delicate a lady in captivity and he immediately went to comfort her mother, the lady Sisygambis, and all her children. Alexander's grief was intense as he looked upon the sorrowing family and he once more held the small Ochus, seeking relief from his own mourning in the comfort of the small boy's body. Alexander arranged an impressive military funeral for Queen Statira with magi performing all the prescribed Persian rites. As well as our Persian prisoners, they were attended by our entire expedition. The king allowed the eunuch Tyriotes, the royal Persian chamberlain, to slip quietly away to carry the sad news to her husband, Darius, the King of Kings. When the chamberlain reached that doomed, unhappy king, his first thought was that his queen had died from the vilest treatment at the hands of Alexander. The eunuch, even under threat of torture, maintained that Alexander had been the gentlest of captors. He allowed the royal family to retain all their possessions, attendants and even the burial rites for the Persian dead. Darius at first refused to believe him and lamented: "O, Alexander, you who hate me without cause, now must you take revenge on women and children, a revenge so terrible that it is worse to them, and to me, than every defeat?"

Tyriotes invited Darius to torture him, but said that he must speak the truth and, when he finally convinced the Persian king, Darius weeping in bitterest anguish for his dead wife, lifted his hands to heaven and cried: "O God of my father, if all is finished with me, allow none to be Lord of Asia, other than my enemy Alexander, so fair and just in victory."

And now Darius, although defeated in great battles, hoping that he might find a change in his bleak fortune, was persuaded by Tyriotes' account of Alexander's character to sue again for peace. This time his envoys praised Alexander for his clemency and offered him, once more, all the territory to the Euphrates as a dowry for his daughter and added the custody of small Ochus, as a hostage, in exchange for Queen Sisygambis and his daughters and all the other Persian prisoners.

The envoys withdrew and we sat in silence with Alexander, while he considered his answer. Parmenion broke into the tense quietness saying that he recommended ransoming and releasing the royal family and the Persian prisoners held at Damascus and so relieving the army of guarding and feeding them. Alexander made an impatient gesture, and Parmenion continued by pointing out that Alexander was offered a rich realm and all the immense lands that it contained, to take in peace and to rule from Macedon. He continued that it was a better alternative to an advance into Bactria, Areia and India, all lands unknown and full of perils. We stirred in interest, but unhappily Parmenion's advice was contrary to Alexander's own vision and he angrily said: "Indeed, if I were Parmenion, I too would prefer riches to glory; as it is Alexander, being Alexander, already has security against poverty and I am not a trader but a king. I have nothing for sale and would more honourably return my prisoners as a gift than ransom them for any price."

The king recalled the Persian envoys into his presence and ordered them to report to Darius that clemency was his natural way and should not be taken as a token of his friendship for the Persian king. He continued: "I also do not wage war against women and children, nor do I barter them for money. Darius works with bribery as proved in the death of my father and he has used his gold to try and suborn my men. I tell you that we shall meet your king to the east of the Euphrates, for I am already beyond the boundary which he foolishly offers to me. Finally, tell Darius to sue for peace and I will consider it, but let him not try to make terms as if he were the victor."

The dejected envoys left the camp of Alexander to advise their master that it was too late to make peace and that he must prepare for battle or submit to Alexander's terms.

Macedonians quietly crossed the river to scout again for the camp of Darius. Their efforts were unsuccessful, and we concentrated on the task of ferrying the whole expedition across the deep and fast flowing Tigris. The horses refused to take the plunge and they, together with the men who could not swim, and all the camp followers, supplies, and equipment, were towed across on rafts during the next two days.

There was an eclipse of the moon during the first night on the eastern bank of the Tigris, which gave forth a light as red as blood and struck terror into the soldiers' hearts. They wailed and clamoured in hostility to foreign lands and stated that, against the will of the gods, they were dragged far from home to endure hardships of deserts and empty lands and battles and every kind of danger and misery. Some even muttered that it was all to satisfy the vanity of one man who disdained his homeland and denied his own father, King Philip, a great king of Macedon.

The king reacted to this near mutiny and called the commanders to his tent together with the Egyptian seers. The Egyptians immediately declared that Apollo represented the Greeks and the moon the Persians and, since the moon was eclipsed and was the colour of blood, the augury foretold a Persian defeat and the flowing of Persian blood. The soldiers, after much argument, finally accepted the omens as favourable to us, which brought an uneasy quiet to the camp. Alexander granted the men three days' rest during which time he offered solemn sacrifices to the gods for their help and guidance. We also celebrated the king's twenty-fifth birthday with athletic contests, feasts for the men and a banquet in Alexander's tent for the King's Companions.

At the end of this respite, we turned south east, away from the Tigris, finally to seek the camp of Darius. We came to a small hill where Alexander halted the expedition and, with a few Companions, he climbed to the summit. We looked down on to a vast plain, which seemed to have been flattened of all its natural features and it was covered by the greatest camp a mighty army had ever assembled.

Alexander dispatched orders for the expedition to make our own camp near the base of the hill and then coolly studied the Persians' strength and disposition until the sun was so high that it distorted our vision and we returned to our own expedition. The king called a Council of War and when he spoke, his face was alight with an inner fire and his body was rigidly controlled. Unusually for Alexander, he asked those of us present if we had any suggestions or observations to make before he gave the order for battle on the next day. After a tense pause, Parmenion spoke: "Sire! If we do not delay and attack under cover of darkness, we shall surprise the enemy and throw him into confusion. He will have no time to harness his scythed chariots, his elephants will be shackled and his men asleep. We should seize the advantage of a surprise attack that only this first night will offer to us, for the Persians seem unaware of our presence."

He sat down to murmurs of approval and Alexander answered him: "Parmenion, you speak, of course, as my father's general and you speak well, but I am Alexander and we face Alexander's enemy and I do things differently from King Philip. I refuse to go as a thief in the night to steal a victory. The whole world must know that Alexander conquers without an unnatural ally such as the dark of night. We are some distance from the enemy, and our men shall receive a hot meal and a good night's sleep before the battle. The horses will be fed and rested so that they will be fit to meet the enemy. Please note that the Great King has flattened the plain for our reception and tonight I intend to ride across it to look for any traps which he may have set to surprise us. Parmenion, Craterus, Coenus, Hephaestion and Jason will ride with me; the rest of you will eat and sleep in readiness for the morrow."

We rode as cautiously as possible to avoid raising the alarm. As we approached, the noise from the Persian camp was like an angry torrent of water rushing down from the mountains after the snows melt. As we drew ever closer, we realised that the enemy seemed to be aware of our presence in the nearby camp. They had posted watchmen; and they were all awake as though they were expecting an attack. Their camp was a blaze of fires, which made it as light as day, and in the distance we saw a few small lamps, which possibly came from the distant town of Gaugamela.

We crossed their occupied plain in total silence, seeking the shadows, but we were so few that we caused no interest amongst the great hordes from many different lands. We found no traps and Alexander concluded that Darius had flattened the earth for the easier deployment of his scythed chariots, and we returned as swiftly as possible to our own camp to eat and rest. When day finally dawned, Alexander's army was fresh from sleep and the Persians were hopefully exhausted from their night-long vigil as predicted by Alexander. He slept well beyond the dawn, until he was shaken awake by Parmenion's order. This gave the men great confidence that their own king was in control of the coming battle, and we started the day with the first advantage. The king commanded the army into battle order as we left the civilian train in our camp. We advanced towards the plain where the Persians waited. Alexander halted us some distance from the enemy to give his battle speech, and final orders as was his custom. At the end of the speech, Aristander, the Lykian seer, dressed in white, flowing robes with his head veiled, led the king and army in prayers to Zeus and Athena. When the rites were completed, we advanced again. Our right wing was drawn up opposite Darius, who was mounted in his chariot of gold, and in command of the central section of his army. The Great King of Kings was an imposing figure in his purple cloak and high crown; he was surrounded by his best infantry and mounted guards on either flank were covered by Greek mercenaries. When we saw them, we marvelled and wondered if there was no limit to the traitors who had fled to Darius? Beyond them were the Bactrian and the eastern cavalry on the left and on the right were Armenian and other western contingents.

Drawn up in the centre of the Persian army were fifteen Indian elephants. Few, if any of us, had ever seen these large and terrifying beasts. They towered over us loudly trumpeting and their noise filled the air and the very earth trembled from their movements.

On the Macedonian side of the battle-line, Alexander commanded the Hetairoi on our right wing, as at the Battle of Issos. On the left, Parmenion commanded the Thessalonian cavalry and our phalanxes occupied the centre of the field. We opposed a vastly larger army, which extended far beyond the horizon. To protect us from encirclement, Alexander deployed troops in our rear, which faced away from the battle-line, and so we formed a solid square to resist attack from every quarter.

Alexander, mounted on Bucephalos, rode the entire length of his army crying: "If I am the Son of Zeus, the god will lead the Greeks to victory over the barbarians."

He was cheered with wild enthusiasm, especially by the Thessalonians, and the whole army shouted his name: "Alexander! Alexander!"

In battle order, we advanced toward the left wing of the Persians, which was under the command of Mazaeus, and they retreated before us. The enemy abandoned the levelled ground and they followed Alexander's battle plan. Darius countered and ordered the Bactrian cavalry positions on his left to attack our flank. Alexander had anticipated the Great King's strategy and our light cavalry, under Hephaestion, swiftly rode to engage the Bactrians. From the centre of the Persian army, their scythed chariots charged towards the phalanx and, at a prearranged signal, the men parted to allow them to gallop through harmlessly to the rear of our lines. As they passed, our men pulled the drivers to the ground, where they were cut to pieces on their own scythes and many others fell to our archers. The pride of the Persian army was now a useless force. Alexander, keeping a watchful eye on the whole field, saw Darius order other cavalry units to the support of the Scythians and Bactrians and, with a mighty shout, the king ordered the hetairoi to advance against them. The Persians rushed to close their centre against our phalanx, which now advanced towards them in oblique order with their pikes forming a solid wall of sharply pointed blades directed at the enemy. Before they reached the Persians, to our astonishment and the shocked horror of the demoralised Persians, Darius, the Great King, King of Kings, wheeled his chariot and fled once more. Those nearest followed him. Alexander, although greatly tempted to pursue him, saw that Parmenion was under heavy attack and his lines were already breached; he allowed Darius to escape and galloped to the general's aid.

As we tried to recover from the shock of Darius' flight, the wild Asian cavalry rushed through our lines to seize our camp, which they rifled, and they offered their idea of freedom to the Persian Royal Family. The Lady Sisygambis, the mother of Darius, using all her queenly dignity, refused to flee from Alexander, whom she loved as a son. The second line of the cavalry now wheeled to defend our camp and we took a great toll of the Asian cavalry. After we finished them off, we returned to aid Parmenion but we found the Thessalonians already in complete possession of that sector of the field. Victory was indeed ours but, without Darius, incomplete for he lived to challenge us again. When we took toll of our losses, we found that many men were dead of wounds, including about sixty members of the Hetairoi, all close friends of the king. Hephaestion was amongst the wounded and an anxious Alexander helped to carry him back to his tent.

That night, when he was sure that Hephaestion would live, Alexander rode in pursuit of Darius. A small band accompanied him, including Craterus, Coenus and myself. The king was shocked by the loss of so many of our men in the battle, especially that of his personal friends, and he was furious to be cheated of his full victory by the flight of Darius, and he rode off in grim silence to hunt the Persian king.

We were forced to ford a small river where we rested and dried out on its eastern bank until the break of dawn, when we continued our wild pursuit. We arrived at the town of Arbela and discovered from the local people that Darius, with a small band of the Persian cavalry, had galloped straight through the city. They showed us a large cache of treasure that the Persians had previously deposited there, which Alexander seized for our depleted treasury. The king decided that Darius had too great a lead and, by now, he must be in familiar territory over the Armenian mountains, where he would find refuge from our pursuit, and we returned to the battlefield in silent frustration.

Alexander immediately upon our return, made straight for Hephaestion's tent. He was overjoyed to find that his friend's wounds were only superficial and the two of them relived the battle until our final moment of victory. Our dead were given all the military honours in a mass funeral, and when this melancholy duty was finished, Alexander paraded the army to hear himself proclaimed "King of Asia!"

The Macedonians reacted in stony silence to this calumny, although they acknowledged that we could not return home until Darius was deposed by capture and trial, or by death in battle. In those first days after the battle, the king dispatched couriers to Antipater, Olympias, the League of Corinth and to all the governors of the provinces to inform them of his great victory and of his new style and title. Philoxenus was sent, as ambassador, to Susa, with instructions to announce the imminent arrival of the new King of Asia and to claim the city's treasury on behalf of Alexander. Eumenes and Callisthenes were particularly busy writing their accounts of the battle, which was given the name of 'Gaugamela'.

We gave the Persian dead a funeral, using their own rites, for they had fought gallantly, and finally we burned the carcasses of both the Greek and Persian horses for their stench hung thickly over the land. And now we lit great fires to celebrate Alexander's victory in the wastelands of Assyria. An enormous feast was prepared for the entire expedition. When it was ready, Alexander sat with the Royal Squadron, and we were surrounded by Macedonians and our excitement was so high that we shouted and laughed together and all our exhaustion was forgotten in that glorious hour.

We slept for two or three days and then, with the whole expedition present, Alexander made solemn sacrifices to the gods. At the end of the rites, the king proclaimed the freedom of every city in Greece but warned Sparta to stay within her own boundaries or face annihilation at his hands. The treasure, which we had seized in Arbela was gathered into piles before the men and Alexander divided it up between the living and the heirs of our dead. He sent gifts, of liberal generosity, to all the Greeks and even to a city in Italy, which had sent a representative force to the Battle of Salamis, between Athens and Persia, almost seventy seasons before. The king always acted with a clear motive and in sharing the fruits of victory he bound diverse states and people to his cause. No detail ever escaped his vigilance nor did he lack the courage to turn every event to the general advantage of the whole expedition. I now felt, after these events and all that followed, a tiredness of body and spirit which always came after a battle. My sleep was haunted by the cries of the dying and the memory of gaping wounds sickened me in body and mind. There are some who glory in the carnage of war, lusting for blood as much as victory. I saw their distorted faces in my dreams and I heard the loud, savage clash of metal against metal, and metal against bone in those troubled hours once more.

Alexander was able to turn violence to a noble purpose and he found no glory in pitiful necessity; had he been otherwise, I must have quit his service. He held me, by his genius, and especially by his dream of universal peace and maybe also by his ever-strengthening conviction of 'One God, the common Father of all mankind'. My life seemed always conditioned by hated war and Alexander was a promise for a different future and from this came my consolation.

There were many thick heads from the extended celebrations. The king relaxed military discipline and he went amongst the army with congratulatory words. He visited the wounded and made many remarks of praise and compassion and he personally applied his soothing salves to their very worst injuries.

We rested for three more days and then we prepared to advance south across the Tigris to Mesopotamia, and through the city of Opis to Babylon. The splendours of Babylon were famous to us, even in Greece. We had heard of the beautiful tiled gates which led through mighty walls 300 feet in height. They enclosed palaces and temples, the fabled Hanging Gardens, broad avenues and public and private buildings of such splendour that they outshone every other city in the world. We wondered how much was left standing by the Persian plunderers. Babylon was once the greatest city of Asia, a glittering prize and especially desired by Alexander.

Spies rode into our camp with reports that Mazaeus had fled the Battlefield of Gaugamela to organise Persians for Babylon's resistance. He had already locked the city's gates against the king's arrival on the banks of the Euphrates, in a vain hope of defeating Alexander. We were only a short distance from Babylon as it lay distorted in the shimmering haze of the foetid heat. The scouts who rode ahead returned to report to the king that a great procession of people, defying Mazaeus, had already left the city gates and was headed in our direction. The king directed the army into strict battle order until he made sure of the Babylonians' purpose. This was a special burden on the men who were exhausted by the march from Gaugamela, the heat and the everlasting mosquitoes and dust. Our tongues stuck to our mouths from thirst and those with open wounds and sores were especially plagued by the flies which flew round us in great clouds of buzzing fury.

The king, by contrast, was clear-eyed and rode proudly in front of his army. He was of medium height, but authority gave him stature and, on the noble Bucephalos, he was the tallest of us all. Alexander rode to Babylon that day dressed in shining armour and he was in every way King of the East as he claimed by right of conquest. And we saw a messenger leave the city and he brought its surrender to Alexander as the procession of Babylonians approached us. We were amazed to see that they were led by Mazaeus, walking beside another high official who was identified to us as Bagophanes, the commander of the city's fortress. Surrounding them were the high priests of the Persian fire religion and a whole concourse of the leading citizens, which was followed by multitudes of ordinary people. Alexander greeted the leaders of the procession with grave courtesy and we continued towards the gates, now followed by the Babylonians. When we reached the city, thousands of people swarmed over the broken walls. They had not been repaired following their destruction when Persian Cyrus conquered the city. We learned that wiser councils in the city had prevailed against Mazaeus and he had quickly abandoned his plan to resist the irresistible Alexander. Now all Babylon, it seemed, came to surrender their city and pay homage to Alexander of Macedon, their new Great King.

Alexander took over the city in a brief ceremony and we rode into Babylon. Most of the Greeks and myself were dazzled and awed by the magnificence that we saw. From the Ishtar Gate, down the wide, ceremonial way to the Hanging Gardens, which were a collection of storied buildings where trees grew at every level of the structures and created cool shade in the awful, damp heat.

The city was surrounded by verdant lowland on which the people grew abundant crops. They were dependant on an ancient irrigation system for water drawn from the Euphrates, and they were never short of food. We marched along great avenues decorated with wreaths and altars and costly incense burned in great clouds above our heads. The people lined the streets and hailed Alexander as their liberator from the Persians and the restorer of their ancient freedoms.

The Babylonians arranged elaborate ceremonies to offer Alexander their country. He accepted and to all his titles he now added that of King of Babylon and King of the Lands, two dignities restored from Babylon's ancient past, abolished by the Persians. To the great anguish of the people, the Persians had also destroyed the temple of Marduk, the Babylonian god. Alexander, as their new king, announced that he had set aside enough treasure to re-build the temple, with a further sum to fund a temple for our Greek gods. Tears of joy streamed down the faces of the Babylonians as they acclaimed Alexander in mighty paeons of praise.

In reality, the separate parts of Alexander's empire were ever more diverse and distinct and their only common bond was in the person of the king. We Macedonians anxiously discussed the possibility of his death; he would leave no heir to his empire and we also saw chaos in all the vanquished lands as our numbers shrank in proportion to the conquered peoples. In Babylon, every known tongue was spoken by the polyglot multitudes who made the city their home. They were natives of every state in Asia, and even Greece, and they all enjoyed fabulous wealth and a life of leisured ease. The morals of the city were consequently very lax and the people practised the utmost depravities; even our Macedonian and Greek soldiers were easily corrupted by the women of Babylon. We were quartered in palaces of royal splendour and they were equipped with baths and there were girls in attendance. One of them especially stood out from the others. She was doe-eyed and graceful as a gazelle and she made my nights less lonely. She spoke Aramaic in a Hebrew dialect. I had studied this language spoken in so many places of the east, but not by the Persians, and there were many local variations, which added colour and interest to the speech of the people. I told her of my home and my father's vineyards and olive groves and of Macedon and of Aristotle and of campaigns and battles and long, hard marches; of Penelope I could not speak. She, in turn, knew the traditions of the Jewish people and taught me the psalms of their King David and the mystical poetry of his son, named Solomon, expressed in words of infinite tenderness and love. She also told me the story, which we had first heard in Jerusalem, of her ancestors brought to captivity in Babylon by Nebuchadnezzar, King of Babylon. They were freed by Cyrus, King of Kings of the Persians, and allowed to return to Jerusalem, but her own family had chosen to stay and live by the waters of Babylon. Her name was Aiysha and with her I found brief peace and happiness. I wrote to my father and I told him of Aiysha and of her gentleness and especially of her gift for music. She played a harp and the haunting music brought the peace of desert nights back into my heart and in Babylon I found healing in the sweetness of this daughter of Jerusalem. Many times we sat together on a terrace overlooking the River Euphrates as day gently merged with night. Together, we found amusement in the loud noise of huge frogs and we listened to the voice of the wind as it rattled in the palm trees. Above us, the ethereal moon rode high and blessed us with its gentle radiance and the stars illuminated the dark in sparkling glory. By such tranquil interludes is life made bearable and for such brief periods do we endure a thousand sorrows as we walk the stony road to death.

The expedition was in Babylon for about thirty days. As the men recovered strength from Gaugamela and the march from the battlefield, the nights were made loud with the noise of soldiers' revelries. The pleasure houses did a huge business and many Greek children would be raised in Babylon. Our men spent freely of their booty and they found that money purchases every favour, even those not willingly given.

Alexander's days were filled with the complex reorganisation of the government of Babylon. Mazaeus kept his job as satrap, in recognition of his surrender of the city to the king. Macedonians muttered angrily against Alexander's too generous treatment of defeated enemies, which was contrary to all the traditions of warfare. He appointed Macedonians to command the garrison and the fortress and to collect taxes, which further depleted the number of experienced officers in the expedition.

Alexander, with his new style of King of Babylon, made a ceremonial visit to the temple of Marduk. It was first destroyed by Sennacherib of Assyria and then by Cyrus, founder of the Persian Empire, and in the ruins the king offered a sacrifice to the Babylonian god. Macedonian voices were loud in protest as the Babylonian deity was a very different god from our Olympians. It seemed, however, that Alexander now denied us the ancient right of Macedonians to criticise their king and that stupendous success had conferred omnipotence upon him for we did not change him. Occasionally, the king relaxed and he and Craterus rode out to hunt lions. One such expedition nearly ended in tragedy, when a wounded beast turned the king's sword and it might easily have torn him apart but for the quick action of Craterus. In a fast movement, he rushed to the king's side and pierced the animal through its stomach with his sword and so saved Alexander. A plan of the incident was designed by an artist and sent to Pella, where I heard that a mosaic, from this design, was installed in the palace floor.

Amyntas, son of Andromenes, arrived in Babylon with mercenary reinforcements, sent by Antipater for the army. He also brought sons of noblemen, who were of an age to serve as pages to the king and they replaced those grown old enough to enroll in the cavalry. My idyll with Aiysha ended when we marched east to Susa. Its ephemeral quality had given it the charm of perfection for there was no time for her to discover my flaws. I shall always remember her gentle ways. We marched from Babylon to Babylonian music, with chanting magi waving censers of smoking incense, and the people decorated us with garlands of flowers. Wild beasts, gifts to Alexander, with their keepers, were added to the civilian train. The Chaldean magi became permanent members of the expedition and they read the stars and seasons and they practised many arcane arts in making their predictions to the king.

The farther east that we travelled, the more gaudy and gorgeous were the clothes of the leaders of the defeated people. Alexander was happy to march the army away from the corrupting influence of Babylon, and he again enjoyed, with many friends, the nights round our campfires. We marched for twenty days between the rivers Euphrates and Tigris, in the land called Mesopotamia. The villages were of sunbaked mud huts and we passed through reed-filled swamps inhabited by

183

people who built reed houses on small islands and showed us a way through the difficult terrain. We crossed stretches of desert where clumps of grass grew to a great height. We passed camel trains and often reality disappeared in the hazy heat, and we all saw trees, parks, palaces and lakes, but they existed only in the shimmering air. It was a land of heat and humidity, fly and mosquito-ridden and we suffered from a searing thirst, for our drinking water was severely rationed.

We crossed the Tigris and neared Susa, the capital of the Persian Empire. The city was the great climax of Alexander's conquests so far, for here Greek ambassadors had shamefully waited in antechambers as suppliants to the King of Kings. The king intended to wipe out the memory of their humiliation when he took possession of Susa.

Philoxenes, who had ridden in advance from Babylon, sent a messenger to the king confirming that he held Susa in Alexander's name. He also reported that the city's treasure was intact. The king immediately relayed the good news to the tired army and the spirits of the exhausted men quickly revived. They knew that, given Alexander's generosity, they would all be rich and have the independence that only money and land procure, all without the horrors and losses of another battle. I rode into the city at the side of Ptolemy and he spoke again of the girl whom he had left in Egypt. He asked my advice on whether he should send for her to join him in Susa. He added that his share of the plunder would allow her to travel in great comfort, escorted by armed men, and that he would have enough gold to buy her a magnificent house in the city. I cautioned him against premature action. We knew that the king planned to stay in Susa only for the time that it took to establish his government and to seize and distribute the contents of the treasury. The Egyptian girl would then be a stranger amongst hostile Persians and exiled from Egypt.

I also pointed out that we might be long gone before she arrived in the city. My advice was unwelcome to lovesick Ptolemy but sane enough to convince him to leave the girl in her homeland, amongst her own people by the River Nile. Alexander, riding Bucephalos, led our splendid entry into Susa, the ancient Elamite capital and power seat of the government of the Archaemenid Empire. The people stood in the streets in vast numbers, silent and afraid for they were mostly Persians and expected Greek vengeance to be their fate. The king rode first to the royal palace where the magnificent, tiled walls dazzled us with their reflected light. They were decorated with reliefs of winged lions, bulls, warriors and lawgivers who were forever arrested in poses of extravagant beauty.

We found Persian officials in the public halls of the palace. They wore robes of sumptuous beauty and their high headdresses gave them great height and dignity. We came as conquerors but the lavish, showy, magnificent splendour of the Persian court and city temporarily dazzled our wits and numbed our Macedonian pride.

In contrast to the Persian courtiers, Alexander entered the apadana, the great audience hall, dressed in the simple chiton and greaves of our own land and escorted only by his sword and shield-bearers. When he sat on the throne of Darius, he was too short for his feet to reach the ground and a footstool was hastily brought for his use. We marvelled at the height of Persia's kings. Later, we discovered that they also required a stool and the high throne raised them above all other men, a strange conceit, but a king's dignity often demands symbols of immortality and power. The barbarians are impressed by such tricks, but we Macedonians only admire leaders who have personal qualities that are far superior to the trappings of authority. The treasury of Susa contained a wealth of jewels, bullion, silver and minted coins beyond anything that we could have dreamed of possessing. We also found, above the price of gold, the sculptured figures of Harmodias and Aristogeitron, delivers of Athens from the tyrant Hipparchos and valued by every citizen in Greece. They were stolen from Athens by Xerxes. Alexander immediately gave them into the charge of an Athenian escort who returned them, in triumph, to their own city. By such signs did Alexander mean to show the Greeks that he fought the campaign for all of Greece against Persian oppressors.

Alexander ordered the mints in Susa to design and produce coinage with a representation of his own head and he declared that Persian money was illegal. He fixed the exchange rate, and the people were freely allowed to change their old coinage for the new with the representation of their new king. Alexander also freed a Persian general named Abulites, who had been imprisoned by Darius. The king, confident of his gratitude, appointed him satrap of the Elamite province but he, again, made Macedonians military governors and collectors of the taxes. Alexander arranged for the government of other conquered territories. Menes left Susa to become the governor of Cilicia with Syria and with Phoenicia included in his province. Alexander was satisfied with the work of Cleomenes in Egypt, Mazaeus in Babylon and, most importantly, with Antigonas in Phrygia, who controlled all the land to the Hellespont, and guarded the strait to Greece. And the law of Alexander was firmly in place in all the provinces west of Susa.

When the king had arranged the affairs of empire, he was free to visit the Persian Royal Family of Darius. The Persian queen was dead, but to Sisygambis, her mother and also the mother of Darius, and to the royal children, he gave a palace and adequate funds for them to live in comfort and security in their own city. He appointed tutors for the children and he gave orders for their lessons to be taught in Athenian Greek. Their long ordeal was over and Alexander said an emotional farewell to them all, especially to Queen Sisygambis.

Parmeneion, Craterus, Ptolemy, Hephaestion and others of the king's friends, including Coenos and myself, gathered in the throne room the night before we marched from Susa. We looked out to where the setting sun turned the distant Zagros Mountains into peaks of fire. It was already late in the year and there was a welcome coolness in the wind blowing through the palace, as we talked of our days in Persian Susa. The army had been reorganised into smaller formations, which was intended to give us greater mobility and the experience of command to a greater number of officers. There were many new recruits, and they were distributed amongst seasoned soldiers, and we discussed these changes before our talk turned to the Persians, their religion and different ways of life.

We understood that they believed in only one god whom they called Ahuru-Mazda, revealed to them by his prophet, Zoroastra, and they reverenced particularly his element, fire. Unlike our Greek pantheon, the Persian god made man his chief concern and to each he gave a value in soul as well as in body. The Persians, as a consequence, did not enslave conquered people whose customs they often adapted to their own ways, and they were always anxious to learn, especially of arts new to them. The priests of their religion taught truth as the greatest virtue and they punished crimes of perjury with the utmost severity.

Corrupt officials, especially judges, were flayed alive until they were dead. We heard of one famous case in which King Cambyses had forced a man to sit on a chair covered with his venal father's skin. We learned that fundamental to the Persians' beliefs was that god and man were co-joined in constant conflict with the spirit of evil. They also believed that justice must be impartial, regardless of poverty, and they especially showed mercy to slaves for a first offence.

We were totally absorbed in our discussion and we sat far into the night until we whispered of the discontent of Macedonian officers at the appointment of so many Persians to high office. We openly despised above all the servile proskynesis, practised by the Persians, which obliged a man to fall humbly on one knee and kiss the king's hand. Persians deferred to Alexander in this revolting way and by his acquiescence in such homage and all his new titles, he drew away from us and we were appalled. Macedon was now but a fragment of his vast empire and we Macedonians a small minority of the people over whom he ruled.

The king joined us and, when he was seated, Philip's old friend and our most respected general, Parmenion, addressed him in solemn words: "O! Alexander, your Macedonians watch the distance grown between you and them with very heavy hearts. They see our enemy given high offices, against all the rules of war. Our men have fought for you and with you, and suffered great hardships and they have buried many friends and endured the privations of the campaign far away from their homes and families. They do not like Persian customs, nor do they wish to become Persians. They have conquered, for you, Alexander, a mighty empire and they would like to share the sweeter parts of victory."

In the tense silence, Alexander had listened and then he spoke: "Parmenion, when my father lived you were his greatest general; you shared his thoughts and helped execute his dreams. I do you honour for this and for the additional service which you have given to me. Now we know very different circumstances, for we have not only Greeks who share our way of life and believe in the same gods, speak the same language and share a common history, but peoples removed from us by these and many other barriers. We must use Persians, who know the customs of the people and can pacify them into submission to our rule, in order to bring stable government, and for the safety of the expedition as we march on, for we are far fewer in numbers than those whom we have conquered.

"When I arrange for the government of a conquered province, I am not the son of Philip, King of Macedon, but the son of Zeus/ Ammon and king of a foreign land. I must fulfill my destiny, prophesied by many oracles and seers. The conquered people would not accept Alexander of Macedon as their ruler; I therefore take the guise of the god-king to secure their recognition. I am no less king in Macedon and, in that office, my ways are the ways of Macedonians. If Macedonians desire to share, more fully, in the rule of the conquered territories, they must change and adopt many of the customs of the people or I am compelled to appoint rulers familiar with the conventions of the local government and religion. I show mercy to conquered Persians who willingly surrender to me, and I confirm them in power in order to take away any incentive, which they may harbour to rise up against us, when we have gone beyond their territory. We have saved many Macedonian lives by making peace and avoiding battles and I have always appointed Macedonians to watch over the Persians in my absence. I will not have my advance halted by intrigue in our rear, or our supply lines threatened by marauding gangs of unpacified dissidents; nor do I intend to waste the riches of our treasury on revolts against us in the cities. We have peace in the lands which we have taken because I rule through Persians known to the local people. How long do you think that it would last if I came bringing only the conqueror's sword?"

As the king finished speaking, we all looked towards Parmenion. He was old and defeated by the policies of a much younger man which were contrary to all his own laws for the conduct of war. They had proved, however, only too successful in the administration of Alexander's new and vast empire. I thought that the king tried to conceal his impatience with old ideas, because of the general's boundless service in the past, rather than acknowledge his contribution to the present campaign. I reflected that it cannot be easy to grow old and realise that a new generation has taken your place and the high service, so faithfully rendered, now commands only an irritated gratitude.

I was a little disturbed by the king's speech. All my life, Parmenion had been the close friend of my father, honoured by him and honoured by King Philip and all other Macedonians. I was relieved that my father was now retired for, had he been present, he must have felt a very bitter distress to see his old friend so deeply humiliated. Parmenion replied to Alexander with great dignity, saying: "Sire, there is no doubt that you are king and rule with absolute authority. Beware lest the gods grow jealous of your increasing power for they may destroy you. In trying to please all men, eventually there may be many who make common cause against you. I was honoured with the trust, confidence and friendship of your noble father and because he was your father and I know of no other who may have sired you, you may command my duty until my life has run its course. I also see it as part of my duty to speak out against whatever I consider might threaten your advance. I have come this far with you to destroy the Persian King of Kings and now that much is accomplished, I remain uncertain whether you can build and hold an empire in these exotic lands so far from home. However, wherever you go, there will I also go using only my best endeavours to carry out your plans and satisfy your ambitions. You should mark what I say, Alexander, for I speak without regard for my own safety. Do not trust the Persians, their allies or vassals, for they must hate the fall of their own empire and the end of their power in the world and they will seek to destroy you. Building an empire is the easiest part of this expedition. To hold it, a man needs more than mortal powers. Gods and man grow jealous and will plot against you; with a cup of poison, a quick sword thrust, by stealth in the night or even in the bold confidence of day, and ambition will be stilled as, in great grief, we saw was done in the death of Philip, our King, in Macedon."

Alexander's face had hardened and he flushed at Parmenion's brave words. Much of the old equality we had enjoyed with the king was now gone and the time was long passed since he had heard such frank words or arguments challenging his policies and ambitions. He spoke quietly in reply however: "Parmenion, I must be grateful for your council and now I tell you that, if I wish for any more of your advice, I will send for you. I cannot live by my father's ambitions, for he is dead and not part of this expedition, and I have sole responsibility for its success or failure. Nor can I be bound by King Philip's general's limited vision. I did not know that you were in my mother's bedchamber at my conception and I have her word for it that I am the son of Zeus.

I am also acknowledged by all the conquered people as their king and, in Egypt, the son of their god. I acknowledge that my high destiny rides upon the world in fulfilment of the oracles' prophecies and that whomever opposes Alexander opposes the gods, and must surely know their wrath."

We were silent. Apart from Hephaestion, who shared every thought of the king's, the rest of us were plain Macedonians, not able to respond to mysticism or comprehend the distinctions by which Alexander divided his life. On this day, Parmenion had spoken for many of us and there was a general unease at the bold assumptions in the king's words. Coenus spoke up amidst murmurs of approval: "Sire, we have great reason to admire Parmenion. At all the battles and sieges since we crossed the Hellespont under your command, he has led us to many victories. In Macedon, his fame and esteem are surpassed only by your own. From being an outside state on the borders of Greece, under King Philip, he brought Macedon to the leadership of Greece which made possible all that has since been won from the Persians. I would indeed shame my father and his house were I now to remain silent. If there is no justice for Macedonians, the barbarians will fare the worse and then, as Parmenion says, will plot to rid themselves of Macedon's king."

We murmured approval and admired Coenus for such frank speech and honest words by which he might even risk his life. The atmosphere was tense, as before the moment when a mighty storm is about to drown the earth and then the king relaxed a little and said to Coenus: "The air is full of the advice and opinions and even wisdom of my friends. I value you all, especially when you speak your minds; Alexander knows the worth of honest advice. I intend no disrespect towards Parmenion and I need him for the future as in the past. We have reached the time for honest exchanges of thought and if we disagree on matters in degree, we are all surely agreed to march on the morrow for Persepolis. Therefore let us save our energies for use against the Persians in our path and stand united before the world.

"Together, we have achieved much, but there is still much more for us to do. We must seize the heart of Persia and when we take Persepolis, we take the world. I give you all goodnight and wish you many pleasant dreams."

The king had ended the discussion leaving many of our doubts unresolved and he dismissed our fears as though they were of no great importance to him. Neither Parmenion nor Coenus was ever motivated by any ambition other than the king's service and we continued to speak of Alexander's ambitions after he had left the hall. Parmenion had bravely voiced the fears of many of those present that last night in Susa. To serve in a great cause is often justification for the horrors of war and all its privations, but to serve the ambitions of one man enslaves in blind servitude.

Hephaestion had departed with the king. I walked the courtyards of the palace with Craterus, Ptolemy and Coenus. We admired the beautiful building, its gardens and its great sculptures and then we went out amongst the crowds who thronged the streets; they were from every corner of the world. There were Arabs, Jews, Edomites, Moabites, Canaanites, Philistines, Syrians, Hittites, Bactrians, Areians, Asiatics, Assyrians, Cappadocians, Cilicians, Egyptians and even a few Greeks; they were representatives from all the satrapies of Persia. Missing only were the Persians who were afraid of the vengeance of their former subjects and they had stayed within their own doors.

Susa's history goes back before Agamemnon and the Trojan War. The city stands high above the surrounding plain and it is built on the layers of previous ruins. Here, Persian law was codified with that of the Medes and sent out, never to be changed, when Cyrus, the Archaemenid, first seized power. Royal messengers had carried the laws to every satrapy of his empire travelling along the Royal Road from Susa to Gordion and Sardis and now the road belonged to Alexander. His messengers travelled with his orders to all the conquered provinces. We stood where the road began and I thought of the fleeting days of empires and of all that had happened since Sardis and Gordion had submitted to the king.

I thought, too, of all that we had seen in Susa, of the Persian Magi who interpreted signs from smoking incense, oil in water and in the casting of lots. They inscribed curses on clay cylinders and practised every occult art and I wondered how they secretly treated the name of Alexander.

Coenus was silent after his exchange with the king, and he remained thoughtful until we reached a crowded tavern. After a few cups of wine we were easily led to a pleasure house next door. The girl was black and very young. She told me that she came from southern Egypt and had been brought to Susa by a merchant and that after his death, she found the pleasure house

191

her only way to survival. Purchased pleasures have melancholy in their price and I gave the girl double the asking price as I felt that the world had meanly used an orphaned child.

Chapter 19

The following day the entire expedition left Susa for the lands in the south east. We soon discovered that the local tribes opposed our advance, when they attacked us at night. They crept into our camp and stole horses, provisions and even a few women. Our guards captured some prisoners, who begged for their lives and had the temerity to cry that they only desired peace with Alexander and all the Greeks. They audaciously put a price on their peace by demanding the equivalent of the bribe money that they had customarily received from Darius. For their impudence, the king sent swift detachments to hunt and kill members of their tribes, until their will was broken and the whole province of Susa, to the Zagros Mountains, was pacified.

We studied the geographers' detailed charts and found that there was only one pass marked through the mountains. To add to our problems, local spies informed us that the pass was extremely narrow and already held by a large force of Persians, Sogdians and Mardians led by Ariobarzanes, the Satrap of Persis and a commander at the Battle of Gaugamela. It was obvious that Ariobarzanes could cut us all down as we entered the pass, which I believe that the enemy called 'The Persian Gates'. Alexander's usual good fortune held, as a rebel prisoner now volunteered, probably hoping to save his own life, that he knew of an alternative route through the mountains. After intense questioning of the prisoner, Alexander set off, taking the informant with him, and a small detachment to circumvent the Persians and attack them from their rear.

It was already winter again and the snows lay deep upon the mountains and we left the civilian expedition in the foothills when part of the army marched towards the entry to the pass.

We waited several days before we heard the clamour of battle, which was our signal to advance and attack the Persians, in their rear, as they defended themselves against the king. He had taken them completely by surprise and after we joined the attack, there was a bloody battle until their remnants fled the field and the pass was Alexander's.

We counted our dead, and when this sad task was completed we joined the king in his tent and he told us that the way that he had taken through the mountains was not a path and that he had lost many men in ice and rockfalls and others had slipped over precipices to their deaths in the icy wastes below. We listened in silence, but we were close again that night in the victory of battle and our common losses. The expedition struggled to join us and once again we had food, tents and clothing to help deal with the bitter cold. The wind howled in winter's fury and our road forward was mostly concealed under drifts of snow and our clothes froze to our bodies, in an icy embrace, until we marched down the mountains and reached Persepolis.

We found a party of Greeks wandering over the plain. They were half-mad with pain, for they had been horribly mutilated by the Persians to prevent them deserting and finding service with the king. We were sickened by their wounds and their howls of protest as our physicians tried to dress their injuries and, as we amputated their shattered limbs, they filled the air with awful screams. Alexander detailed a strong escort to take them to Susa to gain strength enough before they returned to Greece, and he gave them a generous bounty to take care of all their future needs.

Alone in the night, I thought of the king's generous treatment of those Greeks who had served in the army of Darius. I wondered, secretly, if he had acted on a forgiving impulse or if he calculated the effect on Greece when they reached their native cities and they praised Alexander for his compassion and magnanimity. If this were so, I thought that I had lived my life in the shadow of a tyrant, to whom I had given my willing service as an accomplice in all that he did. Yet now I mourn him, with an aching grief, for he was greater than any man in all the aeons of time and especially because he was my friend. I grieve for him in misery and anguish, for my days are lonely from his death and my nights dark with sombre melancholy from the loss of him and so many other friends. We reached

Persepolis. I had seen the great splendours of Athens, the rougher cities of Anatolia, the mighty pyramids and wondrous temples of Egypt, the faded glories of Babylon and the stately beauty of Susa, and now Persepolis, which was the most splendid of them all. The foundations of the city were raised on a vast platform high above the level of the plain. It seemed to float in the air, dominating the land from every direction as it looked across to the wild and desolate mountains which were the burial place of the Archaemenid Kings of Persia.

Approaching the palace from the east, a wide staircase, decorated with reliefs of the Persians' Kings, Immortals, courtiers and tribute bearers from every satrapy of the empire, led up through halls to the vast apadana, which was the audience chamber of the palace. The straight road from the south approached another broad staircase, with shallow risers to facilitate the dignified entrance of the King of Kings, followed by his army, courtiers and family. The monumental scale of the city was for the sole glory of the Great King and his empire. Mighty columns of extravagant wood soared to support the sumptuously decorated roof, and sculptured, mythical beasts towered above, to dwarf us into insignificance. The surface of all the walls was richly carved with scenes of Persian majesty. A relief of Darius, with his son Xerxes, surpassed in beauty everything that I had previously seen. The name of the Great King was scratched, in Greek, above his head and I wondered whose hand had dared to blemish so perfect a work of art.

At sunset, it seemed, every day a mist rolled in from the mountains shrouding the massive buildings and softening them into an ethereal wonderland in that harsh wilderness. During the day, by contrast, the strong sun illuminated the temples and palaces, decorations and columns of Persepolis into a city of royal strength and power. I thought it ironic that we, rough Macedonians, should look upon this ostentatious symbol of Persian extravagance and yet take it for our own. In those days, when the air was clear, a light shone upon Alexander in Persepolis. He was favoured of the gods, bold in all his undertakings, brave beyond any fable and, unlike the heroes of myth, alive amongst us. I felt his reflection glowing upon us all and making us greater men for serving such a king.

Alexander, in elaborate ceremonies, took possession of the treasury of Persepolis. It was overflowing with gold, priceless ornaments, exquisitely worked vessels and platters and mountains of coins and jewels and unminted bullion. A treasure almost beyond the wit of man to comprehend.

The king paid the army and gave each man a generous bonus. He sent money to finance the work in his city on the coast of Egypt, more treasure to build or repair temples in the cities of Greece and all the conquered satrapies and bullion to finance the government and army in Macedon.

Alexander minted a vast number of coins, impressed with his own likeness, to stimulate trade and bring prosperity to every corner of the empire. He reasoned that the more wealth people enjoyed, the less likely would they be to plot revolution in his rear, for a man in search of personal treasure had no time for the mischief of politics and government. He also distributed the wealth of Persepolis, with bounties to the soldiers and generous gifts to the civilians attached to the army. A messenger arrived from Antipater; he brought a letter confirming the defeat of King Agis of Sparta and declaring that all Greece was now at peace. By the same messenger, the king also received a letter from Olympias, the queen. She repeated all her previous complaints against Antipater, protesting that she was held as his prisoner and demanding to rule Macedon as his co-regent or travel to join the king. Alexander ignored both her complaints and her demands. We were gathered with the king one morning, breaking the night's fast with bread, meats, fruit and diluted wine, when a guard rushed into the small hall shouting that one of the palace sculptures had been mutilated in the night. The king left hurriedly to personally inspect the damage. We discovered that a relief, representing a man bowing before his king in the proskynesis, had been hacked almost beyond repair with both figures equally defaced. Alexander demanded that the culprit be found and brought before him, but luckily for him, the criminal was never found for the king judged that this was no ordinary act of defiance but a protest against his adoption of Persian customs. He never referred to the incident again.

The king and Craterus left Persepolis for many days to explore and hunt in the surrounding countryside. Alexander gave a banquet for hundreds of people, including Persians, when he returned to the palace. We were served on plates of gold and our wine was passed to us in golden goblets decorated with the mythical beasts of Persia. Jewels glittered everywhere and the

Persians' clothing was the richest that I had ever seen in texture and colour. There were many courtesans present that night in Persepolis, of whom the most beautiful was the Athenian, Thais. The scene was of such sumptuous and barbarous extravagance and splendour that I felt as a stranger and especially ill at ease under the scrutiny of the Persian kings, who looked down upon us almost with contempt. They were frozen in statues and reliefs of immense dignity and elegance. The feast was over and wine was passing freely amongst us when I overheard Hephaestion say to the king: "Alexander! You owe it to Athens and all Greece to destroy this city of Xerxes in revenge for the destruction of Greek cities and temples by the Persians."

The king laughed in response; I think that he was a little drunk with power as well as wine. He now occupied Persepolis, the spiritual heart of Persia, where her kings were crowned and their funeral rites recited by her fire-priests. It was also the place where the enormous treasury of the Archaemenid House was stored, which they had stolen from the conquered lands. We discovered that most of it had belonged to the unfortunate King Croesos of Lydia after he defied the Oracle of Delphi and crossed the River Halys. Hephaestion continued speaking, backed by Thais, who coiled herself on the king's couch, a brazen, wanton temptress: "This palace is the centre of the world from which the King of Kings claims every corner of the earth. The power of Persia will vanish for ever when it is destroyed."

Silence descended on the assembly as men listened and they heard the mischief intended by Hephaestion and Thais. Many were already drunk and ready for vengeance after the hard campaign, and now the heady wine of victories in battle, separation from homes and families and, not least, the loss of so many friends all worked against reason. I think that there was a madness in the air that night. We were already enslaved by our successes and power and gold. I dimly knew that Persepolis was glorious in its majestic splendour and a unique and holy place to countless people and that to destroy it could only be an act of the most wanton folly. Hephaestion's influence on the king was sometimes sinister. He was very handsome with fair hair curling round a broad brow. His height gave him an advantage over most men, and he had the appearance of the northern tribes who invaded Macedon and Greece when the world was young. He excelled in athletics and he was a brilliant scholar but he gave his friendship to no man, except the king, from whom he bore the special title 'Friend of Alexander'. His devotion to the king was extreme and perfect; they were as necessary to each other as breath and water are to life. Hephaestion excelled as a soldier but even with these virtues, other men were reticent and discreet in his company.

Craterus, a much simpler man, also bore a special title, 'Friend of the King'. He enjoyed hunting, good company, wine, women and especially camp life. His Macedonian ancestry gave him a ready appreciation of all good things in life. He was generous with his friends, quick to laugh and slow to anger and, above all, swift to make decisions for the benefit of the whole campaign. He was a man with whom to enjoy the good and share the bad in this very uncertain world ruled by inevitable Fate.

His eyes narrowed as he listened to Hephaestion but he waited for the king to speak and Alexander said: "I came to Persepolis to destroy Persian power and how better to demonstrate to the people that this is accomplished, than to consume its throne in flames? Even so, until I catch Darius, he remains a symbol of that power. He may hide in his mountains, a fugitive from our wrath, but he shall never again rally an army from the apadana of Persepolis nor pay his Greek mercenaries with money hoarded in the treasury here. Give me a torch and I will light the sacred fire."

Craterus rose to his feet and stepped before the king, shouting: "Sire, do not match the barbarism that we came to avenge with new barbarities. Let Alexander's fame rest on mighty deeds, not on acts of destruction. You found no resistance from the people here, therefore show them clemency. Olynthos, Thebes, Tyre and Gaza knew the wrath of Alexander. Do not now confuse the annihilation of those cities with the mercy shown to others who willingly surrendered to you."

Hephaestion answered him scornfully: "Craterus, do not be faint of heart. The king's power is absolute and he may choose his methods for subduing the Persian. When Persepolis burns in the ritual fire, all Persian resistance must turn to ashes. Their roads lead here and Darius will no longer look to the city for support. The sacred flames will tell his people that a new king reigns. Let the fire be placed in Alexander's hands."

The atmosphere in the great hall was charged and shouts went up: "A torch! A torch! Give Alexander a torch."

Parmenion rose and walked before the king to say: "Craterus advises you well, O! Alexander and it is madness to destroy what is now your own!"

Hephaestion laughed and waved him away and the shouting grew louder and louder and the harlot, Thais, brought the first torch and gave it to Alexander. She was followed by other dancers, all bearing flames on high. I shall ever be convinced that Thais seized a torch and was the first to set the fire beneath the throne of Darius but Alexander, wine-drunk, and laughing shrilly, was swift to follow the wanton's lead. Parmenion shook his head and left the great hall; I followed him and behind me came Craterus and Black Cleitus. We walked away from the palace and turned to watch the flames as they leapt towards the sky. The roaring sound of fire grew like thunder and the black smoke billowed towards us as we silently stood regretting Alexander's worst deed; but he had fulfilled his promise as written to Darius after the Battle of Issos, to destroy the seat of Persia's power.

We shortly discovered that once the king had fired the perfect Hall of a Thousand Columns, he was overcome with remorse and he ordered the men to douse the surrounding buildings with water to prevent the spread of the flames, but the great columned hall was scorched ashes. The following day, after this barbarous act, Alexander withdrew into silence. He expressed no regret, as he had after the destruction of Thebes; instead, he asked Craterus to join him on a lion hunt. They left the acrid, smoking ruin and thus the king avoided enduring the reproach for his reckless deed in the destruction of Persepolis. Before he rode away, he ordered all the native, young men of Persepolis to enrol in his army and he banished Thais from his presence and from the court forever. During the king's absence, I rode towards the mountains to visit the sepulchre of Darius the Great. As I approached, I saw that the rock surrounding the tomb was carved with a parade of soldiers and covered with inscriptions, no doubt giving the record of the history of the Medes and Persians. I dismounted and in the lonely silence I felt myself sympathetic to the Persian way of Zarathustra and his boundless god and that, in coming this way, I must become a small part of the mystery of life, in the continuing march of all the human generations. The vastness of the great plain and the towering mountains dwarfed each man and his endeavours into the secrets of infinity. The silence was so great that the movements of my horse were magnified, and the least fall of rock was an avalanche of sound. It was spring, and tiny wild flowers thrust their way through the inhospitable earth. Insects crawled across the land and the sun shone on the smoke rising from Persepolis and gave a harsh reality to the metaphors of philosophy and the mysteries of religion.

I reluctantly returned to Persepolis and discovered that the Persians interpreted the burning of the city as a sign from heaven that the Archaemenid dynasty had been replaced by a new king, which bloodless victory partly justified the fire. Alexander had been accepted in Susa and all the satrapies but I feared that he took Persepolis from the seed of his own self-destruction, which is as much a part of the nature of man as high purpose and noble ideals. The king returned to the city and the last trace of winter had gone from the land. The wild winds were tamed to gentle breezes as the army marched north to Parsagadae, the birthplace and capital city of Cyrus the Great, founder of the Persian Empire. We crossed the dusty plain, a limitless waste, where we only occasionally met a nomadic caravan or a boy with a few goats and sheep. Summer advanced and it was not easy to see how the people found sufficient grazing for their animals or enough water for them to drink. It rarely rained and when the cooling showers came, the earth turned into a sea of mud, which quickly dried into hard clay under the scorching sun.

We sometimes saw nomads, with their black tents lined with bright, colourful rugs. They were woven and dyed by their women from the wool of their flocks into elaborate designs. The tribes had few possessions; the animals were their wealth, except for their finely-worked, copper cooking pots. Their camps looked lonely in the empty vastness of this land, but they seemed contented with their simple life.

We climbed into the mountains, to reach the valley of Parsagadae, where we found that most of the buildings were empty and in ruins, a sad, silent memorial to Cyrus. There were a few priests living in the abandoned city whose sole duty was to guard the great king's tomb. They wandered like shades in the ruined halls of the palaces. A winged genie looked down on us from a high column in mournful solitude, but from the earth delicate flowers blossomed amongst the fallen stones.

We found the tomb of Cyrus, in a neglected park, beside a

broad stream. His bones lay inside, on the bare and dusty earth. When Alexander saw the desecration, for he was ever mindful of the respect due to even a dead king, he angrily ordered the priests to be brought before him. When they were fearfully grouped in his presence, he pointed to the inscription above the door, which read: 'O man, I am Cyrus, Founder of the Empire of Persia and King of Asia, therefore begrudge me not this monument'.

And he put Aristobus in charge of the priests with instructions to clean and repair the tomb and to restore the body of Cyrus inside the sarcophagus. He assured them that any neglect of this duty, from now onward, he would punish with the utmost severity. I returned to the desecrated tomb that evening and felt a melancholy chill. Parsagadae is a place of past majesty and too lonely and neglected for the tomb of such a king. We rested for a few days in the 'Camp of the Persians' and during this time we celebrated the king's twenty-sixth birthday with parades and games, and we continued to feast in the king's tent far into the night.

A spy brought news of Darius to Parsagadae. He reported that the Persian had now reached Ecbatana, below the mountains of Media, where he was recruiting a new army. The spy added that Darius expected Alexander to return to Persepolis from Parsagadae and that he planned an attack against us as soon as we reached that city. Darius had also considered an alternative plan to retreat to the remote lands of the north east, scorching all the crops as far as Bactria if the king advanced to Ecbatana. Alexander closely questioned the man and when he had satisfied himself that the spy's information was genuine, he gave orders for the army to march at once in search of Darius. We took the road north, through the valleys of the Zagros Mountains, and as summer advanced, the scorching heat of the sun reflected back from the earth in shimmering waves and we burned as if in a furnace. Some of our men died suddenly with fever, their tongues swollen and blackened and their eyes sunk deep in their heads. We had very little water to relieve our terrible thirst and we all craved salt but none was available to us. Tribesmen, who lived high in the mountains, rode down to plague us and force us to fight constant skirmishes against them. The king sent small, swift-mounted detachments to subdue them, but there always seemed more of them and we lost too many good men in fruitless action.

An ever-growing army of spies brought us news that Darius was mustering a large army using recruits from all the tribes of the north and east of the old Persian Empire. More ominously, we discovered that his cavalry had found him again after he had fled from Alexander, following the battles of Issos and Gaugamela.

The king held a council of war and reported that: "Darius is preparing to meet us in battle once more; therefore we must hurry to find him before his new army is trained for war. Some of his generals, I have heard, are now ready to desert him and they plot to ride to Bactria and to make Bessus, a kinsman of Darius, the satrap of that province, and their new king. I have decided that we must advance more swiftly; therefore most of the army will go ahead of the supply train and of all the civilians. To protect them, I shall leave with them detachments of both the cavalry and the infantry, under the command of Cleitus, who will guard them from attacks from the pestilential tribesmen. We shall no longer pursue these into the mountains and the women and children, at all times, shall walk between detachments of soldiers and all the equipment will be used, as usual, to encircle their tents at night. Cleitus will post soldiers beyond the baggage carts to maintain a constant watch for the protection of the people and the safety of our supplies.

"I now mean to finish Darius. If he fights, I shall kill him, if he surrenders, he will be my prisoner, and if he flees again, I shall pursue him wherever he may go. We are only three days from the city of Ecbatana and three days from our final victory. After that, I shall, in truth, be the new Great King of all the Persian Empire which is bounded only by the limitless Ocean."

We reached Ecbatana and to our surprise, the chief citizens came out to greet the king. They told him that Darius, with the satraps of the eastern provinces, a cavalry force of 3,000, double that number of infantry detachments, and a vast treasure had left the city four days in advance of our arrival. Alexander's quarry had once more eluded him. The king was bitterly disappointed, and he immediately sent back a large detachment of the army to escort the civilian train to Ecbatana. The rest of us prepared a camp for their arrival and to shelter our supplies. Ecbatana in Media is on the road from Babylon to Hyrcania and we were again dazzled by the glories of a Persian city. The great palaces were decorated in gold and silver and the supporting beams of the buildings were made from cedars brought over the long road from Lebanon. The temples were sumptuously decorated, even though the fire-altars were outside the walls, in accordance with the Persian belief that this gave them closer communion with their universal god, Ahuru-Mazda, and his prophet, Zoroaster or Zarathustra.

There were public gardens throughout the city, which were oases of exotic flowers, fruits and quiet walks and decorated with pools of water and tiled pavilions. Even in daily life, the people used vessels of gold, exquisitely decorated with birds, animals and designs from geometry. I purchased a few worked pieces and sent them to my father. I knew that he would enjoy the elegance of abstract shapes in Persian art, in contrast to the flowing human forms of Greek art. Cleitus and the civilians soon arrived in Ecbatana and the army was again united and ready to train to fight Darius once more. Alexander paraded every unit before him and addressed us all, saying: "The gods have been with us constantly on our road from Macedon and Greece and they are now ready to give us the final victory over our enemy, who again has taken flight from my invincible army.

"We left our homeland, as you all know, to avenge the destruction brought on us and our cities by Persian kings and to end their constant threats of war against us. We have succeeded in that purpose. I have therefore decided to release from further service all the troops of the Greek allies. They will receive their full pay on the journey until they reach their own cities, when they will be given their part of the great treasures which we have together taken from the Persians. Properly spent, they will have enough to make them independent for life and free of any future labour. I now go in pursuit of Darius, wherever he is hiding, and when I have taken him, I shall also be Great King of this eastern empire.

"If, however, any Greeks desire to remain with me, you may enlist as mercenaries, since I now consider that your service to your own cities is at an end. Should you decide to continue the campaign in my army, you will be very welcome and the equal of the Persians who have joined me. As you know, they are given opportunity to serve in every military and civilian capacity. We do not have enough administrators to fill more than a few of the vacancies and civilians are welcome to undertake these duties.

"I intend that Persia will become an independent ally of

Macedon under my rule. I consider that in order to hold the loyalty of the people, it is essential that Persians take part in their own government. They shall advise me on their laws of justice, their religion and their learning and customs. Ahead of us lies completely unfamiliar territory, and very different peoples who are strangers to our ways. Therefore we shall observe some of their customs as they must abide by many of ours. These then are my orders.

"Parmenion, with 6,000 Macedonians, will return to Persepolis to collect the treasure which we left in the custody of Harpalos, and he will bring it here to Ecbatana.

"Epillocos will command the allied soldiers returning to Greece, and he will take sufficient funds to pay them on the journey and to dispense their final bounty. He will make arrangements for obtaining all the supplies that he will need on the march, to hire ships to cross the Hellespont, and for the journey across Thrace, until all the men under his command have dispersed to their own cities.

"Here in Asia an advance party from my army will go into the satrapy of Hyrcania, to a city named Rhagae, which is not far from the Caspian Gates, and there prepare a camp for the rest of the expedition.

" Craterus will command and reorganise the army here in Ecbatana, in preparation for the march north and the final battle against Darius.

"And now, I say to those of you who are returning to their homes, you have served Alexander well and you have brought great credit to your own cities. I tell you to go with light hearts and heavy purses and tell your children of all the days when you marched with Alexander across Asia, and broke the Persian yoke.

"I must also speak to those Greeks who decide to join me. I give you welcome, but this is no longer the war of the Greek cities against Persia, but Alexander's settlement with Darius for personal injuries. I intend to establish a new empire on the ashes of the old.

"Finally, in memory of Macedon's fallen, we shall erect here a copy of the Lion of Khaeronia, that all men may pay homage to our dead."

The king rode away from the parade ground and the men were dismissed. But they remained standing together in dismay at Alexander's words. A great noise rose amongst them as they tried to understand the real meaning behind his speech. He had changed the entire course of the war and excluded the Greek allies from any part of his future conquests, even from the fate of Darius, and they would be denied the fruits of victory which he had previously shared with them. I know that many of the Greeks felt that, far from rendering service to their own cities, Alexander had used them only to fulfill his own ambitions and that he now unceremoniously dismissed them with the contemptuous alternative of mercenary service. To him alone would belong the glory of the final victory against the Persians.

I walked away with Craterus from the angry men. He told me that he was most disturbed by his own appointment from the king, because it must challenge the status of Parmenion in the army. The old general, full of years and service, was now relegated to a secondary position, even if Alexander had not yet taken from him the title of Commander in Chief. We discussed the king's plan to continue the campaign, for most of us had expected to return to Macedon, and especially did we talk about his intention to found a new empire and a separate alliance with Persia. Alexander held a banquet that night; I arrived at his tent with Coenus and we saw in shocked amazement that he was wearing Persian dress and that he had also assumed the royal purple of the Persian kings. Even worse, there were many Persians present in his company and they sniggered behind their hands at Macedonians gathered in uneasy groups, as they enjoyed the courtesies and attention now bestowed on them by the king.

Macedonian faces hardened as they looked at the barbaric scene before them lit by a thousand torches, which shone on gaudy, Persian robes and illuminated their dark faces and beards as they clustered round the king. Many took their leave of Alexander at the end of the feast when the wine had only once been passed amongst us. Alexander was always swift to take advantage of military, diplomatic or civilian opportunities to advance his position, but his assumption of the hated Persian style betrayed us all. We were Macedonians, conquerors of the world, and we felt that this was the proud part which the king should take and by affecting the dress and manners of the defeated enemy, he slighted all who had served him.

By the time that Parmenion returned to Ecbatana, the

command of the army had smoothly passed to Craterus, which left the old general only in charge of communications between the king, Macedon and the satrapies, and supplies, which were commandeered and paid for as we advanced. We left Ecbatana and marched into the rising sun along the Royal Road and across the waterless steppe, until we observed mountains looming on the distant horizon. As we drew close to Rhagae, we saw that the mountain peaks were covered in snow, despite the terrible heat, which we endured on the plain. We heard that they were the barrier between our position and the Hyrcanian Sea. We camped long enough in Rhagae for Alexander to study all the many new reports brought to him by spies and his advance scouts. We learned that Darius had fled once more. This time, he had taken the road through the mountain pass, known to the local people as the Caspian Gates, towards the Hyrcanian or Caspian Sea. We also heard that Bessus, his kinsman, and the satrap of Bactria, Barsaentes, also a kinsman, and several other eastern satraps were with him but that many others, especially those from the western satrapies, who had heard of the benevolence of Alexander towards other Persian governors, had deserted their Great King.

Alexander appointed Oxadrates, a Persian, as the satrap of ancient Media and he safeguarded his loyalty with a Macedonian in command of the army detachments, which he left to garrison the city. The king took a small detachment of the cavalry in pursuit of Darius. I rode with Alexander and in two days we reached the Caspian Gates where we were met by Antibelus, a son of Mazaeus, and Baghistanes. They saluted the king with the miserable proskynesis, which we forgot when we heard their sordid story of duplicity and treason. They told us that Bessus, Narzabarnes and Barsaentes had plotted together and arrested Darius as they all fled towards Hyrcania. After this miserable deed, Bessus was saluted as their new king by the other two. They were supported by Persian cavalry and other units of Darius' army. To their credit, the Greek mercenaries, under Artabazus, had tried to aid Darius but, when they failed, they had fled to save their own lives. Many other Persian chieftains had deserted with their men. They fled to their homelands and then we were told of the final treachery plotted by Bessus. He intended to use Darius as a hostage, to bargain with Alexander for his own confirmation as satrap of Bactria. How little the

Bactrian knew Alexander of Macedon. The king was furiously outraged by the Persian's treachery to his king, and he set off in immediate pursuit to rescue Darius from his betrayers. He abandoned his intention to seize the Persian king and condemn him to death. For Darius, a king must still command the respect of his own people or all kings might fall.

We rode swiftly through country a little like Macedon, with rivers and streams running through verdant valleys. We crossed primitive bridges which were intended for the slow passage of nomads and their animals. A few of them collapsed and we lost men and horses as they fell beyond our rescue in the dark night. We could not halt our reckless pursuit of Bessus. We sensed our way blindly, until the dawn gave us some relief from the awful dangers of the rough road.

We reached a village at midday, exhausted and hungry, except for the king who had reserves of strength unknown to other mortal men. The people gave us food and told us that Bessus and the other conspirators, with their royal prisoner, had fled that way the previous day. Alexander, excited to be so close to his quarries, asked the villagers if there was a shorter route through Hyrcania. They gave him directions to follow a disused road which crossed abandoned land. The king looked at some of the Companions who were exhausted beyond further effort, and told them to wait in the village for his return. He mounted Bucephalos to continue the pursuit with Nicanor, Coenus and myself in the lead, accompanied by a few other Companions and about 40 cavalrymen. Soon after, we passed the junction with the new road. We saw horsemen ahead grouped round a chariot and as we drew near, they parted and galloped off at high speed, and there was Darius, Great King and King of Kings, sprawled on the floor of the chariot. He was dead, bound in chains and bleeding from multiple stab wounds. We leapt from our horses and his body was still warm even though his life had gone. Alexander gently brushed the swarms of black flies from his wounds and covered him with his own purple cape. A pair of vultures already hovered overhead, waiting to devour the body of Darius the Persian, who in death was no different from other men. A little, pet dog set up a pitiful yowling nearby. We improvised a bier and laid the King of Kings upon its crude form. Alexander detached a few men from our small band to escort the body on the first part of its melancholy journey to

Persepolis for burial with all the rites appropriate for a King of Persia.

Thus did the King of Kings, mighty ruler of the east and the west, miserably die and in that desolate place, Alexander of Macedon inherited his styles and titles and all the lands over which he had been sovereign lord. And the murderers of their king had fled in terror before the wrath of Alexander.

Chapter 20

We rode back across Hyrcania into Media to rejoin the expedition. As soon as we arrived, Alexander called a Council of War to give all the commanders a report on the murder of Darius and at the conclusion he continued with these fateful words: "The man who murders his king shall immediately find his own life forfeit. There is no more foul deed, for the safety and security of all kingdoms lies in the stability of the throne. A king's authority comes from the gods and, even in defeat, he must command the respect due to his unique and high office. We shall therefore pursue Bessus, Narbazanes, Barsaentes and the other traitors with them, wherever they may hide, until we have avenged their foul deed. At the same time, we shall inform the Persian people that we no longer conduct a war of attrition against them. They have already submitted to our rule, but we shall now pursue justice against the murderers of their 'Great King'. Bessus has had the infamy to proclaim himself the successor to Darius, which is now treason to me, for I am the heir to the Archaemenid House. He and the other conspirators have fled into Bactria and they have taken the Persian cavalry, and the remnants of the Persian army, intending to set up a stronghold in that province. These are my plans. Craterus will take half of the army by the western route into Hyrcania, subduing the tribesmen who oppose him and making terms with those amenable to our rule. The rest of the army, under the command of Erygius, with the civilian and baggage trains, will take the route through a town named Shahrud. I, with some of the Companions, will ride by the direct road over the mountains and we shall all meet in the city of Zadracarta. In that city, I shall install a permanent government and garrison; it is territory which the Persians have been unable wholly to conquer. From now on there will be a union between Macedon and Persia and both peoples will enjoy the same privileges as subjects of the same king."

Parmenion spoke up as he paused, saying: "Sir, the army has come far enough across Asia and I must speak on behalf of the men. They want nothing more than to return home to enjoy the rewards of their victories. They have no wish to join hands with Persians or to live in Persian territory. They have given you a great and complete victory over Darius, even to the point of his death at the hands of his own traitors, and they see no legitimate reason to settle a score with those who slew him.

"Your star is still ascendant and we ask you to lead us back to our homes in Macedon. Your great triumph will be honoured there, and in all the world, and the name of Alexander will be known as the greatest conqueror of all time.

"Empires, at this great distance from our home, are none of our business. As we stretch our resources to try and rule these vast and terrible lands, so do we become ever more vulnerable and, if a new leader should arise in the eastern Persian satrapies, all that we have gained, at great cost, will be in jeopardy, including the Greek cities of Anatolia, which you have liberated. Many of the Persian ways are obnoxious to Macedonians and also obnoxious is the notion that our victory should be shared with defeated Persians.

"Those who so readily deserted their own king for service with you will just as readily abandon you. It is time for a grand, triumphal march through Asia to Macedon and the cities of Greece, including Sparta, that all the peoples of the world may acclaim your victories and the benefits of peace. Let these distant, eastern jackals destroy each other. When we return home your victory over them has left them without a government and if any should arise, there is no treasury left to sustain it. Therefore, they will have neither the heart nor the means to march against Macedon or any of the cities of Greece."

Everyone present had listened to Parmenion in tense silence; his courage came from his sense of duty to the army as he voiced the longing of the men to return to their homes. He had surely risked his personal safety and perhaps he knew that it was his last great service to the army and to Alexander, whose plans for the future meant ever greater danger for the king and the army. His own danger was in Alexander's words as he replied:

"Parmenion, you hold great honours in my army and amongst all Macedonians for your service to my father and, since his death, to me. I will now reward you with even greater honours for you shall take up the appointment as my commander here in Media and you shall, also, take charge of the treasury which you brought from Persepolis. At your age, you are entitled to an appointment which spares you from the dangers of the battlefield and the hardships of the campaign. You left your home to pursue my father's plans, which together we fulfilled on the banks of the Granicus and the Plains of Issos and at Arbela. My mission, on the other hand, which was revealed to me at Siwah, is to join Greeks and Persians into one world under God, and to make an end to war. Therefore I must go on to fulfill my destiny even without your support.

"As my father was born a king, I also am a king, and so was Darius, and my honour demands that I punish a king's murderers. Tomorrow I shall receive the Persian satraps who have now come to surrender to me. We shall also enrol all the Persians who have asked to serve in my army, together with the Greeks who have volunteered as mercenaries for the rest of the campaign.

"There are some of you who desire only to return to Macedon, and they may do so, but without taking any of the spoils which we have recently added to the treasury. Those of you who remain with me will advance to immortal glory and riches beyond the possessions of Croesos. The choice is yours but the others who intend to return home shall depart by sunset tomorrow, before we begin training to integrate the army into a cohesive whole."

After Alexander had finished speaking, Craterus and I left the conference together. He, at least, had no thought of leaving this great adventure only part of the way along our road. Few Macedonians wished to return home without the king, or with the conditions, which he now offered to them with no further share of the spoils. Alexander always demanded absolute loyalty from those who served him, which was very different from service to a city-state and elected officials. A king shows constancy of policy and friends, in contrast to the tides of change brought with the rise and fall of political favourites. We also discussed the differences in what we saw as our simpler, if not, easier terms of service.

We also discussed the fall of Parmenion and we agreed that

Alexander wished to be quit of all his father's men who had shared only the limited dream of King Philip. For men, when they serve a king, risk exile from home and the honours bestowed upon them may so easily be taken away if they fall out of favour with their lord. My own father had retired for just such reasons. I doubted that Alexander could have conquered this far from home without the military experience and advice of Parmenion but, even so, the king's spectacular successes on the battlefield and successful campaign so far into Asia, made criticism from such a mentor especially irksome to him.

We saw a few of our comrades depart during the next day and we all wondered if they could safely make it back to Macedon. Most had such compelling reasons to leave the campaign that we could only wish them well on their long and hazardous journey. We trained, without respite, to integrate the new recruits into the army and when the king was satisfied, he divided us into the three commands for the march to Zadracarta.

Craterus led his column through the mountains with half of the army. Erygius had already left with the baggage train, and all the civilians, guarded by the other half of the army, save only for the few Companions, who accompanied the king. We set off, when the camp was completely deserted, for the short route through the mountains.

We reached the city of Zadracarta where, within thirty days, we were joined by Erygius and the civilians and baggage train. Soon afterwards, Craterus arrived with grim stories of the difficulties which he and his men had encountered. He was constantly under attack by the tribes who lived in the heights of the mountains. They had never been under Persian domination and they fought for their freedom, as though they were Greeks, until both sides had lost so many men that they sat down and negotiated terms and, finally, they swore allegiance to Alexander. I think that most of us doubted that their loyalty would last much beyond our passing, but it was sufficient now to have Craterus and his column through the mountains, without further loss of life. We established camp outside the walls of Zadracarta, and it was not long before the local people brought their fruits, vegetables, clothing and carpets to trade with the expedition.

Alexander enlisted many more Persians into the army, but his most important work was to interview a group of ambassadors who had been on their way to pay homage to Darius. They were informed of the death of the Persian king and sent back to their own cities to proclaim the accession of Alexander.

The new men replaced many of our fallen in the army, and those others who had returned to Greece. We also found many Greek mercenaries, who had served in the Persian army, hiding in Zadracarta and they were allowed to enrol after they had unconditionally surrendered to Alexander.

We were surprised to find envoys from Sparta lurking in the city. Alexander spared their lives but held them hostage for the good behaviour of all the Lacedaemonians no matter where they lived. Less fortunate was a delegation of Athenians, whom Alexander soon discovered had treasonously left Greece after Athens had signed the treaty, which established the League of Corinth. They were immediately imprisoned and their possessions confiscated.

We now felt ourselves a small minority in the king's army and many Macedonians were either excluded from his company or voluntarily withdrew rather than endure the presence of Persians. The nights when we were alone with the king in his tent were less and less frequent and he wielded authority, made decisions and formulated policies in lonely sovereignty. I did not envy him the separate strands of his authority, for in seeking to show justice to allies who shared no common interest, he risked creating anger and enmity amongst those less favoured and incited them to conspire against him. We were now in the land of Hyrcania, which stretched between the mountains and the Hyrcanian Sea. It was a favoured land and the rich harvest filled the air with the scent of fruit and carpeted the earth with the glowing colours of ripened cereals. The Persians called it a paradise by which they meant a heavenly park normally found only after death. The snow-capped mountains rose above the coastal plain and the sea stretched to the north beyond the limitless horizon. Many of us hoped that Alexander had discovered Ocean but the geographers assured the king that we had only reached another inland sea. I liked to walk in the dawn as it glowed opaquely from the east, before the rising sun fired these eastern mountains, earth and sea with an incandescent glow of great glory. Later in the day the fires dimmed and the light shimmered across the land until the sun once again withdrew from the earth, leaving the sky blazing with the fiery radiance of Apollo, as he rode his chariot below the western horizon. The expedition ate gloriously of the rich harvest from the sea, and it seemed of the foods of Macedon, for this was a land very much like our own and there were grapes and cereals and dried fruits for everyone's satisfaction. New to us was a delicacy prepared from the eggs of royal fish with which we drank the local wine and we enjoyed feasts fit for the gods and the kings of this ancient earth.

We waited long enough in Zadracarta to repair the war machines, buy sufficient supplies for the next stage in the campaign and receive more foreign ambassadors and the ever-growing number of spies who were well-rewarded for their information. The king wanted Bessus even more than he had desired the capture of Darius, and the night before we left the city he paraded the army, the members of the secretariat and the leaders of the civilian train.

He addressed the army, saying: "I, Alexander, King of the Macedons, Hegemon of the Corinthian League and Successor of the Great King, King of Kings of the Persians, and to all his other styles and titles, pay honour to the men who have campaigned the long road with me from Macedon. You have fought with great valour to bring us so far into the lands of Asia, and you will surely be recognized in all future generations of men. We now stand at the threshold of our advance towards the rising sun, to regions of which we have no previous knowledge and amongst peoples of very different beliefs and customs from our own. We shall continue our journey of exploration, discovery, high adventure and great spoils and I promise that all of you will return to your homes ever more richly rewarded for your service to Alexander.

"Those men who have recently joined us are a welcome addition to the expedition. You are now an equal part of a great campaign aimed at pacifying the world. Our first duty, however, must be to pursue, capture and punish Bessus, to avenge his terrible crime of regicide. When this is accomplished, we shall go on and establish my government in all the eastern satrapies and far beyond, wherever the road may take us, until we reach Ocean.

"My Persian subjects have now nothing to fear except the consequences of revolution against me which, if it comes, I shall put down without mercy. Together, on the other hand, Macedonians, Greeks and Persians, we can work to build a great and prosperous future in which all men will be free to worship

214

god and pursue their lives under the guarantee of the justice of Alexander."

The king's speech was calculated to integrate the new recruits into the expedition and formulate his policy towards them. Mounted on Bucephalos, he was irresistible to all of them and they cheered him with great ringing shouts and a clattering of swords against shields. For the time being, at least, even the Macedonians forgot that they had no desire to advance beyond Zadracarta, nor even to pursue Bessus. Leaders of men relieve them of making hard decisions, the most difficult obligation in this life, which does not prevent those, so relieved, of bitterly complaining at every order which they must follow. Eumenes and Callisthenes recorded the king's speeches in their histories of the campaign, from which the public record was used to inform the world of the progress of the expedition and the official policies of Alexander. He sometimes lamented that there was no-one the equal of Homer to record his deeds, for the ancient epics had kept alive forever the histories of heroes and kings, which still inspired us all. Yet Alexander was far greater than any who had come before him I reflected.

Parmenion left the expedition and returned to Ecbatana in Media. He had an escort suitable to his rank of Commander-in-Chief. I did hear that the king had offered the office to Craterus who refused to take it out of deference to Parmenion and his son Philotas who, according to our Macedonian custom, was entitled to succeed his father. We watched his departure in silent unease as we remembered his great service to both King Philip and Alexander and to all Macedonians.

The king organised many small expeditions of scientific discovery during the time that we spent in Zadracarta. He most desired confirmation that the Hyrcanian Sea was entirely a separate, inland water with no connection to other seas or even Ocean. He, personally, collected samples of the plants, trees and animals, which were carefully packed up and sent to Aristotle for his growing collections. The country here was rich and fertile and the people relied on rainfall for their crops and gardens and there were none of the ages-old surface and underground irrigation systems, essential to the people south of the mountains.

I was sorry to leave Zadracarta, when we marched away from the city to cross the limitless plains which, it seemed, stretched endlessly before us, day after day, to an ever-expanding horizon of mournful steppes. We captured a few small charts from some of the tribesmen and they were given to the scouts who rode ahead to find the often difficult road which connected the eastern provinces.

The army was silent and the men were even sullen; we were cut-off from the world in a dusty, limitless wilderness. South of us, scouts reported that there was nothing but a great, salt desert and ahead, perhaps, was Ocean, an uncertain reward for our present weary condition. The sun beat down on the shadeless earth and burned us all, and at night the icy chill warned us of coming winter. Food and water were short and many of the women and children died from the hard conditions of the march.

We finally reached the town of Susia, in the province of Areiana, where Alexander received a visit from Sartibarzanes, the local satrap. He offered his submission to the king who rewarded him by confirming him in office. The satrap immediately asked Alexander for permission to return to Artacoana, his provincial capital, to prepare the people for the arrival of their new king. After his departure, scouts arrived with the news that Bessus had been proclaimed King of Asia with the chosen name of Artaxerxes and that he had assumed the royal purple and the tall, royal, eastern headdress.

A furious Alexander hastened south to Artacoana where he appointed Macedonians to the government of Areiana and detached troops to garrison the city. We continued by the southern route towards Arachosia. We were about three days march from Artacoana and resting in camp, when we were overtaken by messengers from the garrison commander in the city with reports that Sartibarzanes had declared his independence from the king and that fighting had already broken out between his forces and the Macedonians. Alexander left the civilians and baggage train at our present position, with a detachment of the army to guard them. The rest of the army turned back towards Artacoana to put down the rebellion. Alexander rode ahead at high speed, with a small cavalry detachment, archers and two phalanx brigades in his rear. We were met by more messengers who informed the king that Sartibarzanes was using religion, and the zeal of the people, to fuel his revolt and that many of them were ready to die in his cause. We reached Artacoana in two days and found the city seething in unrest. Sartibarzanes had fled and, to our surprise, Barsaentes, one of the conspirators who had murdered Darius, was to our south in the Province of Dragiana.

Alexander, ruthlessly, restored order amongst the population of Artacoana and destroyed the city in the process. When Craterus and the army arrived, the king marched a few miles to the east to look for a suitable site to found a new city as the capital of Areiana and he named it Alexandria Areiana and established a civilian government.

He appointed a Persian, Arsames, as the satrap of the province with a strong garrison to control the wild, but brave Areian people. When the king was satisfied that he had pacified the province, we rejoined the supply train and continued the march to deal with Barsaentes who, alerted by his own spies, fled at our approach towards the River Indus in the east. We reached Zarangia, the capital of the province of Dragiana, and found that a delegation of Indians waited for the king and they brought with them in chains Barsaentes.

A court of Macedonian nobles, presided over the by the king, convicted the regicide and he was executed according to all natural law. After the execution, Alexander gave a great feast, in the palace of Zarangia, for all his commanders, Macedonian, Greek and Persian. We were, already, assembled when Alexander, dressed in gaudy Persian splendour, arrived surrounded by more Persians in their fine silks and they condescended to Macedonians as though they, indeed, were the victors and we the vanquished.

We were now asked to salute the king in the Persian proskynesis, as Persians sniggered behind their hands. Craterus, Philotas, Ptolemy, Coenos, Seleucos and many others ignored the order and I, too, followed them. My father had always advised me to compromise in the lesser follies of the court but on such a painful issue, I could make no concessions and I felt intense anger rise within me.

I took my seat with the barest salutation to the king. Macedonians, all round me, were muttering in sullen protest. We had come these long and weary years, lost so many of our friends and endured the terrible horrors of battles, scorching deserts, torrential rains, which continued often from season to season, winter's bitter cold in snow and ice, forced marches and, for most, the separation from home and family only to find that the Persians were now our equal and valued as highly by our king, who was dressed before us in their tawdry finery. Our loyal service counted no more than their defeats or their squandered empire. The cool night air was tense with the contempt of Macedonians. We left the food and wine placed before us unconsumed. Alexander, contrary to all custom, drank undiluted wine and gave quick glances around so many hostile faces, trying to show no concern for the anger of the majority of his old friends. He finally spoke to Hephaestion, sitting at his side, in mocking tones, taunting our resentment, and then he called to Craterus: "Did you ever think to dine with the Persian king or sit with his great nobles as you grew up in Macedon?"

Craterus, suppressing his anger, replied: "I dine with the King of Macedon and that is sufficient honour for me."

The king turned to others, amongst them Philotas, and called out: "Philotas, do you also refuse to dine with the King of Kings on Persian soil?"

Philotas gave no answer. He rose and with a slight, mocking bow to the king, he left the banquet. Many other Macedonians followed him, for the last of Parmenion's sons was, by tradition, a very powerful man in the army and destined to succeed his father as Commander-in-Chief. His family, for many generations, had served the kings of Macedon in this high office. He was a proud man and proud of Macedon and of his family. His arrogance sometimes grated on, and alienated his closest friends, but he was the king's near contemporary and despite his youth, he had, successfully commanded the cavalry at the Battle of Gaugamela. We had mourned the death of his brother in the River Nile and Nicanor, the second son of Parmenion, had recently died of an unknown fever so that Philotas was the sole heir to his father's rank, wealth and lands.

In the days following the banquet, the strain between the king and the Macedonians was still raw and tense, and the happy comradeship between us was over forever, when Craterus was informed of a plot against the life of Alexander. In anguish, he took the messenger before the king who named Philotas as the chief conspirator. Philotas was arrested; at first he refused to betray his accomplices but, under torture, he, finally, revealed their names and they were all tried by a tribunal of Macedonian generals, according to custom. They were convicted and executed (by spearing with javelins) for high treason. They had planned to end the merging of Greeks and Persians, to replace Alexander with Parmenion, and to rule the conquered territories from Macedon.

Alexander, immediately after the executions, secretly sent emissaries with a letter to Parmenion. We later heard that they reached his camp in the dead of night and immediately roused the old general to hand him the king's letter. As he read the news of the death of Philotas, they stabbed him to death, and the assassins returned to report the success of their crime to Alexander. We were all sickened when the news quickly reached into every Macedonian tent. We whispered quietly amongst ourselves and grieved for not only Parmenion, but also for a king who felt it necessary to commit such a detestable deed. Alexander, night and day, now feared more conspiracies and he became feverish with anger and, in his fury, he also ordered the murder of Alexander Lyncestis whom he had always distrusted.

None of us believed that Parmenion was part of any conspiracy. Alexander tried to convince us that as the old general controlled the supply line, he could, with his son, threaten the entire expedition. A very few backed the king's position and they argued that once Parmenion heard of the execution of Philotas, he would have organised a revolt in Media. I felt sick with this new sorrow and concerned for Alexander's reason, for guilt is a terrible burden to carry, even for the simplest of men.

I wrote, in anguish, to my father for he had served a lifelong duty with the old general and together they had helped to lay the foundations in Philip's army, essential for Alexander's victories. I knew that his sorrow would be deep and personal and, not least, for the tarnished name of Alexander, son of the always revered King Philip.

I received word from Macedon, before my letter had time to reach my father, of his death. I tried to console myself that now he had been spared my terrible news, but my personal grief for him and the knowledge that he was forever gone from my life added to the depth of the unease that I felt serving in the army of Alexander of Macedon.

The king acted swiftly after the murder of Parmenion. He divided the command of the army between Hephaestion, always his most constant friend, and Black Cleitus who had saved his life at the battle on the Granicus. From now on, he divided authority, as he became more suspicious of even his closest friends, with the exception of Hephaestion.

The king suspected the Captain of the Bodyguard of plotting with Philotas and removed him from office and gave his command to Ptolemy. Additionally, all Macedonians who had disagreed with the king were separated into a newly created unit. The news of Parmenion's death travelled the long road home with remarkable speed and soon the king received dispatches from Antipater, and the Greek cities, expressing disgusted horror at the murder of the old general. The king's anger and disappointment sent him into seclusion for a few days. When he emerged, he sent back bitter replies, even to his mother, forbidding any further mention of Parmenion and he stated that he alone ruled the empire and must answer only to the gods for his decisions. I thought often of the teachings of Aristotle and remembered how he despised the corruption of power, as a darker side of Alexander was revealed and I saw his common inhumanity, despite the great gifts bestowed on him by the gods. We marched away from the black deeds done in Zarangia, but there was a grim change in the spirit of the Macedonians as we lamented the death of Parmenion. We no longer felt the lure of high adventure and the trust between us and the king was blunted and stained. We were older, and youth seemed far behind us. We were a demoralised minority in the army of Alexander. At night, Persians sat with the king and he carefully listened as they told him of their god, their history and their empire. We Macedonians were left outside the tent of Macedon's king in the season that followed the deaths of Philotas and Parmenion. Winter settled over the earth again and we once more endured snow and ice and the great hardships caused by lack of fuel and a shortage of food and clothing. We were forced to burn precious equipment to cook raw food and we often lost our way in the vast, white wilderness. The cruel winds cut us to the bone and many men and civilians lost limbs and even their lives to the bitter cold.

The stream of spies, however, never seemed to stop and so we heard that Satibarzanes, the rebellious satrap of Areia, had visited Bessus and returned to Susia, with a large force of Persian cavalry, to lead his revolt. The king dispatched Artabazes to deal with this threat and he killed Satibarzanes in battle and relieved Alexander of this necessity. Thus did the king cause Persian to kill Persian and we wondered, in secret misery, how long it would be before they murdered Alexander and ended the rest of us. Arcaces, yet another Persian, became satrap in Areia. We moved slowly towards the great mountain range, which sheltered Bessus, who was organising an army in Bactria. When we reached the foothills, the king founded a new city, and he named it Alexander Arachosia. As was his custom, he gave the city his own name combined with that of the province, as an administrative centre for the whole region. Menon, a Persian, was appointed satrap to administer civil affairs and Macedonians, as usual, commanded the garrison in the city, and collected taxes and sent reports to the king on all aspects of government.

At the turn of the year, we climbed into the mountain range and we found no relief from the snow and cold for conditions were now far worse with the increasing height, and the narrow path was concealed under snow and ice. Our supplies rapidly dwindled and men and horses were desperately tired from the weather and the continuous marches; too many were lost again to the weather, in avalanches and over concealed precipices.

Most eastern people live in tribal groups in the mountain passes and valleys. They are nomads and ever on the move with the changing seasons. The king held consultations with some of their leaders and informed them that he pursued Bessus to avenge Darius. They laughed at him and told him that now that Darius was dead they chose Bessus as their natural leader and they returned to their tents to launch lightning raids against us. Alexander formed special units to ride against them, including mounted javelin men and archers, with some remnants of Darius' army, and he also dispatched special units of the phalanx, which were trained as mobile columns.

We paused to rest the expedition at a rough city named Kophen, which was little more than a marketplace for the camel trains travelling north and south. It was situated on a river in a high valley between two mountains. A rough citadel rose above Kophen and towered over the vast bazaar where traders, it seemed, from every country in the world exchanged their merchandise. There were Syrians and Phoenicians from the west, and tribesmen, Indians, Persians and narrow-eyed people from unknown regions far to the east. They offered an abundance of carpets, gold, fabrics, jewels, frankincense, glass and even Greek ceramics in this city named Kophen, in the province of Arachosia.

Emissaries soon arrived in Kophen from Indian rulers. They came to pay homage to the king whose fame had reached into all the corners of the world. They were dressed in vivid colours and wore turbans of folded silks, which were ornamented with enormous jewels. They brought Alexander lavish gifts of rare spices, silk, gold and jewels of ornate and costly design and in exchange they received from Alexander for their lords, promises of peace and arbitration in their internecine feuds. On behalf of their kings, they invited Alexander to visit India, but the king sent them home, to our intense relief, for none of us hoped to travel so far, and Alexander planned nothing beyond the capture of Bessus for the murder of Darius, King of the Persians. The king closely questioned many of the local people and found that we had a choice of seven routes through the mountains as we made preparations to march from Kophen. Alexander took the advice of the majority of the local guides who joined the expedition, and we advanced through the glittering, treacherous, snow-covered mountains. The thin air, in the heights, reduced our progress and many more men died in the ascent through the Hindu Kush. Our food was even more scanty and the cold was so intense that we lost weight as we constantly shivered in the frigid air. The sun shone overhead with brilliant intensity and reflected back from the snow until men were blinded by the hard light. It mocked us, for we were too high to feel Apollo's warmth and we were even relieved when it was obscured by thick, dark clouds from which the soft, silent snow descended on us and brought more deaths. Men and horses slid on the ice and many more were lost when they fell into hidden chasms. I am still haunted by their screams as they slipped down beyond rescue.

There was a grim magnificence in these towering, lonely mountains of the Hindu Kush which were named by the Persians and meant 'Killer of the Indians'. We Macedonians are a mountain people and understand their beauty, power and gift of sanctuary but we were tried to the limit of our endurance by these much greater heights and survival obsessed us all.

Spies, somehow, managed to find us and they brought reports to the king that Bessus had fled before us over the Oxus River. He had burned all the boats that he had commandeered after reaching the northern bank and he was now destroying the crops as he fled across the land in a province called Sogdiana.

We descended from the mountains, with thankful hearts, into Bactria, and we reached the fortress of the province, which we only seized after a hard fight. It was a strategic victory as we were able to establish contact with Susia, directly to our west, instead of using the circuitous route of our march into Bactria. We received supplies and new soldiers to reduce our desperate plight and we stayed in the city of Zariaspa until winter slowly turned to spring and then the expedition marched towards the River Oxus. We were again attacked by tribesmen, allied with Bessus, and the king dispatched units of the army, which had been especially trained, to make instant raids against them. They pursued and killed all the men whom they overtook, sparing their camps and the women and children. I think that Alexander admired the tribes' independence, courage and way of life and he did not want to destroy them beyond regeneration.

The expedition continued to the River Oxus, where some of the geographers declared that we had reached the River Don; others disagreed, but they all had to alter their charts for we were still nowhere near Ocean nor did any of the local people speak of it, much to Alexander's disappointment.

The river, swollen by the melting snows in the mountains, was an angry torrent of swirling, foamy waters reaching far out of its normal boundaries. A vast area of fertile land was irrigated by the river and we were able to purchase food once more, stored beyond the water, from the previous harvest, by the farmers of the river's bank. Alexander surveyed the difficult crossing and expressed his concern for some of the older Macedonians, many of whom were suffering from diseases or battle injuries. He decided that the most disabled should now return to their homes and he sent them off with many honours and great wealth taken as their share of the treasury. Stasanor was appointed satrap of Areia, and in command of the first part of their journey to Macedon. He took over from Arcaces whom the king suspected of intriguing with Bessus. The engineers had no wood to make rafts for the river crossing and the men cut tents into strips and sewed them together into bags, which were then filled with straw; several of these were sewn together to make larger rafts to ferry the equipment. We supported ourselves on the bags as we held the horses' bridles, trying to encourage them to swim the torrent. Very few men or horses were lost and we remembered crossing the Danube by the same method, when the world seemed young and more beautiful to our, then, unwearied bodies.

Once across the river, the ever resourceful spies arrived in the camp bringing Alexander the news, which he so dearly longed to hear. He showed very little emotion, however, as he was told that some of the Persian satraps, with Bessus, including Oxyartes, the brother of Darius, Spitamanes, Catanes and Dataphernes had arrested their leader and, hoping to save their own miserable lives, they were now holding him for the king.

Alexander dispatched Ptolemy, suspecting a trick, in command of no less than 6,000 men, to bring him back alive. Taking the spies with them, they surrounded the small town where Bessus was alleged to be held and they found him alone and abandoned in the deserted town. Ptolemy seized him and ordered him to be placed in chains, with a wooden dog collar round his neck, and all along the road back to our camp he was exhibited naked to the jeering people, a customary, local punishment for a captured, mountain brigand. Many of the Persian leaders had intrigued to use Bessus as their rallying point after the murder of Darius and they now abandoned him to a shameful spectacle, which most of us thought a very unsuitable fate for a brave soldier. When Ptolemy arrived with his captive, Alexander paraded the army and read the charges against Bessus while the wretch cowered before him. He was accused of high treason, first against Darius and then against Alexander, his new king, who asked him in anger: "Why did you capture and murder Darius, your lord and king? Had he not shown you every confidence, as his kinsman, and favoured you with many personal kindnesses?"

Bessus replied from the depths of his misery: "I did not act alone, but together with all the satraps gathered in the tent of Darius during his retreat; we hoped to gain your favour by his death."

Alexander, in greater fury, replied: "Did you think the crime of regicide likely to please me? You should have thought more carefully for I am also a king, and the son of a murdered king, and find your crime the worst that any subject of a king may commit. I order you to be whipped and then handed over and given into the charge of Oxathres who will escort you for trial by a Persian court."

The miserable procession escorting Bessus departed the next day and we later heard that the Persian court condemned him to be first vilely mutilated and then dispatched to Ecbatana for

execution by crucifixion. By such barbarities did Persians seek
to gain the favour of Alexander. Most of the Macedonians were
sickened by the punishment of Bessus. We conjectured that it
was a possible warning for conspirators and at the same time we
thought of Bessus as a brave enemy. We complained bitterly of
Persian customs adopted by the king, and we expected that the
punishment of Bessus would stir up new hostile action against
us. We were correct, as it was not long before news reached
us that the Choasmians, Sogdians and Areians, under the
leadership of Spitamanes across the River Oxus, were organising
a new rebellion. He sent guerilla bands to attack us all along our
route. We had lost many horses crossing the mountains and the
River Oxus and the king used these attacks to send out punitive
expeditions to subdue the rebels and confiscate their horses,
which we desperately needed, as replacements for the cavalry
and to carry our stores. After a hard march, we reached the
fabled city of Maracanda, the administrative capital of the satrapy
of Sogdiana. The city straddles the east and west highways and
we were once again dazzled by the stocks of luxuries on sale in
the bazaars. They were brought to this famous marketplace by
the camel trains which travelled the roads of Asia transporting
all the treasures of the world for sale and barter.

The Persians had made the roads of their empire safe for
men to travel immune from all dangers, and the merchants
complained to Alexander that they were no longer free from
marauding thieves and brigands. The king, gravely, told them
that he would restore the patrols on the highways and severely
punish every robber caught plundering their caravans. They were
delighted with Alexander's promise as they had been forced to
hire mendacious guards to protect their merchandise. These often
fled at the approach of danger. In gratitude, they gave the king
expensive gifts from their priceless stocks but, as usual, every
one of these he gave into the treasury chests of the expedition
and he kept nothing for himself, except the golden casket
taken from the Persian treasury on the Plains of Issos in which
Alexander carried Aristotle's copy of Homer's *Iliad*. I wandered
amongst the camel drivers and listened again to the language
of Phoenicia, Canaan and Syria. They spoke in many dialects of
the strangely beautiful but guttural sounds of Aramaic for they
were men apart from all others and they fiercely protected their
independence. They were prepared to defend their caravans,

even with their lives, against the thieves who preyed upon them. The weary civilian train finally arrived in Maracanda and many children, who were fathered by men from Greece and Macedon, were born later in the city to Persian women.

We had been gone from Macedon for five long campaign seasons and it was summer again, and we once more endured the oppressive heat and maddening insects of the high steppes of Asia. Alexander led several expeditions against hostile tribesmen who suddenly appeared in lightning raids, even in our camp, just within the city. In one of these encounters the king suffered a deep wound in his leg and he was forced to rest while it slowly healed. To celebrate both his recovery and his twenty-seventh birthday, he planned a great feast to which he first invited Sogdian nobles and powerful Persians who now swarmed round him. For the benefit of these guests, the king intended to introduce more of the Persians' social customs, which he found pleasing and, which were so offensive to us and contrary to our Macedonian traditions. We Macedonians were also invited by the king to join in the celebrations, but many of us were reluctant to endure further humiliations and we refused to attend. We heard later that the king silently raged against our absence during the feast and the following morning he rode away from Maracanda with Hephaestion, Craterus and Coenus and a small cavalry escort. We soon realised that he had gone without leaving us his destination or any orders to follow him. Macedonians felt an icy fear and loneliness and we quietly discussed amongst ourselves the dangers, which we faced without him from tribesmen or treacherous Persians, and as each day passed our fears grew and we were very afraid.

Finally the king returned to Maracanda, and the cheers and shouts of the Macedonians echoed round our camp. We soon heard from Craterus that they had camped on a river named the Jaxartes. Alexander stood on the river bank planning a crossing for the whole expedition. Coenus had spent many days advising the king that the Macedonians would go no further into these barbaric lands. At first Alexander had argued that he was the king and must make all the decisions, until Craterus and even Hephaestion had joined Coenus in protest, and finally, but reluctantly, Alexander accepted this truth. He immediately looked for a suitable site to found a city, which he named Alexandria Eschate or Alexandria the Furthest, to announce that he had reached the end of his expedition. For the shortest time, with this news, we were happy beyond our expectations, for we truly believed that we were about to begin our long victory march to Macedon; our joy was short-lived. We had learned from Aristotle, long ago, that the Jaxartes was the eastern branch of the River Danais, which separated Europe from Asia. Alexander had quickly calculated that no river could cross the mountain ranges, which, we now realised, divided the continents. He ordered the geographers to correct all our maps and charts and, when they were ready, he sent copies to Aristotle marking the mountains and the newly discovered course of the river.

Our hopes of home dimmed when the king ordered most of the army to prepare for yet another expedition to the Jaxartes. I remained in Maracanda, happy with the city's amenities and content to spend my days with the camel drivers and to learn more of their language, journeys, customs and homelands. Soon after the king's departure, spies arrived in the city to report that Spitamanes had crossed the River Oxus at the head of a great horde of Scythian tribesmen and that he was attacking every town on his way to Maracanda. We were poorly defended and when he arrived before the walls of the city, we dispatched local tribesmen to find the king and alert him of our danger. Within a few days, we saw the clouds of dust as Alexander approached, and Spitamanes raised his siege and retreated north with his savage tribesmen. Polymetus pursued him to the Jaxartes where they fought a brutal battle. We lost many men in the fighting and when our army was within sight of victory, Spitamanes, as Darius before him, escaped and fled even further north across the river and beyond pursuit. He was a brave, bold and able general and he immediately recruited more tribesmen for his cavalry.

They were all expert horsemen and seemed to live on horseback and they played wild games for the possession of beheaded calves, which they propelled on the ground with short sticks, when they had nothing better to do. They were short, squat men and they dressed in animal skins and they knew nothing of written languages. They dwelt in circular, felt houses, which they erected over wooden frames for easy transportation, as they moved unceasingly from worn out pastures to new grazing lands. The army returned to Alexander's camp on the Jaxartes and Spitamanes once more laid siege to Maracanda and messengers secretly stole out at night to report his arrival to the king. In little more than three days, Alexander covered the great distance to the city and Spitamanes, again, fled across the steppes. Alexander pursued him until he reached a large Scythian camp where he ordered the execution of most of the men, allowing a few to escape to take a warning to Spitamanes. He reasoned that this would deter the mutinous rebel from further hostile action and discourage any other tribesmen from enlisting in his service.

Alexander returned to Maracanda and, before hard winter once more settled upon the land, the entire expedition marched south from Maracanda back to Bactra, the capital of the province of Bactria. We all thought that this must be the first stage on the return journey to Macedon. Our first duty, once in the city, was to build a huge camp for the army and the civilians, whose numbers had swollen by the children born during the march from Greece, a great number of Persian women, who had attached themselves to our men, and the spies, craftsmen, traders, and the provisioners of food and, especially, the fodder for the animals. Alexander, in order to devote himself entirely to the administration of the vast lands under his law, gave the command of the army to Craterus. It was a difficult time for most of the Macedonians as we still mourned Parmenion. We could have accepted no other in his place, except for Craterus, who enjoyed the respect of every soldier and the affection of all who knew him.

The king sent messengers to the military commanders of every satrapy in our rear, giving them reports of all our latest moves and he received and studied their replies for a great part of each day. He also received many ambassadors from as far away as Magna Graecia, in the west, and the Indian kingdoms of the unknown east. He did not forget Spitamanes, and sent out several expeditions to hunt him down, for he was indeed the most resolute and brave adversary during the entire campaign up to our present position.

A new spring, at last, gave us relief from the aching cold of winter and with it came news of the many raids, which Spitamanes had conducted against our garrison in Maracanda. The king's response was swift. Craterus remained in Bactra, with a strong force, to protect the civilians and our supplies. Alexander divided the rest of the army into five columns which were commanded by Hephaestion, Coenus, Ptolemy, Perdicass and himself. They had orders to march by different roads into Sogdiana and search out the rebel leader. Hephaestion had the second duty of establishing new towns throughout the region, and to detach enough men from his column to garrison each one of them. Spitamanes' spies must have been quick to inform him of the departure of army units from Bactra, as he now led his tribesmen into the province of Bactria, attacking even to the outskirts of the city. Ptolemy had anticipated his moves and had remained close enough to the city to pursue him. Spitamanes lay in wait for an attack and he inflicted a severe defeat on Ptolemy's men. The news quickly reached Craterus, who left the city and found the enemy camp still celebrating their victory. Their merriment soon turned to grief as Craterus successfully attacked them, but Spitamanes once again escaped, this time briefly, as we soon learned that he was murdered by those same tribesmen whom he had so ably led. They dispatched his severed head to Alexander, camped in Maracanda, as proof of their submission to his rule. I joined the king in Maracanda to help integrate recruits, who had newly arrived from Antipater, into the army as much needed reinforcements. We were overjoyed to receive the Macedonians with fresh news from Macedon, although for some it was a time of grief and despair when they learned of the deaths of their family members.

Many tribal kings and chiefs came to pay homage to Alexander, as the news quickly spread amongst them of the death of Spitamanes. Some of them even offered their daughters in marriage to the king. He treated them all with grave courtesy but he refused their proposals, except one for a few men to join his army. Kings, chiefs and a multitude of foreign ambassadors were received, according to the customs of the Persians, with the king sitting on carpets in a madjlis, surrounded by Persian nobles. Once more, Macedonians protested as we discussed every new concession that the king made to our defeated enemy. Some of our men mocked Alexander in his absence. They decked themselves in fine, Persian robes and addressed each other in the exaggerated Persian style and laughed hysterically as they found relief from bitter feelings in childish antics. The king's policies of reconciliation with the Persians, and giving them high appointments at court and in the government, were naturally appreciated by the defeated enemy but when Alexander failed to become a Macedonian amongst his own people, the insult was an ever-widening chasm between us. Coenus had bravely warned him, on the banks of the Jaxartes, that the Macedonians would go no further and now he spoke again, in his official capacity, of the men's hatred for Persian customs, supplanting our Macedonian ways. Alexander responded to his warning and invited only Macedonians to a symposium in the Platonic manner, and so familiar to us all.

We sat on low couches and drank from our stocks of wine and discussed our victory over Spitamanes and debated from which direction our next challenge would come. And then, Hephaestion began to speak, to murmurs of approval from men who sought to rise in the king's favour. He compared Alexander's courage and deeds with those of the gods and heroes. The king, somewhat confused with wine and not listening too closely, seemed to accept the vain words with a half smile until Cleitus the Black, the brother of Lanice, the king's old nurse, and mentor to us all, spoke in protest saying: "Nothing has been achieved in these barbarian lands, on this expedition, without the courage and loyalty of all the Macedonians on the long road from Macedon, which is marked with the graves of our Macedonian dead, and ending here in Maracanda."

Alexander's face reddened in anger. He was a little drunk on the raw, local wine and nervous sycophants tried to distract him with other comparisons, some even citing that Alexander was much greater than his father, King Philip. This was too much for Cleitus, who rose to his feet and shouted: "Alexander! The gods are not to be scorned for they guided the army all the way here from Macedon. You may never prefer Persians above Macedonians, for we gave you your victories over them. Persian customs imposed upon us are a vile insult to Macedonian soldiers, and I have the right to speak for did I not save your life on the banks of the Granicus?"

The king jumped to his feet, as if to attack Cleitus. Craterus and others restrained him, but Alexander tore himself loose from them as Cleitus continued shouting contemptuously: "Son of Ammon! Son of Ammon! Son of Ammon!"

The king called for his bodyguard. They seized Cleitus and hurried him out of the king's tent amidst a tense and horrible silence. Cleitus managed to free himself and he rushed back into the hall, as the king grabbed for his dagger which someone had removed from his reach.

Later, a distraught Alexander told us that he took this as a sign of a plot against his life and he ordered the trumpeter to sound the alarm. When the man hesitated, the king knocked him to the floor. Cleitus continued yelling insults as he rushed towards him. Alexander seized a pike from one of the bodyguards, threw it at Cleitus and ran him through; he died instantly and the horror caused us all to sober up in that gaudy, tawdry scene of Persian finery, spilt wine, Caspian fruit, oriental silks and the blood of Cleitus gushing from his mouth and round the pike sticking out from his chest.

The king vomited and ran out from our sight. He went to his quarters, bitter with remorse, to mourn a faithful friend and lament the sorrow of Lanice. To the grief of losing her own sons in battle, she must add the wanton waste of her only brother. She had been Alexander's nurse and given him his only experience of tenderness in his early years, which was now rewarded by murder. A grim and terrible depression settled over the army after the death of Cleitus. The king was prostrated by grief and remorse. He remained in his tent, refusing all food, for three days and nights. Persians dared to whisper that the gods had provoked the quarrel from jealousy and they persuaded the king that he was not entirely responsible until he finally left his quarters lured out by their honeyed words.

The same issues still divided the king from the Macedonians, but none now felt free to challenge his policies without risking the same fate as had befallen Cleitus. Even though the king suffered such terrible remorse, none of us felt safe criticising anything that he might order us to do.

We Macedonians were sick of war and death and mourning and the privations of the expedition. We acknowledged the king's grief, but we knew that Cleitus had spoken for us all and we were angry and afraid in these dark, barbarian regions of a hostile earth.

Chapter 21

Summer was again turning into bitter winter during the lost days after the death of Cleitus. Alexander was consumed with guilt for the loss of so great a friend and a superb general and he could no longer stand the bloodstained city of Maracanda. He announced that the army would leave immediately for Nautaca, a newly founded and strategic city between Maracanda and the River Oxus to our south. He appointed a Macedonian as governor of Maracanda, with orders to subdue any tribal uprisings in the area, which might survive the death of Spitamenes. The king detached a strong force of cavalry and two Macedonian phalanxes to garrison Maracanda, under the command of Coenus, before we marched to Nautaca.

Even, before we had completed our camp and headquarters in that city, spies brought the king reports that Oxyartes, a famous Bactrian chieftain and warrior, was holed up for the winter on the Sogdian Rock, a natural, and reputedly impregnable fortress deep within the mountains of Sogdiana. They also reported that there was yet another fortress, far to our east, which remained in enemy hands.

Many new recruits arrived in Nautaca from Antipater and some came from local tribes and other former Persian lands under Alexander's law. The Macedonians and Greeks were easily integrated into the army but, by now, the king took great care in selecting and testing the loyalty of renegade Persians. He personally questioned them about their beliefs and family histories before accepting them into the army. He listened to their recommendations on raiding tactics and he trained a column of volunteers from the phalanxes, for the assault on the rebels of the lofty fortress. He also questioned the local people on the physical characteristics of Sogdiana, beyond Maracanda, especially the notorious Rock, occupied by Oxyartes.

The long winter finally turned to spring, but the night winds still howled through the camp and bit us with raw cold until, gradually, irrigation ditches were freed from ice. The people depended on them for water for their growing crops, and they were happy to ignore our presence and work their farms. It was a rested and vigorous army that marched from Nautica. New local recruits made us a less homogenous expedition, but they did give us greater experience and strength to fight the various kinds of warfare, which we must employ in these barbarian lands. Macedonians were also learning to speak the Persian and other local languages, both from the mercenaries and from the women who thronged to join us. The generals' greatest concern was the king's inconstant moods, an evil and dark consequence of the deaths of Bessus and Cleitus. He was haunted in a lonely and black part of his soul and, as he withdrew, almost in shame, from Macedonians, it meant that he spent more time with insidious Persian nobles. Rarely, we Macedonians were summoned to his tent, in the night hours, when the talk had been of everything beneath the sky's remote bowl but, unlike his behaviour in former convivial days, he often spent his days alone and withdrawn or alone with Hephaestion. Not even Craterus was at his side for this loyal and devoted friend frequently departed on expeditions against tribesmen who continued to ambush the campaign, until he had routed them all. Finally the Sogdian Rock and that other distant fortress were their last strongholds. We all expected that we had started on our final march before we turned into the setting sun on the long journey home to Macedon. If Alexander was aware of the bitter chasm which divided him from the Macedonians, he gave no sign, other than to choose Persians above Greeks and to affect Persian dress, as if to prove that he ruled primarily as King of the East. We resentfully felt that we were valued as no more than mercenaries in his service.

As we approached higher ground, the snow still deeply carpeted the earth and slowed our progress until, finally, we arrived at the Sogdian Rock where we found the people gathered in a small town, high above us. It was perched on a crag beneath a much loftier peak, and it was protected by sheer cliffs, which fell to the ground on every side of the mountain. Local spies reported that the people had enough food to last for many seasons in their impregnable fortress and that they used melted snow as an abundant supply of water. The best news for us was that Oxyartes was away from the Rock. Alexander studied an almost comic situation and he ordered a Persian, possessed of a mighty, carrying voice, to call on the Sogdians to surrender.

They loudly shouted in reply: "Get celestial flyers, O! Alexander! and then we will deliver ourselves, for our oracle has prophesied that these cliffs will not be taken except by winged soldiers."

With a show of his old enthusiasm when he met the challenge head on, the king offered large rewards to the first twelve Macedonians to scale the cliffs. In response, 300 came forward, most of them from the especially trained phalanxes, and they hurriedly unpacked ropes and iron pegs and started the ascent from a position hidden from the jeering Sogdians.

They were soon gone from our sight in the darkness of night, until the next morning we beheld them waving flags from a pinnacle high above the town. We miserably counted thirty brave men who had fallen to their deaths from loose rock and snow and these brave men we could not afford to lose. The king himself called to the Sogdians to turn and look upwards and chaos broke out amongst them when they saw our soldiers, for they were without their leader, Oxyartes. It was not long before they shouted back to us that the prophecy of celestial soldiers was fulfilled and, without a fight, they surrendered their fabled rock. We entered the town to find that it was much larger than had appeared from the ground below. I was in the king's party when he first beheld Roxane, the daughter of Oxyartes. In all the lands of Persia, only Queen Statira had been more beautiful. The girl was about fifteen years old, with hair the blue-black colour of a raven. Her cheeks held the bloom of a ripened peach and her eyes sparkled with the vigorous health and joy of youth. The king abruptly stopped as she knelt before him, and he stretched out his hand to gently raise her to her feet. He walked slowly away and because of Roxane, daughter of Oxyartes, the king was merciful to the people of the Sogdian Rock.

Alexander sent a messenger to Oxyartes and informed the chieftain that he intended to marry his daughter. The happy news brought that prince in a great hurry to take part in the rejoicing and to make peace with the king. He also brought his two sons, who immediately volunteered for service in the

Macedonian army and they brought with them their Sogdian, Bactrian and Scythian cavalry. They were all quickly enrolled and Macedonians, once more, felt the sharp sting of resentment. We wanted no more conquered Persians diluting our numbers and setting themselves up as the equals of their conquerors, especially from the favoured base of a family relationship with the king. And now we marched from the Sogdian Rock on our last journey in Sogdiana to the territory of the Paraetacene, to take the final stronghold at the furthermost limit of the Persian Empire. Chorienes, the local prince, had retreated to this stronghold; it was known by his name as 'The Rock of Chorienes'. The turncoat, Oxyartes, with his sons and all his followers and the lady Roxane, with her attendants, rode by the king's side. Oxyartes was now chief advisor to the king in Sogdiana. At his suggestion, we halted two days' ride from the Rock of Chorienes and the king received many local spies and listened to Oxyartes as he described the physical features of the fortress in careful detail.

He moved amongst the Companions, barely disguising his sly satisfaction in his new role, bitter gall for Macedonians to digest. Persians were notoriously skilled in the ways of intrigue and they had bested each other from ancient times. We were simple Macedonians with a single loyalty to the king and foreigners to any similar deceit.

After a few days, we marched to within sight of the fortress and looked across the pine-covered ravines and we saw that it was much higher and larger than the Sogdian Rock. We cut down trees and made ladders from their limbs, which we placed at the narrowest part of a ravine and we constructed bridges to cross its width. When we reached the walls of the fortress, we bombarded the Sogdians night and day. Oxyartes spoke directly to Chorienes and persuaded him to surrender his fortress in exchange for the guaranteed safety of the inhabitants of his Rock. Oxyartes claimed this as his personal victory, and the king granted him the honour. Macedonians were angry; the king's strategy had always been to take a city in only one of two ways, either by its surrender or by victory in battle; this was the first time in the campaign that Alexander had made terms with an enemy.

Once inside the city, however, our feelings were laid aside for we rejoiced in the king's wedding. It was simply done. Alexander and Roxane held a sword between them and cut bread, according to eastern custom, in the presence of the Companions, Oxyartes, his sons and their principal followers. Cupids decorated every available space, for the king loved Roxane, the beautiful daughter of Oxyartes. Coenus had rejoined the king and many other Macedonians rode in to share in the celebrations. Alexander's personal desires also served his ambitions and now great benefits came to him from his alliance with the tribes. They were finally pacified and all the Persian Empire was at last conquered and subdued. The king was now part of a family, which he so much needed as he grew more isolated from the Macedonians. We did not share Alexander's dream of one empire, nor did we wish to die, as Cleitus had died, in a drunken brawl. When men of power lose control over self, they disintegrate from within; and, as the worm destroys the apple and disease eats the body, a touch of corruption spreads to the perimeters of their power and all within its limits must suffer a decline of virtue.

We were young when we left Macedon, full of truth, bold hopes and limitless dreams. We were now much older men and witnesses to corruption, murder and the misery of vanquished peoples. We felt as grains of sand, blown by strong winds in the desert and that when the day came for Greeks to leave the shores of Asia, there would be none to remember our passing and the years of terrible hardship, which we had suffered to fulfill a king's ambition would be in vain.

After the wedding came a week of celebrations during, which the king held games to commemorate his day of happiness – in the city, on the Rock of Chorienes. He awarded palm leaves to the victors, telling them that no reward could equal the honour that they held that day. To all of his new relatives and friends he gave very rich gifts from the treasury. Hephaestion was jealous of Roxane and Oxyartes, but when he discovered that they did not diminish Alexander's affection towards him, he managed to suppress his antagonism. He, like the rest of us, must ever be mindful of the fate of Parmenion, Philotas and Cleitus the Black, brother of Lanice, the king's beloved nurse.

Alexander spoke to the army at the end of the celebrations. He told us that his marriage to Roxane also symbolised the marriage of east and west and that he favoured the Persians from a genuine affection and regard, which he felt towards them, as well as out of political and military necessity. For the eastern Persians, the marriage had brought them nothing but riches and positions of power and prestige and a king's favour. Macedonian bitterness blazed again as we sat round our campfires.

We remembered Parmenion, Philotas, Alexander of Lyncestis and Cleitus the Black, and we talked in low voices that no spy might listen and report our words. Some even whispered that the king was mad; others suggested that he was only mad with power and yet others said that the eastern gods had taken his soul in exchange for his Persian victories. I was deeply troubled, for I loved Alexander. I did not love his Persians, but loyalty must surely stand the test of other, strange alliances and I remembered that the king had led us all to victory after victory, and most generously rewarded us. My life was wholly bound to him in duty and friendship.

One night, the king attempted to repair his breach with the Macedonians. He held a symposium and invited many of his old friends. After drinking a little wine, he passed the chalice to Hephaestion, who drained it, and fell before the king in the homage of the proskynesis, and they exchanged the Persian kiss of friendship. The cup was refilled and Hephaestion passed it to Coenus and so on down the line, and they all remained seated until it reached Callisthenes, who took it in a silence grown tense and sour. He drank, but stood up emphasising that no true Macedonian knelt to any man. The king refused his kiss and Callisthenes strode from the hall shouting: "I go the poorer by a kiss!"

Many in the hall muttered against Callisthenes; he was resented as a civilian, for his airs of intellectual superiority and his influence with the king. From then on, however, he was watched nervously by all of us and the king treated him as an enemy and accused him of being the leader of Macedonian opposition to himself. He now lived apart, in the company of the pages, who idolised him as their teacher and as the nephew of Aristotle.

At a conference, shortly after Callisthenes fell from grace, the king addressed us, saying: "We have explored these wide lands of Asia searching for Ocean and we have found only rivers, with mountain ranges beyond their banks or limitless steppes. We have received no reports indicating that beyond the rivers, steppes and deserts lies the sea, fertile land or sufficient people to threaten our hegemony.

"Many men have visited us from India, and they tell us of roads through the mountain passes and of streams which accumulate on the great inclines to descend into broad rivers and empty into the sea and, I believe, may very well reach Ocean.

"We have also met many traders, who carry merchandise between east and west and spread civilisation wherever they travel. We have learned that India is not a land united under one king but rather divided into small quarrelling states and I consider that we can use their disputes to quicken our advance. We already have alliances with some of the princes and more will follow as we march eastwards. Then, indeed, shall Macedonians have dominion over all the world and discover the true geography of the most distant places. We go to India not only as conquerors but primarily as explorers, and we shall seize the opportunities to widen the frontiers of knowledge and to give Greek civilisation to the most distant barbarians.

Bactria will be our northern frontier, and I appoint Amyntas as satrap of the province, with 10,000 infantry and 3,500 cavalry to guarantee the borders. Hephaestion and Hystapes will share command of the agema, which will continue as the footguard in the headquarters' camp of the expedition. We are now a mighty army of Macedonians, Greeks and mercenaries from all the old Persian provinces. I intend that Persians will no longer serve in separate units but that they will be fully integrated into the army, even into the cavalry. To our great victories shall be added the new learning, which will change the world and we shall find wonderful challenges for every soldier, philosopher, writer, geographer, scientist and craftsman in our expedition.

"From now on, we shall use only the language of Greece until it spreads amongst all people and, with a unified army, we shall be one world under God for he is our common Father. Our deeds have already far surpassed any others in history and our empire will stretch from Hellas into India. We all now prepare to march to the east."

As the king finished speaking, the Persians applauded, but Macedonians were silent. We had been in these remote and haunted regions for two full seasons and we wanted only that Alexander should lead us home. We were tired of foreign lands and the ways of barbarian people and we ached for Macedon. Wives grow weary of the absence of their husbands and children mature beyond the recognition of their fathers. Most of us thought that Sogdiana, and the city of Alexandria Eschate, had concluded the expedition and we wanted no part of India. There were a few younger men, of course, who were anxious to prove themselves in war and gain a share of the spoils and the mercenaries hoped that Alexander would continue the campaign and keep them employed. The Persians benefited from every possible developing situation. I walked with Craterus and Ptolemy, after the king's speech. Craterus was a soldier and, after Alexander, the best of us all. He rarely discussed politics; he was loyal to the king and he had a noble character incapable of the smallness of most other men. Ptolemy was generous and he loved to study science and all the arts with the Persian magi in the great cities, but most of all he cherished his memories of Egypt and her people.

As we walked together, we remembered Aristotle and our days with the great teacher in Mieza. We talked of King Philip and the tempestuous Olympias, and of the campaign since we had crossed the Hellespont. Ptolemy kept a personal, daily journal of the expedition and I asked him how it progressed. He answered: "From my notes, which are now filling a large box, I shall work for a few years when we return to Macedon and, in my old age, I shall publish a true account of the expedition so that the whole world will know how it was to serve with Alexander. He has accomplished more than any other man known to history and has always shown great kindness to me. If the king has faults, they are manifest for the cause to which he has dedicated his life, and he cannot tolerate dissension in the army. Without our complete loyalty, which he has always generously rewarded, none of the expedition could have succeeded. I grieve most of all for Parmenion. The king truly believed that Philotas was guilty of a conspiracy when he sentenced him to death. He surely risked Parmenion's revenge when this news reached him and Alexander was forced to safeguard the expedition by the general's own death.

"The pinnacle of power carries a heavy crown of loneliness and well may we pity the decisions a king must make for the good and safety of us all. For myself, I am a soldier and desire only to do my duty and leave dangerous politics to other men."

Craterus answered him saying: "Those are wise words, Ptolemy. At any time, the Persians may combine and attack our rear and then we must be lost as we are too thinly stretched from here to the Hellespont. The king, therefore, binds them through service and the rewards that he gives to them. They will more readily accept his rule if he adopts some of the customs of their land, which do offend us. However, Macedonians cannot bow before a man or call him a god and Alexander must respect our ways, also, and be content to be deified only by Persians, if that is his wish, and not by us."

At that point, we reached a tavern and we entered to enjoy the warmth, food and wine. There was a pretty serving girl and I found some comfort with her that night. Since the king's marriage, there was peace in the whole region and many Macedonian children were born the following season on the craggy Rock of Chorienes, as well as to the women who joined the expedition when we marched to India.

Chapter 22

The camp was full of activity as we prepared to leave the Rock of Chorienes. Engineers and craftsmen had manufactured a great amount of new equipment and our stores were swollen with necessities and captured treasure. The personal possessions of the soldiers were far greater than when we left Macedon; with their huge shares of bounty, they had made many purchases in the markets of the Persian Empire. All this had to be loaded on to pack animals, and the civilian train had swollen with the many new soldiers and camp followers and their possessions. Alexander invited a few of the Companions to join him on a hunt to pass a few days, as a diversion from all the commotion in the camp. The surrounding country abounded in game and we were concealed in a small wood when a large boar charged across the path, immediately, in front of our position. An impudent page named Hermolaos rushed forward and killed the animal with his spear and so usurped the king's ancient right to be the first to strike.

Angry shouts denounced the page, and he was immediately arrested and brought before the king. Alexander quietly questioned him, and he freely admitted that he had acted out of shameless impudence and the king, for this reason, ordered him to be whipped.

The humiliated Hermolaos, as soon as he was released, rushed back to our camp and complained to his tutor, Callisthenes. He was still living in isolation, except for the pages, since the night of his quarrel with the king, when he refused to give the Persian proskynesis to Alexander. We heard later that Callisthenes taunted the page, saying that the Greeks of old would not have tolerated so great an insult as a whipping and he urged him to take his revenge. Slyly, he added that we were all become slaves, in the service of this king, and that there were none left to challenge Alexander.

The simmering Hermolaos, in even greater fury, rushed to confide in another page, his close friend, Sostratos, and together they hatched a plot against the life of Alexander. They brought into the conspiracy four more pages who were Antipater, the son of Asclepiodoros, Anticles, son of Theocritos Philotas, son of Carsis, and Epimenes, the son of Arseus. Together they chose a night to murder their king when it was Antipater's turn for guard duty, which gave them easy access to Alexander. Epimenes, who was the youngest, lost his nerve, and told of the plot to Euryloches, his elder brother, who was also a page. In great alarm he rushed with the tale to Ptolemy, hoping to save the lives of both his brother and Alexander. Ptolemy immediately reported the facts to the king and the six pages were arrested. They were tried before a military tribunal, Hermolaos made matters far worse for himself and the other conspirators when he tried to defend himself by saying: "The king has murdered Philotas, Parmenion and Cleitus, and he has raised eastern slaves above we Macedonians. We are now all pawns in Alexander's hands for no man may speak the truth without finding his own death. We planned to deliver Macedon from this tyrant, who demands the honours due only to a god ..." and his voice trailed off in nervous misery.

The guilty verdict of treason brought a melancholy end to the trial and the six were condemned to death by stoning, to the great grief of all but the most hardened Macedonian. Later, even the king felt a deep remorse for the lives of his young pages and, after further investigation, he discovered that Callisthenes had bitterly criticised him to all of them. He decided that Callisthenes was the real instigator of the plot and he was arrested for both inciting the pages, who were entrusted to his care, and for treason. The king had to consider whether, as a Greek, Callisthenes should be returned to Corinth and there tried by the Synhedrion of the League of Corinth, or whether, he should be tried by a military court in the camp. He was, meanwhile, held in chains and heavily guarded to prevent his escape. The king had sent for Nearchos to join him at the time of his marriage to Roxane and he now arrived to a great welcome on the Rock of Chorienes. The number of Macedonians in the army was so greatly reduced by death, garrison and administrative duty in the provinces, and by settlement in Alexander's new cities, that the king needed his support and that of the men whom he brought with him. Nearchos expressed great surprise at the size of the army, especially of the swollen enlistment of so many men, Greeks and Persians, who had served the defeated enemy. We were ready to leave Chorienes in the spring, and we moved out towards Bactria, the Hindu Kush, and beyond their heights into Arachosia. The lady Roxane rode in a litter near the king. She was as beautiful as a rose but seemed to show no strength of will which, when I remembered the epic battles between Philip and Olympias, had to be a vast improvement and we were all relieved that she demonstrated no interest in the affairs of state.

Although the Persians were integrated into the army, we lived separately from them and many of our men became more demoralised by every new favour granted to the foreigners by the king. Histanes, the brother of Roxane, was enrolled in the cavalry and so was with us by day, and we found his arrogance particularly offensive and hard to bear as we talked amongst ourselves. There were even ugly rumours that Alexander planned to rid himself of all Macedonians and found a new eastern empire with himself as a god-king.

To add to our misery, we endured terrible heat on the open steppes and many of the women and children and even some of the men died from lack of water and the accumulated miseries of the march. At last, we found some relief when we reached the mountain passes. This time, remembering the cruel crossing, when we had marched in the opposite direction during harsh winter weather, we were fortunate to find that the snow only rested lightly on the surface of the earth.

The lofty mountains were improbably beautiful, and around us the peaks and precipices echoed back our voices and all the other noises made by the expedition. Above us, the luminous air was brilliant with sunlight and warmth, until night fell, when the cold air descended and we huddled round the warmth of campfires endlessly talking of Macedon and our lives in our native land. We, also, remembered all those who had died in battle or by murder at another's hands since we had crossed the Hellespont. Alexander lived apart from us in his tents with Roxane and her Persian relatives and Macedonians whispered of his ingratitude with bitter words. Perdicass, Coenus and Ptolemy attempted to warn the king, but he brushed them aside, and their words were as useless as leaves falling from the trees in the chill of autumn. From the mountains, we descended again to the valley of the River Kophen, where we camped for a few days of rest. The king offered sacrifices to Athene in gratitude for the safety of the expedition. At the end of the rites, Alexander summoned us to a generals' conference and when we were all assembled, he said: "Ahead lies the great Indus River. In order to secure our supply lines, we must subdue all the tribes between our present position and the river. Hephaestion and Perdicass will leave in advance, in command of separate columns, and they will construct a bridge across the Indus. As usual, geographers will go with them to chart the route and send back copies with all the details of the road marked for our use.

"The rest of the army will follow, pacifying the tribes as they advance. I anticipate that our new conquests will yield us great riches to add to the treasury already in our hands, which will be distributed after the needs of the expedition have been met."

There were angry mutterings of dissent from the Macedonians who had expected the king to concede to Macedonian feelings and announce a return to our homeland. Alexander ignored our bitter concerns and spurred us instead to action and further conquests in the lands beckoning him to the furthest east and resentment festered in the hearts of his countrymen.

Hephaestion and Perdicass worked on the arrangements for their separate expeditions. They enrolled pacers to measure the distances that they travelled, engineers, a few scientists, geographers, and writers to record their progress for the official diaries of the expedition. They each took a small part of the supply train, together with some of the women and children attached to their men. Craterus, under the king, commanded the rest of the army, and we marched east some time after the departure of Hephaestion and Perdicass. We came to a city named Nyssa, which we heard had been founded by Dionysos, and that the people preserved many of the traditions connected with the god. We visited a grove on Mount Neros to find laurel and ivy growing, as on our own mountain heights, and here Alexander offered sacrifices and held a great feast to honour the local people, their gods and their customs.

After this unexpected interlude, we continued eastwards,

and we were amongst tribesmen who were so fierce and brave in protecting their territory and homes that they had never been entirely subdued, not even by the might of the Persian Empire. Alexander and Ptolemy were both injured in the first action against the tribesmen and we were delayed for seven days as they recovered from their wounds. The local town was destroyed and the women enslaved, by command of the king, as a warning to all those other towns, which lay in our path. We came to the territory of a tribe, which was in alliance with the King of Kashmir. He had sent massive reinforcements to their chief fortress; this we seized only after a savage battle. Even the women resisted us as they fought and clawed our soldiers in the tradition of Amazons. The losses, on both sides, were extremely heavy and the stench of blood running in the streets and the screams and groans of the injured, especially of the children, filled the air with misery. Alexander severely punished the people left alive in the fortress, through taxation and enslavement. Many of them escaped and, under cover of night, fled eastwards towards their ally in Kashmir.

They left behind a strong fortress, which the king garrisoned, and he called on veteran volunteers to leave the army and settle in the town with their women and children. When all this was achieved, we continued the march, using charts sent back to the king by Hephaestion, which led us to the valley of the Peukelaotis, until we finally reached the banks of the River Indus. We now turned north following the river to the fortified Aornos Rock. The great crag appeared to be impregnable, and the tribesmen, behind its high walls, were free to attack the expedition in lightning raids and then retreat at will. The king, once he had surveyed the Rock, gave orders to prepare for an attack against the fortress. The engineers began work on a ramp wide enough for our siege machines, with room to spare for the men to manipulate them up the slope. As they worked, the army trained intensively for the assault until the king ordered us to rest for two days. On the first night, we gathered in his tent and he spoke to us of his ancestor, Herakles, who had delivered Prometheos in these mountains of the Indian Caucasus. Alexander, all his life, had longed to surpass the legendary deeds of his hero and even weary Macedonians found a new inspiration in the ancient story and comfort from being, once again, close to Alexander.

The siege machines were finally in position against the walls.

We pounded them night and day until a breach allowed us to fight our way into the fortress. The king led the attack and, after a hard and bloody battle, we reached the top of the great Rock, and Alexander held all the lands of India from the Indus to the Parapamisos Mountains, which bordered the old Persian Empire. He named this conquest Cis-India, and he appointed Nicanor of Stagira, to be the new satrap with Siscottus, an Indian, to command the garrison – a new and unwelcome departure. Macedonians held this position in every other conquered city. We now turned south to find Hephaestion and Perdicass, who were camped together on the banks of the Indus. By the time that we arrived at their position, they had built a bridge across the river, made from confiscated boats lashed together. Alexander ordered the army to rest for thirty days and sent messengers and an army escort to bring the civilians and supply train to our position. It was already winter and we spent the time repairing our clothing and equipment, a very welcome break from the hard march from the Rock of Chorienes, and the eight long seasons since we had crossed the Hellespont. Amongst all the foreign embassies who now arrived to greet Alexander, one of the most important was from the Prince of Taxila, a country across the Indus. He acknowledged the king's succession to Darius, and he offered Alexander his own capital, without any conditions. He had previously sent a petition, during our march through Sogdiana, when he asked for an alliance with the king against his hostile neighbours, Abisares and Porus. Alexander sent his ambassador back to this prince and when he returned, the king accepted, in tribute, the city of Taxila, which we heard was the principal town between the Indus and the River Hydaspes.

Chapter 23

The civilians and supply train arrived safely on the banks of the River Indus. At the end of a thirty day rest period, we crossed over the river by the bridge of boats built by Hephaestion and Perdicass and their men. It was a hazardous undertaking, especially for the women and children and horses, which required a great deal of coaxing and help on the swaying boats. When all were across, the king offered sacrifices and he gave heartfelt thanks to the gods for our advance. It was early spring and the earth was bright with flowers, matched by the dress of the local women, as we began our march into the unknown lands of the far, distant east. To our north loomed the great mountain range of the Caucasus, known to the inhabitants as the Himalayas, from the heights the rivers brought down alluvial silt to the plains, and they were made richly fertile and the soil grew abundant crops of food. We marvelled at all that we saw. The land was densely populated by a dark-skinned people who wore loose, colourful robes and bright cloths wound round their heads. Most of them kept a few goats and sheep for domestic use and we saw many wild animals and brilliantly coloured birds. The people worshipped a pantheon of gods, and they were quite different from the Greek Olympians. It was a land of noise, colours and the fresh beauty of a new spring season.

As we neared the city of Taxila, an embassy arrived from that Prince. They brought his submission and that of all his people to Alexander, the new Great King. They were all dressed in fine silks in the gaudiest colours and jewels sparkled on their fingers, in their headdresses and robes and on the daggers which they wore in their waist sashes. They rivalled the profusion of flowers blooming to the distant horizons. We Macedonians were dazzled

247

by the sun and colour and we breathed the scents of flowers, exotic spices and humanity and our minds were more than a little confused by the people and their alien customs. We came across a party of ascetics who were quite naked in the sun and oblivious to its burning rays. We were told that they were equally indifferent to the chill of night. Alexander was curious about their detachment from the world, and he asked them many questions, through interpreters, about the religion which inspired them. He carefully listened to their answers, but for the most part the rest of us were gone too long from home and so were indifferent to their strange beliefs. Much more exciting was the arrival of King Taxiles mounted on a great elephant. It was splendidly decorated and he was escorted by his armoured soldiers and local princelings, as we advanced to the gates of his city. Amongst the magnificent gifts which he offered to Alexander were 200 talents of silver, thousands of sheep, sacrificial wild beasts and 30 elephants and these animals were fervently desired by the king as a mighty new machine of war. After the welcoming ceremonies, Taxiles and Alexander entered the city together to the wild acclaim of the people and they rode side by side to the palace in Taxila. Before entering, the king addressed the people in rather strange words as they were already free from foreign domination, but it was his standard greeting of reassurance and peace to a newly conquered people and he said to them: "We come to you, not as conquerors, but as liberators. We intend to negotiate with King Porus of Pauravus to free you and his own people from any future threat of war between you. Taxiles is still your king and all those who serve him loyally also serve Alexander and they will be rewarded accordingly."

Alexander then gave Taxiles his own costly gifts including Macedonian horses highly trained for war, which added great prestige to the local ruler. Taxiles had even more gifts for the king; his subjects carried a king's ransom in money and great boxes of drinking vessels and plates worked in the purest of gold. We recognised them at once, for they were the finest products of Greece and they were powerful symbols to Alexander of the unity between east and west in his cherished conception of his own unique empire. The city was alive that night with the excitement of a great feast held for all the people. It was mysterious to us that they should rejoice to lose their freedom to Alexander but, we reasoned, that they possibly preferred an easy capitulation to a benevolent conqueror who showered them with gifts, rather than to endure a siege and a certain, bitter defeat. The king's reputation had preceded his arrival in Taxila.

Within a few days, the generals were gathered in Alexander's tent. He advised us that he had no desire to fight Porus, in the neighbouring kingdom, unless he was denied the right of passage across his land, which must lie between Taxila and Ocean. He sent an embassy to Porus to negotiate terms for peace between them. We marched from Taxila, after a few exciting days spent in the city enjoying the people's friendly hospitality. I am sure that they were all glad to see us leave, after they had met the expense of their magnificent gifts to Alexander and the hospitality that they had shown to us. They were, however, left the consolation of their city intact from the ravages of war and their way of life undisturbed by a large garrison of alien troops. We moved towards the River Hydaspes and an uncertain reception by King Porus. We had, already, neared the west bank of the river when we met his embassy to Alexander, escorted by the king's own ambassador to Porus.

The Indians were richly dressed, but extremely nervous when they presented their master's letter to the king, and they carefully watched as he read its contents. Porus wrote that he would meet Alexander on his own territory but that he would receive him with weapons and not the surrender of his kingdom. The wretched members of the embassy shook in anticipation of death at the hands of Alexander but they had nothing to fear from the king; he was ever punctilious in his courtesy to accredited ambassadors and he always sent them home in complete safety.

Alexander held a council of war with the generals to plan his strategy for meeting with the rebellious king. He concluded the council by saying: "We are two days' march from the Hydaspes, where Porus is waiting for us. The rainy season has already begun and I have heard that as the rains increase, the land is flooded and everything manufactured by man rots. We must therefore march at once, before we are bogged down and unable to continue the expedition or purchase supplies for our survival. I understand that Porus is waiting, with a great army, across the river, and we accept his challenge to war in the certainty of our victory. The army will be ready to march at sunrise."

We reached the river and found it swollen by the rains into a mighty torrent. We made our camp as we endured great cloudbursts of solid water and our weapons immediately rusted in the continuous downpour. Many of the men developed high fevers and dreadful, open sores on their skins as the rain made a complete tribulation of our lives, tormenting us with its ferocity, and men died either from sickness or dreadful despair. Then, miraculously, the rain stopped, and we could see the enemy camp on the other side of the river. Most alarming, to us, was the great number of elephants drawn up on the opposite bank and their loud trumpeting filled the air with dreadful menace. A huge army stretched behind them beyond our sight. Alexander rode amongst our men reassuring them, by his confidence in our victory.

He ordered a part of the army to line up on the bank to give Porus the impression that our attack would come from opposite his position. The rest of the army marched up and down the river to keep the enemy always on the alert, in an effort to exhaust them as they kept watch over our movements. Our spies discovered a ford south of our camp, and Alexander made preparations to cross by this, under cover of darkness. Enemy spies must also have been alert and reporting our stratagems, for once we were across the river on the eastern bank, we encountered chariots leading detachments of their cavalry.

We soon saw that the enemy force was very small and that the chariots were quite unable to manoeuvre in the mud and their cavalry consequently lost rank and floundered about in disorganised chaos. They did come together at our approach and fought fiercely against us, but they were no match, and soon most of them lay dead on the ground, including their leader, a son of Porus. Alexander sent the enemy survivors back to Porus with news of their defeat in the hope that this was sufficient incentive for him to concede a Macedonian victory. The king always tried to avoid battles, to spare lives and property, but he never hesitated to meet resistance with war. Our army now regrouped, advanced along the river bank and crossed over to join us. As we approached the enemy positions, we saw arrayed before us the greatest army since the Battlefield of Gaugamela. In addition to the elephants, there was a cavalry force at least four times greater than our own, which was supported by infantry units of proportionate strength.

The elephants were spread amongst many of the enemy units and we were a tiny army against their enormous numbers. The king ordered the phalanx into position opposite the enemy, with the cavalry, under Coenos, flanking it at either side. Under the king's orders, we attacked every weak point in the enemy positions and then regrouped after each skirmish. The elephants almost proved to be our ally, as they prevented the enemy units from responding quickly to our manoeuvres and we found them more terrifying, because of their size, than as a weapon used against us. They quickly panicked in the ugly noise and confusion and they trampled many of their own soldiers to death.

We gradually gained ground from each small victory until, all along the battlefront, Macedonians were on the attack and by nightfall Porus was routed.

The second son of Porus, together with many of the other enemy commanders, was also dead and thousands of their ordinary soldiers had been killed. It was a scene of carnage and horror to sicken the most seasoned soldier on either side.

Porus signalled to his men, from his position on the back of the largest elephant in his army, the end of the battle. We watched as an attendant touched the animal gently with a stick. The elephant knelt and gently lifted Porus with its trunk, and then carefully placed him on the ground. An aide escorted the enemy king towards Alexander, who dismounted from Bucephalos and walked to meet him across the blood-soaked field of battle.

The old man was much taller than most of the Indian people and of a high and noble bearing. He was bleeding profusely from an ugly shoulder wound and obviously in great pain. He greeted Alexander with a courteous salutation which was returned by the king who asked him, "How shall I treat you?"

Porus answered him with one word: "Royally!"

And the king replied: "That was my intention, but what do you desire personally?"

Porus answered Alexander and said: "With that I have covered everything."

Alexander immediately turned to address the two armies and confirmed Porus as king of his country and satrap over all the neighbouring lands and people. He not only showed his personal admiration for the gallant old warrior, and his great dignity in such adversity but, also, respect for the civilisation which we found amongst these barbarian people.

Alexander, by his generous treatment of first Taxiles, and now Porus, hoped to show his policy of pacification to all the other kings of this vast land of India and convince them, in advance, not to oppose his expedition. He intended to use his successes to spread Greek culture and the koine, the language which had evolved from Greek since we crossed the Hellespont, and the concept of unity throughout the conquered territories.

We cleared the battlefield and both sides cremated their dead with great sorrow and respect. It was time for a conciliatory feast beyond the city to celebrate our victory amongst the living. The king shared meat and wine with Porus and his men, to cement the alliance, which he had forged between them. Alexander was particularly careful to show honour to Porus amongst his own people so that his authority would not be diminished after so spectacular a defeat.

The feast was a great state occasion. Alexander was dressed in Persian robes, which emphasised his Asian title 'King of Kings', and his rule over all the Asian peoples gathered together on the battlefield. We Macedonians were far outnumbered by Greeks, Persians, Indians, Medes, Arabs, Babylonians, Phoenicians, Cypriots, Jews and Egyptians attached to the court, army and civilian train. We sat apart and now that the battle was won, we felt again sorrow and anger to be so far from our home in Macedon.

The food that night was the best of all the lands between Macedon and the River Hydaspes and peacock proud were all the furnishings of the king's banqueting tent. Hephaestion sat on Alexander's right hand and Porus was honoured on his left side.

Hephaestion soon succumbed to the influence of wine. His face was bloated and red and his speech was slurred, but Alexander, neither then, nor at any other time, showed any displeasure with his friend's excesses. In his case, the king waved the Delphie rule of 'moderation in all things'.

The celebration was at its height when a page approached Alexander and, as he stood nervously waiting for the king's attention, it was obvious to all of us that he brought terrible news. The king turned to him and gave him permission to speak and, amidst the hush that fell, his clear young voice faltered as he said: "Sire! Bucephalos has died this hour."

Alexander, with all happiness drained from his face, rose to his feet and rushed from the tent, followed by Craterus, the staggering Hephaestion, Ptolemy, Coenos, Seleucos and myself amongst many others of those present that night. We arrived at the stable to a melancholy scene. The area was lighted by torches and in the flickering shadows we saw the grooms gathered round the body of the old warhorse who was dearer to the king than any living man on earth. Alexander knelt beside the noble animal and cradled his head in his arms. I had seen him moved by many emotions but by none so deep as that caused by the death of Bucephalos, the most trusted companion of his life and heart, to whom he owed so many victories throughout his campaign. His grief showed in the stark misery of his face and in his anguished voice as he spoke his farewell to the great horse. We all shared his sorrow and bitter grief but not one of us could comfort Alexander on this darkest day of his life.

I walked away from the sorrowful scene, and I thought back to the day, now so long ago, when a young prince had gently tamed the wild horse with the strangely blazoned head, on a Macedonian plain. I remembered, also, all the other great moments when Alexander, astride the great black stallion, had paraded before his army and I saw so clearly in my mind's eye the many times that they had galloped together into battle and overcome every adversary. Bucephalos was almost as great a legend as Alexander himself and, amongst the Asians who prized horses above every other possession, the stallion was the talisman of the king's invincible march across their lands.

Alexander built a town nearby and he named it in memory of Bucephalos and he garrisoned it only with Macedonians. The civic and cultural centre was entirely Greek in architecture and a noble statue of the beloved stallion dominated the agora. The city of Bucephalos perpetuated, for all time the most famous horse in history and, in case other men forget, it is true that he had never been ridden by any man except Alexander of Macedon and, with his death, died the youth of the king. The day after the death of Bucephalos, Porus, with his courtiers and the remnants of his army, returned to his own capital and left Alexander to his grief. Macedonians criticised the king's generosity to this defeated enemy and Meleager even risked his life making adverse comments in the presence of the king when he remarked ironically: "Alexander has found a man worthy of a thousand talents."

The king bit his lip, and his face flushed, as he replied: "I have paid a cheap price for peace and saved many Macedonian lives, which would have been lost in prolonging a war. Porus has paid a very bitter price, the death of his sons and so many of his men, in fighting against us."

His words were conciliatory, for ever in his heart did he regret the death of Cleitus and he always tried to turn away from words of provocation amongst his Macedonians, and the tense moment was over with the departure of Meleagar to his own quarters. The rain held off, and new recruits arrived from Greece. They were absorbed into the units, which had suffered losses during the recent battle. We repaired our weapons, dried out our clothes and threw away food ruined in the deluge. The civilian train caught up with us and when the expedition was restored to working order, Alexander held a council to lay out his plans for our next advance. He first said: "Craterus will remain here to build the new city of Bucephalos according to the plans, which are now ready.

"I have studied these regions with the geographers and we are far beyond where we expected to find Ocean. The Hydaspes, I learn, is a tributary of the Indus and there is yet another river, which also flows into that great river and is beyond our present position, called the Acesines. Not far beyond must lie Ocean, which, I am told, joins with the Hyrcanian Sea and when we reach it, the whole earth will be ours and our mission will have found its furthest limit. We shall then take time to explore all the lands now under our rule and establish sea-lanes for trade in every province. We shall spread Hellenic laws and customs and our liberal government for the benefit of all the people.

"We have suffered too many grievous losses, especially in this last battle against Porus, and we have also left many of our best men in our rear to administer the provinces. Therefore, all of you, who are still with the expedition have more than a double value to our enterprise and all the new recruits, who have flocked to join us, are most welcome replacements.

"I intend to offer sacrifices to all the gods for our arrival in this distant land and we shall organise games to celebrate our victory over Porus. These will be followed by seven days' rest and we shall then march in the final part of our great adventure."

The king and Craterus hunted during the seven days of rest. They killed tiger and wild boar and captured peacocks and many other exotic animals, which were sent back to Aristotle, now living in Athens. Alexander returned to the camp a little more reconciled to the death of Bucephalos, although he felt the loss of the great horse at every day's dawning. Grief saddens a man's heart for all time and, unlike joy, may not be fully shared. Few of us, except Hephaestion, were still close to the king. His position over so great an empire, and his successes against all adversaries, provoked jealousy, rivalry and even murder, as we had seen, and his place was lonely at the pinnacle of power. His loss was the greater, for Bucephalos had been entirely his, although the great horse was honoured throughout the army in fact and legend. Alexander turned to those who most loved him, especially Hephaestion, although Craterus was the better man, always honest and the finer soldier, but the king needed a sympathetic heart. I was sorry, for many reasons, to leave Craterus when we marched into the rising sun, towards the River Acesines. Friendship, in the army, can play no part in military duty, but the men were always easier under his command and they were not afraid to approach him with a grievance or to request a favour. From him flowed an impartial and ready justice down through all the ranks to the newest recruit.

The land between the rivers was similar to that of Egypt. Certain of the food staples were identical and the crocodiles of the Indus region seemed to prove that we must have reached the source of the Nile. The king sent reports of this great news to Antipater, Olympias and Aristotle as now the knowledge of all mankind was so much greater and the king could establish trade routes for the benefit of commerce and the spread of knowledge. As we marched, a constant stream of merchants, recruits, suppliants, ambassadors and administrators arrived in the camp from all the districts of India and far beyond. The king questioned them all on their homelands and learned that there were three more tributaries of the Indus before us and that they all joined together and flowed into the southern sea.

The king was disappointed that all the reports agreed that beyond the rivers was not eastern Ocean, but an immense desert, and maps were drawn to chart this new information. Aristotle had believed, but we found that he was in error, that the eastern coast could be seen from the Indian Caucasus, or Parapamisus range of mountains. We felt that Ocean must indeed be far beyond our present position and even beyond the reach of Alexander, whose leadership and invincible spirit had brought us so far into the lands of Asia.

Alexander held a council to show the new maps that the geographers had drawn as far as the Acesines. He called in a courier and gave him copies to take back to Craterus with suggestions of places to explore and with orders to send soldiers, and enough slaves, into the mountains to fell trees and to build a great fleet of ships. Alexander spoke to the council, as an explorer gripped by new discoveries of lands and people still unknown to us. He pointed out all the rivers, plains, deserts, mountains and seas marked on the charts before him and in his voice, we heard the enthusiasm of his youth and the keen edge of his leadership. We were exhilarated and relieved that his grief over the death of Bucephalos was not so sharp, but his face was deeply lined from the pain of his terrible wounds and the cares of the expedition. He turned from his charts and said: "During the time, which it will take Craterus to build a fleet, I propose to continue the campaign further to our east to confirm all the reports, which we have gathered on these new lands. I am informed that there are hostile tribes across the Acesines and I intend to subdue them in order to leave a pacified border. I plan to avoid the worst of the sun's damaging heat by marching in a more northerly direction, where my guides assure me that there are wooded hills and sufficient water for all our needs.

"Nothing in the campaign so far matches the importance of what still lies before us. We must fully open the east to the west and the west to the east and uncover all that is mysterious to us in these lands.

"We shall continue to collect animals, plants and minerals on our route for Aristotle to examine and record. The astronomers will chart the stars as we advance, and we shall keep tables of the rainfall and the sicknesses, which ravage the people. Instructors will remain in the town to teach the people the Koine as the common language of us all. We shall then have the necessary means of communication to establish our government over all the territory of India.

"I say to you that, because of this expedition, there will be written the most glorious chapter in history and the greatness of our achievements will echo down through future generations. When scholars write their accounts, they will look back and date a great turning point by our achievements, for our little army has indeed given us control of the world.

"To these most ancient civilisations, we shall give the

Hellenistic ethos, and to the spiritual values of the east, we shall bring the rational and scientific learning of the west. All men will live under God, and the excellence of the government which we have given to them and justice will rule throughout our new empire. The seas will become highways for scholars and commerce and a new enlightenment will cover the earth with truth. The gods have truly favoured our whole enterprise and only with their blessing have we come this far.

"We have met and overcome so many hardships, which would have defeated lesser men, and through them all I, Alexander, have served you well as you have served me and together we have given our thanks to the gods. We shall now march until Ocean lies before us and at last we are at the end of the earth."

We soon heard, if spies are to be believed, that the subject people received the news of Alexander's speech with enthusiasm. They believed that they were offered, in exchange for their submission to the king, an equal share with Macedonians in peace and the administration of the empire. The Greeks and Macedonians, however, were grown weary of a lifetime of campaigns, wars and marches, and they very reluctantly prepared to continue onwards.

As we reached the Acesines, a spy brought in a report that a nephew of Porus was leading a revolt against Alexander. The king was confident that his new ally would put it down and honour their alliance. Hephaestion was more often drunk than sober and when we crossed the river, Alexander left him behind to build a new city and to administer the land between the Acesines and the Hydaspes. We all hoped that the work would return him to more sober ways. We soon found that the land across the river was indeed infested with belligerent tribes and we were forced to fight many skirmishes against them. We approached the fortified city of Sangala and the gates were closed to our advance. Many of the local tribes had sent their men to defend the city against us. We camped outside the walls and we woke up one morning to find that the enemy was drawn up on a hill on our side of the walls and near to a gate and that they had protected themselves behind a great barrier of carts.

The king placed the best archers in front of the hill, flanked by cavalry detachments, to hold the enemy to his position. Behind the archers, the phalanx waited to advance. Perdicass and his mounted regiment, with the Royal Squadron in support at either side, and beyond them archers on the extended line, were in position. The reserve units of the phalanx and cavalry waited in the rear to fill gaps, as they occurred, in the front line. It was a typical Macedonian battle order as we took up our positions.

Alexander gave the order to advance. The enemy was concentrated on the hill making it impossible to launch an attack. Along the whole line, as we advanced, we were met by a hail of arrows. The king immediately realised that we were at a disadvantage and he dismounted from his horse, to lead the phalanx against the carts which concealed the enemy.

The tribesmen fought a hard battle as we grew closer up the hill near to hand-to-hand fighting; they gradually retreated into their town. When the last of them was inside, they closed the gates and appeared on the walls to shower us with their arrows. We lost some men and horses, especially from amongst the Persian mercenaries and more of these than all the Macedonians killed in the battles against Darius.

The king ordered the army to encircle the city and many of the enemy tribesmen were killed as they tried to escape over the walls. On the fourth night of the siege, the gates of the city were suddenly flung open and the Indians came rushing through them. Ptolemy was ready and waiting and most of them were cut down before they had advanced more than a few steps.

We now easily breached the walls. After bitter fighting against the few remaining tribesmen, we overcame their defence and the king razed the city to the ground to punish the people's resistance. Porus had arrived to visit the king during the siege and he was dispatched, with all his elephants, as the emissary of Alexander, to receive the surrender of all the towns, which had sent men to the aid of Sangala. He had made a recovery from his wounds, and he and Alexander honoured each other as brave, soldierly kings.

We left the desolation of Sangala and crossed the River Hydraotes, where we were greeted by Phageus, the local ruler. He had heard of the fate of Sangala and readily submitted his city and land to Alexander and he agreed to the appointment of a Macedonian satrap. He was confirmed as king of his province and he quickly gave advice and offered guides for the next part of the expedition. He told Alexander that we should cross a river called the Hyphasis which was also a tributary of the River Indus. Beyond the Hyphasis, we would find an immense desert, a full twelve days' march across, and then the River Ganges and more lands of great wealth. Porus confirmed his report and we all questioned amongst ourselves where Alexander might find Ocean, if it existed, and where indeed was the limit of earth and Alexander's ambition. The king pointed out that the River Ganges must either completely flood the land or flow into a sea and eventually reach Ocean. The words of Phageus, describing all the new lands before us, were as tinder in the fire of Alexander's ambition and he questioned everyone who came into the camp for their knowledge of the countries which lay before us.

During the march to the Hyphasis, we were drenched every day by the rains of the Indian summer. We were exhausted by our efforts to deal with the flooding waters, trying to keep our equipment in serviceable condition and caring for the horses when they fell sick. They quickly died. Many of the men, the women and children also died from fevers and unknown diseases. Our food stores were ruined and we all suffered from insect bites, infections of the skin, ulcers and a horrible loss of weight so that our bones stood out as they pressed against our skin. The mercenaries were in an even worse state and they whined of the hardships incessantly until the sickest were out of their misery in the arms of death. We were, for the first time, a demoralised army. It is far easier to fight a brave and well-trained enemy than the elements, and many read the weather as a sign from the gods that they wished us to leave these hostile lands and return to Macedon.

Alexander admitted that, although no enemy had defeated us, we were lost to a far greater adversary and he paraded the army and we faced west, so that when he rode out before us, his eyes still looked to the east in the lonely solitude of his ambition. The ranks of men were tense as we waited for him to speak. I wished that Craterus had been present to lend his strength to the king; he was alone and diminished in size on a smaller horse than Bucephalos. Finally he spoke: "Men of my army, you have nobly borne all the hardships of more than eight seasons of campaigning. You have endured hardships, which lesser men could never have faced, you have crossed searing plains and deserts and high, snowy mountains, you have survived disease and wounds inflicted on so many battlefields and lost many of your friends. You have forded impossibly wide rivers and destroyed the Persian threat against Greece forever and you have gained the greatest empire the world has ever known. I have shared all the same hardships but now before us is a grand new challenge. There are lands still undreamed of between here and eastern Ocean and I ask you to unsheathe your swords and come with me to discover these new worlds, which shall belong to Macedonians ..."

The rest of his words were drowned in a mighty roar of anger and revolt. Without the Macedonians, Alexander could not cross the river for his Persians were miserable fighters in the cause of this King of Kings and the Macedonians now would go no further. Coenos, as the noise died down, rode his horse out towards Alexander's position and he spoke for us all to the king and I clearly heard his words: "O Alexander! You speak the truth in describing what the men have endured, for your sake, since we crossed the Hellespont. Now we are weary unto death and we yearn for our families and the land of our birth. We are tired of alien ways and would again breathe the clear air of Macedon. We long to regain our strength and refresh ourselves under the skies of home.

"We say to you, lead us back to Macedon as Macedon's King, for we are wearied by barbarians and their vain ways. Too many of our brothers and friends have already died in your service and the few of us who are left expect to enjoy a retirement from our labours on your behalf. Under your rule has fallen so vast an empire that not all our resources can contain it. If we venture further, our supply lines can be cut and we shall be stranded far from home, amongst hostile people, and then we shall die as exiles.

"You, O King! cannot wish to command the Macedonians by decree; for you say yourself that you will lead us only when you have persuaded us, and that you will not enforce your will, if you are persuaded otherwise by your Macedonians. It seems, therefore, that the only question between us is, who offers the best argument for our next objective?"

Coenos spoke in conciliatory words which were met by shouts of approval from Macedonian throats, although most of the eastern mercenaries were unable to understand his words; none present could fail to sense the mood of the Greeks or hear the loud groans as the heavens opened up again to join the earth with sheets of rain. Over army and land lay the strong stench of urine, wet horses, clothing, leather, dirt and men. Rain streamed down our faces; it saturated our clothing, turned the earth into a sea of slimy mud and settled in puddles and lakes. The water roared, as it lashed down, in the fury of unknown gods and drowned out every other sound. It made each one of us, even Alexander, small in our helplessness to fight and conquer such an unnatural enemy.

The king sat watchfully astride his horse, as the army fell into a sullen silence. His image was blurred by rain and the light of Apollo no longer shone upon him. He turned his horse and rode away. Ptolemy gave him time to clear the parade ground and then dismissed the men. I rode across the field to join him and together we went to Alexander's tent to see the king, but the guard refused to admit us and he remained secluded for two long days.

During that time, Ptolemy walked amongst the Macedonians to calm the men. He listened to their problems, which had festered dangerously into near revolt, for he was a true Macedonian and the bravest soldier, and he shared many of their feelings. He quietened the voices raised against the king, and shamed the most vociferous for their excessive language. Ptolemy, in the absence of Craterus, was the leader, after the king, of the Macedonians and Alexander needed him, if we were to survive as an army, and not disintegrate into a rabble; a prey to revolution amongst the mercenaries or from murderous attacks by conquered people. The time was here for a final confrontation between Alexander and the Macedonians.

When the rain ceased the hot sun drew moisture from the earth in vaporous steam and everything rotted until it decomposed into a filthy slime. This was surely a land of morbid extremes, parched by searing sun or inundated by torrential rains. It had both steaming jungle and sterile desert and, not least, it had a teeming population and starving beggars displaying malignant sores and deformities in the hope of compelling pity and so extracting money from passers-by. There were also ferocious animals, dangerous snakes, birds of iridescent, brilliant plumage, and scores of holy men indifferent to the world, in their pursuit of abstract mysticism.

For Macedonians, a most disagreeable land. Some years, the people reaped an abundant harvest; in others, they endured a total failure of their crops because the rains failed or came in torrents and flooded the land. We heard of famines, pestilences and wars ravaging people and animals. We weary Greeks felt a profound misery and homesickness and a longing for our own temperate land. Many of us had children, now grown into strangers, and others of us were orphaned or widowed during the long campaign. We offered no threat of personal danger or treason to the king. We only begged him to end his dream of ever greater dominion, ever further from Macedon and Greece.

The king emerged from his tent on the third day following the last parade of the army. He sent for Indian priests to join him and then he walked to the bank of the Hyphasis and stood gazing across to the far side. The priests offered sacrifices for a safe river crossing and Macedonians gathered to watch, in a sullen crowd, unwilling witnesses to vain ceremonies. Greek and Chaldean seers read many omens from the sacrifices and declared them all unfavourable towards a river crossing and in the tense silence, Alexander walked in the direction of the crowd and spoke to all his men gathered there: "Macedonians, your will is obvious and I must heed the omens so unanimously shown to me, therefore this river shall be the limit of our expedition. You have all been given many opportunities to return to Macedon so why do you continuously reproach me, at every advance that I make, for you serve me voluntarily? In gratitude to the gods who have brought us victoriously across the world to these eastern boundaries, I shall now erect twelve altars to honour them. They will also honour Herakles, my own ancestor, who also raised twelve altars at the western limit of the world. When the masons have completed their work, we shall dedicate the altars and then we shall turn to march with the sun, until the light of Apollo once more shines on us on the distant shore of the Hellespont."

As Alexander finished speaking, a heartfelt, mighty cheer went up to heaven from every Macedonian throat. The men were wild with joy and, by conceding to them, Alexander bound them back to his leadership. The king walked away from the river bank, a remote and lonely figure and I suspected that he was already planning a future for the expedition.

All of the Macedonians celebrated throughout the day and their wine cups were filled and refilled. Alexander's praises rose to the heavens in impromptu song and every scribe was occupied writing letters for dispatch to Macedon with the good news of our return.

The king held a great feast that night and, in the absence

of Hephaestion and Craterus, Ptolemy sat at his right hand and Seleucos, the son of Antiochus, to his left. Coenos was several couches away, slighted because he had spoken for the Macedonians, but not banished altogether from the presence of the king. That night, Macedonians were happy and they loved Alexander more than at any time since he had adopted Persian ways. He still wore Persian dress, as if to use this happy night to gain acceptance amongst Macedonians for the hated foreign customs.

The Persians were, this night at least, in the background and Ptolemy deliberately led the conversation into the affairs of Macedon by remarking in the following words: "O King! The lady Olympias and Antipater will rejoice at the news of your return home and all Macedon and Greece will celebrate your victories and their deliverance from the Persian threat. Your homecoming will be the greatest in all history, for you bring not only stories of countless victories and great wealth, but also the promise of peace for all time and a prosperous life for all your people. They will be free to travel throughout the world and to trade and the best of our young men will train as administrators and soldiers to bring the benefits of your government to all the countries that have fallen to you. Our return journey will be a triumphal march in every land through which we pass and your army will now enjoy the rewards so rightfully theirs."

The king answered, after a pause in which all grew quiet: "Ptolemy, you speak the truth and I am glad that my army will enjoy the rewards for their labours, which you describe. In the past, I had thought that to serve with Alexander, conquer the world and gain immortality would be a sufficient prize. I was wrong, however; most men do not want the heroic in this life; rather they crave ease and comfort and they have no vision beyond their own mortality. It is, after all, granted to few men to alter the course of history, to right the ancient wrongs, which were done to a people, or to receive the loyalty of a superb army. That has all been given to me and my life is fulfilled. No man may set his ambition beyond the limits of those who must share in its fulfilment and so I return to Macedon, not having failed my men in any particular but rather having given them the world as a homeland. One day, God will send favourable omens, if not to me, to my successors, and this eastern frontier will be pushed to Ocean and every last mysterious land will be opened for full exploration. In all my undertakings, I have honoured the gods and received their favour. Without them, I could accomplish nothing. Therefore, today, I accept what all their omens tell us and I shall await that more propitious moment when I shall find other men to share in my further endeavours."

As he finished speaking, he turned to his page and proffered his goblet for more wine, and raising it, he said: "I drink to life, to the men who have heroically given theirs and to the men who will follow me in the future to wherever their horizons beckon."

We all raised our cups. The happy and excited Macedonians, eager to leave for home, did not properly hear nor heed the king's words and I knew that in his heart he had not abandoned his dreams of conquest and exploration and that he still desired above all to look upon Ocean. The gathering broke up with noisy laughter and Alexander stood alone, silently watching us leave his tent.

The next day, the king gave orders for the masons to build the altars to the twelve Olympians and the Greeks worked with a ready zeal and they did not allow Persians to share in their labours. While they worked, we prepared to march with the rising sun. Men shouted to each other and talked of their families and their lands, some bought with the Persian booty, which they had sent to Macedon. They speculated on the harvest soon to be gathered, and of their wealth and how they would increase their holdings and of how they would always be free of labour for another's profits. Even the rain held off, and we dried out our clothes, tents and supplies. We washed in the river and at last prepared food over rekindled fires.

The blacksmiths set up their workshops, the geographers corrected their charts and the scientists busied themselves gathering rocks, flowers, herbs and some animals. The whole camp bustled with activity; and happiness glowed on the men's faces but not on those, which belonged to Persians, for their future was uncertain. The few Macedonian women left in the camp shared in the general rejoicing. Most had children who had never known a settled home and there were many orphans to be cared for and escorted to their fathers' houses where Alexander intended to establish their Macedonian identity. Alexander gave the Persian women in the camp a choice of returning to their own homes, making new ones in the lands of India, or continuing with their men on the journey to Macedon; even they shared in the booty, which gave them freedom to make their best personal selection.

Alexander sent dispatches to Craterus and Hephaestion and to Antipater and to all the satraps and military commanders to announce the end of the campaign.

I felt no desire to return to Macedon. My life was now with the king for I had lost all that I held dear in Macedon. I hoped for an appointment in one of the western provinces and my first choice was Persis, ancient land of the Persians where Persepolis majestically reached up to the sky and Persian history was written. The Twelve Pillars were finally ready and dedicated by Alexander, in ancient ceremonies, on a day when the sun bathed the wet earth in glorious light. We broke our camp and King Alexander rode at the head of his army, at the beginning of the return journey towards the Hellespont and home.

Chapter 24

We marched across the pacified land between the rivers Hyphasis and Hydraotes. For the first time since leaving Macedon, we were at ease, free from the threat of attack from hostile tribes and armies. The men sang and danced all night in their joy and they willingly undertook every task necessary to keep the expedition on the road home. Even the rain had eased, and local people assured us that it would soon completely cease. Fewer men fell sick and the numbers, forever, exiled in shallow graves, under alien skies, were reduced as the earth dried up and the beneficent sun spread its light and warmth across the land.

Alexander was sombre and apart. He was deeply wounded by the Macedonian refusal to follow him across the Hyphasis. I felt that he was much less concerned that he had been forced to turn back than by the final defection, which proved that he no longer commanded the unconditional loyalty of his own men. He rode alone, burdened in solitary thought and always Ptolemy was just behind him, to give council or comfort whenever the king called him to his side.

We crossed the River Hydraotes and marched by desolate Sangala, until we reached the Acesines, where Alexander was reunited with Hephaestion. Joy and happiness shone on his face and that day we gathered in the king's tent to celebrate our arrival, and to exchange our news. As we drank wine far into the night, Alexander spoke: "I have studied the new maps and charts of the climate, crops and animals drawn up by the geographers and scientists. They carefully questioned the local people and I am now convinced that we are not at the source of the Nile, but that we have come to lands of which no-one in Greece has had any previous knowledge ..."

There was a buzz of excitement at the king's words and we paid close attention as he described to Hephaestion our arrival on the Hyphasis and, with pain in his voice, how he had been forced to discontinue the expedition and return to the Acesines. We were quiet as he continued: "And so you see, Hephaestion, I had to accept that the omens were all against any advance across the river. I was convinced that our forces were not great enough to subdue the lands beyond, for all the reports showed that they were densely populated and heavily defended. I was especially concerned that our supply route and means of communication would be in jeopardy. However, because of the revolt by the Macedonians, we are left without a garrison on our eastern border and this Alexandria, which you are building must be our last outpost until I return. We must make sure that it has a strong garrison and indestructible walls and that we have the loyalty of the local rulers before we leave their countries."

He paused, in the uneasy silence, which had fallen, and then continued: "I see that the detestable rains have undone a great deal of the work, which you had already finished in this city and tomorrow we shall make a start on all the necessary repairs and reinforce the walls and public buildings. We have many soldiers eligible for discharge and I shall offer them large rewards to settle in Alexandria-on-the-Acesines."

Hephaestion replied: "We are all amazed to find that we are not at the source of the Nile and we must conclude that the earth is a far larger place than we ever imagined possible. Therefore, it is better that you did not cross the River Hyphasis, for as you say, our army is too small to control all these vast new lands. The men, here, are also delighted that the expedition has turned back to Macedon. They have had a hard time trying to build the new city, as the rains destroyed more each day than we were able to rebuild. We have completed strong storehouses and once the public buildings are ready, a new town quickly attracts settlers, particularly if it has a strong garrison to protect the population.

"We also fought against the revolt led by the nephew of Porus; he is now dead, and if you add all the new territory to that administered by Porus, then he will be strong enough to keep the peace between the Hyphasis and the Hydaspes so that you may easily return, and continue the expedition, when the gods are favourable to a new enterprise."

His words seemed to calm the king and he answered: "What you say, Hephaestion, supports what I have planned. Porus is a king and a man of royal honour. He will rule in my name and collect only those taxes which are fair and just to the people. The country between the rivers will remain pacified under Porus and we can, therefore, leave assured of a welcome return in the future. The army is all impatience to march to Macedon, but I plan to open the sea routes to Babylon from the east, and that means that I must conquer the southern satrapies, which once were the frontier of the empire of the Persians, and at last to find Ocean."

There was a deep stillness over the gathering as it now dawned on us that Alexander, rather than take the known route to Macedon, planned a new campaign of conquest and exploration in more strange lands and so outwitted all those who had refused to cross the Hyphasis. By what means, he intended to beguile the men into new adventures was not yet apparent but I feared, once they realised that the campaign had taken a new direction, he risked an even greater defection than on the banks of the Hyphasis. We parted for the night in a sombre mood trying to weigh the consequences of the king's plans. The following day, Alexander paraded the army and outlined his plans to the men, telling them, "We are on the road home ..."

He paused to the roar of applause from the men and continued when it died down: "I intend to find an easier route rather than again cross Asia's deserts and mountains. The geographers have shown me their charts, with proof that India's rivers flow into the Indus and that flows into the same sea as the Euphrates. Craterus is building a fleet to sail down the River Hydaspes and, while Alexandria-on-the-Hydraotes is being built, I ask for volunteers to go into the mountains and cut trees so that we may build more ships in this city. We can then sail down and meet those sailing from the city of Bucephala, until we reach the point where the rivers come together, and flow on as one towards the Indus.

"Craterus reports that many new recruits have arrived from Harpalus. Nearchos has also joined him and he has brought sailors to man the ships.

"Once we reach Ocean, we shall found the trade routes to Macedon, and they will carry the world's commerce to all our people and bring us great prosperity. I expect to discover huge treasure stored in the southern satrapies and, after the cost of the expedition has been met, it will be divided, as usual, amongst you. No man in this expedition will ever want again and his heirs will be men with lands and riches to make him the first in all the world."

Alexander rode away to his tent and left the men subdued as Hephaestion dismissed them. They talked amongst themselves but few yet realised that Alexander intended to lead them on a new expedition through unknown lands. Their knowledge of the geography of Asia was limited to the parts that we travelled on the outward journey. The choice now was either to trust the king or once more rebel against him. Most of them realised that as long as Macedon was their final destination, they must accept Alexander's leadership for there was no-one else to take his place. He had made the southern way sound shorter and far easier than the hard trials of the outward journey and, until rumours of more fighting and more risks filled the camp, he had gained their acceptance for the southern route.

Porus arrived to a glad welcome from the king who gave him his dead nephew's land to add to his own and he made him satrap of all that part of India between the Hydaspes and the Hyphasis. It marked the king's high esteem for the old warrior and they continued to treat each other as equals in rank, if not in destiny.

King Abisares sent an embassy to greet the king, and they brought a large troop of elephants amongst his gifts to Alexander. The king already doubted the animals' value in battle but the gift pleased him and increased his prestige amongst the local people. Alexander received countless foreign embassies and many local leaders as we built Alexandria-on-the-Hydraotes. The fleet of ships, designed to sail down the river to where it flowed into the Indus, were built, in haste, day by day. Many of the younger men volunteered for the adventure of serving as crews and they were trained by sailors who had served in the navy under Nearchos. When, at last, the walls of the new city were standing proud and strong, Alexander held dedication ceremonies for the city and ships and made many sacrifices to the gods in gratitude for our safety, the future of the new town, and the success of the newly dedicated fleet. Some of the older men, eligible for honorable discharge, volunteered to stay behind in the city and they were given their share of bounty, with land

and farm animals for their daily sustenance. Detachments of the army, and more volunteers, were permanently assigned to man the garrison for their protection.

The expedition marched with the sun towards the River Hydaspes. The king was no longer a lonely figure at the head of the expedition. He rode with Hephaestion at his side and even from behind, we knew that he was happy again.

When we reached the banks of the Hydaspes, we marvelled at the mighty fleet under construction by the orders of Craterus. Day by day, fresh supplies of wood were brought into the camp from the mountains and they were quickly turned into planks by the carpenters, mostly Greek, Phoenician and Indian, who were all skilled and experienced craftsmen. They were transformed into our standard ships by other carpenters and specialised shipwrights.

The two new cities of Bucephala and Nicaea were rapidly nearing completion; the latter, still under construction, commemorated the victory over Porus. They, like Alexandria-on-the-Hydraotes, had been badly damaged by the rains whilst they were being built. The new walls were much stronger and many sailors and civilians were ordered to speed the repairs to both cities. As the houses were completed, discharged soldiers with their women and children moved into them and both sites bustled with noise and activity. The din from the shipyards continued night and day and it mingled with the ringing clatter of the metal workers.

Harpalus had sent a large force of 4,000 cavalry with spare horses, 12,000 men for the infantry regiments, and armour to equip many times that total. The new, combined army drilled constantly on every available piece of land and expeditions left by ship to explore the channels of the river. They brought back reports of navigational hazards, such as islands and sandbanks, and even of hostile tribes, which secretly watched them from the river banks. The king had charts drawn according to the men's observations and ordered soldiers to serve in the ships for the protection of the vessels and of the sailors.

Alexander approached several of the generals and asked them to take command of the fleet but they all declined on the grounds that they had no experience of ships or sailing. Nearchos had only recently arrived in the camp and the king very reluctantly asked him to take command of the fleet. I think that he was hesitant to put so close a friend in an unknown and dangerous appointment. Nearchos immediately accepted and the confidence of the men on the ships grew accordingly; not only was he Alexander's most trusted admiral but he was also his close friend and we were all sure that the king would not risk his life in too hazardous a venture. He was grown more cautious with age and with the loss of so many of his friends and men. There were too few Macedonians in the army and each of their lives grew more precious to Alexander, as even more were also lost to sickness and other hazards of a campaign.

About this time, Callisthenes died from overweight, dropsy and an infestation from fleas. He received all the rites common to dead Macedonians and it fell to me to write to Aristotle and inform him of his nephew's death. It was not long before many rumours of his end grew into legends in which men would blemish Alexander's name, but his death was a natural occurrence and the king had long since grown indifferent to Callisthenes' fate.

The expenses of the expedition now exceeded Alexander's ability to pay the bills. He invited thirty of his generals and friends to bear the costs of an agreed section and, in exchange, to receive a larger portion of the new wealth that the king was confident the expedition would capture as we journeyed into the south.

When the new cities' walls were completed and the fleet ready to sail, Alexander asked for volunteers to man the ships and Cretans, Egyptians, Phoenicians and men from the Greek islands readily came forward and they began training for their new duties.

The rains had altogether ceased by the time that all was ready for the journey down the Hydaspes and appropriate ceremonies were held on the river banks to mark our departure. Thousands of people, from far and wide, arrived to watch us leave and they joined in the festivities which lasted for a complete day and night. They drank enormous quantities of wine and beer and consumed vast piles of meats, which were cooked over huge, open pits. Alexander boarded his ship to the deafening shouts and cheers of a great multitude of people. Never had any of them seen such a display of power or so comely a king.

He had spent freely of his vast treasury to the immense benefit of the local population. I did not, therefore, believe that they cheered because they were thankful to see us leave their territory, but rather because of the respect that the king had earned amongst them. As his ship moved into midstream, he poured a libation over the side and then he stood motionless in the prow as the oars dipped into the water until the ship was caught in the current and carried downstream.

The army was divided. Craterus took command of a column on the west bank and Hephaestion led on the east bank. Philip, newly appointed satrap of the province known as Ghandara, remained behind with a third column of the army, to protect us against attacks from our rear. His orders were to rejoin the expedition when all danger had passed.

I boarded a ship with other members of the cavalry and a detachment of archers for our defence on each vessel. The whole expedition must have been one of the bravest sights in history. There were over 2,000 ships setting off, with the army marching along both banks. The rowers chanted the rhythm of their strokes, to the trumpeting of the elephants as they lumbered along the banks, adding to the general noise and excitement. More and more thousands of the local people streamed down from the hills adding to the kaleidoscope of colour and the clamorous noise. High in the sky, above the sensational scene, in full glory, Apollo rode across the skies and his light shone on golden Alexander and, if for this hour alone, he will have everlasting fame in these far-distant lands.

During the first days on the march, the usual spies arrived to advise the king that hostile tribes were gathering together to fight against us in areas through which we must pass. They also told the king that where the Acesines flowed into the Hydaspes the banks of the rivers were wide enough apart to build a camp. Alexander ordered us to increase speed to reach this confluence of the rivers without delay. At various points, cliffs towered on either side of the river and we lost sight of the army, which opened us all up to separate attacks. The captains of the ships had to keep exactly on their stations to avoid collisions amongst so many vessels. We had discovered that the voyage was not without dangers, but all proceeded safely until the river narrowed and we heard a loud sound of rushing water. We sailed through dangerously sharp rocks and high waves and swirling whirlpools. Many of the ships suffered damage and some of the horses fell into the water due to the ships' motion, and they broke their legs and we were forced to destroy them; not an easy task for Macedonians, but we eventually reached the confluence of the rivers.

We were in calmer waters and we found that Craterus and Hephaestion were camped by the river. We secured the ships to the bank, separating those which had to be repaired, and then we began intensive training to prepare against an attack by the local tribes, who were known as the Malli and the Oxydracae. They were brave warriors who usually fought each other, but had now combined to defend their territories against the arrival of Alexander's army.

The Macedonians had lost their bright happiness in the realisation that they once more prepared for war, and they muttered that if the king had returned to the Hellespont by the familiar and pacified routes of his outward journey, our progress would not be challenged. They also spread fear amongst themselves of the unknown and unmentionable dangers to be encountered whenever we reached Ocean and the fearsome edge of the world. They argued that the gods had sent many signs to halt Alexander's march to the place of the sunrise and that now he had tricked them into turning south, in defiance of the dark mysteries which hold dominion where the sun and moon secretly meet. The king soon heard of this fearful talk and he gathered the Macedonians round him and said to them: "I have heard from various people of the terrors, which you imagine amongst yourselves and I assure you that there are no great evils in our path, as you foolishly suppose. You must know that other men constantly travel these ways and have safely reached the sea and sailed across it to the River Euphrates. Shall all of you be as old women frightened to death by your own shadows or shall you be as soldiers in the invincible army of Alexander? You, who have conquered the whole world, shall not be afraid of tribesmen who will quickly surrender when they see our strength. Shall you risk an ambush and death at their hands because you refuse to take the initiative and defeat them in an easy battle and so gain their hoarded treasure? Have we come all this way together only to disintegrate as an army and be destroyed on the way home by simple tribes-people? I have brought you safely through far greater dangers than we now encounter, and three times together we battled against the mighty Persian armies and three times they fled before us; shall you now die of fright before undisciplined and untrained tribesmen?"

The veteran Macedonians were shamed into silence by the king's words and they were forced to acknowledge that they had no other leader to take them back to Macedon, or even into the unknown lands of the south. In the early seasons of the campaign, they had followed Alexander with unquestioning loyalty and even now, when they scorned his road home, they realised that they were doomed without him and as they slowly dispersed, they were once again fully under his command.

The king next sent most of the fleet down the river, with the army marching south along the banks. He expected to deceive the watching tribesmen into believing that he was leaving their territory. He himself took a small expedition of swift horsemen further east to assess the strength of both the tribesmen and their fortified towns. At the end of this exercise we re-joined the army and Alexander held a council of war and he spoke to the generals: "To our east, I have discovered that a vast desert stretches far beyond our present position. The Malli tribesmen are gathering in the north and the Oxydracae are to the south of this river. They plan to settle their differences and join together to attack our rear whenever we leave it exposed. I intend to defeat them both in their towns and in the desert. Nearchos, and the rest of the ships, will sail back to the confluence of the rivers to defend our rear; and I shall take part of the army, with Perdicass in command of the infantry, to attack the tribes wherever we find them. Craterus will wait for three days, and then return with units of the army to join the navy. Hephaestion and his men will make preparations to leave and continue south along the riverbank. If the Malli fighters join the Oxydracae, they must abandon their towns to us and we shall destroy them, but I am informed that they will not leave their families, but rather that they will fight to the last man to prevent their towns falling into our hands.

"I shall reward our men with all the treasure that we find hidden in the cities, so that they will be less inclined to continuously trouble me with their rebellious talk. We can only advance when our rear is secure; therefore, if the men wish to see their homes in Macedon again, they must fight with goodwill and defeat our last enemy. This river, I am assured, flows into the Indus and follow it I must until we reach the southern sea and return to Babylon by the ancient trade routes."

Alexander clearly intended to leave the area pacified and open for exploration and he planned to remain in the tribal lands until this objective was realised, without heed to the soldiers' protests. Hephaestion left the camp the following day and Nearchos sailed his ships up the river on his return journey. Craterus waited for three days and led his column north along the river bank to join Nearchos. I rode out from the camp, with the king, across the desert with half of the Companions, a corps of hypaspists, several companies of archers and a battalion of the phalanx, a sufficient force to defeat a large army of the Malli. We left the civilian train and the women and children, the supplies and the treasury in the camp under a strong guard to protect them against marauding tribesmen.

We had guides to lead us to the towns but no native interpreters had volunteered their services. The first day, we covered a distance of about 100 stades when we reached a watering hole and made a fortified camp for the night. A detail of the men prepared our food and the rest filled all the water skins for the onward journey. As soon as the meal was over, we dropped to the ground and fell asleep. We were too exhausted to even talk amongst ourselves, except for the guards who took the first watch. Even Alexander slept in preparation, for we were in unknown territory and possibly at a great distance from the next watering hole. Every day we must reach water, for without it, in the burning sun and shadeless desert, we should soon be as dried as the embalmed corpses of Egypt or so weakened that we would be devoured by carrion, and our bones exposed to the elements until they were so bleached and brittle that they must intermingle with the sands of the desert in lonely, unburied anonymity.

We broke camp before the rays of the sun were above the eastern horizon and the march continued right through the following night. The king and the cavalry rode ahead of the column to survey the land and, when we came to a small inhabited town, we slaughtered everyone whom we found outside the walls. We waited for the rest of the expedition to reach our position before we broke into the city and completed the grim work started beyond the walls. We allowed a few men to escape, to carry a warning to other members of their tribes of their fate if they failed to surrender to Alexander.

Perdicass left the city in advance, with a small detachment

to surround the next nearest town, but he discovered that it was already deserted when he arrived outside the walls. He immediately set out towards the river in pursuit of the fleeing people and when he found them, they also were slaughtered. Only a few escaped into the desolate marshes along the river banks.

When Alexander arrived outside the deserted city, we rested before we marched back to the river where we found a few remnants of Oxydracae warriors They fought bravely, having only their lives to lose, which were dearly bought by our many dead. We killed all of them. We buried our dead, dressed the wounds of our men and rested, after the slaughter, and we marched to conquer the land of the Malli. Every town and village that we found offered fierce resistance to our attack until we were sick of blood and destruction. Alexander seemed almost indifferent to the suffering, driven only by his desire to pacify the people and continue the march down to the sea. He was unapproachable and very different from the king who had led us across the Hellespont so many seasons past. We lost so many men during the annihilation of the Malli and many of our wounded died from loathsome infections. The morale amongst the men was destroyed in the unprotected heat of the endless day and the bitter cold of desert nights, for winter was fast approaching and the land no longer held any warmth after the sun had set in the west.

Finally, we came to the chief city of the Malli, which was situated on the banks of the Acesines. We observed a mighty citadel behind the strong outer walls, the Mallis' last great defensive position. Our weary and depleted army had lost the will to fight and when Alexander called for volunteers for a storming party across the walls, not one man came forward. The king looked over the men in chilling silence and saw nothing but a sullen resistance and he rushed forward alone and grabbed a ladder and placed it against the city's wall. He climbed to the top and stood exposed with his sword in hand, protected only by his shield. We all felt shame as we saw his lonely, exposed position and we rushed to follow him as he leaped down into the city. Peucestas, the King's Shield-Bearer, with Alexander's bodyguard, were the first to reach him. Many other Macedonians rushed for more ladders of which dozens collapsed under the weight of too many soldiers. As we reached the top of the walls, we were met by a shower of arrows; one of them pierced the king's amour and I watched, in fear and horror, as he fell onto his shield. Peucestos leapt to cover his body with the Shield of Herakles, which he always carried into battle, riding at the side of the king.

We all thought that Alexander lay dead upon the ground; that concentrated our anger and we made a furious attack against the Malli. They advanced towards the king's body and we grouped around him to a mighty onslaught from the defenders of the city. We gradually overcame every last heroic one and by nightfall not a man, woman, or child was left alive in the doomed town and the stench from the bloodstained streets rose in a terrible protest against the insanity of war.

We lifted Alexander and, to our amazement, he still breathed. The men were already desperately mourning him in the carnage and isolation of that dread city.

We left the dead, even our own, unattended, together with the stench of rotting, raw flesh. The grim, carrion birds were wheeling overhead and animals were preying on decaying flesh. Both Greek and Indian dead combined in silent protest to the gods on high. We carried away our wounded on horseback as best we could.

We dressed Alexander's wounds and he gradually regained consciousness but he was very close to death. We told him that the men believed him dead and he ordered us to carry him to the river, and take him on board a ship, and get him back to the expedition with all speed. We arrived to the sorrowful lamentations of all the Macedonians, who thought that we carried only the corpse of the king, and then he raised his hand to us all in feeble salutation. Their fearful sorrow was stilled and to convince them further that he lived, Alexander ordered us to bring a horse and place him on its back and the misery of the Macedonians turned to hysterical joy and the shouts and cheers echoed from the hills as they all pressed forward to see and touch their king. There were tears in the eyes of Alexander as the sun shone in benediction on his golden hair, and the men were wild in their praise of him and all opposition melted as snow in the fires of war. We helped him from his horse and carried him back to his tent where he lapsed into a coma and we watched beside him with anxious hearts until consciousness returned to him during the night. The king's recovery was slow and the news of his victory over the Malli soon reached the Oxydracae and, with it, the tales of all his exploits grew until they even believed that he had risen from the dead. They came in great numbers to offer their submission to this invincible conqueror.

When we returned inside the city to count our dead, we found the body of Coenos, a close friend of the king's, and of us all, a brave leader and soldier and hero of all the men for his stand in their defence against the king. He was given a military funeral with all the rites of a valiant Macedonian soldier. Alexander mourned him and he was sick of the bloodstained lands of the Oxydracae and Malli and we quickly marched away to escape from the grief and carnage.

Chapter 25

We returned to our camp on the banks of the Acesines, and we were much relieved to find that the civilians had escaped an attack. Alexander sent messengers to Nearchos, carrying orders for him to bring his fleet down to the junction of the River Indus. During our absence, many more ships had been built to replace those damaged in the turbulent waters of the Acesines.

As soon as the army was sufficiently recovered from the hard campaign against the Malli and Oxydracae, we marched south into a land inhabited by a fanatically religious people who, without any fear for their own lives, attacked us, often simultaneously, from both sides of the river. The king sent out several small expeditions to subdue and pacify them and he founded many new towns on the banks of the river, with strong garrisons to guarantee peace after his departure.

Ptolemy was pieced by an arrow during one skirmish with these fanatics. He was brought back to camp and, though his wound was not serious, the weapon had carried a poisoned tip and he was already delirious with a high fever and he seemed close to death. Alexander's anxiety and care for him were very great and when he did not improve, in desperation he sent for Calanus, a famed holy man of those regions, who applied local herbs to Ptolemy's wound and it miraculously began to heal and he came out of his coma. The king was so overjoyed that he sent a sample of the poison and specimens of the healing plant to Aristotle, hoping to discover other cures from so common a resource and Calanus joined the expedition as a cherished advisor to the king.

About this time, Oxyartes, the father of Roxane, also rejoined the expedition. Alexander now added a territory known as the

Parapamisidae to his satrapies and so replaced a corrupt governor with his own barbaric relative. Craterus, also, returned to rejoin the expedition. Philip, the brother of Harpalos, and governor of northern India, arrived in the camp to report on his satrapy to the king and he was given all the newly pacified territory to join to his own. We learned from Philip that the latest attacks against us had been led by a sect of people known as Brahmins. Most of their leaders were in our hands and, to punish them and to make them an example in all the region, Alexander sent the prisoners into exile and confiscated the sect's treasury.

At last we reached the Indus River. The king ordered Philip to build yet another Alexandria at the confluence of the two rivers, which was at the border of his satrapies, and he personally selected the civilians to serve in Philip's administration and gave him a strong garrison for the defence of such vast lands. The king planned to create a separate satrapy of lower India and named Peithon as its first governor.

It seemed, for a brief time, that the world was at peace until spies brought us news of violent disturbances between different tribes to our west. Alexander made the hard decision to send Craterus to pacify that region. He took with him three battalions of the phalanx, and several companies of archers, and the largest part of the civilian train, with most of the women and children. He also took the sick and wounded, to spare them further hardship, and they were carried on the backs of elephants. The king gave Craterus orders to pacify every stade of land between the Indus and Carmania, a huge and inhospitable country quite unknown to us. The mighty elephants were a disappointment, especially to the king. They were not a great weapon in war for they panicked in the noise and confusion of a battle, but they proved their worth to the expedition as excellent beasts of burden. They were slow, they required vast amounts of fodder and a great deal of specialised care, but for our wounded, their worth was priceless on their road to Babylon.

It was now nine seasons since we had crossed the Hellespont and, before winter was over, the fleet set sail on the Indus, which indeed, we had found, just as Alexander had predicted, and the army marched for the south, the sea beyond, and Babylon. The men were at last satisfied that they were on the road home to Macedon. We continued with pacification of the people living on either side of the river as we moved south. When they resisted

Alexander, their cities were destroyed and we seized their gold, jewels, and their elephants, which they used to work their fields and to gather wood from their forests. The king of Patalla, a city-state in the delta of the Indus River, arrived to visit Alexander and he brought the king a royal ransom in gifts of gold, jewels and spices. It was all conveyed into the expedition's treasury for the king kept nothing of value for himself.

The King of Patalla was received with the usual courtesy by Alexander and before he left the expedition, he had promised the king a welcome to his land, which he offered in homage to Alexander. However, as we approached his capital city, he fled before us and we occupied it without shedding any of the people's blood or losing any more of our own men.

Our craftsmen immediately built boat yards for the construction of ships capable of crossing the seas. We employed local people who were experienced in building such large transports and while the work progressed, Alexander took a small expedition down the river to find the sea. We were amazed to discover that, as we sailed south, the level of the river changed twice each day. The first time that this happened, several of our ships, which were close to the bank, were left high and dry and they suffered extensive damage as they fell onto their sides. The men were truly frightened by this strange occurrence and many of them interpreted it as a warning from the gods. Calanus, the Indian holy man, however, assured the king, and all of us, that the ebb and turn of tides was natural in these waters and that they must be calculated before every voyage.

And so the day came when Alexander fulfilled his dream and, because of the tides, he looked not upon a sea but on Ocean. He was overjoyed and made many sacrifices to Poseidon. Calanus advised Alexander that, by sailing out west and north from the land, he would reach the mouth of the River Euphrates, and he confirmed that this was indeed the sea route to Babylon. Alexander's plan was now a reality and he was happy beyond words.

The chart makers worked night and day to turn their sketches into maps and charts. They found that their earlier predictions were false, for no-one had dreamed that the Indus delta stretched so wide across the country. Alexander paid the local people for their knowledge of tides and currents, the land, and especially of the route to Babylon.

We returned to Patella and we told the rest of the expedition of our discoveries, particularly of the tides and of Ocean. As the construction of the new fleet was nearing completion, Alexander invited his commanders and closest friends to a symposium, in his tent, to discuss the next part of the expedition. He had nearly recovered from his wounds and Ptolemy was also regaining his strength and preparations were well-advanced for the departure of the army.

When we were all assembled and seated on couches and the wine was served to us by beautiful Persian and Indian women, Alexander spoke. As we all listened with great attention, he said: "My friends! Finally, we have reached Ocean and the last part of our great enterprise. The army will march overland to Babylon, which is the centre of the world and the natural capital of the east. The wise Calanus assures me that India can also be ruled from the city as both the north and south are accessible along the ancient Royal Roads of Persia. Macedon and Greece, in the west, are also reached by the well-travelled roads from Babylon. I am advised, however, that the end of summer will be the optimum time for Nearchos and the fleet to sail across the sea, when the winds change and they will give him the most favourable conditions, as the tides will be less strong and the waters more calm.

"In a few days, the army will march to the coast, with all the civilians who remain in the expedition. We shall establish supply bases and dig wells for the use of the navy wherever we find water along the shore on our route.

"When we reach Babylon, those of you who wish to do so, may return to Macedon, with all the honours that they have so richly earned and their full share of the spoils. For myself, I have heard many stories of the lands of Africa, even further to the south and west of Egypt and of Arabia in the east. To our north lies the Hyrcanian Sea and all the lands between there and eastern Ocean must be pacified and explored. In Babylon, I shall recruit a new army to go to the furthermost ends of the earth and a navy to sail all of Ocean in search of new routes and lands. Those who remain with me will bring their experiences of hardship and leadership as priceless gifts with which to leaven unseasoned men in so many great new endeavours. All of you may look for the rewards of your service in a share of the treasures which we have taken together, and in the administration of the empire.

"Your king may never rest, but must ever seek to fulfill his destiny to enlarge the empire, promote trade and bring peace to the world under one god.

"I shall dismiss the troops who are native to India and they shall take their share of the bounty with them and bring prosperity to their villages. Their people will welcome them back and they already show goodwill towards our governors whom we are leaving to rule over them."

I, and many others, went to see Nearchos for our final farewells. This time, our next meeting seemed more uncertain for he was about to sail uncharted waters of which none of us had any knowledge. He was a great naval commander and handled ships and men with an easy confidence. Since our days at Mieza with Aristotle, he had remained close to the king and they spent many hours alone together before the army marched for the delta of the Indus. Alexander had been reluctant to give Nearchos the command of the sea voyage, and risk his life in so hazardous an undertaking, but it gave his uneasy men some confidence as they argued amongst themselves that the king would not expose the life of so dear a friend, if the unnatural dangers were greater than the rewards that he expected at the journey's end.

We turned into the setting sun, when we reached the river's delta, and our miseries increased daily. The vegetation was sparse and held no moisture, except for myrrh trees, which were recognised by the Phoenicians and from the bark of which they extracted a strong and sweet-smelling resin that they burned as a sacrifice to their gods. They told us that the men of Arabia brought it on their camel trains to the markets of their towns.

Overhead, the sun burned as a naked furnace, and we were forced to march at night and make what shelter we could during the day. The Persians studied the stars and advised Alexander on our path forward, though few expected to make it alive back to Babylon. We had little food or water in the arid, waterless waste and women and children, men and animals died each day and were left to birds and wild animals as awful prey. We were also attacked by tribesmen, who found some kind of an existence amongst the rocks and hard earth. The king sent small detachments to pursue and kill all whom they found and this made it a little safer for the expedition.

For Alexander, the mountain range which paralleled the coast between us and the sea was the most difficult evil. We were forced to travel long distances inland and we could not establish supply points or dig wells on the coast for the benefit of the fleet as we had promised Nearchos. We all worried daily about Nearchos and his men, and the king was silent and despairing, tormented by such a failure in his plans to supply water to the sailors.

Alexander, the commanders and the Companions marched on foot to endure the same hardships as every member of the expedition. The hot wind blew incessantly, carrying clouds of sand, which covered us in choking, sharp particles of dust. We were forced to kill our pack animals for food and dump our treasury of gold, jewels and money in the bleak wilderness.

One night, a few of the desperate men broke open some of the supply boxes and ate the contents, for our condition had worsened day by day, and our food stocks were almost exhausted. Alexander, uncharacteristically, feigned no knowledge of this unheard of breach of discipline, in order to avoid having to take disciplinary action against such pitiful culprits. We were most desperate for water. When two of the men found a tiny pool shaded deep within a rock, they managed to fill a hat, which they brought to the king. He gravely thanked them and poured the water into the desert saying as he did so: "A king must serve as well as lead, and especially share the hardest part of that duty which he requires from others, or he must naturally fall. We have come the hardest part of our journey, and I am confident that we shall soon arrive at a spring and, wherever that exists, then we shall find people who will be glad to sell us supplies and we shall probably find a city where the people will be happy to see us and offer us their hospitality and we shall rest and bathe."

Alexander was gaunt and pale, some of his old wounds had opened and when the men heard his brave words and noticed his wounds and general frailty, they were shamed into better discipline.

A few days later, we camped in a dry river bed. Unknown to us, a storm raged far to our north and the wadi flooded, without warning, while we slept. The royal tent was destroyed, but by the grace of the gods, neither Alexander nor Roxane were within. Many of the other women and children were drowned and we lost a great part of our meagre supplies. Alexander gave the order that we must camp, in the future, at least 50 stades from any water course or valley floor.

It took us several days to dry out our clothes and stores. Most had to be destroyed for they were damaged beyond repair. Alexander decided to follow the watercourse, believing that the flood waters must empty into the sea, and at last we stumbled out to the shore where we found springs of fresh water and, best of all, a settlement of people.

We were able to cleanse ourselves and wash our clothes and a few coins and a little gold bought us fish and bread. Our guides were told by the village people that we were not very many days away from the city of Pura, which was the capital of Gedrosia. Once rested, we returned to the desert and completed the march to Pura and we had travelled for 60 days from the Indus delta when we finally reached the city. We had lost half of our men, most of the women and children, and nearly all our stores crossing that desolate wilderness. Alexander immediately asked the people of Pura if they had any news of his fleet and he offered a reward for accurate information, but we heard nothing and we all felt, even Alexander, a great anxiety for our missing friends.

The king removed the satrap, Appolophanes, from office for failing to obey his orders and send supplies to Nearchos and to meet the expedition in the wilderness with food and water. To add to all the bad news, messengers arrived in Pura to report to the king that Philip, the satrap of India, had been murdered; another great loss for us all. Alexander sent a commission to Taxiles, adding Philip's land to his own, and he now ruled over an area so vast that it seemed impossible for one man alone to administer it.

We were all relieved to be out of the desert, even though Pura was a miserable town of huts, poverty and disease. The men found a source for a rough, fomented drink and they all drank a prodigious amount and their revelry was beyond control. Our deliverance was great and the local women and children stayed in their houses in fear of our men, even by day.

Alexander waited, but no news came to the city of the fleet, and he reluctantly gave the order to march from Pura towards Carmania. We had bought supplies and tent material and the remaining pack animals were laden down with skins full of water.

We reached a river which we believed to be the border with

Carmania. We crossed over to the other side and made a camp and lit fires, not only to cook food but as a protection against the early winter chill. We sat round the blaze and listened to the guides and even a few spies who had found their way to our position. Suddenly, into the light and warmth of the fire, a small party of wild and beggarly men approached Alexander. The guards advanced to protect the king and he ordered them to seize them all. We saw, in the flickering light, that they were emaciated, dirty and that their hair was wildly uncombed. The guards pushed their leader in front of the king and this man croaked in a voice dry from lack of water and hoarse from his effort. It was almost beyond comprehension when he said: "Alexander! I am Nearchos and these are some of my captains."

Once the king had taken in his words, he fell on them all in great joy, weeping tears of relief and thankfulness. As soon as the first shock was over, he ordered the stewards to bring water, clean clothes and food and when Nearchos and his men were sufficiently recovered, we all sat together by the fires and, in silence, we listened to their story. Nearchos began: "O! King! Soon after you had left the Indus, we were attacked by hostile Indians and I decided that we should sail down to the delta before they could damage the ships or kill many of the men, for we had no reserves of either to take their place. We were forced to sail before the wind changed, as was predicted by Calanus. Once we reached the open sea, we were becalmed and we ran very short of water and we were in a great heat, which rose out of the sea. Suddenly, the wind did change, and it brought violent storms and enormous sea creatures, which blew huge columns of water from their heads into the air, and they menaced the ships by their hulking size as they swam amongst us. I ordered several of the boats to ram them together, to the sound of the trumpeters as everyone shouted and made a great noise. Fortunately, we scared them off and the men were less terrified when they swam away.

"We now had more than enough wind for our sails and we put into a small harbour expecting to find you. Instead, we discovered villages of men who lived in caves on the shore and used primitive stone tools to skin animals and fish. They allowed us to use their wells to draw water but we had no-one with us who could speak their language.

"We sailed again, and passed by swamps where the trees grow upside-down and in such a dense mass that we were unable to find anywhere to put ashore.

"Finally, when we were desperate for water, we found the mouth of a river and when we landed, we were told that you camped but a distance of only eight stades. We have therefore come to find you and report on our voyage and to assure you that very few of our ships or men are lost, and of these, some may yet join us."

Alexander was near to despair during the terrible trek across the Gedrosian wilderness for the loss of so many lives and anxiety for the fate of Nearchos and his men. For their safety, and our salvation, he now offered many sacrifices, in gratitude to the gods and for the survival of both the expedition and the navy. These were followed by games, which were religious and symbolic rather than celebratory and then by a parade of our remnants led by Nearchos. To fill the king's cup with happiness, Hephaestion rode into the camp and we drank and celebrated wildly in thankfulness for his safe return.

When all was quiet once more in the camp, the king in his concern for Nearchos, asked him to give up the command of the fleet. He relented, after Nearchos insisted on completing his task, and quickly left the camp to rejoin his ships. I suspect that his haste was caused by a suspicion that the king would change his mind and insist on keeping him safe with the expedition. Hephaestion, also, left the camp; he took his men, most of the army, the remaining women and children and the elephants, by a southerly route into Persis. As soon as they departed we hurriedly made preparations for the last part of our march into Carmania.

Many officials from the old Persian satrapies came to greet the king in Carmania. Amongst them was Stasanor, the satrap of Areia, who also represented his father, the satrap of Parthia. Cleander and Sitalces, the murderers of Parmenion, also arrived; they were received by the king, but for the rest of us, we avoided them and we refused to eat or drink with them; the pair jointly ruled in Media.

It was not long before resentful Medians arrived to lay before the king many accusations against Cleander and Sitalces. They told him of their rulers' corrupt and greedy ways and they especially complained that their holy temples had been ransacked and plundered. The king first listened carefully to all of their accusations and then to the replies of both men, and they were judged guilty and speedily executed. At last, revenge for old Parmenion and a warning to all who would abuse power in the king's name. Alexander never mentioned them again, but he was probably glad to be relieved of both of them or they must constantly remind him of Parmenion's cruel end.

Our spies and scouts led us to the camp of Craterus and the men greeted each other with tumultuous shouts of pure joy and laughter. The women, whom he had safely brought to Carmania, rushed to find their men again, but for too many of them, they simply learned of death and they could only mourn their losses in the solitude of their grief. That night, so many stories of battles against hostile men, of hardships, hunger, danger and triumphs were told, and some of the tales grew in the telling to mythic epics of challenges, courage and tenacious heroism. We laughed at each new exaggeration and easily forgave the storyteller for each of us had known too much fear and danger, and we all felt a common relief to be back in civilised and inhabited lands.

The king appointed Peucestas, his sword-bearer, to be satrap of Persis in advance of our arrival, to mark his gratitude for saving his life in the battle against the Malli. He was given an especial duty to raise and train a corps of young Persian men to personally serve Alexander. We marched from the camp and travel was now easier. The air had already cooled with the coming winter and our rests were longer at each stop. The soldiers, and even the civilians, showed a new spirit as we drew ever closer to familiar territory for the first time since our departure from Macedon. We passed through many lush villages amongst the fertile oases and we were able to purchase food and stores to satisfy all our needs. The village people made us welcome and gave us a place to rest and allowed us to freely use water from their springs and wells.

Messengers rode into the camp from all the satrapies and some brought disturbing news of official corruption and insurrection by oppressed people. The king listened, in anger, to all of them and he promised to deal swift justice to those who had betrayed his trust. He was now the lord of the greatest empire in all history and he sometimes spoke to us of his plans to consolidate his rule. He typically said: "To hold this great empire, every official must be above graft and corruption. I intend that my government shall be just, that taxes will be fair and that all the peoples will enjoy a new prosperity. Those who have failed in the responsibilities entrusted to them shall find swift justice and those who have been faithful will receive rich rewards. There have been many rumours of my death, during our absence, and many men have taken advantage of such hearsay for their own profit and they must now find their reckoning with me in person.

"I have always promised that the union between Greece and Persia will bring equal benefits to all peoples and if we fail in this undertaking then there will be constant uprisings to disturb the peace.

"I am returning not only as King of Macedon and Hegemon of the League of Corinth but as King of Kings of the dead Persian Empire, as Pharaoh of Egypt, and as the conqueror of India. My authority is sovereign, but my generosity for loyal service is well-known to all men and my judgment will be against those who, for personal gain, would try to destroy the unity that we all worked to achieve."

When the king stopped speaking, we broke into little groups. I saw that he no longer glowed with the youthful vigour of earlier days for he endured constant pain from his many wounds. The disillusion from the betrayal by trusted servants weighed on him far more than all the hardships of the campaign. It is impossible for the man of integrity to understand the sins of greed, jealousy and spite – all motives of far lesser men.

Finally, we reached Persis and the road over the barren country before we returned to Parsagadae. The king immediately inspected the tomb of Cyrus and his fury was terrible when he found it, as he had left it, derelict and ransacked, with the bones of the great founder of the Persian Empire still exposed and scattered on the floor within. The gold sarcophagus was broken and the gold scimitar and ceremonial vessels were gone. Alexander had given the Magian priests, the custodians of the tomb, a great sum of money to repair it to its original condition. The priests were brought before him and tortured but none of them would admit responsibility for stealing the gold and the money which the king had donated for the restoration.

The satrap of Persis was dead and his unauthorised usurper, Orxines, was brought to the king and tried and condemned to death for corruption. To add to the king's grief, Antropates arrived in the city, escorting another usurper, this time the new satrap of Media, who was bound in chains. He had declared himself King of the Medes and Persians and for this treason against Alexander, he was hanged. Antropates was appointed, in his place, as satrap of the fabled province. Next, it was the turn of Ordanes, the satrap of Carmania, also condemned for the gross abuse of his office, and then the saddest blow to the king came when he received reports of the renegade Harpalos, a trusted friend from the school of Mieza. He had been treasurer of the expedition and we found that he had appropriated vast sums of money and financed a life of extravagant luxury, wild by even Persian standards. He had also recruited a private army and obliged all Greeks to bow before him in the Persian proskynesis. In Alexander's eyes, his worst crime was to raise his mistress, the notorious Thais, to the status of a goddess, an unprecedented impertinence and blasphemy. Unfortunately, when news reached him of the king's approach, he had fled to Athens, from which city a messenger arrived to tell Alexander that he was held under arrest.

Many others in authority had also recruited private armies and the king ordered these to be disbanded and he organised embassies to journey to every part of his empire and announce his safe return. When all the work was done to Alexander's satisfaction, we left Parsagadae for the great Persian ceremonial capital of Persepolis. The king looked upon the burnt ruins of the apadana in bitter shame and remorse at the wanton destruction of so magnificent an edifice to the power and glory of a King of Kings. I remembered Parmenion's words of caution to him before the flame was lit and Alexander's grief was made keener by the discovery of so many other men's abuse of power.

From the palace, Alexander strode to the treasury and discovered the full amount by which Orxines, the satrap, had stolen from the store of coins, jewels and bullion, left by Parmenion. The people told the king of the heavy taxation which he had imposed on all of them for his personal benefit, and of how he had murdered and oppressed them to steal their land, possessions and even the dowries of their wives.

I had dreamed of an appointment to the governorship of Persis, the most romantic of all the satrapies and centre of the Persian Empire. I do not think that the king considered me for any great admininstrative office. I was his friend and always rode close to him and listened as he spoke his thoughts, and I kept my counsel at all times as I was advised to do, long ago, by Aristotle.

Alexander sent for Peucestos and confirmed him as satrap of Persis. When this Macedonian rode into Persepolis, he was dressed in Persian clothes. He had adopted Persian ways and spoke the Persian tongue. He was an acceptable governor for proud Persians but, from then on, an exile amongst the Macedonians. With this important work in Persis now finished, the king was eager to ride away from Persepolis. He was haunted by the destruction of the palace and the daily reminder of his youthful revenge on the long dead Xerxes.

We marched in easy stages to the Persian Gates. It was winter again and cold winds tempered the heat of summer. There was snow in the Zagros Mountains of Susiana but once we were through them, we reached the lowlands, and at last the plains of Babylonia. Our guides led us to the mighty city of Susa, capital of the Persian Empire and beginning of the Royal Road to Sardis of Lydia and Gordion in Phrygia. The men, already, felt nearer Macedon and all the dear and familiar life of home. They were relaxed and full of hope that, at last, the long, arduous campaign was drawing to an end. The satrap of Susa, Abulites, with his son Oxathres, was waiting for Alexander at the gates of the city. They were both as taut as the strings of a lyre as they fawned on the king, to his unconcealed disgust. Once inside the city, it was not long before we knew the reason for their servile conduct, as delegates from all parts of Susa arrived to accuse them both, before the king, of endless acts of brutish oppression. Abulites had been the satrap under Darius and confirmed in the office by Alexander. He and his son had acted in Alexander's name and had lost the king much of the favour of his Persian subjects. For this reason, as much as for their crimes, when they were found guilty of misuse of power, they were put to death. Even more disturbing to the king was that he received daily reports from distant parts of the empire of more acts of tyranny by his appointed officials and of uprisings of the people against their oppressors, even amongst the Greeks. In answer to each report, Alexander sent embassies to replace the corrupt officials, most of whom were executed for their abuse of power. The king was occupied with affairs of state for many days, but when the last messenger was finally seen, listened to, advised and satisfied,

Alexander planned a great feast to celebrate our return to Susa. He called Macedonians to a council and unfolded his intentions and received our startled attention in the following speech: "This great empire, which together we have vanquished, shall only be held by a true union between Macedonians, Greeks and Persians, as I have frequently explained to you. When this is achieved, all the other peoples of the world, lacking a separate and sufficient strength to challenge us, will then willingly accept our government. Therefore at this great feast, to which all Macedonians and many Persians are invited, I shall marry Statira, the elder daughter of Darius ..."

Alexander was interrupted by a great stir of interest, but he quietened the noise and continued: "Hephaestion will marry Drypetis, Darius' second daughter. All the Macedonian generals will wed daughters of the Persian nobility and 10,000 of the men will legalise the unions which they have already made with Persian women, or wives will be found for them. I intend to give a dowry to all women who marry on that day and, after the wedding, the Macedonian soldiers will be discharged with enough money to live either in Macedon or in any other city of the empire.

"I know that many Macedonians have borrowed money against their share of bounty from Persian moneylenders. I invite all of them to give their names, with the amount that they owe, so that I may discharge their debts and remove a source of complaint from the Persians.

"I have sent for Peucestas to bring his Epigone recruits from Persepolis, and they will be integrated into the army with no distinction between their status and that of Macedonians and with an equal opportunity to serve, even in the royal Agema Guard.

"I have punished many of the men who were charged with the government of the satrapies, whose infamous conduct towards the gods and the people could not be tolerated. Few of them have been punished for personally disobeying me, for it is by far a lesser crime and comes under the reforms, which I have already ordered to take effect and which I shall take care of as I visit each province.

"Now to turn to Greece, I have reports of disturbances in the city-states where bands of discharged soldiers have returned and chosen to live as outlaws and even as mercenaries in the armies of quarrelling cities. I shall issue a decree of amnesty for all ex-soldiers and order some of them to go back to their native cities and I intend that they will take care of that difficulty. Nearchos is going to the Olympic Games and he will request that I shall be deified so that I may legally act above the law, but only in the pursuit of justice.

"I am taking all these measures to bring peace and prosperity over all the lands under our government. There are not enough Macedonians for every task to be done or every office to be filled; we must, therefore, take the best men of all nationalities to carry out the civilian administration and the command of the army, which is scattered to so many different cities."

We had listened to the king's words in a tense silence, for all of us were closely affected by his orders. The silence now was broken in a roar of noise similar to a rush of water flash-flooding across a barren desert. Many of the officers and men had contracted permanent liaisons with Persian women and for some of these, legalisation of their unions would cause no great change. Many of them, however, had wives in Macedon and they were deeply offended by the king's proposals; others of them despised the Persians so much that they had lightly used the women and fully intended to abandon them before they returned to Macedon. For myself, my memories were still green, even after the eleven seasons of the campaign, and I had no desire to take another wife, whether Greek or Persian, nor could I think of entering my father's empty house with a Persian stranger. I left the audience chamber in the company of Craterus and Ptolemy and we continued to discuss the king's plans and how we would be personally affected by all that had been revealed to us. Craterus had already proposed for the hand of Amastris, the daughter of Oxathres, who was the brother of Darius. Oxathres had fought gallantly at Issos, even after Darius had deserted the field, but he was captured at the end of the battle. He was now numbered amongst the Persian hetairoi or 'Friends of the King'. Amastris had been taken captive by Parmenion when he occupied Damascus and she had recently come to Susa to join her father after the campaign in India.

Ptolemy, at last, was over the Egyptian girl, and he had chosen Artakama, the daughter of Artabazus, known to Alexander when, as a young prince, he had received Persian ambassadors at his father's court. He and his family were also taken at Damascus.

293

He had remained loyal to Darius until the King of King's murder beyond the Persian Gates, when he had submitted to Alexander, who rewarded him with the satrapy of Bactria.

We were joined by Seleucos who was already married to Apame, the daughter of Spitamanes, that same Persian noble who had arrested Bessus and delivered him to Alexander. After that treacherous deed, he had continued to rouse opposition to the king and he had fled to Bactria, where he was murdered by his own wife who then delivered his head to Alexander. Perdicass was with Seleucos and he planned to marry the daughter of Antropates. These, my friends, were marrying for the first time; they were all men of ambition and fully understood that the way to promotion was by obeying, without question, the commands of Alexander, the King.

The Persian women, especially those from Bactria and the northern satrapies, were very comely, with strong characters, and they made excellent wives for most of our men, so long from home, who were hungry for domestic comfort, particularly that which was financed by Alexander's generous dowries to them; it was not an unwelcome arrangement.

The men who faced enforced discharge were far from content and linked their retirement with the summons to Peucestos to bring the Epigone to Susa and so replace themselves with Persians. They complained again that the king wished to free himself from Macedonians and to become entirely Persian. They grumbled that it is the Greek custom to take only one legal wife whereas the Persians had many, simultaneously, and that the king was already married to Roxane and they interpreted his second marriage as another indication of his contempt for Macedonian ways, ignoring the king's true motive to gain peace and integrate his empire. The men also felt deeply suspicious of the king's offer to pay off their debts to Persian usurers. None of them came forward to volunteer their names and the amounts for they feared a trick to uncover and punish their personal extravagances. Alexander was deeply distressed when he was told of their lack of confidence in him and he gathered them round him and gently spoke to them: "A king must always treat his subjects with respect and honour and to show my faith in all of you, I intend to pay your debts without you registering the amounts."

They crowded round him and many wept as they reached

out to touch him for they truly loved him and especially trusted him as their leader and they shouted out to him that he was the greatest hero in all history. By such small gestures did he bind them to him and he settled their debts to their satisfaction and that of the Persian moneylenders.

During the next few days, by order of the king, an enormous tent was erected in Susa to hold the many thousands due to attend the mass wedding. It was sumptuously lined with carpets, which had been woven in every district of the old Persian Empire. The wall hangings were costly silks brought from the lands beyond India and many trees were uprooted and placed throughout the pavilion to provide an additional, luxurious decoration. Servants and soldiers built great tables for the food and Macedonians gathered to celebrate their return from India, to honour the king and to marry the daughters of Persia.

The festivities began when Alexander joined the Macedonians at a banquet, during which all the foods available in the markets of Susa (purchased and prepared) were served. Hunting parties had brought down birds and game to go with the fruits, nuts and grains from storage warehouses. The wine flowed in rivers of gold and red poured into cups with exquisite decoration. They were taken from the treasury. Toasts were constantly shouted across the spaces, but before everyone reached a state of drunken debauchery the women arrived and stood beside their husbands. Their brightly coloured robes made exotic butterflies of them all and their jewels sparkled on their hands and the trumpeters sounded off outside the tent … altogether a barbaric scene and it took five more days to conclude the celebrations. I married a girl who was quite unknown to me. She came from the satrapy of Media and I sent her home, with her dowry, and that was the end of my marriage in Susa.

Many other Macedonians made similar arrangements to satisfy the king's command and at the end of the celebrations, he discharged all the newly married men and they returned to Macedon with their wives, the dowries and their share of the treasure seized since we had crossed the Hellespont.

The king's marriage to the daughter of Darius made him the legitimate heir to their throne in the eyes of the Persians. Day by day, once again, Alexander seemed to become more Persian than Macedonian and the anger of the few remaining Macedonians boiled to the surface in frustrated rage, but we were too few to influence the king or change his policies. His marriage had been conducted according to Persian rites and now that the 10,000 had departed, we Macedonians were far outnumbered in a mighty army from every country of Asia. Peucestos arrived leading the Epigoni, and Macedonian distrust was expressed in voices full of angry scorn as he swaggered, like a Persian, in command of the ceremonies in which they were integrated into Macedonian units.

Alexander, well aware of the wrath of his countrymen, organised a great feast, where he awarded golden crowns to Peucestos, for saving his life in the battle against the Malli, to Leonnatus, his kinsman and a trusted advisor, who had also saved his life in another encounter with the ferocious Malli, and finally, a crown to Hephaestion for his enduring friendship and to celebrate their new relationship through their marriages to the daughters of Darius.

Alexander's happiness was marred by all the reports, which came to him of internecine wars between the city-states of Greece. Most disturbing to the king were the details of Antipater's involvement in many of the disputes. Contrary to Alexander's orders, he had continued to divide and rule in the traditions of King Philip. The king took counsel with many of the generals, particularly with Craterus. They spent nights together and, as a result, Alexander dispatched decrees of amnesty to all the contending cities, on condition that they kept the peace from now on amongst themselves. He ordered them to welcome their own discharged soldiers and their exiles who were roaming the countryside seeking employment as mercenaries, thus fuelling the strife.

Chapter 26

And it happened that about this time Calanus, the Indian holy man, being full of years, felt that Death approached him. To avoid the corruption of his body, he requested that the king build a pyre on which he desired to be burnt alive. Alexander, deeply distressed, at first refused his appeal until he sorrowfully gave way and he ordered some of the men to fashion the funeral pile. As the flames consumed the holy man, the last words of Calanus were addressed to the king and he said: "We shall meet again in Babylon."

None of us knew his meaning and we felt that his death was barbaric, but his faith made it acceptable and he was given a ceremonial funeral when the grisly business was over. The king grieved deeply for Calanus and for the loss of his wisdom for he was the lodestar of Alexander's east.

To seek relief from sorrow, we marched from Susa. Hephaestion, in command of the infantry, went due west to the Tigris and the king and the cavalry rode south to the delta of the Euphrates where we found Nearchos and his ships, which were tied up to the river bank. The air was full of the joyous shouts of the men as they danced and sang in glad reunion. We drank and feasted all night and once everyone was sober and fit again, Alexander held a military parade to award Nearchos a golden crown for the successful completion of his hazardous journey from the delta of the Indus.

We made the nights loud with our stories since we had parted in Carmania. For his part, Nearchos told us that he had safely returned to his ships. He had then followed the Persian coast until he reached a narrow strait, which he had crossed to the Arabian shoreline. He continued north until he found a small island with water wells where he had camped to wait for all the other ships to sail in from the open sea. To pass the time, the sailors had built a small temple and a few rough shelters and they named the island Icaros. When only Soteles of Athens had failed to join them, they had left a ship, with a few volunteers, to watch for his vessel and continued the voyage until, as Alexander had so often predicted, they had reached the delta of the Euphrates. A few days after our arrival in the delta, Stales and his crew straggled into camp and we rushed to greet them. They were given baths and clean clothes and food and when they were rested, we sat down to hear their story. Soteles told us that they had been shipwrecked and found refuge on a small island, which we assumed to be Icaros, as he reported that there were a few buildings, including a small temple. There were some native inhabitants living on the island, but he had found no sign of the men left behind by Nearchos. One of his men had engraved a stone for the temple, dedicating it to Poseidon and Artemis in gratitude for their deliverance from the sea.

He continued that he and his men were taken by local fishermen to the mainland of Arabia and he spoke of seeing long camel trains carrying fabulous shipments of myrrh, frankincense, cinnamon and other unknown spices, which were brought from the south for the trade routes across Asia.

Soteles, and his men, had been guided by men from different tribes of Arabs to the king's camp. They already knew and told Soteles of Alexander's arrival in Susa as well as the docking of the fleet in the delta of the Euphrates. As he concluded this new odyssey of the expedition, the king questioned him, saying: "Are there many people in Arabia and what kind of towns do they have and are they prepared to pay me homage and what weapons do they use in their own defence?"

Soteles replied: "We only found on the shore, a few stucco huts, thatched with palm fronds, and these belong to fishermen and seafarers. Most of the people live in tents made from the hair of goats and we have already seen many of them leading their caravans in the lands of Asia. They are hospitable to strangers but ready to defend themselves to the death. They use daggers and swords similar to those forged in the fires of Damascus. They are a proud people, even arrogant, and might be persuaded to voluntarily serve Alexander, as most of them have no wealth, but as a people, they would never accept foreign domination.

Their land is a parched desert and hotter than the iron-maker's furnace. They have no water and are forced to ferry it by ship in animal skins from the rivers of Mesopotamia. They trade across the world, eat dates and nuts, and fish for pearl-bearing oysters far out in their seas."

As he paused, Alexander next asked him, "Do these people have any harbours that are suitable sites on which to build cities? Are there any wild animals in the desert and are there plants or trees for food and fuel? Is it possible that deep down, below the surface of the sand, we should find water; if not, to carry enough for an army would seem an impossible task?"

We all became very attentive at these words of the king. He clearly was inspired by fresh challenges in what sounded to us to be a very miserable country without natural resources for our Greek way of life.

Soteles replied to the king: "I think that there are many possible sites for harbours. The sand meets the sea and it would be easy to build moles out into the water where ships could dock, if we could find enough hard material. We did hear that in distant places from the shore, there are water wells and around them grow trees, grains and other food crops. Most interesting, we found patches of the oily substance oozing out of the ground, which we have seen in Mesopotamia and other countries, and it can be used as fuel.

"The Arabs are a nomadic people; if not travelling with their merchandise with their camels and horses, they are herding sheep and goats, which they use for food. They cure the animal skins for leather and the wool is woven for clothes and tents. They must constantly move to fresh pastures for the animals quickly exhaust the sparse vegetation. They are the most hospitable of people, which, for strangers, is limited to three days.

"At certain seasons, great sandstorms blow across the land and sky, and the dust penetrates into the eyes, mouth, nose and every crease of skin with a stinging ferocity. Sand blocks out the sun and it is neither night nor day but always as hot as fire and men crave salt and water and they burn with fever from which they often die. Then the vultures devour their flesh leaving only their bones to whiten and turn to dust in the fullness of time.

"Strangely, in the spring, the earth is covered with small flowers, and we saw gazelle and also other tiny animals. Lizards grow to an enormous size and snakes and scorpions are underneath and behind every rock. The Arabs hunt with trained hawks and elegant dogs, which are called by them ' salukis'. The sea, fortunately, gives an abundant harvest of fish but locusts swarm in the summer and devour every living plant. Arabia is a flat hostile country quite unsuited for Greeks, especially Athenians."

We let his impish insult pass as he continued his vivid account: "The sun comes out of the sea in the morning as a fiery chariot. It crosses the arc of heaven and as it passes over the land, the air shimmers so that the eye creates pictures of lakes, forests and cities and mountains and they all disappear as if the gods of that place delight in mocking men, and when the sun finally descends into the earth, desert and sky come together in flaming colours of reds, oranges, greens and violets.

"It is a land quite close to heaven, for at night the stars are near to the earth and they glitter in brilliant radiance from the deep, dark sky. In that land loneliness, thirst, hunger and heat were our companions and in such a waste, a man must know himself, and the limits of his endurance, or perish. Maybe a Spartan might willingly endure such privations but Macedonians never. O King! It is a wilderness deserted by our gods!"

Alexander had listened with very close attention to Soteles' description of Arabia and he replied: "Soteles, your description of the land and people is a spark lighting the flame of a torch, but if the people will not pay me homage or even send an ambassador to declare their submission to my rule, I may find it necessary to campaign against them. We need their knowledge of the trade routes of the world, their harbours for the sanctuary of our ships and the spices of their desolate wilderness for markets everywhere. We shall require caravan stops on the road to India and distant Africa. The island of Icaros may serve our purpose for our fleet but we must have many more rest stops in pacified territory, for the overland merchants. We must, therefore, establish cities and harbours on the mainland. When I am assured that civilised government has been restored throughout Greece and the empire, I shall ask for volunteers to come with me to explore Arabia.

"I am anxious to personally see how the people have organised their lives that they survive where Soteles thinks that we should perish but, meanwhile, he and his crew must rest and one day we shall tame his 'wilderness'."

We separated for the night and by the next day Alexander was ready to leave the camp and we continued to explore the reedy marshes of the delta and the king sent many lingering glances towards the lands of Arabia. We took the eastern route until we reached the River Tigris; we continued along the river bank and found the camp of Hephaestion. After a few days' rest, the united army marched to the city of Opis. It was here that we had crossed the river, after the Battle of Gaugamela, eight long seasons before. Soon after our arrival in the city, Alexander ordered the Macedonians still with the expedition to parade before him. To be singled out was now so unusual that the men speculated on the king's purpose. We had not long to wait to find out. As soon as we were assembled on the parade ground, Alexander rode out in front of us and along the ranks of the men; he then halted his horse and when it was still, he began: "I now intend to honour the promise which I made to you, that when we returned from the east, all the veterans who have served throughout the campaign will be honourably discharged and may return to their homes. They will be richly rewarded for their long service and their wealth will be the envy of everyone else in their cities and villages. Amongst those who do not qualify for discharge under these terms, any of you who have been wounded or have reached an age when they are no longer fit for hard campaigns, will be similarly dismissed. You have my gratitude ...."

But the rest of his words were drowned out in a sullen roar of anger. The few Macedonians still with the expedition understood only too well that any loss in their numbers must diminish their privileged position in the army and they suspected that this was the king's hidden intention. Many angry voices were raised to demand of Alexander that if he now planned to separate himself entirely from Macedon and become a Persian king, no less a tyrant than the Archaemenids. One resentful voice even shouted, and his cry was taken up by others: "Alexander! Why don't you take the field with your Egyptian father, Ammon?"

The king's claim to divinity rankled with the men; it was, to them, a disastrous denial of his father King Philip, a true and beloved Macedonian. The cry went up again and more insults were added: "None go or we will all go, and there will be none to fight your battles but your Persians and Ammon, your Egyptian father!"

The ugly situation grew worse as some of the generals closest to Alexander joined the protests. The king, in fury, leapt down from his horse and called the guard. He pointed out thirteen men who were the first to raise their voices and they were led off and summarily executed for treason.

Alexander had restored order and in the black silence he mounted a podium and addressed the men: "Macedonians! I am King Philip's son and to my great father do you owe everything that you have. When he became king you were herdsmen, in rags and hides, climbing the mountains and tending to your flocks. Go, if you wish, but first hear the truth from me, you who are as unreasoning as cattle. Ammon is my spiritual father and King Philip my natural father. From Ammon comes the source of my divinity and from Philip, my royalty.

"King Philip made you soldiers and lords of all Greece. He gave you clothes and learning, he gave you bounty and he secured your borders and brought wealth to your families. My father gave you peace and an alliance with all the city-states of Greece, save only Sparta, to fight against the Persian plunderer.

"King Philip died at the miserable hand of a traitor and I became your king. I have led you to Ionia, Lydia, Aeolia, Caria, Lykia, Phrygia and through Cappadocia to Cilicia, Phoenicia, Canaan, Egypt, Syria through the Persian Empire, to the vast lands of Asia and India and back again, after winning every battle against the mighty Persian army.

"I discharged my father's debts and built up the public treasury to sustain our great campaign. At the same time, I lined your purses with the largest share of all the treasure, which we have secured and for myself I kept nothing. Your inheritance is not your only share of the treasure, but the rich provinces over which you are appointed as governors and commanders according to your abilities. I have paid your debts and given you a glory unmatched in history and your deeds will be known in every future generation, for we have changed the world.

"Go, if you will, and tell the Macedonians how you left Alexander to the wild tribes, which he has conquered. Tell them how you deserted your king on the Hyphasis and at many other places. I have not only conquered every enemy who came before us, I have held you together when you grew faint-hearted and gloomy and turned into a rebellious mob. Go and be proud of the story that you will tell to them."

At the end of his scornful words, the king leapt down from the podium and marched to his tent. The men stood round in groups, not saying very much. They knew that they were without a leader, save the king, and they were still far from home. They also considered that if they carried out their threats and all left Alexander, then their promised share of the treasure would vanish like a mirage in the deserts of Arabia and all their hardships of the long campaign would be cancelled out in the bitter equation of life. Alexander remained in his tent for the rest of the day and the watching Macedonians heard him call the Persians to him. He gave them appointments already held by Macedonians, and exchanged the family kiss with them and promised them great positions in his army.

The Macedonians watched in horror as the king's response played out in their estrangement and disgrace. Finally, they could stand it no more and they rushed to greet him protesting their loyalty and faithful service. Alexander truly loved his Macedonians and, with tears in his eyes, he greeted each by name until one of his father's old soldiers cried: "Alexander! We are bitterly hurt that you place Persians above us in the army and that they are received as members of your family and given the kiss which has never been ours."

The king replied: "O! Macedonians! I make you all my family."

He then reached out and first kissed his father's friend. The Macedonians were hysterical with joy but it was the king's victory. He had them back even though he had irrevocably strengthened the Persians' place in the hierarchy of the campaign. None could now doubt his right to reorganise the army with Persians enjoying every rank and title.

To make the reconciliation complete, the king invited the Macedonians to a feast, which he gave exclusively for them. He spoke to them of his vision of uniting Greek humanity with the spirituality of the east and tried to make them understand that for the happiness of all, there must be peace amongst his subjects. The discussion went on far into the night and libations were poured from the same bowl to all the gods of Greece and Persia. Alexander prayed aloud for a true partnership between all men. He was surrounded by Greek seers and Magiian priests of the Persian religion were invited to add their prayers to his own.

The king continued the festivities for several days until all was peace between himself and his Macedonians and then the veterans prepared to leave and many, indeed, were glad to take their pay and bounty and the extra talent the king awarded to each man. He gathered them round him and said: "My Macedonians and brothers, your gallantry has brought us to the rule of the world. You have endured improbable hardships with terrible courage through the long exile from your homes. Now your return will be a great triumph and I have decided that Craterus, the 'Friend of the King', and your great general will lead you back to Macedon ..."

He was interrupted by the cheers of the men for Craterus was well-beloved and the most respected of all the generals since the death of Parmenion. To be led by such a renowned soldier would give their own homecoming great prestige and dignity. They knew that all Greece would watch their arrival and understand the immense honour done to them by Alexander of Macedon.

In this great, dramatic moment, as the noise died down, the king continued: "Antipater will replace Craterus in the army here and when he departs from Macedon, he will bring your replacements with him. He has served both my father and me with great distinction and he will now exchange offices with Craterus in the army.

"I am exceedingly happy that Craterus will have you all in Macedon to serve him with love and loyalty. I have received many dispatches reporting quarrels, and even wars, amongst the Greek cities and, as you know, I have sent them an edict to take back their own many exiles and discharged soldiers, who have fomented a great deal of the trouble, but the Greeks are Greeks and do not obey my commands from this distance. Craterus will arbitrate their disputes and see that my orders are carried out and your experience will be of great help to him. He will not hesitate to quell disturbances with military force."

Alexander had skilfully brought the discharged Macedonians back into useful work and he spoke with deep emotion to the men: "And so, my beloved Macedonians, I must bid you farewell. The bonds between us, which distance will never sever or time diminish, are forever and when you reach your homes, may you all enjoy the honours to which your great service has entitled you."

As he finished speaking, the men crowded round him and

many were not shamed to shed tears as they clasped the king to them in loyal and affectionate farewell. They were soon gone and gone also was the cloud of dust which hid them as they left the camp on their long journey home.

Alexander had cleverly deposed of Antipater in Macedon and Greece and replaced him with Craterus to ensure that his policies would be carried out amongst the warring cities. He had also sent the aged men home and removed their bitterness among the younger serving men. He was surrounded by his own generation and could more easily enforce his will in the government of the empire. His confidence must be high or he could not have spared Craterus and all of us should know that Alexander 'the Great', as many men now called him, ruled the world.

I had turned down my right to leave the army and I had asked for and received Alexander's permission to stay with him. To part from Craterus was yet another sorrow that I must endure but I had no duty to take me home. My steward looked after my father's estates, my son was cared for by his mother's parents and tutored by an excellent teacher and I could not reconcile myself to a lonely country life. I had wearied early in my youth of all the intrigues at the court in Pella; they made life both uncomfortable and dangerous. Alexander was already making plans to explore and conquer other lands, now that he had successfully settled his administrative problems. Arabia was close; it beckoned me and I longed to reach its shores, but we marched again across the mountains, once more to winter amongst the beautiful, deserted palaces of Ecbatana. When we arrived in the city, there were many ambassadors waiting to greet the king. He received them all and sent them back to their own provinces and countries with instructions to keep the peace. He also wrote long reports to Aristotle and spent days with the geographers and chart makers and he only occasionally hunted, the wild birds and animals.

With the departure of Craterus, none could take his place in the companionship of the chase for the king. Alexander held feasts and symposia for both Macedonians and Persians but hostility flared again. The king tried to keep the peace between us but we were as far from them as life is from death. The Macedonians also spoke amongst themselves of all the powers that Alexander had assumed. In the traditions of Macedon, our king was the first among equals with supreme authority only in time of war and in settling legal disputes amongst his people, but Alexander claimed to be divine with absolute powers. He no longer confided in his generals and often acted without seeking advice in wars of words. He gave summary judgments and for treason, death was his only penalty. The Macedonians were now numerically very weak and could not oppose his will. The Greeks, who might have been our allies had long departed for home, except for a few mercenary soldiers, and that left the Persians in Alexander's tent. They, of course, were delighted with their new position. Accustomed to autocratic rulers, they had a king, a former enemy, who gave them positions of great power. They fawned upon him and offered him the servitude of a conquered people as though they were still uncertain of their fate.

None of us shared in Alexander's decisions, yet all bore the consequences. We had to be grateful to the gods that Alexander was innately just, of noble character, a great leader and general, for our lives were in his hands.

Alexander sent for Archios of Macedon, who had sailed his ship, under Nearchos, from the delta of the Indus south to Mesopotamia. He gave him orders to set sail south again to find suitable ports for the navy, preferably on easily defended islands or, failing that, along the shores of Arabia. The king's new vision was to find a sea route linking Babylon with Egypt, Africa and west, to seek lands beyond the Pillars of Herakles. By the spring, the army prepared to march back to Babylon and those who knew the city and relished its diversions, were full of excited anticipation.

Before departure, Alexander held a feast for all the governors, satraps and high officials who lingered at the court in Ectabana. The king arrived, dressed in Persian finery, and accompanied by Hephaestion similarly attired. During the evening, Hephaestion fell ill and, with an anxious Alexander at his side, he was carried to his own quarters.

For seven days, Alexander remained beside his couch as he drifted into unconsciousness, only to watch, in a terrible agony of grief as his beloved friend gently slipped away in death. Alexander's sorrow was beyond consolation. He lay beside the body for three days, taking neither drink nor food. He finally aroused himself, in the bitterness of mourning, to make arrangements for the funeral. He first sent a swift messenger to the Oracle of Siwah begging to know if he should sacrifice to Hephaestion as a hero or a god. He ordered Perdicass to take the body to Babylon, to arrange for a state funeral for his friend and to wait for his own arrival. After the cortege left Ecbatana, guarded by a huge military escort, the king fell to the ground, where he stayed motionless until the procession was no longer within our sight.

Hephaestion's title of Grand Vizier lapsed with his death for, in the king's heart, none could fill it and so did the office of 'Second After the King', making the chasm between Alexander and the few Macedonians deeper, for his rank as King of Kings was far beyond our reach, and there was no-one to intervene on our behalf, but none raised his voice in protest.

The fever which took the life of Hephaestion is endemic to the east. Some recovered from its ravages but doctors whispered that too much wine had aggravated the disease and helped bring Hephaestion's end.

Alexander was possessed by grief and was distant from all other men. He prayed wildly to the gods and revived the ancient rites of the Kaiberoi which, so long ago, he had practised with his mother. The men whispered of his excesses and everyone was dejected and in despair. Excessive mourning can make men mad and I remembered Halicarnassos where I had grieved for Penelope. At last, the king came out from his tent and gave instructions for the march to Babylon. We were glad to shed so much despair in the work of preparation, which consumed our days. We were attacked several times on the journey by hostile tribes, but the battles seem to help Alexander as he drove the attackers off with his practised skill and he turned from seers, priests and mystics to become a soldier once more. Eumenes forgot his hostility to the dead Hephaestion and wrote poems and paeans of praise in his official report of the hero's death. It delighted the king to read of the deeds of his friend and did no harm, even where the praise was far greater than the exploits eulogised.

Embassies endlessly arrived in the camp as we marched from the king's domains and far beyond. There were Italians, Carthaginians, Aetheopians and tribes from Europe, the steppes of Asia and many other unknown lands. They had all heard of Alexander's safe return from India and wished to pay respect and honour the king on his great achievements. He welcomed them all and closely questioned them about their homelands, as he had so long ago questioned the Persians at King Philip's court in Pella.

The king sent a sea captain and his crew to build a fleet on the shore of the Hyrcanian Sea. He was impatient to confirm that which he had been told, that the rivers of Asia emptied into its broad waters. He planned to send Nearchos and his men to explore the sea as soon as all the ships were ready to sail.

Mazaeus, the satrap of Babylon, was waiting for the king on the west side of the Tigris. He was attended by a mighty assembly of Persian nobles, Macedonian officials and soldiers and the leading citizens of the city. The Persians greeted Alexander with their hated proskynesis; they were gaudy peacocks in their brilliant robes and no more intelligent, or so it seemed to me. We joyously greeted the Macedonians and eagerly exchanged all their news from home with stories of the eastern campaign.

We marched to Babylon and at the gates of the city Chaldean seers and priests urgently asked to be received by Alexander. They entered his tent and stood before him and their spokesman gave him a warning from the oracle of their god, cautioning Alexander not to enter the city. The king heard them out, in courteous silence, and dismissed them as he said to the Macedonians: "I have heard, from many sources, that the Chaldean priests have used the monies and revenues, which I assigned for the restoration of their temples, for their personal enrichment. I suspect that they now would keep me from Babylon to conceal their cupidity. I shall therefore disregard their warning."

The priests overheard Alexander's words and they turned back to plead with him saying that if he must enter the city, then he should approach it from the west as all the omens were unfavourable from the east. The king, ever mindful of the auguries, accepted their council, and marched round the city's walls, at the head of a large detachment of the army, to the western gate. We soon discovered that the marshes across the saturated ground, on that side of Babylon, made a triumphal entry impossible. We therefore returned to the eastern gate and Alexander entered Babylon, leading a great procession of people, which had formed behind the army.

Alexander was welcomed into the city with exotic, formal ceremonies and, at their end, he addressed the huge crowd, proclaiming that Babylon was now the capital of the world. To honour the occasion the priests, in solemn rituals, made many sacrifices to the gods and, swinging their censers, they created incense clouds above us all and the air was perfumed in fragrant opulence. The ceremonies and rituals were followed by celebratory games, although only Macedonians and Greeks competed, and we feasted for seven days and nights. Ambassadors, at this time, departed Babylon to proclaim its new status throughout the world. Nearchos brought his ships into the city and he planned a great new fleet with which to explore the rivers, seas and lands beyond our present limitations. Heiron, a sailor from infamous Soloi of Cilicia, sailed in advance to find a passage to Egypt from the south. Coinciding with his departure, Alexander dispatched messengers to Memphis ordering the satrap to send a naval expedition in the opposite direction, in expectation that it would cross Heiron's ships somewhere round the great landmass of Africa. Sailors also left Babylon to recruit seafarers from the coasts of Phoenicia, Syria and Canaan and to invite people of those countries to settle the lands of Mesopotamia and the coasts of the Arabian Sea.

About this time, Archias arrived in Babylon, after sailing down the Tigris into the open water. In great excitement, he reported to Alexander, saying: "We found the island which Soteles called Icaros and our men who were left there by Nearchos. They had temporarily gone to the mainland and they have now returned with sheep and goats, which they use for food and clothing. They are busy digging wells, improving the temple, housing and public buildings. One of the men is a potter and he is making storage jars, while some of them have already married local women. We explored the island and the coast of the mainland and found it just as reported by Soteles, a wasteland of dry desert and unbearable heat. We sailed further to the south of Icaros and discovered a much larger, inhabited island with many date palms and abundant water. It has an excellent harbour and the island is well able to support a fleet and a garrison. We named it Tylos, although I believe that the local people call it Dilmun, and this was the furthermost point of our voyage."

The king was gratified with the report of Archias; it answered some of his questions and left many more to be resolved. He, therefore, ordered Androsthenes of Thasos to take his ship beyond Dilmun and find the next harbours for the use of the fleet. The king supplied him with gold and silver coins to use for trade with the merchants of the island. Alexander instructed him to bring back some of their works of art, their plants, food and animals. Androsthenes also returned without going beyond Tylos and Alexander told us that he intended to lead the next expedition himself through the Arabian Seas. The king received many envoys from the Greek cities and they brought him golden crowns and recognised him as a god, all save the Spartans, who alone sent no crown but a typical laconic message saying: "If Alexander wishes, he should call himself a god."

The king would have prized the homage of Sparta above all the other Greek cities; but he thought the message a much better option than an open declaration of war. This was the year of the 114th Olympic Games. I sought Aiysha in Babylon, but she was gone and her memory only faintly lingered amongst her friends in the city. Some of them thought that she was dead, others declared that she had journeyed to Jerusalem. She was to me as perfume, a fragrance of subtle and elusive memory.

Babylon was bustling to obey the king's orders and on every unused space men were training for future expeditions. The dykes and canals of the whole region had fallen into disrepair through neglect. Alexander personally supervised the work of restoration to end the devastating inundations, which had destroyed parts of the city and most of the crops season by season. We received many volunteers from Macedon and Greece and the king reorganised his army with every nationality of the empire serving in each unit. The ratio was now approximately three Persians for each Macedonian in the expedition. He disbanded the Macedonian phalanx and placed the men in other units of the army. Alexander gave many Macedonians senior command positions, which was a small consolation for our hurt pride. In early summer, the king's embassy returned from Siwa. Alexander received the members with great emotion and he asked the spokesman: "How does the Oracle say that we shall honour Hephaestion?"

He replied: "O King! The Oracle gives you the authority to honour him as a hero and not as a god."

Alexander was deeply grieved at this reply but he later understood that the deification of Hephaestion was an impossibility and he accepted the compromise.

Much more ominously, the same envoys brought reports that Cleomenes, the satrap of Egypt, was planning an uprising against

310

the king and that he had disgraced Alexander by exploiting a famine in Greece and charging the Greeks enormous prices for Egyptian grain. Alexander, hoping to reform the corrupt official, sent him orders to change and reform and warned him of his own imminent arrival by ship. He also commanded him to erect worthy memorials to Hephaestion throughout Egypt.

The king made elaborate preparations for the funeral rites of Hephaestion, who would live again as a hero in all his last ceremonies. He built his friend an immense tomb in Babylon and it was the most magnificent in the history of the world, easily excelling the mausoleum of Mausolus the King of Halicarnassos in Caria. It was decorated with gilded ships, torches and statues, golden crowns, snakes, soaring eagles, lions and bulls and surmounted by the weapons of Macedon and Persia. Great hollow spaces crowned the edifice to conceal the singers who chanted during the rites. The funeral ended the king's long period of mourning for Hephaestion and he continued the preparations for the sea voyage around the coasts of Arabia. Alexander made many sacrifices to the gods for a safe journey and he gave a feast for the army with plentiful supplies of food, beer and wine.

Finally, a few days before our departure, those Macedonians who were staying in Babylon to administer the empire arranged a symposium for the king and all the generals who were leaving on the expedition. With only a short break, the party continued into the second night. Alexander fell ill and returned to his pavilion, at first attending only his religious duties. He was forced to postpone the voyage around the coast of Arabia.

We watched in terrible anguish as Alexander's illness consumed him, until one night at sunset, his condition grew worse. All the generals gathered by his bed and together we carried our king across the River Euphrates to the ruined palace of Nebuchadnezzar, once King of Babylon. The rest of the Macedonians, in awful sorrow, followed the procession and we filed past his couch. Speech had left Alexander, but we each saw faint recognition in his eyes as he raised a finger in salutation. Seleucos, in desperation, sent to the temple of Marduk, the Persian God of Healing, and asked for the help of his priests. They sent instructions to leave the king where he lay in the pavilion and that night Alexander of Macedon died from a fever which infested the river marshes or, it was whispered, by the hand of malice. The warning of the Chaldean priests not to enter Babylon from the east tormented us all, and the prophecy of Calanus, the Indian holy man, that he would meet Alexander in Babylon, was fulfilled that fearful night. Macedonians were shocked, frightened, dazed and consumed by the loss of their beloved and great king. They were unable to attend to routine tasks. A few, finding work better than idleness, began to construct a crystal sarcophagus to hold Alexander's body as Egyptian embalmers went about their terrible work.

Chapter 27

And now the sword of Alexander is sheathed and his eyes are closed to further horizons. Silent is the voice which inspired other men to deeds of courage far beyond their natural limitations. If he was a man, he was greater than any before him; if he was a god, he gives a new meaning to divinity. Alexander was not capricious, selfish or corrupt; whatsoever he did was for noble ideals in a quest to end the searing misery of war and give the world unity and peace. To me, he was a friend, compassionate in my adversities, gentle in criticism, stern with himself and silent in the affairs of other men. His sense of royalty and destiny guided his life and, unlike any other king, for his few deeds of cruelty he suffered sorrow and a bitter remorse. He was a fearless and incomparable leader and dearly loved by his Macedonians.

Alexander civilised the world and Hellas flowered in the lands of the barbarians. The gods know that other men will destroy his empire, and greed and jealousy will fuel the fires of war. The voyage around Arabia, exploration to the east, the north and in the far west are dead, for they were the dreams of Alexander and his alone to accomplish.

We are escorting the king to Egypt for burial in his city of Alexandria. Ptolemy arrived from that country, and seized his body, as the other generals continued to quarrel over the partition of Alexander's empire. They were taking him for burial at Aegae in Macedon. We are led by Ptolemy, and the heat of summer far out in the Syrian desert is the last hardship that we shall undertake in Alexander's name. There are no complaints from the men and they march in the silence and solitude of their sorrow.

When this last duty is done, I shall go to Icarus and Tylos, to the satrapies of the east and the south and, finally, I shall return to Macedon, but only if the gods permit me, for no man may plan, with certainty, beyond a moment of time for they scatter dreams and take away our breath as the winds disperse the sands of the deserts of Arabia.